The Abyss line of cutting-edge psychological horror is committed to publishing the best, most innovative works of dark fiction available. ABYSS is horror unlike anything you've ever read before. It's not about haunted houses or evil children or ancient Indian burial grounds. We've all read those books and we all know their plots by heart.

ABYSS is for the seeker of truth, no matter how disturbing or twisted it may be. It's about people, and the darkness we all carry within us. ABYSS is the new horror from the dark frontier. And in that place, where we come face-to-face with terror, what we find is ourselves.

"Thank you for introducing me to the remarkable line of novels currently being issued under Dell's Abyss imprint. I have given a great many blurbs over the last twelve years or so, but this one marks two firsts: first *unsolicited* blurb (*I called you*) and the first time I have blurbed a whole *line* of books. In terms of quality, production, and plain old story-telling reliability (that's the bottom line, isn't it?), Dell's new line is amazingly satisfying . . . a rare and wonderful bargain for readers. I hope to be looking into the Abyss for a long time to come."

—Stephen King

Please turn the page for more extraordinary acclaim . . .

Death-walker

R. Patrick Gates

A DELL BOOK

Published by
Dell Publishing
a division of
Bantam Doubleday Dell Publishing Group, Inc.
1540 Broadway
New York, New York 10036

ISBN: 0-440-21467-X

Printed in the United States of America

Published simultaneously in Canada

April 1995

10 9 8 7 6 5 4 3 2 1

OPM

To all the gang at the Hill—you know who you are.

To Leo Hurley for helping me realize this book was possible.

And especially to Lisa for her love, devotion, and a great idea.

I

Relapse

We admitted we were powerless over alcohol and drugs—that our lives had become unmanageable.

> —Step One of AA's
> 12 Steps to Recovery

A definition of insanity: Doing the same thing over and over and expecting a different result.

> —AA slogan

1

 The bottle came out of the drawer less than a month later. He'd put it in the drawer under the TV with the intention of never taking it out again, but that was not to be.

Down the road, when he looked back at that moment, the turning point of his life, Bill Gage would realize that if he'd really never intended to drink again, he wouldn't have put the bottle in the drawer in the first place—he would have thrown it away. Later he would be able to see that there were many reasons why he relapsed into alcoholism and worse. But at the time, he saw only one: the dream, *the nightmare,* that wouldn't go away.

And he felt guilt over that; immense guilt. It wasn't the loss of his wife Cindy to the Video Killer, Wilbur Clayton, that caused his relapse. It wasn't the sadness, torment, and depression he felt, nor often saw in the eyes of his children. It wasn't the loss of his position with the Crocker Police Department. It wasn't even the fact that he had killed Wilbur Clayton in cold blood and had got away with it. Certainly, any of the above were very good reasons for any *sane* man to pick up a drink and lose himself in the escape of alcoholism, but they weren't his. No, he had to lose nearly four years of sobriety due to a *stupid dream* (and as they say in AA, to some "*stinking thinking*") that in the light of day was as silly as a bad B horror movie.

The dream had first visited him the day after his sister-in-law, Evelyn, and his kids moved back to the house to live with him. Evelyn had protested, saying it wasn't wise nor healthy for the children to go back to the house where their mother had been murdered and where they had actually *seen* her dead body floating in the tub. She thought it would be the most unhealthy for Sassy, who had been stalked by the killer in the house after she had seen him kill her mother. Evelyn had also expressed concern for Bill, arguing that it wasn't good for him to be back in the house either, what with all its reminders of Cindy and their life together.

But Bill saw it differently. For him it was *because* of those reminders that he'd chosen his kids over the bottle that day of the inquest into his actions concerning the apprehension and fatal shooting of Wilbur Clayton. Those first few days and weeks after the wrap-up of the case, Cindy's funeral, and the inquest, he had drawn strength from the house and the feeling of Cindy's presence everywhere. It was because of her that he had been able to quit drinking the first time, nearly four years ago. It was because of her, and the family and home life she'd provided, that he had been able to stay sober on his own. He had dismissed Evelyn's arguments with the sure knowledge that the memory of Cindy, so strong in the house, would be sufficient to keep him sober and help him do right by his children.

It was not to be.

The dream saw to that.

The first night he had it, he woke in a cold sweat, shivering and reaching for Cindy only to find her cold empty pillow. He had clutched it to his chest, hugging it for surrogate comfort as dry sobs wracked him and the dream flitted through his memory in bits and pieces. Mostly, he remembered darkness and a clicking sound accompanied by flashes of bright light and the touch of a hand clutching at his arm.

That was all. Certainly nothing to wake up sweating, shivering, and near to tears over. He had lain awake a long time that night, trying to remember more of the dream but unable to. He had dozed off again toward dawn and woken a few hours later convinced it had been nothing but a senseless indigestion nightmare brought on by the Chinese food he had treated Evelyn and the kids to.

By bedtime of the next evening, he had forgotten all about the dream, but it didn't forget about him. The second night he woke as he had the first, sweating, shivering, and reaching for the comfort of a wife who wasn't there. This time, as he sat in the darkness hugging the pillow, he remembered more of the dream.

It started out in darkness, but it was a different darkness than he had remembered from the previous night. This darkness was lighter, alive with sound. Not just the clicking sounds either, but human ones. A soft moan. A whimper and a sob. And the clearest sound, one that made the hair on his arms stand up and sent a tingling wave of fear over his scalp, was a whispered plea: "Help me!"

The bright flashes of light came next, blinding him more effectively than the darkness had, followed by the clutching hand and something else—something he couldn't remember for the life of him but that he *knew* was so *horrible* that it had catapulted him completely out of sleep.

He went back to work the next day at his K mart cop job and had to put in four hours of overtime to just begin to get caught up on the work left from his leave of absence. That night he had slept the sleep of the exhausted, and if he had dreamed the dream he didn't remember it. The next few nights were similarly spent in deep, exhausted sleep untroubled and uninterrupted. But less than a week later, the dream returned with more force than before and then continued its visits right through tonight, which had been the worst so far.

Bill Gage poured a generous amount of Jack Daniel's into the glass and inhaled its heady aroma. Though he sat in the darkness of his living room, he imagined he could see the dark, mysterious caramel color of the liquid, swirling with transparent images drawn in silky liquid currents like an op art painting filled with hidden sights and meanings.

"Four years," he whispered softly. *Do you really want to do this?* his rational side asked him. He contemplated the question for a long time, and as he did, the memory of the dream rose in his mind like a specter. Tonight the dream had been horrible, the worst yet. And unlike other nights, tonight he could remember every detail of it.

It was obvious to him now what the setting of the dream was. It was the tunnel under Crocker Hospital. In the dream, Bill was back in the tunnel. He could hear the water dripping, could smell and feel the dampness. His breathing was rapid, wheezing in and out of his lungs, and his heartbeat was so loud it seemed to be coming from somewhere outside of himself.

The tunnel was dark, pitch-black. Suddenly it was illuminated for a brief second by a flash of light that let him see his surroundings, then left him blinder than before. In those few seconds he saw the wet walls of the tunnel and the trickle of water running at his feet. The flash of light came again and he saw more—large, dark green trash bags piled against the sides of the tunnel. Another flash and he saw a dismembered arm hanging from one of the bags.

He staggered back as if from a blow. The flashes of light began to speed up until they reached a strobe effect. The bags of dismembered bodies were all around him, some closed tight, some half open spilling their contents of mutilated body parts. In the flashing light the arms, hands, and legs seemed to come alive and move, reaching for him as if seeking revenge.

"It wasn't me," he whispered to the moving limbs. "It was Wil—"

A hand clutched at his arm and he screamed the last half of the name, "—*buuur!*"

Bill whirled, expecting to see one of the chopped hands grasping his arm. But it was worse, it was the corpse of Wilbur Clayton, the poor demented killer he had tracked down and shot like a dog because he'd reminded Bill of his own serial-killer father.

The breath froze in Bill's lungs.

Wilbur was on his knees, reaching his dead hand up to cling to Bill's arm. His face was mottled blue and white, his eyes cloudy with death, the bullet hole in his forehead Bill had put there crusted with coagulated blood that glistened blackly. Using Bill's arm for leverage, Wilbur pulled his deadweight up until he was standing. He swayed, almost toppled, then leaned close and breathed a cloud of foul air into Bill's face.

"You think this is bad?" Wilbur whispered, his voice bubbling in his throat and a shiny, viscous green fluid trickling from his lips. "This ain't bad, Billy-boy. Why don't you go look over there. Over there is *bad.*" Wilbur's words brought such a deep terror to him that Bill began to tremble. Wilbur was pointing in the direction from which the flashing light was coming. It was a circle of light that seemed to be receding into the tunnel until it was a faraway dot, then it would grow again, strobing all the while. Bill was overwhelmed with the feeling that there was a presence beyond and hidden in the light, visible only by the faint reflected gleam in its eyes like two tiny ghosts suspended in air, but capable of stirring in Bill such momentous fear and terror, it made all other aspects of the dream seem as harmless as a child's cartoon by comparison. He didn't know why, or how, but he knew that the presence beyond the light had immense power and was somehow directing the dream, and directing him, wanting him to do something horrible, something unspeakable.

Bill Gage sighed and breathed deeply. The heavenly aroma of the Jack Daniel's filled his head. With it came fleeting memories of all the hell he had gone through while in the alcohol's embrace, and he thought that if anything, those memories of hell should be enough to keep him from taking a drink.

But this was different, wasn't it? Before he had submerged himself in alcohol because of the awful truth he had learned about his father. Now it was . . . the dream? Was it really? No, it wasn't the dream exactly, it was the lack of sleep the dream caused.

Yeah, that was it. He wasn't escaping or trying to run away this time, he was merely taking a drink to help him sleep. He was in control this time, unlike before when he had been half crazy with grief, rage, and guilt. If Cindy's death and everything else that had happened in the last month hadn't driven him to drink, surely he had proved that he wasn't an alcoholic and could control it, and surely one drink for the purpose of getting a little shut-eye couldn't hurt, could it?

With a quick turn of his hand and wrist, Bill downed the whiskey and answered the question once and for all.

2

Naked in the midnight darkness of his cell, he sits. On the floor at his feet, a newspaper lies spread, the headlines and story depicting the saga of Wilbur Clayton, The Video Killer, and Bill Gage, the cop who killed him.

The night guard has just passed by and will not return for another hour at least. He gets off the narrow bed, lifts the mattress, and plunges his hand into the small slits on its underside. He sighs with growing excitement, touching the metal that lies deep in the mattress's ticking. Carefully he removes the object, delighting in its gleam and how it catches and burns with the faintest rays of light.

He stands and straps the object on, fitting it snugly over the deformed object of his shame. Where before he felt like half a man, a freak, now he feels fully masculine, a superman.

He touches the metal lightly, thrilling at the sensation of the cold steel against his fingertips. In his mind's eye, he begins to run the fantasy that has sustained him for over fifteen years. Eyes closed, mouth twisted in a grin, he imagines dealing death to his nemesis with the thing between his legs.

Softly, but lightly and with growing excitement, he begins to caress it. His breathing comes quicker until he is panting. He grips the base of the metal and pulls it, stroking, stroking. Up and down, excitement building closer to a climax with every stroke and every imagined atrocity he will perform with the thing in his hand.

He has imagined this for so long that if he concentrates hard enough, long enough, he can actually feel the blood, and the feeling is good. It is warm—the warmth of life itself.

Suddenly, he is there—climax! His back arches, his body shudders. He grips the object fully and blood flies from his hand.

He sits on the bed and looks dumbly at the deep gashes in his palm, knowing he should have been more careful, but not being able to control his lust. That bothers him. He can't afford to lose control like this, not now.

The conviction that it is at last time to act overwhelms him. He will wait no more. The cop is in the news again and it is time to reap the fruits of the past fifteen years that he has spent in captivity. If the cop can face the most horrible truth of his life and survive it, then so can he.

And the cop will not survive him.

Horrible truth? He laughs. That which others would find horrible, he delights in, is proud of. Yet there is one horrible truth that he fears: that he might be stuck inside the gray walls, the iron bars of prison forever.

Ever since the Ravaging and the ensuing Revelation in his first year of prison, he has worked slowly toward changing that truth, taking his time, inching his way along like a soldier over a minefield in the dark. He has played the game with the prison psychologist and chaplain—the game of remorse; the game of repentance; the game of rehabilitation; all subtitles and categories under the main game: the game of freedom. He has played these games so well that he almost believed them himself, but there was always a part of him deep within, hidden from reason and sanity's touch, that knew he was just playing along. Playing and waiting. If playing the games got him paroled, so much the better—that was the easy way. But even if they got him nothing more than an increase in privileges, he could use that to his advantage. Each bond that is removed, each restraint that is loosened, causes the powers that be to regard him with an increasingly lazy eye. Soon, the lazy eye will droop, will doze, and in the time it takes to blink, he will be gone.

Until recently, until reading of the cop's return and success in catching the so-called Video Killer in Crocker, he has been willing by day to create a sincere facade of change and play the waiting game for as long as he has to. But by night, with the death tool he fashioned for himself in the prison machine shop and bribed a guard into letting him smuggle back to his cell, he lets his innermost self, his secret monster—his *true being*—shine forth.

After all, what is time to him? Is he not immortal? He can certainly afford to wait with the endless patience of a predator snake for its prey to move within striking range. But now, with the cop in action, recovered no less, he can afford to wait no longer. The cop is getting old. Who knows how long he has?

He knows he must set the wheels to a faster turn and hope to Lady Luck—always a dear and close friend in the past, until the cop came along—that the eye of authority has grown lazy enough that it can be lulled, even hypnotized into closing just long enough for him to disappear. But it must be done right, just right. Then the cop, the bastard who broke his promise and put him away in this eternal hell where he has been ridiculed and tortured beyond the limits of sanity, will have to face a horror a thousand times worse than the one that ruined his career with the state police.

He smiles, thinking of the pleasures he will have and the exquisite pain he will create in the bodies of the cop's children and in the mind of that bastard as he is forced to watch. The thoughts bring arousal again, but he dares not allow himself to touch the deadly thing again. His hand is *cut badly enough. He looks to his cell mate's bunk. Carefully he unstraps himself and returns the lovely object to his mattress, then he is on his cell mate, waking the thin, twenty-year-old junky. He grabs the boy's hair, nearly yanking it out, and muffles the screams by pressing the boy's face against his own body. He imagines it is his instrument of death that is giving the youth such pain instead of the embarrassment that he was born with.*

He laughs with release and joy at the pleasure of the violation and the pain he has given. He knows it is an omen of good things to come.

3

Why do they call it a big head? Bill Gage wondered painfully. His head felt anything but big. In fact, it felt excruciatingly small, and getting smaller, as if it were in a vise that was applying pressure to all sides, and top and bottom, closing, tightening inch by inch, millimeter by millimeter until he was afraid his skull would pop under the pressure.

He tried to get up too fast, and someone began pounding on the vise, and he was quickly forced back to a prone position. Now there was a great Chinese gong in his head and some idiot who had to be *deaf* was ringing it for all he was worth.

Bill found that if he lay absolutely still and breathed as shallowly as possible, the banging gong subsided into a dull yet still painful thumping in time to the pulsing heartbeat in his temples.

The inside of his mouth felt covered with fur, his throat like sandpaper. He swallowed with difficulty and tried again to sit up, moving very slowly and carefully so as not to increase the gong alarm. He managed to make it and sat resting on the edge of the bed. The digital clock on the night table read 10:30 A.M. For a moment, he panicked, thinking he was late for work, but then remembered it was Saturday and gave a sigh of relief. With this head he didn't want to deal with irate managers or grill petty shoplifters today.

But if it was Saturday, where were the kids? Usually the twins, Sassy and Missy, were playing their stereo loudly enough to wake the dead, and little Devin, no matter how many times Evelyn told him to let his father sleep, always managed to sneak in and use Bill's stomach as a trampoline. Bill was thankful to have missed that particular mode of awakening today. Devin would have found himself wearing the contents of Bill's stomach if he'd jumped on him this morning. Still, he missed waking to his son's smiling face and happy laughter. The house was quiet, too quiet.

Moving cautiously, he struggled to his feet, put on his shirt, pants, and slippers without the gong getting too bad, and shuffled to the doorway. "Hello?" he tried to call but the word came out as a dry croaking sound. With a swelling of the pain in his head he cleared his throat and tried again. No answer. Suddenly an eruption of nausea forced him to rush to the bathroom at the end of the hall where he spent several gut-wrenching, head-splitting minutes calling *Ralph!* until his stomach was empty and as sore as his throat and head. He splashed cold water on his face and struggled to swallow and keep down a couple of aspirin.

The twins' bedroom was empty. Sassy's bed was neatly made, as usual, though Bill noticed that Sassy had removed her dresses and other clothing from the closet and had hung them on the curtain rod over the room's sole window. Missy's side of the room was a mess, also as usual, with clothes and stuffed animals strewn around her half of the room in direct contrast to Sassy's side.

Bill looked at the latter's orderliness and marveled at how quickly Sassy had recuperated from the trauma of all that had happened to her. She was seeing a psychologist, as was Missy, but they both seemed to be doing so well he often wondered if it was a waste of money. Little Devin was doing the best of all, though he often cried for his mother at night and at times when he was hurt, but thank God Evelyn was there.

But where was she now?

Bill gingerly made his way downstairs. The dirty dishes in the kitchen sink told him the children had eaten their regular breakfast of Cheerios and OJ, but they were no longer in the house. He ambled into the living room and was reproached by the sight of the quarter-full fifth of Jack Daniel's on the coffee table next to the dirty glass. He felt a flush of hot shame at knowing Evelyn and maybe the kids had seen it.

But maybe they didn't see it, he told himself and knew it wasn't true. They saw it. The fact that Evelyn had hustled them out of the house before he woke was proof enough of that. She knew Saturday was his day with the kids. She also knew that if he had been drinking, he'd be in no condition to be with them.

He felt like a louse; a very *sick* louse, his pounding head and churning stomach reminded him.

Hair of the dog.

The thought came unbidden to his mind. It had been one of his favorite sayings when he was mired in the depths of drinking over four years ago.

"No," he told himself aloud. Last night was just a splurge, a deviation. It was *not* a return to the drink-soaked days of the past. His drunk last night had been therapeutic, medicinal. He'd needed it because of the damned dream that wouldn't leave him alone, wouldn't let him sleep.

Yeah? Well, if taking a drink to get rid of a killer hang-over isn't medicinal, then what is?

That was logical. It didn't mean he had to get falling-down drunk and stay that way. Just one drink to rid himself of feeling sick. That was all he needed. Just one drink.

With a muttered curse of "What the hell?" he took the one drink, then another without a thinking pause. He felt better. He took another. When the bottle of Jack Daniel's was gone, he found a half-full bottle of Tanqueray gin, Cindy's brand, under the TV. Like a man in a trance he poured one drink of that and downed it. He had another *just one* and another until that bottle too was empty and he was passed out on the living room couch, mouth open, snoring loudly.

4

Ivy Delacroix woke to Henry's licking his face and nuzzling his ear. "What's the matter, boy? You hungry?" he asked the puppy, scratching its neck. He picked the dog up, got out of bed, yawning and stretching with one arm, and went into the living room. A flood of rage and anguish stopped him in the middle of the room when he saw his mother passed out in the easy chair, an empty bottle of Sangria on the floor next to her.

It was starting all over again, he knew. This was the third week in a row he'd found her passed out on a Saturday morning after she'd worked a late shift at the restaurant. And all her old behavior was slowly returning, all her old walls were going back up, shutting him out. The closeness and renewed love they'd shared at Christmas such a short time ago now seemed like something he must have dreamed or fantasized.

Ivy caught his reflection in the long mirror over the couch. His dark mulatto face, offset by his reddish hair, stared back at him, full of anger and hurt.

He didn't know what had gone wrong; things had been so *good* for a while. They'd been talking, close, and she'd stopped drinking. Then for no reason at all that he could see, she'd just started shutting him out again and had returned to wallowing in self-pity. For all his intelligence and maturity, he was lost, didn't know what to do, and it frustrated him. He knew he should be doing something, that the burden of making her see what she was doing fell squarely on him, but he felt helpless. After all, she was still his mother, and eleven-year-old sons don't tell their mothers what to do, even if he did feel and act more like a parent than she did.

Henry whimpered in his arms, and Ivy went into the kitchen. He got the dog a dish of leftover tuna fish from the refrigerator and put it in a plastic bowl next to the dog's water dish.

"Mom?" He went into the living room and knelt by the chair. He gently shook her shoulder. She snorted and mumbled. "Mom? Wake up."

"Lea' me 'lone," she muttered.

"Come on, Mom. We have to talk."

"Go 'way."

"Mom, please?"

"Go away!" She shouted and turned her face to him, her eyes barely open but bloodshot. "Don't you understand English? Leave me alone!" She rolled away from him again, shifting awkwardly onto her side, hunching her shoulders in to herself.

Ivy rocked back on his heels and got up slowly. Tears filled his eyes, but he forced them back, replacing the hurt with anger and coldness. If that was the way she wanted it, then fine. He didn't need this crap. He was better off on his own, like he'd always been.

He returned to his room and hurriedly threw on some clothes. He packed all his favorite books into his knapsack. Going to the kitchen, he tied the length of rope he used for a leash to Henry's collar, grabbed his coat, and stormed out of the apartment, making sure to slam the kitchen door good and hard in the hopes that it would wake her and give her a splitting headache.

The day was gray and cold but he didn't notice. It fit his mood perfectly and seemed but an extension of it. He didn't know where he was going to go, he just knew he didn't want to be around his mom for a while. He took Henry for his morning walk, circling the neighborhood until he found himself back at his tenement house.

Ivy looked at the building, thinking of his mother passed out inside, and felt the old rage building in him. Why did things have to be this way? Couldn't she see that she was screwing everything up?

I wonder how she'd feel if I just disappeared, or died? he thought self-pityingly. Maybe that wasn't such a bad idea. If he disappeared for a while, maybe she would so- ber up.

Ivy's look brightened. He ran around to the back door of the garage and found it was unlocked. He went in and cleared a space in the corner, then arranged some boxes and a dilapidated chair cushion into a makeshift bed.

"She'll never know we're here," Ivy whispered to his dog as they settled together on the cushion. "She never comes in here. Okay, Henry, we've got our own place now." The only problem was that it was cold in the garage and certain to get colder, especially at night.

"What are we going to do?" he wondered to Henry, who was licking his face. He'd just have to find some way to keep Henry and himself warm in there.

A memory of something he'd read came to him and he opened his backpack, digging among his books. In the bottom was an issue of *Popular Mechanics* he'd taken from the school library with an article in it about a guy who had invented a space heater out of old washing-machine parts. The heater ran on very little electricity and no heating fuel. He flipped the pages until he found the article and sat, nodding his head, his smile growing wider as he read.

5

Bill woke to Devin's screaming happily and jumping up and down on his stomach. His son's screams detonated a headache of nuclear proportions in his skull, and his use of Bill's gut as a trampoline threatened to bring up all the booze he'd imbibed.

"Get the hell off me!" Bill bellowed in pained rage, sitting up too quickly and setting off further explosions in his head that were fiercer than the mad gonging of earlier.

Startled and scared, Devin shrieked, at the same time reflexively propelling himself backward away from his father. With Bill's body rising beneath him, Devin lost his balance and fell off the couch.

Bill was sinking back to a prone position from the force of the pain in his head and saw his son falling. He tried to grab the boy, but his alcohol-dulled reflexes just couldn't make it. Devin fell, tears already welling in his eyes, his face screwed up to bawl even before he hit, and whacked the back of his head against the edge of the coffee table as he tumbled to the rug. He lay, stunned, blinking water from eyes that looked at Bill with hurt astonishment and accusation.

Bill's voice and the crack of Devin's head against the table brought Evelyn and the twins running from the front hall where they had been hanging their coats. As they reached the door, Devin's stunned silence erupted into a scream of pain.

Bill sat up, despite his raging headache, and reached for his son, who squirmed away in terror as though he thought his father meant to harm him more.

Evelyn ran into the room, taking in the empty bottles on the table and Bill's bleary-eyed, rumpled state in one judgmental glance, and picked Devin up, clucking to him and shushing him softly as she hugged and kissed him. With a hard glance that spoke nasty volumes at Bill, she carried Devin out of the room and upstairs. He could be heard wailing at the top of his lungs all the way up to his room and then some before his crying began to sputter, stall, and subside.

Bill held his aching head in his hands, wincing at the needles of pain Devin's shrill screams had sent shooting through his head. He felt eyes on him and looked up. Sassy and Missy still stood in the doorway, staring at him. Missy looked scared and confused, on the verge of tears herself, but Sassy stared at him with more contempt and disgust than Evelyn had shown.

Neither of them moved, and Bill's head hurt too much for him to do anything but hold it and hope it didn't fall off his shoulders during one of the booming rhythmic explosions of pain that rocked it in time to his heartbeat.

Missy looked at the bottles on the table, at Bill, then quickly away, becoming suddenly interested in the pattern of the hooked rug on the floor. Sassy kept her accusatory stare on him and seemed about to say something when Evelyn called them upstairs to help her with Devin.

Bill tried to stand, retreating twice from the pain and nausea it caused, and succeeded in gaining a very stooped upright stance on the third try. Groaning, he picked up the bottles and glass and carried them in slow motion, wincing at every step, into the kitchen. He couldn't bend over to throw the bottles in the trash under the sink without feeling as though he was going to pass out. Instead, he put them in the sink with the glass. He remained there, staring at them and clutching the porcelain edge as if for dear life until the dizziness passed.

Using the counter for support, he baby-stepped to the refrigerator, opened it, and began a slow, painful-at-every-move search of the shelves, pushing aside jars and bottles and Tupperware holders of leftovers. Hanging on to the fridge door, he lowered himself slowly to a squatting position, legs bowed out, back straight to avoid the dizziness bending over would bring, looking ridiculously like a ballet dancer doing an arthritic plié.

The four wire rack shelves and the shelves on the door didn't contain what he sought. Frustration brought him to attack the perishable-goods drawers. He yanked open the top, sliced-meat drawer hard enough to make it jump its runner and get stuck. It was empty. He tried to push it back in, banging it furiously with the side of his fist until it righted and closed. His head throbbed terribly with the effort.

He grabbed the bottom, and last, drawer, the crisper, and pulled it open with less force yet still hard enough to cause a can of Budweiser stuck behind a package of carrots at the back of the drawer to come tumbling forward, ricocheting off the inside front of the drawer and bouncing halfway back to its original position.

Eureka! He'd *thought* there was a beer down there—dimly remembered putting it there several years ago right after he and Cindy were married. Some company had brought it, a cousin of Cindy's whose husband had guzzled all but one of a six-pack while Bill had sat there, still young in his sobriety, and made believe it didn't bother him. He had been tempted by the beer after the company left, and had almost dumped it out to keep from succumbing to its call, but had stuck it in the fridge drawer, telling himself it was to have on hand in case of more company, but really to prove to himself that he could know it was there and leave it alone (*and* maybe *just to have there in case of an emergency like this, eh, Billy-boy?*).

He tried to deny the cutting self-accusation, but the answer to the question of why he had been able to refuse to take the drink then, when he'd been only a few months dry, but couldn't now, after nearly four years of sobriety, seemed obvious: He'd been able to keep it there not as proof of his willpower, but because he always *knew* it was there, just in case he ever needed it—no, *when* he needed it.

He tried to argue that it was impossible. His taking the beer now was just one of those things. He could refuse the drink if he wanted to, but he didn't want to. After all, it was just a *beer.* But deep inside was the knowledge that he was lying to himself. Before, he'd had Cindy and an entirely new life to keep him strong. That had kept him from drinking the symbolic beer for four years. Now he had nothing and no one to blame but himself.

The knowledge seared his brain, and in defense he automatically pushed it from the realm of conscious thought and back into the miasmic depths of his subconscious. He couldn't face it, just couldn't. He made believe he was ignorant of the truth and devised excuses, as a good alcoholic does, that sounded right and good and justifiable to him and that he could believe with a minimum of effort—to hell with what anyone else thought.

These thoughts sloshed around in his brain as he retrieved the beer can and pulled himself up by the door. He closed the fridge and leaned against it, fumbling with the pop-top until he got a numb fingertip under the edge and pulled it up, pushing the tab into the can.

Heady beer sprayed the kitchen like seawater foam.

The sudsy stuff expanded from the opening rapidly, threatening to spill over the top, but he got it to his gaping mouth, inhaling the foam and slurping the liquid thirstily, losing only a tiny trickle down his chin.

Eyes closed, he drained the can, belching loudly as he lowered it from his lips. For a moment he thought it would all come back up with the belch, but it stayed down and, *yes*, it worked as he knew it would, like the proverbial charm, and he felt better.

Same thing as a Bromo-Seltzer, he thought, opening his eyes, and was confronted with Evelyn staring her steely stare at him.

"Great!" she said in disgust. "Just great." Her eyes glistened with anger.

To Bill, for that moment, she looked so much like Cindy that he wanted to cry. He gulped hard and turned away from her, walking more steadily now with the beer in him. He went into the front hall and grabbed his coat off the mirrored rack.

"Bill, I want to talk to you," Evelyn said harshly, following him.

He ignored her, looked right through her, and put on his coat.

"Bill, don't leave!" she shouted angrily and added in a more controlled tone, "Please, Bill. We have to talk *now*."

He zipped his coat and walked out the door.

He woke shivering. It was dark and at first he thought with terror that he was in the tunnel of his dream. The lights of a passing car dispelled that thought, thankfully, and he realized that he was in his car.

It was funny, sort of, that he'd thought of the dream just now. He hadn't had the dream since . . . since when? Oh, yeah. Since he'd started drinking again, and that was . . . he wasn't sure. In fact, he wasn't sure what day, or more rightly what night, it was. He felt like shit—worse.

He looked at his watch, hit the date button, and saw that it was Monday, 3:00 A.M. He closed his eyes and tried to think. He remembered leaving the house Saturday afternoon and going to the Quarry Tavern for a drink, but could remember nothing after that.

Blackout!

The thought tried to push its way to the front of his mind, but he kept it out. He turned on the dome light and discovered a bottle of Jack Daniel's, half full, lying on the seat next to him.

"Hello," he whispered through trembling lips. He couldn't remember having bought it, but he was glad he had. He picked it up and had trouble unscrewing the cap, his hands were shaking so badly. *Must be damn cold,* he thought, though he didn't feel cold. He got it open and took three quick swigs, then three more. His hands grew calmer and he took another long pull. His hands, his whole body, stopped trembling.

You had the DTs, you fool, he thought and accepted the knowledge as though it was nothing out of the ordinary. He capped the bottle, looked at his watch again, and realized he had to be to work in six hours. He felt a sudden urge to pee and got out of the car. The night was unnaturally warm for February, confirming that his shakes hadn't been from the cold, but his feet were chilled. He was still wearing his slippers.

He looked around as he stood by the car relieving himself and saw that he was in the parking lot of a Leominster nightclub, The Toreador, on the outskirts of the Searstown Plaza near Route 2. The lot was empty. He zipped, got back into the car, and took another drink, trying to decide whether to go home or not. He figured that might not be such a good idea, considering the state he was in. It was warm enough to sleep in the car—he'd already proved that—might as well stay where he was and go home after

Evelyn had left to take Devin to day care and go to work herself. And by then the twins would be in school.

He set the beeper alarm on his watch for eight o'clock, finished the bottle, and curled up on the seat. He was asleep in seconds.

As expected, Evelyn and the kids were gone when he staggered into the house. He took a hot-as-he-could-stand-it shower and dressed for work. His hangover wasn't as bad as it had been Saturday, but it was bad enough, and by the time he was ready to leave for work, over an hour late, he noticed the return of the tremors in his hands. He took six aspirins with a cup of instant coffee for breakfast and stopped on his way to work at a package store that had just opened. He bought a dozen nip-size bottles of Jack Daniel's, drank two immediately in the car, and stashed the rest in his suit pockets to get him through the morning.

For once he was glad it was a Monday. It meant he wouldn't be in the home office in Crocker all day. Every Monday he had to drive to Fitchburg, Worcester, and Springfield to collect the weekly reports and time cards of the store detectives that worked the K marts in those cities, and go over any problems with them.

He spent the morning in the Fitchburg office, laboring over his own reports while his assistant did the daily inventory of high-risk theft items—small tape recorders and Walkmans, cassette tapes, candy, condoms, and women's lingerie were priorities; the merchandise that seemed to attract shoplifters the most. By doing a daily inventory of these and most of the other small, easily concealed goods in the store, he could tell where security needed to be beefed up.

By noon his stash of nips was exhausted and he was ready to hit the road. After a quick stop at a liquor store within Crocker Plaza itself for a quart of Jack Daniel's, a six-pack of Bud, and some Clorets for his breath, he was on his way.

Between Fitchburg and Worcester he drank a quarter of the whiskey and two beers. He did his duties at the store as quickly as possible, avoiding talking to anyone as much as he could, which was easy: the staff there resented him ever since he'd become the regional director and corporate headquarters had moved the Central Massachusetts home office to Crocker to accommodate his living situation. He was back on the road in forty-five minutes.

The longer trip to Springfield consumed the rest of the beer and all but a couple of finger widths of the whiskey. He did his work in record time there, also, and hit the closest bar—a small pub called The Wall—that he could find. By four thirty he was well on his way to another stupendous drunk but still had enough presence of mind to call the home office and explain that he wouldn't be back in today and was going to head home from the Springfield store.

He remembered nothing after that until he woke in his car again with the sun shining in his eyes. He was still parked in the small lot behind The Wall, so he knew—thank God for small favors—that he hadn't tried to drive anywhere during his blackout.

His watch told him it was seven thirty, Tuesday morning. He would never get home, cleaned up, and to work by nine. He noticed a pay phone next to the pub's rear entrance and staggered to it. With hands shaking so badly he could barely put the money in the slot, he punched up his assistant's home number and told him he'd be out sick for a couple of days.

"About time I took a goddamn vacation for myself," he grumblingly rationalized when he'd hung up the phone. Winter was back and the cold increased his DTs. He hobbled back to the car and sucked the last few mouthfuls of whiskey from the bottom of the bottle—what he had always jokingly referred to as the "backwash"—and searched the floor for the discarded beer cans, tipping each upside down to his mouth to slurp out any last drops they contained.

It wasn't enough. He still felt sick and shaky. He looked at his watch—eight o'clock. At least an hour to go before any package stores opened. A sweaty panic filled him. *An hour to wait! A whole hour!* He didn't think he could last. He had to have something now or he was going to be so shaking sick in an hour that he wouldn't be able to drive to a package store, much less be able to act normal enough to go inside and buy something.

An idea came to him, something an old wino had told him about stealing bottles of NyQuil when he was really hard up for a drink and had no money. "Stuff's twenty-five percent alcohol," the wino had explained. Bill started the car and drove until he spotted a pharmacy that was open. Like a man in a desperate hurry, or with a desperate need, he went in and bought three bottles of the cold medicine, slapping a twenty on the counter and not waiting for the change.

Back in the car, he ripped open a package and guzzled the bottle down, gagging at the awful taste of the stuff. He started to drive and opened the second bottle. Halfway through it, his nerves calmed, he felt better and actually told himself the stuff wasn't half bad, was pretty good, in fact. By the time he was on the Mass Turnpike heading home, he was into the third bottle and feeling fine. He sang along with golden oldies on the radio and sipped his medicine in high spirits.

Back in Crocker, he didn't feel so good anymore. The thick, syrupy-sweet cough medicine wasn't sitting well in his empty stomach. He couldn't remember the last solid meal he'd had and didn't want one now. Just the thought of food threatened to bring the NyQuil up PDQ.

He got home and made it to the bathroom just in time.

His stomach felt better once he was rid of the NyQuil, but his head was pounding up a storm again. He stumbled to his bed, kicked off his shoes, and lay down, falling quickly to sleep in his clothes.

6

Ivy tightened the fan belt he'd found in the garage and applied a fine coating of motor oil to the washing machine drums he'd "borrowed" from two old machines in the far corner of the storage area. His homemade heater was finished. By scavenging parts from the old washing machines and a lawn mower in the garage, he had managed to build the fuel-less heater described in the *Popular Mechanics* article. He hooked it up to an old car battery—from the local junkyard—and crossed his fingers before flicking the switch. With a hum and a shudder the heater came to life, but he kept his jubilation in check, waiting to see if it would actually throw any heat.

The machine worked on the principle of heat created through friction when the two round drums—actually the inside baskets of the washing machines that hold the clothes during a wash—spin in opposite directions and are closely together, one against the other, so that they barely rub. Though it needed no fuel to run, it did need electricity, and the drums had to be lubricated daily with a fine sheen of oil—he used his mother's cooking oil—so as not to grind.

Ivy held his hand over the revolving drums and turned the knob controlling the speed of the fan belts up a notch. The drums spun faster, humming louder, and with a sense of joy surpassing anything he'd ever experienced, Ivy felt heat radiating up to his hand. He let out a whoop of victory as a warm stream of air washed over him.

"It works!" he crowed in a soft yet enthusiastic voice. "The damn thing actually works!" Now all he had to do was rig up something to keep a slow drip of lubricating oil on the drums and he wouldn't have to worry about remembering to oil it every day.

Struggling with some heavy boxes of dishes someone had left in the garage, he stacked them in a circle around the homemade heater and his bed. When he was done, he had a nice, cozy, warm little room for Henry and himself that would also keep the dog from wandering when Ivy wasn't there.

The only thing he was unsure of was the old car battery. He didn't know how long it would provide power, but the junkyard man had said he would recharge it for Ivy anytime. Still, he wanted to rig something more permanent and dependable; if the battery ran out on a cold day, no amount of recharging would do any good if Henry froze before Ivy got home.

"It'll have to do for now, though. Right, boy?"

Henry jumped at his legs, and Ivy took him in his arms, feeling a sense of accomplishment and victory he hadn't had in a long time.

7

"What happened to your hand, Jack?"

"I cut it on the metal lathe in the machine shop," he lies, and the fool shrink accepts it unquestioningly.

The psychologist is easy. The man plays his game, thinking it is his and he has won, when the opposite is true. The plan is genius, a true jewel. He wonders why it didn't occur to him sooner and knows it is because he didn't need it sooner. Necessity is the mother of invention. Who said that? Frank Zappa, wasn't it?

He laughs and the stupid psychologist laughs with him, not knowing why he laughs.

"What's so funny, Jack?"

He laughs again, and again the idiot joins him.

"I'm just so happy with the change in my life, the change you've wrought," he says, smiling his high-on-life-and-dammit-isn't-it-good smile.

"I'm just so full of joy at the miracle you've performed. I just wish I could truly, tangibly, express what I feel in my heart for you." He laughs again at the truth of the latter statement, which sounds like so much brownnosing bullshit but isn't.

In his mind he imagines using the thing hidden in his mattress on the good doctor, shoving it in a place that will ensure the fool shrink will never have to worry about occasional constipation again.

Ah, but dreams are a dime a dozen. Someday the plea-sure of performing radical proctology on many, perhaps even the psychologist himself, will be his, but now he has other fish to fry and the doctor is a necessary cooking utensil.

The prison chaplain is even easier than the shrink. A saintly expression, a bowing of his head at the mention of Jesus Christ, and a soul-baring confession of past crimes and atrocities—which he enjoys immensely even though all but one of the sins are fantasy. He underlines his tales, each more lurid than the last, with tears of remorse and cries of pain for the suffering he has caused, all the while secretly knowing that what he confesses is what lies ahead, not behind.

He has a special feeling for the priest, too, and a desire to give the holy man final communion with his sharp and secret manhood. But these are hidden thoughts, savored for their nourishment but not allowed to interfere with his true mission.

With the priest and psychologist won over to his side, he hopes the prison authorities will fall to his game of domi-noes, but they are harder and wiser than the men of liberal science and religion. They know his kind—though not who he is—and he knows they know. With time, he's sure he could turn even the crusty old warden to his favor, but time is not a commodity he can invest in anymore.

The game changes from dominoes to poker when the parole board sits at the table, and though he knows he holds only a pair, he believes, must believe, in the power of the bluff and in that old whore, Lady Luck.

And in the batting of the lazy eyelash of authority the game changes again, becomes baseball. It's the bottom of the ninth, two out, winning run on first, and his two slug-gers, the doctor and the priest, due up to bat. Banished from the playing field, like a manager thrown out of the game by the home plate umpire, he sits in his locker room/ cell waiting word of the outcome and imagining he can hear the cheers of the hometown fans just outside the prison walls.

8

Bill Gage woke sober for the first time in days and didn't like it. What he liked less was the guilt and reproach his previously drink-subdued conscience kept serving up to him, like an Italian mother ignoring the pleas of her dinner guests that they've had enough as she heaps more food upon their plates.

He lay in bed, watching flashes of the past few days play across his memory like scenes from *The Lost Weekend* and was ashamed. What had happened? Why had he done the stupid, even cruel things he'd done?

The memory of Devin's look of terror brought tears to his eyes. He wouldn't hurt Devin, or the twins, for anything in the world!

When you're sober you wouldn't, his conscience stated.

And what of the blackouts? What had he done during those? He suddenly felt like a character in a run-of-the-mill detective yarn wondering if he's killed anyone. No. It wasn't in him to kill or hurt anyone.

Really? His conscience again. *What about Wilbur Clayton? What about your own son?* He flinched at the thought.

Well, that's it, he told his conscience. *It's over. Never again. I've got it out of my system. It was just a temporary relapse. If I stop it now, I can repair the damage I've done to my family. I can explain to them, explain to Evelyn . . .*

what? That was a good question. How could he explain to them what had happened, *why* it had happened, when he wasn't sure himself?

The dream.

Yes, the dream! But was that really why he'd gone off the wagon, over a stupid dream? And if it was, could he tell them about it? Could he tell them about the guilt he felt over killing poor insane Wilbur Clayton in cold blood, not to mention the guilt he harbored over Cindy's death?

That was the crux of it. Guilt. His old friend. Guilt had been the driving force in his life for as long as he could remember. Guilt over not wanting to be like his father had driven him to a career in law enforcement, following in his father's footsteps. His father, the cop. Guilt had driven him to the bottle ten years ago when the truth about his father had come out. His father, the serial killer. Deep down hadn't he known all along what his father was?

And how did you know that, Billy-boy? That is something he doesn't want to, *can't* think about.

Guilt over not being the kind of man Cindy could love and want, who could take care of her, had driven him to kick the booze habit (and boy! he'd proved what a great caretaker he was, hadn't he?).

The pain of truth welled in him and he sobbed, hard. The tears brought more guilt—here he was crying for himself when he'd never shed a tear at Cindy's funeral. He shed them now in long mournful cries of hurt and loss. He cried until he had no more tears to give, and then he cried some more, dry eyes burning, throat choked closed.

In the midst of his pain, a redeeming thought came to him: It's not too late to make amends. He could never change what had happened, the past was past, as Cindy had been fond of saying, but he could fix things with his surviving family and do it without mentioning the dream. With all that had happened, surely they would understand and empathize. And if he made a new start with them, he could erase the damage of the past few days and banish it from their minds, and his, forever.

"That's it," he said through clenched teeth. "It's over." With a sense of determination he hadn't felt since he'd decided to kill the Video Killer no matter what, Bill got out of bed and went into the bathroom to shower.

9

Ivy got off the school bus and walked toward his house swinging his backpack lazily by his side. Even with the trouble with his mom's drinking, he was enjoying school a lot more these days, and his grades reflected it. In his pocket he had his second term report card—all *A*'s. His teacher, Mrs. Rayburn, was ecstatic over the change in Ivy's schoolwork, certain that she had *reached* him and turned him around.

Ivy let her think it; he didn't mind. Mrs. Rayburn was nice. She was even talking about having him take the entrance exam for the Crocker School for Gifted Children. He didn't think he'd have any trouble passing it, but he wasn't sure he wanted to go there.

He'd come out of his shell a lot since Christmas and had made a lot of new friends at school. Of course, his fame from being involved in the Video Killer case had helped. After he'd had his picture in all the local papers and had even been interviewed on channels four and five news reports, he'd found the kids at school a lot more accessible. All of them had wanted to know the gory details about how he had discovered that the guy living next door to him, Wilbur Clayton, was a serial killer who videotaped his murders and sent them to the police—hence his nickname. Over and over he'd had to tell of what had happened at Crocker Hospital on Cristmas Eve when Wilbur Clayton had caught Ivy spying on him in the abandoned wing of the hospital and had chased him into the tunnel under the building. The only thing Ivy left out when telling the story was the act of cold-blooded murder he'd witnessed when the cop on the case, Bill Gage, had shot the defenseless Wilbur Clayton in the head.

He turned up the driveway to the tenement house and quickened his steps. He'd been gone from the apartment for two days now, and he was hungry. He wanted to get some food supplies for himself and Henry and leave his report card on the table. He could imagine his mother's reaction when she saw that his grades had gone from C's and D's in the previous term to A's now. Later he planned to go up and see her, after she'd had time to see the report card and think about things. He hoped it would make her realize how hard he was trying and might rekindle the closeness between them they'd shared at Christmas and had lost too quickly.

He went to the garage first to check on Henry. As soon as he entered, Ivy felt the warm air generated by his homemade heater and breathed a sigh of relief. He found Henry on the bed of boxes, curled up and sleeping. The newspapers on the floor around the dog were messed and wet, but were nothing that couldn't be easily cleaned up, which Ivy did by rolling them into a large ball and chucking them into an empty box he'd put nearby for just such a use.

The heater was running smoothly, the spinning drums humming quietly with a soothing sound. Ivy knelt by his dog and let out a low whistle. Henry awoke, yawned, and stretched before becoming aware of his master, then jumped onto Ivy's lap, his tongue and paws brandished in an excited show of affection. After several minutes of this Ivy noticed the dish of dog food from the last can he'd taken from the apartment and the bowl of water he'd left for Henry that morning were empty. Picking his dog up, Ivy shut off the heater and carried his pet up to the apartment for feeding and watering and so he could leave his report card before his mom got home.

Something was wrong, Ivy realized as he reached the third floor. The kitchen door to the apartment was open. It was too early for his mother to be home, which made Ivy think someone had broken in and might still be inside. Quietly he put Henry down on the porch floor and crept to the door. He peered in, careful to expose as little of himself as possible.

The apartment looked empty but was a mess. All the kitchen cabinets were open, their contents knocked over or strewn around the countertop. A lot of the stuff was on the floor: a box of cornflakes, its contents spilled; a jar of peanut butter, shattered in a spray of gooey stuff, a jar of coffee near the refrigerator door.

Ivy held his breath and listened intently for any sound. There was only one, coming from the direction of the living room. It was a familiar sound, raspy, and buzzing.

Snoring!

His *mother's* snoring!

Calling Henry to him, Ivy opened the door and let his puppy scurry inside. Ivy followed. As soon as he entered the kitchen, he could see into the living room, and there she was, passed out in her easy chair. For a moment, because of the mess the place was in, the thought crossed Ivy's mind that his mother might have come home early, surprised the burglars, and been knocked out by them.

Then he saw the near-empty bottle of Sangria by her feet. She was knocked out, all right, but she had done the knocking to herself with the help of the booze. Ivy felt disgust and anger welling in him.

But what had happened to the house? Not just the kitchen, but the living room too was in shambles, as though an earthquake or a severe windstorm had struck. Lamps were knocked over, the coffee table was askew, knickknacks littered the floor—even the ugly Felix the Cat clock his mother loved so much lay broken on the floor.

In a muddled state Ivy walked through the living room to his mother's bedroom. It, too, was a mess. The bureau drawers were pulled out and their contents flung around the room. The bed mattress was half off the frame, and the blankets lay in a crumpled pile on the floor.

He turned and ran to his room, confronting more of the same. His clothes were all over the place, and his bed nearly turned upside down.

In a frenzy he went to the closet and reached in, feeling along the inside wall for the hole where he kept a small cloth bag that contained ten dollars he had saved from his continued bottle collecting. He had forgotten the bag when he'd moved into the garage and hadn't remembered it until just now when he'd seen the closet door open and all his things in a mess.

The bag was gone. Ivy squeezed into the narrow closet, searching for the bag, and found it on the floor. Empty.

Ivy was shocked and perplexed. Had the apartment indeed been robbed? Perhaps it had while his mother was passed out drunk in the living room. It seemed farfetched and didn't answer the question of why she was home and drunk in the middle of the afternoon on a workday.

There was only one other conclusion he could come to, one he didn't want to accept but couldn't deny.

He ran to the living room to wake his mother and question her but made another discovery before he could. Lying half under the recliner was a pink slip of paper. Ivy bent over and retrieved it while Henry tried to snatch it from him. Ivy shooed the pup away and examined the paper. It was a layoff notice, effective immediately, from the plastics factory where she worked. It confirmed his suspicions, and in a rage he shook his mother awake.

"Mom! Wake up!" he shouted.

"Go 'way."

"Mom! Wake up! Right now! I mean it!"

She tried to ignore him, wincing at the harshness of his voice, but couldn't. She struggled to consciousness.

"Mom, I want to know what the hell is going on. Why'd you trash the apartment, and where's my money?"

She roused herself enough to find her bottle and take a swig before answering. "Whaddya mean?" she slurred, wine dribbling from the corner of her mouth.

"I mean this friggin' mess!" Ivy yelled, indicating with a sweep of his arm. "I mean the money I had hidden in my closet!" he added, pointing toward his room.

His mother sat up, hugging the bottle tightly to her chest. "I don't know what you're talkin' about. Musta been your mutt. I tol' you to leave him outside."

At that Ivy exploded. "It wasn't Henry, Ma! He was *outside* all day. You did it, so don't lie and don't go blaming my dog. *You* did it, and *you* stole my money."

"I don't know what you're talking about," she answered guiltily, avoiding his eyes.

"Don't you?" Ivy shot back. "Then who took my money?"

"What money?" she grumbled.

"You know goddamn well what money," Ivy thundered. "The money you stole out of my closet."

Now it was his mother's turn to be angry, but it was a false anger, a bluff anger in an attempt to change the subject. "Don't use that tone of voice with me! I'm still your mother!"

Ivy barked a hard, sarcastic laugh at her. "What a joke! A *real* mother wouldn't drink herself into a stupor every day and steal money from her own son!"

"I didn't steal it," she said meekly. "I . . . I borrowed it."

"Hah!" Ivy challenged her.

His mother roused herself from her chair and pointed

accusingly at Ivy. "What are you doing with that much money, anyway? And why are you hiding it?"

"That's none of your business. It's my money, and you had no right stealing it," Ivy retorted.

"Oh, *really!* What gives you the right to hoard money when every cent I earn goes to paying rent and buying food so you can have a roof over your head and enough to eat."

Ivy was temporarily taken aback with a twinge of guilt.

"If you're making money, you should be giving it to me!" his mother demanded, sensing the advantage shifting to her.

Ivy saw what she was doing and recovered quickly. "Why? So you can spend it on booze and cigarettes?"

"What I do with my money is my business!"

"Yeah, and what I do with my money is *my* business. You don't have any right taking my money."

His mother was silent.

"So why did you take it, huh? To buy this crap?" Ivy kicked the bottle next to the chair over, spilling the wine on the rug. His mother flinched and grabbed it, righting it before too much of her precious booze could escape.

"I got laid off from the plastics shop today," she said in a small voice, picking the bottle up and hugging it to her.

Ivy felt a moment of pity but was too angry to let it stop him. "So that gave you the right to come home, trash the place and steal my money so you could get drunk? How's that going to help? If you had asked me for the money to help out—not for booze and butts—I would have given it to you."

"Oh, right." His mother sniggered. "Look, Ivy, don't give me that crap. Just leave me alone." She lifted the bottle to her lips and took a long pull from it.

Ivy gave her a look of utter disgust, picked up Henry, and walked out of the apartment.

* * *

Henry lapped tears from Ivy's face. They sat together in Ivy's nest in the garage. "Yeah, boy, we have to stay here, now. She's been so drunk she didn't even know I was gone. She doesn't care. As long as I can keep this heater going, we'll be nice and warm. I can even still go to school. I guess I can sneak into the apartment and get food when she's passed out. Yeah . . . it's just us two."

Ivy picked up his dog and hugged him to his chest. But the tears wouldn't stop.

10

The priest comes by his cell just before the dinner bell rings.

"Nothing yet, Jack," he says. "They'll continue deliberations tomorrow. Don't look so disappointed. It looks very good for you. Your exemplary record during your fifteen years here speaks much more persuasively on your behalf than does anything I or Dr. Schultz can say. Pray tonight. Pray for God's will to be done. If you pray that with all your heart, He will do what is best for you."

"Thank you, Father Rosario," he mumbles, hanging his head. "I will."

The priest blesses him and leaves.

He bangs the wall in anger and frustration but stops himself quickly.

What am I doing?

It's all right. What's another day? It's just a minor postponement, a slight game delay due to rain. The game will go on, I will be victorious.

Calmer, he sits on his cot, chiding himself for losing control and for revealing to the priest his disappointment. He looks at the small square mirror hanging on the wall over his cot. His pale blue eyes stare back at him. His close-cropped brown hair seems to bristle with annoyance.

His large mouth is grimacing beneath his fleshy nose. He makes a willful effort to smile, to relax, to appear to be a mindless religious fanatic.

There. That's it. He must remember to always keep his mask on, never let it fall. One glimpse at his true self will have them howling for his blood, will have them locking him away in a dark hole and throwing away the key. He is so close now, he cannot lose it.

Another day is nothing to an immortal. The cop will still be there tomorrow, and the next day, and the next. He's not going anywhere. According to the newspaper, he's not even a cop anymore. Retribution time is coming.

With a quick jerking motion of his head, he spits his false teeth into his hand and puts them in the glass of water on the floor by his bed. He checks his cell mate, who is sleeping, and after a moment of listening to be sure no one is approaching the cell, he removes the cloth-wrapped object from the hole in the underside of the mattress. Unwrapped, it catches the light and gleams with a cold brilliance. He caresses it, careful not to touch it too hard lest he cut himself. He breathes on it and slips it carefully into his mouth so as not to be cut by it. It feels good there. It feels hungry, and he can imagine how it will look and feel ripping into the mouth of the cop and the mouths of his family members.

He removes the killing object from his lips and straps it on. He reaches under the cot for the worn newspaper and lies down, reading the article about the Video Killer again. Oh, how he would have liked to have met him. They would have made quite a team. But even in death, his brother, Wilbur Clayton, speaks to and inspires him through the deeds he performed.

With a sense of growing excitement, he begins to form the secondary phase of his plan in his mind. He hasn't thought about it much, what exactly he will do once he is free. He knows it will come, as all great ideas come to genius. And it does.

He laughs softly, running his fingers over the metal between his legs and letting his mind run wild with fantasies of revenge beyond ecstasy.

11

The twins were home, in their room listening to their stereo, when Bill got out of the shower. Still weak, but feeling much better than he had, he leaned on their doorjamb and smiled at them.

"Hi," he said as brightly as possible.

"Hi, Daddy!" Missy, dark haired and tomboyish in her rumpled sweater and jeans, answered, flashing him a quick smile before subduing it under the glare her sister threw her way. Sassy, light haired and neat as a pin in a suede jumper, remained silent, ignoring him.

Bill took a deep breath, preparing to speak, to rectify, but chickened out. He reasoned it would be easier to tell everyone at once so he wouldn't have to go through it twice, and decided to wait until Evelyn got home. He went to his room to dress, not failing to notice that Sassy turned the volume on the stereo up full as soon as his back was turned. He was buttoning his shirt, about to go downstairs and call out for some pizza for supper, when Sassy appeared in the doorway.

"Why did you come back? Why didn't you just stay away? You think you can just come back here, smile and say hi, and everything will be okay?" she asked in rapid-fire succession, her voice thick with vehemence.

"Sassy, I came back to apologize and explain," he said, palms outward in a gesture of pleading.

"What's to explain? You were a drunk when Mommy

met you and you're still a drunk. You never think about anyone but yourself." Her face was flushed with anger and her voice heavy with threatening tears.

"Sassy, that's not true—"

"Isn't it?" she interrupted him. "Just cuz I'm only nine years old doesn't mean I'm dumb. I heard you and Mommy arguing about your job with the police. I *heard* her ask you to leave it cuz it was wrecking our family, and you *wouldn't do it!* You had to be a big-shot detective!"

"You're right," he said softly, humbly. "I made a mistake. People make mistakes. I was hoping I could make up for my mistakes with you and Missy and Devin. I still want to be your father."

"Is getting drunk and beating Devin up how you make up for mistakes?" she snapped accusingly. "And you're *not* my father, even though you're a loser just like he was. At least he was nice enough to take off and not screw us up by staying around." The tears came.

"Sassy, I—"

"If it wasn't for you, my mother would still be alive!" she screamed and ran down the hall. The slamming of her bedroom door was a thunderous exclamation point.

Bill sat in shocked silence on his bed. He'd had no idea Sassy harbored such feelings and resentment, which obviously went back much further than his recent drunk. He had thought she was doing so well, recovering so nicely. He hadn't an inkling of the hate, blame, and resentment she had for him. How could he have been so blind?

He thought about what she'd said and saw the truth of it in black and white. He *was* self-centered. He always had to have his way. He could never see what was important to anyone but himself, could never focus on anything else but his own little reality.

Talk about tunnel vision!

And he had thought it would be so easy to win his

family back, that they would see everything in terms of
how it had affected *him*, of how it had screwed *him* up.

Evelyn must feel the same way, he thought. Sassy was
smart, but she was still a kid, and she couldn't have voiced
all that she'd said so clearly without having heard it from
an adult first. He had thought it wasn't too late to make
amends, but it had been too late long before he'd picked
up the bottle again. His drinking wasn't the problem here,
as he'd thought. *He* was the problem.

The only rays of hope he could find in this dismal situation were Missy and Devin. Missy didn't seem to feel the
same way as her sister, but then Missy, though always the
one with the smart mouth, was an easygoing person quick
to forgive and eager to be liked. But she was very impres-
sionable and sooner or later would go along with the ma-
jority consensus of Evelyn and Sassy. Devin was *his* son
and was too young to understand any of this, but maybe
he understood on a basic enough level. Bill's outburst
toward him the other day might have damaged that relationship forever also.

God! He had been a damn blind fool!

Self-loathing permeated him to the point that he
wanted to step outside his body and beat the shit out of
himself. It led him to contemplation of the pistol he kept
locked in the strongbox in the top drawer of the dresser,
but he recognized that thinking of suicide was only self-
pity in disguise and hated himself more.

"Daddee!"

Devin ran squealing into the room and threw himself at
Bill, wrapping his arms tightly about his father's neck in
an embrace that spoke of how much he had missed his
dad. Bill returned the hug, pulling Devin close, and broke
down and cried.

"You can't blame her for feeling the way she does,"
Evelyn said softly, holding her coffee cup with two hands

just below her lips. She and Bill were sitting at the kitchen table; the kids were in bed.

"I don't. I . . . I just don't know what to do about it." Bill sighed. He gave Evelyn a measured look. "Do you feel the same way?"

Evelyn looked into her cup for a long moment. "To an extent I do, yes. I don't blame you for Cindy's death—you didn't make that crazy kid kill her—but you have to own up to the fact that it was your obsession with being a detective again that put her in the position of becoming a target. She talked to me a lot about you then. She understood why you had to go back to police work, understood how much your father haunted you, but she couldn't understand how you could be willing to jeopardize your marriage and your family over it.

"Cindy was very practical, as I'm sure you know, and she could never see why people let the past rule their lives. And she was right, you know. You can't do anything about the past, can't change it. You can't even do anything about the future. All you can do anything about is the *now*. But you couldn't see that, you were too wrapped up in your past. And then the strangest thing was that after it all, when you were no longer a cop, all you wanted to do was forget the past, and you expected everyone else to go right along with you."

"Why didn't you tell me this before? Why didn't you tell me I was being such an insensitive idiot?"

Evelyn let out a derisive laugh. "Why didn't you take the crap out of your ears? I did tell you, starting when you wanted to move the kids back into this house, but no, you had decided they were fine and could deal with it. You actually made the absurd analogy that it was like making a kid get back on a bike once she's fallen off!"

Evelyn sipped from her cup, put it down, and shook her head sorrowfully. "Do you know that neither Missy nor Sassy has taken a bath or shower in the upstairs bathroom? They don't even go in there! They use the small bathroom down here. And Sassy won't hang her clothes in the closet of her room where she hid from that killer. You didn't know that, did you?"

Chagrined, Bill shook his head. "I noticed the clothes just today."

"Here's something else you don't know, but should. When I met with Sassy's psychologist—"

"Wait a minute!" Bill interrupted her. "When did you meet with her shrink, and why wasn't I invited?"

Evelyn gave Bill a hard, exasperated look. "You *were*, sweetheart. I told you about it when I gave you the letter from her doctor."

"What letter? I never saw any letter."

"It was with the doctor's bill that you complained so loudly about being too high!"

He remembered now. He had been so incensed at the cost of Sassy's therapy that he had barely glanced at the letter. He also remembered Evelyn's telling him about the impending meeting with the doctor, and he had made the stupid excuse that he had to work to be able to pay for the therapy since his insurance didn't cover it and had topped it off with a smart remark warning Evelyn to make sure she wasn't going to be charged for the meeting. Why had he been such a jerk?

"I'm sorry. I was an idiot."

"You'll get no argument from me," Evelyn replied, a wry smile on her face.

"So what happened with the psychologist?"

"She told me that the thing that weighed heaviest on Sassy, that she had the most trouble understanding and dealing with, was the way you abandoned her in the hospital when she needed you."

Bill started to protest but stopped himself. It was true. He had been so obsessed with killing Cindy's murderer that he had *used* Sassy and then discarded her when he had what he wanted.

"What do I do now? How do I make it up to her? What do I say?"

"I don't think there's anything you *can* say, it's the *doing* that'll make a difference. Just try to be a father to her, show her you love her no matter what she thinks of you. She'll come around. And whatever you do, *no more drinking!*"

Bill nodded his agreement, but couldn't help noticing the scratchy feeling in the back of his throat that cried out for a shot of smooth whiskey to soothe it.

12

He waits, the zebra shadows thrown by the bars of his cell striping his body. His mind is empty but for one phrase: Om nerva shevoya—*I am powerless over everything but myself. The meditative phrase was taught to him by the psychologist and, though he knows its meaning to be untrue (true for mere mortals but not him, oh, no, not him) it helps him to focus, to draw inward, to charge the power. At times, while meditating, he reaches such an intense pinnacle of perception he imagines his senses leave his body, connected to his mind by psychic umbilical cords, and he explores the world beyond his cell.*

He pictures the guards at the end of the cell block; the other prisoners reading, sleeping, writing letters, pissing, performing futile sex acts alone and on weaker inmates as they while away the endless seconds, minutes, hours, days, weeks, months, and years that are the bane of prisoners.

He could feel pity for them, if he could feel pity. They have not learned the secret to immortality that he knows: One day at a time. *Nothing else exists. There is no yesterday, no tomorrow. Today is eternity and he lives it, immortal.*

He imagines his ears can perceive every sound in the vast prison, no matter how small or distant. He pretends he can hear the pans rattling in the kitchen as the inmate cooks prepare dinner; the voices of the watchtower guards discussing Monday Night Football; the snuffling breath of the German shepherd guard dogs as they make their rounds with their guard masters. He thinks he can hear all sounds on earth, and some in hell below.

And he can imagine the smells, too. Oh! how he can imagine the smells! The Alpo breath of the dogs and the scent of their powerful bodies—pungent and damp, almost overpowering the sour-sweet stink of human perspiration from their masters. From the kitchen again, he imagines the odor of onions and fatty beef frying in preparation of stew.

With little effort he can conjure up the body scents of the thousand prisoners he is locked up with. The smells are of death and fear (what a lovely scent) and every emotion known to man secreting from the pent-up humanity around him. Beyond the walls, he can perceive the buried scent of their waste flowing into and filling the massive septic tank under the ground behind the prison.

A new scent, not imagined, reaches him at the same time as the sound of the locked door opening at the end of the block. It is Old Spice mingled with garlic. He knows the smell well, as he does the cadence of the footsteps that approach. It is the priest, his dark clothes rustling like a murmured prayer and the rosary beads he always wears round his neck clicking softly against the buttons of his shirt. The priest has had spaghetti in a heavy garlic sauce for supper—a daily ritual, it seems, for the priest, since he always stinks of the cloying spice.

Slowly he comes down from his visionary heights and opens his eyes, remaining seated until the priest is in view.

"Praise God, Jack! You've done it. Your parole has been approved."

He closes his eyes for a moment, containing his jubilation and keeping his composure before going to the bars to grasp the priest's outstretched hands in a show of mock gratitude. "Thank you, Father. I don't know what to say."

"Don't thank me, Jack. Thank God. Join me now in a prayer of thanks." The priest gets on his knees outside the cell, still grasping Jack's hands through the bars and pulling him down with him. For one delirious moment, as the priest begins intoning the Our Father, he has a crystal-clear image of his hands crushing the priest's until the holy man curses his maker in pain. A powerful, almost irresistible urge to actualize the image possesses him, but he fights it off and joins the priest in humble prayer, head bowed so that his malevolent smile is hidden. His mouth speaks the words of prayer, but his mind races and plans the next step of the game.

13

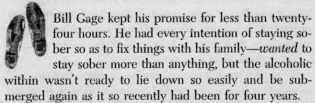Bill Gage kept his promise for less than twenty-four hours. He had every intention of staying sober so as to fix things with his family—*wanted* to stay sober more than anything, but the alcoholic within wasn't ready to lie down so easily and be submerged again as it so recently had been for four years.

He woke with the shaking sweats the morning after his talk with Evelyn. A long hot shower, half a dozen cups of coffee, and a handful of aspirins did little to allay them. Evelyn offered to make him some breakfast before he went to work, but he declined, his stomach souring at the mere thought of food.

If Evelyn noticed his trembling hands while he gulped cup after cup of coffee, she didn't say anything and deftly got the twins and Devin ready for their day and out of the house with as little interaction with him as possible. With Sassy it was easy; she was still angry, holding her grudge, and avoiding him. Missy made a point of saying good morning while her twin was upstairs, and Devin climbed on his lap for a hug and a kiss before Evelyn hurried them all on their way.

Before leaving the house, she slipped her business card, with the phone number of the insurance agency where she worked, into his shirt pocket. She told him not to hesitate to call if he needed to talk to someone during the day. He managed a reassuring smile and a nearly convincing statement that he'd be okay, and then he was alone.

He went immediately to the TV/entertainment center in the living room and began searching its drawers and cabinets, lying to himself that he was really looking for some paperwork he'd left there, and completely aware of the lie as soon as it became obvious the cabinet was empty of booze.

With nothing in the house to tempt him, not even a bottle of NyQuil, he was able to be honest with himself. He argued that it was good that the cabinet was empty and tried to believe his search had been a momentary relapse—he had to expect those—but the building panic he felt belied those thoughts.

He left for work, his coat open in the hope that the cold morning air would invigorate him and help keep his mind off his growing compulsion for a drink, but it only reminded him of how good it would feel to have his gut full of warm whiskey. He drove past several bars and package stores on his way to the Crocker K mart, and only the knowledge that it was too early for any of them to be open kept him from stopping.

"I thought you wouldn't be in for a couple of days," his assistant, John Drake, greeted him as he entered the security office on the second floor at the rear of the store.

"I'm feeling better," he replied, struggling to keep his trembling hands under control while he hung his coat up and poured himself a cup of coffee from the pot they kept brewing on a hot plate in the corner of the office.

"No offense, but you don't *look* like you're feeling better," Drake commented. "In fact, you look like shit. You sure you're okay?"

"I'm fine," Bill snapped. With two hands he carried his coffee to his desk. Drake shrugged and left to do the morning inventory. Bill sat at his desk, hands wrapped around the Styrofoam coffee cup, and watched through the one-way observation glass that lined the office wall overlooking the store.

He closed his eyes and breathed deeply, trying to get hold of himself. "I don't need a drink," he whispered soundlessly to himself. "I don't want a drink." The alcoholic within chuckled at his feeble attempt at exerting his willpower, and Bill hated himself for letting it.

Though he didn't smoke, he took a cigarette from the pack of Camels on John Drake's desk, lit it, inhaled deeply, and coughed uncontrollably for nearly a minute. He gulped coffee and took another, smaller drag, then another, closing his eyes and welcoming the light-headed feeling it caused. He began to feel slightly nauseous, but the smoke calmed his trembling hands and body. He smoked the cigarette rapidly, lit another, and marveled at how much better he felt. He was on his fourth cigarette when Drake returned to the security office.

"Since when did you start smoking?" he asked, eyeing his pack of Camels, which Bill had left open on his desk.

"Uh, just recently. I borrowed a few from you. Hope you don't mind. I didn't have a chance to stop and pick any up on my way here," Bill explained.

"No problem," Drake replied. He picked up the pack of butts, which was half full, and tossed it to Bill. "Here. Keep these. I've got a carton in the drawer. Actually, I'm glad you're smoking. Now I won't feel guilty about poisoning you with my secondhand smoke."

He laughed and Bill managed an accompanying chuckle. Bill had often complained about John's "secondhand smoke" and had made a habit of turning on the overhead fan whenever Drake lit up.

The morning crawled on toward noon. Bill tried to occupy himself with work, especially when John was in the office manning the observation windows, but found it extremely hard to concentrate. When Drake was patrolling the store, Bill found himself pacing the floor and chain-smoking, or sitting and staring at his desk blotter as if something of consuming interest lay there. He finished the pack of cigarettes within a couple of hours and bought another one from John, smoking more than half of them in the space of an hour.

"You going for a world record?" John asked wryly at one point, but Bill ignored him and pretended to be absorbed in an arrest report filed by the Springfield office.

With the help of constant intake of nicotine and caffeine, he was feeling almost okay by noon. His raw nerves healed to an uncomfortable edginess, and he wasn't craving a drink with every other thought. He planned on remaining in the office for lunch, where it was safe, but the store manager came up to the office and invited him out to discuss a rearrangement of the aisles of high-risk merchandise that he'd been contemplating.

Bill strongly disliked the manager, a petty gossipy man by the name of Schroeder, but accepted the invitation immediately. Drake looked mildly shocked at that. The store manager was always coming up with ideas on how to cut down on theft (as if he thought he could do the security job better than Bill or Drake), and in the past Bill had always curtly told him to type his idea up and submit it for consideration.

While the manager went to get his coat, Bill answered Drake's look. "Got to listen to the asshole once in a while, John, just to keep him greased."

"You'll only encourage him," Drake warned in reply.

"Maybe. Maybe not."

He joined Schroeder at the store entrance and they walked across the parking lot to a small French restaurant, The Crêperie. As he walked, Bill tried to convince himself of what he'd told Drake, but knew that the reason he'd accepted Schroeder's invitation was that the manager was well known for his liquid lunches.

That doesn't matter, he argued. It didn't mean he had to have a drink. And he believed that right up until the moment he ordered a Seven and Seven with his chicken-and-broccoli crêpe.

The words came out like a reflex. From that moment on he was like a man in a trance, detached from himself and acting as if under the will of someone else. He drank five Seven and Sevens to Schroeder's seven gin and tonics. Both men ignored the meals they had ordered.

Schroeder droned on about his plan for rearranging the merchandise, but Bill barely heard him. He nodded and appeared attentive, but all his attention was on the succession of drinks in front of him and the wonderful taste of the whiskey and the even more wonderful calming warmth that spread through his body with every sip.

At the end of the lunch he told Schroeder his ideas were interesting but he'd still like to see them on paper. He stood up and relished the rush of the booze to his head, but he didn't totter or sway a bit. He didn't stagger in the slightest as he walked from the restaurant. He felt great. He felt whole. He wondered why he had ever thought having a few drinks was a problem, was something to be ashamed of, something he couldn't control.

He worked well the rest of the day, smoking less than in the morning and not feeling the craving for a drink that had tortured him before lunch. In the back of his mind he began to entertain a revelation: namely that he was *not* an alcoholic; that he could control his drinking, that as he was experiencing, liquor could be used as an asset and not just for escape as he'd always used it in the past.

That night he drove home, unmindful of the few bars and liquor stores along the way, and ate a good, if quiet, dinner with Evelyn and the kids. He felt exhausted after dinner and lay down in his room. He was asleep in moments, and submerged in the dream in a few seconds more.

* * *

"Welcome back," Wilbur Clayton growled in Bill's ear as he clutched Bill's arm. In his other hand he held a bottle of Jack Daniel's, sloshing the liquid around inside and making it sound like the waves of a distant ocean. All was illuminated in the searing white flashes from the pulsating spotlight, while the darkness behind it held only the small twin reflections of the light in a pair of eyes. If he stared long enough, Bill could begin to see the outline of the body beyond the light, and it was huge, hulking, menacing.

Fear swallowed him, bringing shakes worse than any DTs. He reached for the bottle of booze Wilbur Clayton held, but the dead youth kept it teasingly out of reach. He tried to step forward to grab it, but his feet were frozen to the floor.

A plea came out of the darkness.

"Help me! Please!"

"Come on," Wilbur Clayton whispered, pulling him toward the faraway flashing light. "I've got something to show you, Billy-boy."

Bill tried to scream and woke gasping for air. The dream flitted away, leaving him with nothing more than the terrible memory of the fear he had felt during it. He knew the dream had been different this time, had progressed in its action, but he could recall nothing more than seeing the bottle of Jack Daniel's in Wilbur Clayton's dead hand.

He swallowed dryly. He had an immense thirst and water wouldn't quench it.

"I'm going back to the office for a while. There's some work I've got to get caught up on," Bill said loudly from the hallway as he put on his coat. In the living room the twins were lying on the floor watching television. Evelyn sat on the couch, a sleeping Devin cradled in her arms.

She gave him a questioning look when he popped his head in to wave good-bye.

"I won't be too late," he said and hurried out the door before she had a chance to say anything.

He drove directly to the Blue Fountain Lounge, not thinking of where he was going. Parking the car across the street from the place, he had a flashback of the last time he'd parked there, the night Cindy had kicked him out and he'd sat across from the Blue Fountain consumed with the obsession for a drink. But he'd fought it off then.

The memory brought a pang of guilt. He shrugged it off. He'd been in need of escape then, but this was different. He was just out for a couple of drinks, *in moderation,* like a normal person. He avoided thinking about the dream that had brought on the thirst.

I know what I'm doing, he thought. *I don't need to get blind, blackout drunk. I'm going to drink in moderation and enjoy some adult company. I deserve that.*

And he was successful. He remained in control. He sat at the end of the horseshoe-shaped bar and ordered a shot of Jack Daniel's with a beer chaser. He sipped the whiskey slowly, relishing the taste, and nursed the beer. He made both last forty-five minutes before ordering again. He bought a pack of Camels from the vending machine and enjoyed smoking while he slowly drank the second whiskey and beer.

This proved it. He felt no urge to consume as much booze as he could, fearful he wouldn't get enough before last call. He drank and smoked and watched the patrons at the bar, and the tables beyond, do the same.

No alcoholics here, he mused. Just a small crowd of adults enjoying one of the finer things in life. *In moderation.* Yes, that's what he was doing. That would be his new watchword, his new mantra: *In moderation. All things in moderation.*

He smiled. He knew how conquering heroes must have felt in times past.

"Hi! Don't I know you?" A short, slightly overweight brunette had climbed onto the bar stool next to him. She wore a low-cut beige sweater, revealing deep cleavage between more than ample breasts. Below, she wore a black spandex miniskirt that did nothing for her large thighs.

Her face was cute, in a pouty sort of way, but she had several blemishes on her chin that she'd failed to hide with makeup. She wore too much purple eyeshadow, giving her the look of almost having twin black eyes. The only thing saving them from that fate was their very light, pretty color of green.

"I don't know," Bill said, smiling. "I don't think so."

"Sure, I do. You were at the Quarry Tavern this weekend, weren't you? We danced. Oh, you were really bombed, though—you probably don't remember." Her voice was high and slightly squeaky, reminding Bill of Betty Boop.

The Quarry Tavern. He'd found a pack of matches with the name Quarry Tavern in his pocket after the weekend. He must have been there during his blackout. He had no memory of this girl or of dancing with her. Partly to be polite, but mostly to rewrite recent history and forget about the blackout (that didn't mesh well with his recent conversion to social drinker), he lied.

"Oh, yeah. Right. I remember you now. You're—" He snapped his fingers as if her name was on the tip of his tongue and had fallen off and doing so would somehow help him catch it.

"Darlene," she said, her face brightening. "You remember me?"

"Sure. Yeah. I was feeling good, but I wasn't that far gone that I wouldn't remember dancing with someone."

Darlene laughed. "Well, we did more than just dance."

She stopped and clapped her hand to her mouth, giving Bill a coy glance. "I don't mean we fooled around or anything, but we sure tied one on."

"I know. I was there, remember?" Bill said.

Darlene giggled in agreement. She motioned to the bartender and ordered a sloe gin fizz when he came over.

"Let me get that," Bill said, putting a ten on the bar.

"Thanks. You're Jim, right?"

"Bill."

"Oh, yeah." Darlene blushed. "Where did I get Jim. Were you with a Jim that night?"

"No. I don't think so. Sorry."

"Oh, well, Bill. I remembered your face anyway. I was pretty far gone myself that night, but I always remember a cute guy no matter how wasted I get." She giggled and leaned toward Bill, affording him a better view of her cleavage, which was clearly her best feature.

"I remember now," she said slowly. "You suddenly disappeared after last call. I looked all over for you. That really bummed me out." Her naturally pouty expression became poutier.

"I'm sorry." Bill shrugged.

"'S okay," Darlene said quickly and smiled. "The way we danced a couple of slow numbers that night, I thought we had, ya know, connected." She gave Bill a seductive look.

Bill took a drink and said nothing. He was unsure of how he wanted things to go here. The girl's apparent availability had stirred a lust in him he hadn't felt since before Cindy's death. Yet the memory of Cindy, who still felt like his wife, made him feel as though he'd be committing adultery.

Darlene was about to say something else—something suggestive, Bill thought since she put her hand on his leg —but was distracted by someone entering the bar.

"Oh!" she said with breathless excitement and removed

her hand from Bill's leg. "I gotta go talk to someone. I'll be right back."

Bill turned and watched her join a longhaired man just getting to a table at the back of the room. She draped herself over the man, whispering in his ear and giggling while he felt up her ass.

Oh, well. *C'est la vie.*

Bill wasn't terribly upset. He downed the rest of his whiskey, followed it with the beer, and scooped up his money from the bar, leaving a dollar tip for the bartender. Smiling ruefully at himself for being so foolish as to think he might get lucky with Darlene, he left and went home.

He was surprised, and secretly glad, to find the house dark and everyone in bed. He was even more surprised when he checked his watch and saw that it was after one. He didn't think he had been out that long. It hadn't felt like five hours.

He smiled with satisfaction and gave himself a mental pat on the back. He'd had only two drinks in five hours (four if you counted the beer chasers as separate drinks, which he didn't). Could an alcoholic do that? He didn't think so.

He locked up the house and went happily to bed.

And woke sweating and trembling at 3:00 A.M., but not from the dream.

The DTs again.

Oh, no! his conscience gloated sarcastically. *You're not an alcoholic!*

He mentally told it to fuck off and went downstairs, retrieving his cigarettes from his coat pocket. He sat in the dark and tried to smoke the shakes away, but it didn't work.

There must be something wrong with me, he reasoned, refusing to believe his shakes were being caused by alcohol withdrawal. Christ! It had taken him five years to reach this stage before. This time he'd been drinking for less than a week! What the hell was going on?

Maybe I've got Parkinson's disease, or a nervous condition, or something like that, he wondered hopefully.

He made a pot of coffee, his trembling hands spilling the grounds all over the countertop. He drank cup after cup, chain-smoked, and rationalized.

If it is Parkinson's, or some other kind of nervous disorder, then a doctor would treat it with tranquilizers, wouldn't he? And isn't alcohol a tranquilizer?

He went to the fridge, opened it, and stared at its contents. He picked up the bottle of vanilla extract off the top door shelf. He remembered his mother saying once that during Prohibition her uncle Joe used to drink vanilla extract. He read the contents, saw that he was right, and dumped half the contents of the bottle into his cup of coffee.

He took a grimacing sip, then downed the cup of coffee in three big gulps. He poured another cup, adding an ice cube from the freezer to cool it down, and poured the rest of the vanilla extract in. He downed it as soon as it was cool enough to do so.

He felt almost immediate relief in the light buzz that filled his head. The tremors ceased. *Better make an appointment with the doctor about those shakes,* he told himself with no intention of ever doing so, and went back to bed.

He woke at seven with a throbbing hangover, but no DTs. He stayed in bed, feigning sleep when Evelyn rapped softly on his bedroom door and peeked in. After he heard her and the kids leave, he got up, showered, and went through what was becoming a daily routine: drink a pot of coffee and eat a handful of aspirins.

He dressed and sat in the living room watching the morning news shows. At nine o'clock he wrote a hasty note to Evelyn explaining that he'd be home late and left the house, heading for the nearest package store. As he purchased a pint of Jack Daniel's, he noticed his hands beginning to tremble again. He took a long pull from the bottle as soon as he was back in his car and headed the shakes off nicely. He arrived at work in good shape and good spirits, though an hour late.

"You're late," John Drake said kiddingly when Bill entered the office.

"Yeah, but I'm the boss," Bill quipped. He sat at his desk and shuffled papers in a show of work until Drake left the office. He retrieved the pint of whiskey from his coat pocket, took a few good pulls from it, and stashed it in the top drawer of his desk.

He worked all morning in this manner: attending to his paperwork when John was present, and replenishing himself from the pint when his assistant was absent. He got a lot of work done, even managing to get ahead of the endless paperwork the position required. And he felt that the quality of the work had never been better.

The bottle lasted until noon, when he planned to go out for a few at lunch, but before he could get out of the office the phone rang. It was Chief Albert of the Crocker police.

"Hello, Bill. How are you?"

"Fine, just fine, George. And you?" Bill spoke amiably but was mentally cursing his old friend for keeping him from his much-needed liquid lunch.

"I haven't had a chance to talk to you since the inquest," George went on. "I've been up to my ears with the same old budget squeeze and crap from the mayor, ya know?"

"Sure," Bill answered, thinking, *Come on! Come on! Get on with it!*

"I was wondering if we might have lunch sometime, or maybe you and the kids could come over for dinner. Lucille would like that. She's dying to meet you and your children, and she's a damned good cook, if I do say so myself."

Warning bells went off in Bill's head. If he had *any* meal with George, he wouldn't be able to *drink*. The chief knew of his drinking problems; Bill had been the one to tell him. (And that *was* in the past now, wasn't it, since he now drank *in moderation*.) George would think he was an alcoholic if he saw him drinking again. But the worst was the panic at the thought of passing a couple of hours without a drink.

"Uh, I'd like that, George, really. But I'm really behind here at work, what with all the time I missed. The damn place nearly fell apart without me," Bill lied. In fact, he was ahead of his paperwork. "Why don't I give you a call when I get caught up and we can make some plans then?"

"Okay. Sure. I understand." The chief sounded disappointed.

Bill felt a twinge of guilt at giving his old friend the brush-off, but it didn't last as his desire for a drink cut the call short.

"Okay! Great! I gotta go. I'll call you, George, soon. I promise," Bill said and hung up.

He returned from lunch with half a dozen JD and waters under his belt and another pint of the whiskey in his coat pocket. He told John Drake to take the rest of the afternoon off with pay. He reasoned John deserved it, and it was a way of making up for his own tardiness that morning, but it was really so he could be alone. He locked the door and sat at the observation window with his pint of Jack Daniel's and pack of Camels.

Every hour he went down and covered John's rounds of the aisles and returned to his bottle, cigarettes, and chair as soon as possible. On his 4:00 P.M. round he caught a twelve-year-old boy pocketing a package of blank cassette tapes. He took the boy up to the office and gave him the

third degree, threatening him with arrest. The kid broke
down, bawling out a story of how he was stealing the tapes
to record his band. They wanted to make a record and get
discovered.

Bill had to turn away to hide his smile at that. The
dreams of childhood. A sudden inexplicable sadness swept
over him. With it came a sense of shame for scaring the
boy. It was regular practice with juvenile offenders caught
for the first time. The theory was to scare them so good
the first time, they'd never do it again. Though it had
always been an effective deterrent, Bill had never seen
how cruel it was until now.

He let the boy go and felt a little better at the look of
relief and gratitude on the boy's face as he went out the
door. Several swigs from the bottle did the rest in bringing his mood up. Yet deep down, a small sad spot had
appeared and wouldn't go away.

When the night guard came on at five, Bill headed over
the nearby city line into Quarry and The Quarry Tavern.
As he had the night before (and was certain he had *all* day)
he drank slowly, congratulating himself with each measured sip for his moderation and self-control. At nine he
left the tavern, feeling drunk for the first time that day yet
still able to walk steady and appear sober, which, of
course, brought more congratulations.

He had intended to go home but instead found himself
driving by The Blue Fountain. He went in, looking around
with anticipation and feeling disappointment when he
didn't see Darlene. He feigned indifference and sat at the
bar, ordering JD straight up and downing it and another
in a matter of five minutes.

He was very drunk now and knew it.

"In moderation," he slurred softly to no one. "I forgot
moderation."

He bought a fresh pack of cigarettes and made a point

of smoking three of them in a row before ordering another drink, which he sipped.

That's the ticket.

He smiled confidently and lit another cigarette, using it to measure the time he should take between sips: three sips per cigarette.

"Here you are! The disappearing man! Where'd you go last night?" It was Darlene. She'd just come in and was struggling out of her heavy overcoat.

"Oh, hi," Bill said nonchalantly, suppressing his excitement.

"Why'd you take off last night?" Darlene asked, draping her coat over the bar stool next to him and sitting on it. She wore a flimsy white blouse and what looked like the same tight miniskirt as she had the night before.

With a stirring of his loins, Bill noticed Darlene wasn't wearing a bra. He could see the dark round circles of her nipples and the heavy curve of her large breasts through the blouse.

"It was late," he explained. "I have to get up for work in the morning. Besides," he added with a shrug, "you looked pretty intimate with your boyfriend."

"My *boyfriend*? Oh! You mean Davy. He's not my *boyfriend*, he's just a guy I know. A friend. I had to tell him something. I came right back, but you were gone."

"Sorry," Bill said. He finished the rest of his drink.

"Let me buy you one tonight," Darlene squeaked happily and motioned to the bartender.

Remember! Moderation!

"Uh, no, thanks, Darlene. I've had enough for tonight. If I have any more I'll wake up with a hangover I wouldn't wish on my worst enemy."

The bartender was busy serving a couple at the other end of the bar and Darlene stopped gesturing. "Really? I've got something that can fix that."

"Please," Bill moaned with exaggeration. "No hangover remedies. I've tried them all."

"This is no remedy. This is hangover *prevention.*"

Bill looked at Darlene, raising his eyebrows inquiringly. Darlene scrutinized his face for several moments, seeming to be deciding something about him.

"Well? Don't keep me in suspense," Bill joked.

"I don't know," Darlene said hesitantly. "You kind of look like a cop, but you seem okay. You'd tell me if you were a cop, wouldn't you?"

Bill laughed heartily. "No, honey. I'm not a cop. That's one thing I'll never be." He left off the "again."

"You got a car?" Darlene asked, lowering her voice and leaning close to him.

"Yeah," Bill answered slowly. If she was afraid of his being a cop, then the chances were damned good that she was about to suggest something illegal. He stared at her breasts straining against the thin material of the blouse, her nipples hard and protruding.

Was sex with this girl worth breaking the law?

What the hell do you care about the law? What did it ever do for you?

He chose to listen to the latter voice, the voice of his alcoholism, and led her out of the lounge to his car. The only thing he had to worry about now was whether or not he was too drunk to make it with Darlene.

She gave directions as he drove to her apartment, a few blocks from The Blue Fountain. She lived in a bleak, gray, three-tenement house. Her apartment, small but neat, was on the first floor. She told him to sit on the couch and make himself comfortable while she put their coats in the closet and went into the kitchen. She came back a few minutes later with two bottles of Budweiser and a medium-size leather pouch.

She handed him a beer and placed hers on the coffee table in front of the couch. She sat next to Bill and immediately busied herself with the contents of the pouch, removing a pocket mirror, razor blade, short plastic straw, and a rectangular packet of folded magazine paper about an inch long. From the back pocket of her miniskirt she retrieved a teaspoon.

Bill recognized the paraphernalia from his days with the state police and the numerous drug busts he'd been on, but he decided to play the innocent.

"You ever do coke?" Darlene asked, unfolding the paper packet to reveal a squared mound of chunky white powder.

"No. Never. I've heard about it," Bill replied. A part of him told him to get up and leave *right now,* but another, larger part was intrigued enough to stay. He'd often wondered why people of all walks of life seemed to enjoy cocaine so much.

"This stuff will sober you right up and let you drink all night without getting too drunk, *and* you never have a hangover the next day."

She scooped a pile of powder off the paper with the spoon and dumped it on the mirror. With the back of the spoon, using it like a pestle, she ground the coke into a fine powder. She carefully licked the spoon and proceeded to use the straightedge razor blade to chop the powder even finer and separate it into half a dozen long thin parallel horizontal lines on the mirror's surface.

Bending over, she put one end of the straw to her right nostril, plugged the left one with her other hand, and snorted one of the lines. She switched the straw to the left nostril and repeated the process with another line. She sat bolt upright, sniffed deeply a few times while blinking rapidly, shivered, and let out a long whistling sigh. She smiled at Bill, her eyes bright and glassy, and slid the mirror over to him with the straw.

He contemplated it for a moment before picking the straw up gingerly between two fingers. The policeman part of him cried out one more time against what he was about to do, but it was drowned out by the conviction that he was not a policeman any longer, never would be again, and owed nothing to the past. It was gone forever, so why shouldn't he try something new and live a little? So what if it was illegal? And if the coke could do what Darlene claimed it could, wasn't it worth at least a try? Maybe it would even alleviate the morning shakes that always accompanied his hangovers.

Aware that Darlene was watching him, he bent over the mirror, mimicking what she'd done, and snorted a line up his left, then his right nostril. He coughed as some of the stuff went into the back of his throat, which immediately went numb.

Darlene giggled. "Don't snort so hard. The trick is to get it right up here"—she pointed at the bridge of her nose—"without letting it go down your throat. Here, try this." She dabbed the tip of her index finger into the powder until it was coated. "Open your mouth," she directed him and rubbed the coke sensuously over his teeth and gums.

Bill wasn't sure he liked the numbing sensation in his mouth; it reminded him too much of trips to the dentist, Novocain, and drilling.

Darlene snorted the last two lines and prepared some more with the spoon and razor blade. She offered it to Bill and he tried again, managing to keep the stuff out of his throat this time. He snorted four lines and left four for Darlene.

"You do the rest since this is your first time. I'll cut up some more," she told him. She went into the kitchen and brought back two more beers. She put a record on the stereo in the corner of the room before rejoining him on the couch.

Bill finished his first beer and took a long pull of the second, letting the foaming liquid swish around in his mouth in an attempt to wash away the numbness. He sniffed several times, feeling his nose becoming clogged, and gradually noticed that he felt different.

Darlene was right! He wasn't drunk anymore! The wooziness of the booze had evaporated into a subtle yet exhilarating feeling of energy, like a constant mild adrenaline rush. With the clearing of his head came a sharpening of his senses. The beer tasted better, cleaner, fresher. He could smell the perfume and faint odor of sweat from Darlene. He could feel the warmth of her body next to his on the couch even though they weren't touching. He became aware of the sound of the wind outside and the faraway hum of a passing train. The music from the stereo took on quadraphonic depths.

They snorted four more lines apiece, and with each one Bill experienced an increase of the drug's effects until he no longer felt drunk at all. He felt the exact opposite: acutely sober, but high at the same time.

"So, what do you think?" Darlene asked after he'd snorted the last line.

"It's . . . nice," Bill answered, unable to express any better what he was feeling. "I never imagined coke was like this."

Darlene giggled with delight. "I knew you'd like it; anyone who tries it does. And this is really good stuff, almost pure." She paused a moment and gave Bill a crooked smile. "And not only can you drink like a fish all night with it, it makes sex *wild*!" She giggled and licked her lips, staring at Bill with half-closed eyes. "You can *fuck* for *hours* and not get tired." She giggled again and added, "Or soft."

Bill believed her. At the mere suggestion of her words he got a raging erection that felt bigger than any he'd ever felt before.

Darlene got up from the couch, a mischievous smile on her face. "It's *so* hot in here! My landlord controls the

heat for the whole building, and he keeps it sweltering all
the time." She stood in the middle of the room and faced
Bill, her hips moving in time to a slow song on the radio.
She slowly unbuttoned her blouse. "I usually walk around
naked in here just to stay cool, or when I'm feeling really
hot." She pulled the blouse tails from her skirt and let it
slide from her shoulders to the floor.

Bill couldn't help but gape at her breasts, which were
much larger in the flesh. The nipples were dime-size and
erect. He could almost see them throbbing in time to the
beat of his hard-on.

Darlene cupped her breasts from beneath with both
hands and lifted them like an offering to Bill. "You like
them?" she asked coquettishly. "They're my best feature."
She ran her hands up over them, pausing to squeeze the
nipples between her thumb and forefingers.

"Mmmm! Coke always gets me so *hot*!" she breathed.
"It makes me a nympho."

Bill was off the couch in an instant, stepping over the
low table and grasping her tits in his hands before he
realized what he was doing. His lust was animalistic, and
he grunted, wrapping his arms around her, bending her
back, and lowering his head to suck loudly and greedily
on her nipples.

Darlene giggled and moaned, running her hands over
his back and through his hair.

Bill lowered her to the carpet and tugged her tight skirt
down over her nyloned legs and off. He tossed it away.
She wore no panties, only a lacy black garter belt to hold
up her stockings.

Darlene sat up and attacked his belt buckle. He
brushed her hands aside and undid it quickly, deftly, for
her. She grabbed his pants and pushed them and his Fruit
of the Looms to his knees with one thrust.

"Ooh, yeah!" Darlene moaned huskily. She looked hungrily at his freestanding sex. "Give me your big cock. Ooh! I want it!"

For a fleeting moment Bill felt trapped in a porno movie and almost laughed, but Darlene was spread-eagled on her back and he mounted her. He became a machine then, thrusting and grunting, unthinking, *unable* to think, consumed with physical sensation. He rode her, battered her with his lunging, but she took it all and moaned in ecstasy throughout.

Suddenly she began to buck wildly beneath him and gasp for air. Her eyes rolled up into her head and her entire body convulsed beneath him. A high-pitched scream wailed from her open mouth as she came and came again, seeming to Bill to go on forever.

Bill felt himself building and pumped her faster, crying out like an enraged animal when he too achieved orgasm. And Darlene's claims about the coke once again proved true when he didn't get sensitive and lose his erection. In fact, with every thrust he could feel the ongoing tingle of the orgasm coursing through his body.

Laughing with amazement at his newfound prowess, he didn't let up for a second.

After what seemed like hours of hard lovemaking, Darlene slid out from under Bill and crawled to the coffee table for more coke. "Time to recharge," she said and motioned him over from where he had collapsed on the floor. She did two fat lines and handed the straw to him for the remaining two. He barely got the second one up his nose when she pulled him to the floor and began licking his still-hard member as though it were an ice-cream cone. His penis raged in return, and she swallowed it, sucking it in and out of her mouth, her head bobbing until he came again. She took him deep in her throat as he came and sucked and swallowed every last drop from him —causing him to briefly wonder (*very* briefly) if she'd ever heard about condoms or AIDS. He knew he should be worried about AIDS himself, but the combination of drug, booze, and her lust drove such thoughts from his mind.

She released him just long enough to straddle him. "Oh, yeah! God! Yeah!" she crooned, licking her lips and tossing her head. She came very quickly and it seemed she would never stop.

Bill ejaculated twice more during the night for a total of four—a feat he could only marvel at. They made love in every position he had ever tried or heard of, and a few he hadn't, on every piece of furniture and in every room of the apartment. They stopped only to consume more coke and eventually ended in the bedroom until dawn.

By first light Bill was beyond coming anymore. His entire groin was numb, but he still had an erection and Darlene was eating it again.

"Let's take a break," he said, lifting her face from him.

Darlene smiled dopily and nodded. "Let's do some more blow."

Bill wasn't sure. He was starting to feel like shit and told Darlene he needed to sleep.

"Listen, this will fix you right up. You can go for days partying with this and not sleep and everything's cool."

Considering that all her other claims about the coke had been true, he agreed. They did four more lines each, and Darlene proved her honesty once again. He did feel good. And obviously Darlene did, too, for she immediately went back to work on his cock, which led to another hour of sexual gymnastics.

Finally she fell off him and collapsed at his side. She reached for the mirror and packet of coke, saw that it was empty, and swore with disappointment. She picked up the packet, unfolded it flat, and methodically licked any remaining powder from the entire surface of the paper.

"No more?" Bill asked. He'd had enough sex for one night (one *lifetime*!) but he felt as though he could use some more coke to give him a lift as it had before.

"No." She pouted, then brightened. "But if you can come up with three hundred bucks, I can get us some more." She fondled his softening penis. "Then we can party all day."

"Don't you work?" Bill asked, smiling.

"I used to, at G.E., but I got laid off last month. I'm collecting now, but it don't go far, otherwise I'd gladly pay for it. Whattya say? Can you swing it?" she asked hopefully.

"I'll have to go in to work for little while, then I'll go to the bank."

"Awesome!" Darlene crowed. "I'll call my dealer and tell him we'll be over before noon to get an eightball. That's an eighth of an ounce," she explained, not knowing Bill was familiar with the term.

"That costs three hundred dollars?" he asked. She nodded and he inwardly chuckled at the realization that inflation affected everything, even drug prices. When he was with the state police ten to fifteen years ago, three hundred dollars would have bought a quarter ounce of cocaine.

He went straight to the office from Darlene's. A vague feeling of guilt kept him from going home first where there were too many reminders of Cindy. At the office, John Drake was on the phone when Bill walked in.

"Hold on. He just came in," John said into the speaker before cupping his hand over it. "It's your sister-in-law, and she sounds mighty pissed." He handed the receiver to Bill and left the room.

Bill took a deep breath. "Hello, Evelyn. What's up?"

"What's *up*?" Evelyn said, her voice a mixture of sarcasm and incredulity. "What's up? Oh, not much, Bill. I just called to say hi." The sarcasm deepened. "By the way, I noticed you didn't come home last night. The kids noticed, too, especially Devin. I had to lie to them."

She waited for an answer, but Bill could think of nothing to say. His mind wandered and he thought about what excuse he would give Drake for leaving early.

"I'm not your wife, Bill," Evelyn snapped, interrupting his thoughts. "I know I'm sounding like one, and I don't like it. But I've got the *children* to worry about if you won't. I know you're an adult and can do whatever you want, but you've also got children who care about you. Did you think they wouldn't notice that you hadn't come home all night? Did you think Devin wouldn't notice when he went in to wake you like he does *every morning?*"

Bill remained silent, his mind wandering again during her tirade, this time to whether he'd left a nip of JD in his desk drawer. Evelyn's voice was making him thirsty.

"Come on, Bill. Say something!" she demanded. "Talk to me! Where were you last night?"

"I was here," he lied after clearing his throat. "I worked very late and decided to sleep in the office."

"Really? So how some you weren't there when I called this morning?"

"I, uh, went out for some breakfast."

"Tell me another one, Bill. Not only weren't you there this morning, but you weren't there last night at nine thirty when I called. The night guard said you left at five and didn't come back."

Bill winced at being caught in the lie.

"You're drinking again, aren't you?" Evelyn asked, disgust replacing sarcasm in her voice.

Bill's silence was as good as a yes.

When Evelyn spoke again, her voice was devoid of emotion. "You've got a problem, Bill, and only you can do something about it. Right now, Cindy's kids and their well-being are my main concern. Until you get straightened out, I think it's best if the kids and I move into my condo."

Bill didn't protest. He glanced at his watch and wondered how long it would take him to get to the bank.

"All right, then. We'll move this afternoon." She paused before going on, her voice trembling. "Please get help, Bill. Your children love you and need you, no matter what has happened. It's not too late to be a father to them, but if you keep on the way you're going, they'll be grown up before you're ever sober again."

"I'm sorry," Bill stammered weakly.

Evelyn hung up.

What are you apologizing for? the alcoholic within spoke up angrily, trying to drive out the sharp pangs of remorse and justify Bill's recent behavior. What was the *big deal,* anyway, with staying out all night once in a while? If *anyone* had a problem here, it was Evelyn! *He* didn't have a problem. He had proved that! He was drinking in moderation, and an alcoholic can't do that and remain in control, but he was in control, wasn't he?

His conscience, in a voice weak and growing weaker, dared him to take a good hard look at the past forty-eight hours and then honestly say that his life was not out of control and he didn't have a problem. The alcoholic scoffed the conscience into retreat with the pure volume of its argument. It puffed him up with righteous indignation and persuaded him to go and have a few drinks because that was the only suitable answer to her accusation, and he believed the insane logic of it.

Bill slammed the receiver onto the cradle with mock anger and bravado and left the office, meeting John Drake on his way out.

"I'm taking the day off," he told his assistant. "I've got some personal business to take care of. Make sure you draw up the inventory schedule for the Worcester store today."

It was the last time he would ever again give an order to John Drake.

* * *

At the bank he filled out a withdrawal slip for three hundred dollars, considered it, and tore it up. He filled out another for two thousand. Hell, if he was going to cut loose, he might as well do it big time. He picked up Darlene and followed the directions she gave as he drove.

"Did you get the money?" she asked.

"Well, yes and no," he teased.

"What do you mean?"

"If three hundred will buy an eighth of an ounce," he asked, taking the wad of bills from his pocket and handing it to Darlene, "how much will fifteen hundred buy?"

Darlene's eyes widened in amazement. She snatched the money from Bill's hand and began counting it. "Oh, wow! This is fantastic! This'll buy an ounce for sure!" She hugged his arm and reached between his legs, massaging and squeezing.

"I've got another five hundred to get some booze with," Bill added.

"You're great, you know that? We are going to party like it's 1999!" she said, laughing.

Despite having no idea what she meant by that, Bill laughed along with Darlene. He felt good again, Evelyn and the children forgotten.

Darlene directed him to her dealer's apartment in a seedy part of town near the college. He let her off a block away, saying he wanted to hit the nearby package store while she got the stuff, but he really wanted to be sure he was nowhere near the dealer's place just in case a bust happened to go down.

Darlene was surprised and pleased that he trusted her with so much money. She gave him a quick French kiss and agreed to wait at the corner for him to pick her up.

Bill drove to a package store he knew of a few blocks away. It was amazing how much stuff he'd forgotten over the years, yet he could still remember the location of nearly every liquor store and bar in Crocker and for miles around.

The place was called Gippy's. Bill bought two cases of Heineken, a case of quarts of Jack Daniel's, and a case of fifths of Grand Marnier because Darlene had said it went great with cocaine.

"Looks like you're having a party," the clerk, an elderly man, maybe even Gippy himself, stated as he rang up the purchase.

"You bet."

He had to drive around the block four times before he found Darlene waiting for him.

"Where's the stuff?" Bill asked as she got in the car empty-handed.

"Safe," Darlene replied, patting her breasts. "Let's party."

14

The next phase is the slowest but the most important, and he meditates hourly, disciplining himself for patience. He endures and cooperates with the endless red tape/paperwork needed for parole, like the model prisoner he has pretended for so long to be.

On the day of his release, he says good-bye to the priest and the psychologist, who seem genuinely sorry to see him go (the fools). They have no idea that if his parole had been denied he would have taken great delight in killing them, prison or no prison. Death is a form of freedom, too.

His plaything cell mate can barely conceal the joy at his leaving. He would like to strap on his secret weapon and leave his mate bleeding internally, but kisses the boy long and hard instead, whispering in his ear afterward, "I'll find you again someday." That wipes the look of joy from the youth's face and leaves him pale and shaking.

He arrives at the halfway house in nearby Crocker and registers. He endures more paperwork and a lengthy orientation given by a social-worker drone and his meek-looking parole officer. He nods dutifully at the right moments and is pleasant to everyone, giving them his best pearly-white-denture smile.

He puts his few belongings away in his tiny room on the third floor, making a slit in the underside of the mattress to hide his most prized possession, as he did while in prison.

He wore the thing from prison, the base unhinged so that the sharp length of it could be taped against his stomach, the blade wrapped in rags so that it wouldn't cut his flesh to ribbons.

His first week in the halfway house, he does everything he's supposed to do. He attends the daily therapy groups (called "rap sessions" by the earthy-crunchy house counselors), keeps his room clean, helps with meal preparation and cleanup, and sees his parole officer on schedule.

In the second week he informs the parole officer that he wants to find work, and the man agrees, pleased to see his charge showing such ambition. The parole office sets up interviews for him and he keeps the appointments faithfully and punctually, but always acts just strange enough so that he is never hired.

And all the while he hones his plan, dreaming of the day, very soon, when he will strap on his wielder of revenge for keeps and his transformation will be complete.

15

Bill Gage woke from a semiconscious stupor and reached for the bottle of Jack Daniel's on the floor next to him. He took a long hard pull and followed it with several lines of coke, which were neatly laid out on the large mirror atop the coffee table. On the couch, Darlene snored softly, twitching in a cocaine-induced sleep of exhaustion. Bill knew that sleep well—it was the only kind he'd had since . . . since . . . when? He couldn't remember. The only good thing about the sleep was that it was too light to produce dreams—*the* dream. In fact, he hadn't had the dream since he'd started using coke.

A wave of nausea passed over him and he quieted it with another couple of lines and a drink. Better. He got up, nearly fell over, and went to the bathroom to take a leak. As he stood there, pissing for what seemed like hours, he caught his reflection in the mirror of the half-open medicine cabinet over the sink.

He looked like shit. Worse—he looked like death, and not even death warmed over. He looked like cold death, old death—like a cadaver left too long in a morgue freezer and thawing out too quickly. His normally pudgy, roundish face had become gaunt, sallow. His receding hair was greasily matted to his head. He looked like a different person.

His eyes mesmerized him. The pupils were enormous,

huge black holes surrounded with bloodshot red. The more he looked at them the larger they seemed to grow until he could see nothing else there but blackness. They reminded him of twin tunnels, and the image brought guilt and thoughts of Wilbur Clayton.

His eyes filled with tears, his face contorted, and he wept; not for Wilbur Clayton; not for his dead wife, Cindy; not for his kids, whom he had abandoned—he wept for himself, and hated himself for it. He tried to pry himself away from that mirror and the horrifying image of what he had become, but he couldn't. Not until he struck it with his fist, smashing it and cutting his knuckles deeply, could he free himself from his own hellish gaze.

He staggered back to the living room, where Darlene was waking up, aroused by the sound of breaking glass.

"What was that?" she asked, reaching automatically for the straw and the few lines he had left undone on the mirror.

"Nothing," Bill muttered. He retrieved his bottle of JD and guzzled from it while he walked a tight circle in front of the couch. He couldn't stand still, couldn't sit down. His body was alive with a restless anger that made him want to strike out and smash everything the way he had smashed the bathroom mirror.

"I thought I heard something break," Darlene said between snorting lines. When the last one was done, she looked up at Bill. "You okay?"

"Just fine," Bill answered and took another swig. "Just fucking great!"

"You don't sound so 'fucking great,'" Darlene said with a teasing laugh.

Bill glared at her. "Just shut the fuck up and lay out some more lines."

Darlene made a face but obeyed, laying out a dozen thick lines of the white. Bill urgently grabbed the straw from her hand and proceeded to snort every line, switching nostrils every third line.

"Hey! I want some of that, too!" Darlene cried, reaching for the straw. Bill shoved her back hard against the couch.

"What the *fuck* is wrong with you?" she asked angrily, getting up from the couch.

Bill gave her a look of pure hatred and finished snorting. The rush was intense. He felt his heartbeat quicken, along with his breathing, and he broke out in a slimy cold sweat all over his body. Along with everything else inside him speeding up, he felt his anger and self-hatred increase also.

"Are you going to do all of that, or can I have some too?" Darlene pouted. She reached for the bag of white, and Bill caught her wrist, twisting it until she cried out.

"Leave it alone," he said through clenched teeth. "It's mine and you've scrounged off me long enough."

Darlene pulled her hand out of his grip and rubbed it, tears filling her eyes and streaming down her face. "And this is my fucking apartment! You've scrounged off me long enough, too, so get the fuck out!"

Bill was only too happy to comply. He gathered up the bag of coke, razor blade, spoon, and straw and started for the door.

"That's my fucking spoon and razor!" Darlene sobbed. Bill threw them both at her, the razor catching in her sweater and hanging there like a wad of metallic saliva.

He opened the door and Darlene ran to him, grabbing his arm. "Please don't go, Bill. I'm sorry," she pleaded. He tried to shake her loose, but she hung on. "Please, Bill, don't. I'm sorry. Stay, please, and let me have a little snort. I need it."

For a moment he softened, but when she pleaded for more coke, his anger exploded. He turned, shook his arm free of her grasp, and backhanded her hard across the face, sending her sprawling to the floor against the coffee table. He left, the image of Darlene's frightened bleeding face chasing him.

He got in his car and started to drive. He was barely able to steer for trembling so badly, but he wasn't trembling with rage, it was shame that made him shake so. And it wasn't just shame at striking Darlene—the first time he'd ever struck a woman—it was shame at everything he'd done in the past few months since the moment his personal obsession with his father-haunted past had pushed him into not caring about his wife, family, or anything other than exorcising that ghost. But even putting a gun to Wilbur Clayton's head and pulling the trigger hadn't freed him, it had only enslaved him more, leading back to the chains of alcoholism, and now drug addiction.

Why? That was what he needed to know. Why did his past still have such a stranglehold on him?

He drove aimlessly, crying quietly, and felt the recent past he so wanted to escape overwhelm him.

The last four weeks of his life were a blur, a kaleidoscope, a carousel of images; and all the images were wild, drunken images, drug-induced images. He had gone home only twice in the four weeks to pick up clothing. The rest of the time he'd spent partying with Darlene, wasted out of his mind. He didn't go to work, didn't call in, didn't eat. All he did was drink, take cocaine, and have nearly nonstop sex with Darlene.

They went through the first ounce of cocaine in little less than five days. Then Bill withdrew more money from the bank and bought another one. A succession of people came and went through the apartment during that lost month in Bill's life. Thinking back on it now, he realized he had known none of them, and couldn't remember any of their faces or names. They were just a parade of nonentities coming to snort his coke and drink his booze.

There were several very wild parties, one of which degenerated into an outright orgy. Bill remembered (how many weeks or days ago he had no idea) waking to find himself lying in bed with Darlene and two other women he didn't know, plus a young boy who couldn't have been more than sixteen. All of them were naked and sticky, and he had very little memory of what they had done together.

During his time with her, Darlene had proved to have an unceasing appetite for drugs, drink, and sex, and not necessarily in that order. She kept him up for days on end until he could take it no longer no matter how high he was on coke. He'd have to crash for an hour or two only to wake up to find Darlene's mouth on him or her straddling him or plying him with more alcohol and more drugs.

And he had liked it. He had liked not having to think. He liked not having any responsibilities. He had liked the fact that he could do as he pleased and lose himself in a fog of drug- and drink-induced nothingness.

Everything had been going fine until he had run into Evelyn on one of his frequent trips to the package store. Had it been just three days ago? He thought so, but couldn't be sure.

He had been loading several cases of beer, Jack Daniel's, and Grand Marnier into the trunk of his car, which was parked in the mall parking lot outside the store, when Evelyn came out of the supermarket next to the liquor store and spotted Bill.

"Think you've got enough booze there, Bill?" she said, sidling up to his car before he realized she was there. Startled, he jumped, letting the trunk fall on his wrist. Evelyn had received great enjoyment from that. Bill rubbed his wrist and closed the trunk with regret that he couldn't pull one of the bottles of JD out and take a good long healthy drink.

"In case you were wondering, or in case you care— which I doubt—your children are doing fine. Sara, understandably, doesn't seem affected by your absence, but Missy, and especially Devin, are confused and hurt. Tell me, Bill, has your drinking become so important to you that you no longer care about your children?"

He had been stung by the remark precisely because it was true—he hadn't thought of, nor cared about, his kids since hooking up with Darlene.

"You're pathetic, Bill."

He'd almost laughed at that. She said it with the same tone of voice she might use to comment on the weather, but he couldn't help smirking, which was the wrong thing to do. Evelyn exploded.

"You're more than pathetic, Bill," she shouted, drawing the attention of several people nearby in the parking lot. "You're disgusting! What kind of man are you to leave your children so you can get drunk all the time? I can understand your not caring as much about the girls since they're not your flesh and blood, but Devin is your *son*, goddammit! What the hell is wrong with you?"

"Quiet down!" Bill had demanded, looking around. "You're making a scene."

"Really? What's the matter, does the truth embarrass you? Afraid to have people know what kind of slime you really are?" She had raised her voice then and spoken to the people listening. "Tell me, what do you folks think of a man who abandoned his kids because he'd rather get drunk?"

"That's enough!" Bill retorted. "This is too much."

"No, Bill!" Evelyn spat back. "No! You're too much. You're too fucking much."

He'd been taken aback by Evelyn's swearing. He had never heard her use such strong language. Before he could recover, she turned and stalked off to her car. She opened the trunk and literally threw her grocery bags into the car with such force Bill had heard the tinkling of a bottle breaking. She then slammed the trunk lid and turned back to him.

"One more thing. That guy Drake from the store has been calling. When you decide to give up, you give up on everything, don't you? He said you haven't been in to work in over three weeks. Haven't called either. He asked me to tell you to call him if I saw you." She opened the car door and paused for one more shot before getting in. "I hope they fire you, Bill. I hope you lose that job. I hope you lose *everything* that you ever cared about, then I hope you *realize* you've lost it. I think you've already lost your kids."

Though he had craved a drink and coke after his run-in with Evelyn, he had managed to stay relatively sober long enough to stop by the store and see John Drake. He found his name had been removed from the office door and replaced with Drake's above the title: DIRECTOR OF SECURITY.

John had been uncomfortable, even apologetic, about having usurped Bill's position, and though Bill felt angry at him, he knew he had only himself to blame for losing his job. He'd reassured John that he wasn't angry, though he was, and didn't hold it against him, though he did. He even went so far as to congratulate John and say he was glad that his former assistant had been promoted. He then took the severance check the company had issued to him and went out and bought more cocaine, going on a binge that had lasted until this morning.

He pulled up outside a small package store and dug his pinky finger into the bag of coke lying open on the seat next to him. He coated the fingertip well, shoved it up his nose, snorted, and repeated the procedure. Shoving the bag under the passenger seat, he got out and went in to buy some Jack Daniel's.

He had just enough money to buy a fifth and kicked himself when he remembered he'd left nearly a thousand

dollars in cash and his bank account books at Darlene's.
He took the bottle and hurried out of the store in a frenzy
to get back to the apartment before Darlene discovered
what he'd left behind and went out and bought herself
some coke with it.

He was driving with one hand and downing half the
bottle of JD with the other when he ran a stop sign and
plowed into a station wagon filled with kids. The bottle
flew from his hand, smashing into the windshield and star-
ring it with a complex spiderweb of cracks. His head tried
to follow, but the steering wheel kept him in the seat,
crushing against his chest and causing him to ricochet
back and forth between it and the backrest like a pinball.
The last thing he saw before blacking out was the face a
screaming, crying child framed in the rear passenger window of the station wagon. The last thing he thought was:
Oh, my God! What have I done?

II
Rehab

Came to believe that a Power greater than ourselves could restore us to sanity.

—Step Two of AA's 12 Steps
to Recovery

I'm here because I'm not all there.

—AA slogan

16

Bill Gage woke to whiteness and a bruised, sore feeling in his chest. It pierced his skull through his eyes, making him wince with pain. He closed his eyes, took a deep breath, and tried opening them again. Not so bad this time. The terrible whiteness was diminished slightly. After a few moments he was able to focus.

He saw tile, white tile, all around him. He looked up. Even the walls were white tile. He looked back at the floor and had a moment of dizziness, feeling as though the floor were falling away from him. He blinked and the feeling disappeared; the floor *did* fall away, sloping downward to a drain in the middle of it.

The place was familiar, but vaguely so through the muddled haze of his brain. He tried to stand, feeling something hard and metallic beneath him as he put his hand down, but toppled over, rolling onto the tile and setting the pain in his head ablaze with renewed force.

He managed to get to his knees and saw that the metal surface he'd been on was a narrow steel cot with no mattress, bolted to the wall a half foot off the bare tile floor. The harsh fluorescent ceiling lights cast his shadow in triplicate around him, bringing back the dizziness. His eyes were drawn again to the drain in the middle of the floor, and the familiarity of it tugged harder at his memory. He looked up and saw a bare porcelain toilet and sink against the far wall.

A drunk tank! That's where I am, he thought.

He stood on wobbly legs, and his pants fell down. With a great deal of awkward effort, he bent over and pulled them up. His belt was gone, and his pants wouldn't stay up.

I've lost weight, he thought, dumbfounded. His belt had always served as nothing more than something to put through the belt loops of his pants—his pants had always fit his ample waist snugly enough to prevent them from falling down.

How the hell did I lose so much weight? he wondered. The answer came with the question: *When was the last time I had something to eat?*

He couldn't remember. He tried and just couldn't remember putting anything other than booze and cocaine into his body in the last month.

That'll do it, I guess, he thought with a smirk and an overwhelming urge to put more of the same inside himself as soon as possible.

Why the hell is my belt gone? he pondered, picking his pants up from around his ankles again. He noticed his shoelaces were missing too.

So you won't hang yourself, dummy!

Now he remembered too clearly that removing a prisoner's belt and shoelaces to prevent suicide was standard procedure.

"I've been arrested," he mumbled. "What the hell happened?"

He tried to remember and felt sick at the effort. He staggered to the cot and lowered himself onto it. He rubbed his eyes and tried to retrace his steps in his mind. He remembered being at Darlene's apartment. Was there an argument? For some reason the thought made him very uncomfortable and he moved on. He remembered leaving and driving around for a while . . . to cool off? Was that it? Then . . . what? Oh, yeah. He stopped at a package store; didn't have enough money to get more than a pint of JD. He was hurrying back to Darlene's to get his money when . . .

Oh, my God!

The accident flashed before his eyes—the station wagon suddenly in front of him—the sickening crunch of metal on metal and shattering glass—the bottle of Jack Daniel's smashing into the windshield—the steering wheel and the seat back playing Ping-Pong with him—and worst of all the last image, that of a child, screaming through the broken rear window of the wagon.

It was too much for his stomach and he vomited, just managing to lean over enough not to get it on himself or the cot. He watched the regurgitation flow slowly toward the drain in the middle of the floor and began to cry.

"How are you feeling?"

"Shitty," he mumbled. He was sitting in Chief Albert's office. An officer had come and roused him from his crying jag and brought him there. Now he sat, his head hanging in shame, wishing he could have a drink, just one—or a snort—maybe two or three of those.

"What do you remember?" the chief asked.

"Not much."

"Do you remember the accident?"

Bill shuddered. "Yeah."

"What about being at the hospital? Do you remember that?"

Bill shook his head slowly. "No."

"I'm not surprised. You were pretty well out of it. You'll be relieved to know, or maybe not, that you're okay. Some minor bruises to the chest was all that you suffered."

Bill could barely bring himself to ask, but he had to

know. "What about . . . the . . . What about the family in the wagon?" Tears welled in his eyes.

"There's an old saying," the chief said slowly, drawing out Bill's agony at finding out whether he'd killed anyone, "that God watches over drunks and lunatics. I guess today it was true. No one in the wagon was hurt—shook up and scared pretty badly—but not hurt."

"Thank God," Bill murmured. The moment of gratitude was short-lived, replaced by righteous anger. "What the hell was that guy doing driving like that with kids in the car? He pulled right out in front of me!"

Chief Albert's answer was loud and angry, thundering in Bill's ears. "You ran a stop sign, you *asshole*!"

Bill cringed before his friend's anger. His first impulse was to argue, but the image of the stop sign flashed through his memory, and he knew the chief was right. He had run the stop sign because he'd been too intent on his bottle of booze to stop in time.

"So what happens now?" Bill asked meekly.

Chief Albert composed himself, bringing his anger under control before answering. "Normally we'd throw your ass in jail and you'd face charges. We found almost an ounce of coke in the car with you, not to mention the bottle of JD. And with the new tough drunk-driving laws in this state you'd almost certainly do hard time. Plus time for possession of a controlled substance."

Bill's shoulders slumped and an involuntary moan escaped his lips.

"But," the chief went on, "because of the service you provided in the Wilbur Clayton case, and considering all you went through during it, what with the murder of your wife and all, the DA and the mayor have agreed to offer you a deal. The family you ran into have been talked to, and as long as your insurance takes care of them, they have no qualms with what I'm about to say. Of course, they have the option of suing the shit out of you if they so choose, but at least they won't press charges."

"Okay, so what are my options?" Bill asked quietly.

"*Options* you don't have. You either do what I say or into the slammer you go."

"Yes."

"Yes, what?"

"Yes, I'll do whatever you say," Bill said in resignation.

"I know you will, unless you're a lot stupider than I thought. There's a place just over the border into Vermont, a rehabilitation clinic by the name of Birch Mountain Hospital, where we send officers who develop substance abuse problems. The DA and mayor have agreed that if you check into the clinic, get into AA and drug counseling, and stay sober, no charges will be brought against you. The DA has already arranged the deal with the district judge, and it amounts to your being on probation."

"For how long?"

Chief Albert paused. "For as long as it takes for you to get clean and sober, Bill. Then for the rest of your life. I don't know if you realize it or not, but you came damned close to killing an innocent family today. You came close to killing *children.* Whether you want to admit it or not, you need help. I've seen a lot of cops turn into drunks, and frankly I have my doubts that you'll make it and stay sober, but I owe you the chance. Even though I'm so pissed off at you right now that I could knock you down, pick you up, and knock you down again, I'm still your friend."

Silently Bill began to weep. The outpouring grew until he could keep it quiet no longer and he started to bawl like the kids he had often caught shoplifting. "You're right," he sobbed. "I need help. I'm out of control and can't . . . can't . . . help myself." He tried to say but the tears overwhelmed him, closing his throat and choking off his words.

"Though it hurts, I'm glad to hear you say that, Bill. It's the first smart thing you've done in a while. Now pull yourself together, and I'll have one of my men run you by your place to pack a bag, then take you up to Birch Mountain."

Bill mumbled his thanks and tried to stifle his sobs.

The officer was waiting downstairs while Bill packed a suitcase. In the bottom of the top drawer he found a small square packet wrapped in tinfoil. As he opened it, revealing the chunky white powder within, he remembered stashing the coke there during the sole trip to the house while he was living with Darlene. He'd put it there for an emergency, and if ever there was one, this was it.

"I'll be down in a minute," he yelled to the cop from the top of the stairs. "I just have to get some things in the bathroom."

"Don't bother bringing any aftershave or aspirin or anything that might have alcohol in it, they'll just take it away at the hospital," the cop shouted back.

"Right. Thanks," Bill answered and ran to the bathroom with his packet of coke. Frantically he opened the medicine cabinet and pulled out his round shaving mirror, placing it on the top of the toilet tank. He broke the hollow handle off a disposable razor to make a crude straw and dumped the coke onto the mirror surface. Using a bobby pin (and trying not to think that it might have been one of Cindy's), he separated the coke into uneven fat lines. As fast as he could, he snorted all the coke and felt both immediate relief and a burning desire to get more. As he wiped the remnants of the snort from his nostrils, he wondered if he could talk the cop downstairs into letting him stop by Darlene's apartment before going to the hospital. He was certain she had some blow stashed there, and if he was going into the hospital for a month, he was going to need it to get through. Plus there was the matter of the money he'd left behind, which had gotten him into all this trouble in the first place.

"I left a few things at my girlfriend's, and I was wondering if we could . . ." he started to say as he reached the bottom of the stairs but the cop, a young guy by the name of Fisher, cut him off.

"I'm sorry, sir, but I'm going to have to frisk you."

"What?" Bill asked, trying his best to sound outraged but managing only paranoia at best.

"Sir, you've got what looks like coke all over the front of your shirt and smudges of it on the rim of your nostrils. I was told to make sure you didn't bring anything with you."

A dozen comebacks filled with righteous indignation flashed through his mind, but Bill could vocalize none of them. Helpless, he raised his hands and allowed Officer Fisher to frisk him.

"Is there any more cocaine in the house?" Fisher asked when he was done, finding nothing.

"No," Bill answered meekly.

"I hope not, sir. Chief Albert is going to have the house searched, and if he finds anything and knows you're lying, he might not take it too kindly on you when you get out of the hospital."

Bill believed Fisher. George Albert *was* his friend, but he was also a tough son of a bitch of a cop who didn't like to get jerked around, especially when he was doing someone a favor. "No, Fisher, there's nothing left. I swear."

They drove west out of Crocker on Route 2. Half a mile out of town, Officer Fisher took the Westminster exit and stopped at a small package store just off the rotary. "I have to get cigarettes," he told Bill and went in.

Bill looked at the package store with longing. The coke

had made him feel better and though he loved and craved the stuff, booze was still his first love, and he would have given anything to have a drink at that moment.

Officer Fisher came back to the car with a pack of Marlboros in one hand and a brown paper bag in the other. "I've done this detail a few times with some of the guys on the force and I know how you must be feeling about now, especially after the blow you just did."

He handed the bag over to Bill, who opened it and pulled out a pint of Jack Daniel's.

"Chief Albert told me your brand and said not to get you more than a pint. He's a tough old bastard, but he's got a heart of gold. 'Course, don't ever tell him I said that."

Bill looked at the bottle in wonder and back at Fisher.

"This is it, pal. Your last drink. Enjoy it. It'll smooth out the edges on the three-hour drive to Birch Mountain."

Bill didn't know whether to weep or say thank you and did neither. He unscrewed the cap as quickly as possible and took a long, hard, and last drink of heaven.

17

Ivy got off the school bus and crossed the street several houses down from his. He sneaked around the house and made his way toward home via the neighbors' backyards. He climbed two fences and belly crawled under a hedge until he reached the Claytons' yard. He stayed close to the back of the house and looked over at his tenement for any sign of his mom.

The coast looked clear.

It had been nearly a week since he'd started living in the garage, and he'd seen his mother only twice. The first time was the night of the day he'd left. Around nine she'd come out on the back porch and yelled for him for over ten minutes until the fat guy on the second floor opened his door and shouted for her to shut up. The second time was just yesterday, early in the morning. She'd come down to the driveway and looked around the yard, pausing by the garage as if debating to look inside. She didn't, though, and turned away, wrapping her coat about her and heading down the street. When he'd estimated that she was out of sight, Ivy had gone up to the apartment and raided the kitchen for a jar of peanut butter, a loaf of bread, a bottle of soda, and a can of Dinty Moore's beef stew for Henry. He'd managed to make a food run only once before that, the day after he ran away, and he and

Henry were starving. Ivy skipped school that day and he and his dog had a feast.

He ran and broad jumped the rickety picket fence separating the Claytons' yard from his, and didn't stop running until he reached the back door of the garage. He was just in time. Less than a minute later he heard footsteps and looked out one of the small windows in the wide front door of the garage. His mother was coming up the driveway, a long slender brown bag under her arm that Ivy knew from experience could contain only one thing: a bottle of Sangria. She was walking unsteadily, nearly staggering, and Ivy spit in disgust at her drunkenness.

She doesn't even care that I'm gone, he thought with a pang of self-pity. *She never really cared about me at all. She's probably glad that I'm gone, cuz now she can drink all she wants with no one to bother her.*

Ivy went to Henry, picked the dog up, and cuddled him. "That's okay, right, fella? We don't need her. We don't need anybody."

Though he tried to be tough, he couldn't keep the tears from flowing, nor banish the ache from his young heart.

18

Somewhere near Williamstown, Bill Gage finished the bottle of Jack Daniel's and passed into a near-unconscious stupor. He barely heard Fisher mention they were passing over the state line into Vermont, and heard nothing else the young officer said until he announced that they were there.

Bill roused himself, sitting up, and noticed that they were traveling on a narrow, winding, tree-lined country road. Ahead to the right was a large wooden sign with BIRCH MOUNTAIN HOSPITAL—NEXT LEFT painted on it in green block letters.

This is it, Bill thought groggily and raised the bottle to his lips for fortification. Empty. Panic began to creep in like feline fog. He needed another drink—just one more —to face this.

As if reading his mind, Fisher shook his head. "Sorry. One bottle for the road is all you get. It's time to face the music." With that he made the left turn that led up to the hospital.

Traveling that road, Bill didn't have to wonder why the place was called Birch Mountain Hospital. Except for an occasional hairpin turn, the road went almost straight up. His ears blocked, then popped, with the rise in altitude, but he barely noticed for the thirst that was beginning to rage in him.

The trees began to dwarf and grow thinner as they

neared the summit. They passed a huge white Victorian-style mansion on the left that Bill thought at first was the hospital, but Fisher kept going. Another couple of turns and they were above the tree line, driving between shale and granite outcroppings. A large, architecturally modern building came into view at the very top of the mountain. To its right, across the road, was a long, low brick building with barred windows.

Bill decided that must be the hospital and the fancy building at the top must be the staff residence, but Fisher didn't stop the car until they reached the latter building's round driveway. He pulled the car to a stop at double glass doors and shut off the engine.

"This is it. Your home for the next sixty days."

"*Sixty days?*" Bill was hoping he hadn't heard correctly.

"That's right. Didn't Chief Albert tell you?"

Bill supposed George had told him, but he'd been too out of it to listen. If he had, he wasn't sure he would have agreed to this.

You didn't have a choice, dummy! It was either this or jail!

Not much of a choice, he thought, but this had to be better than jail. He hoped.

Fisher got out of the car and retrieved Bill's bag from the trunk. Bill got out and felt the full brunt of the whiskey he'd drunk hit him, almost knocking him over.

"Steady," Fisher counseled and took his arm. The glass doors opened and a male nurse in white came out to help him inside.

Bill Gage was led into a large lobby area done in blond pinewood furniture. The walls were decorated with serene landscape paintings, and everything was lighted by skylights that spanned the cathedral ceiling. The back wall was glass from roof to floor and looked out on a veranda that afforded a spectacular view of the surrounding mountains and countryside. It looked more like the lobby of an expensive hotel than a hospital.

Behind a massive, horseshoe-shaped desk that took up nearly a quarter of the room, a receptionist sat typing at a computer console. The male attendant directed Bill to a couch so plush he sank a good foot into it when he sat, and went over to speak with the woman behind the desk.

Officer Fisher placed Bill's suitcase next to the couch and reached out his hand for Bill to shake. "Good luck," he said, and paused as if wanting to say more but let it and Bill's hand go. After speaking a moment with the attendant and receptionist, he gave Bill a short wave and left.

Bill put his head back and closed his eyes. With the effects of the booze and with the coke wearing off, he was extremely tired. He felt as though he could sleep for a month. He was just dozing off when he felt a light tap on his shoulder.

"William, your reservation has been confirmed, so we'll get you settled now."

Bill opened his eyes and looked at the attendant standing over him. Had the guy really said "reservation"?

"I'll take you to the admissions area, where you'll be examined by a doctor, and a counselor will take your history and ask you some questions. Can you walk, or should I get a wheelchair for you?"

"I think I can make it," Bill grunted, trying to get up from the couch and failing. The attendant, who was a lot stronger than he looked, took his arm and helped him up. Never letting go of Bill's arm, he picked up the suitcase and led Bill down a wide corridor off the lobby.

Bill had all he could do to keep walking and focused on his feet to keep them going one in front of the other. What he did manage to see of the hospital further impressed him. The corridor was painted in a pastel peach and adorned with the same style of serene landscape paintings, plus a few tastefully calm abstracts, as the lobby.

Skylights lined the ceiling, dispelling the need for artificial illumination.

They went through another lobby area, larger than the first, which was filled with an abundance of plushly upholstered furniture interspersed with wooden tables. At a couple of the tables people sat playing cards. A few looked up with curiosity as Bill went by and he wondered if they were patients or staff on a break. He tended to think they were the latter since they were dressed in street clothes. He was still functioning under the idea that in a hospital patients had to wear johnnies.

The attendant led him around a corner, past a busy nurses' station, and into an examining room. He helped Bill to a straight-backed wooden chair and placed the suitcase on the examining table.

"William, I'm going to open your suitcase and search it, then ask you to empty your pockets and remove your clothing so that they can be searched also. This is standard procedure for all new admissions," the attendant explained.

"Why?" Bill asked.

"Well, William, even though people come here to deal with their addictions, you'd be surprised at how many try to sneak alcohol or drugs in with them. You'll be allowed to keep any personal toiletry items that do not contain alcohol, but you will not be allowed to keep any aspirin or other medications, even if they are prescribed. If you are taking prescription medications for any legitimate medical reason, tell the doctor when she examines you and she'll arrange for your medications to be administered by the nursing staff."

"She?" Bill asked uncomfortably.

"What?" the attendant returned, not getting the response he expected. Nine out of ten patients balked at the conditions he'd just explained and would decide they wanted out.

"She. You said the doctor is a she?"

"That's right. Dr. Rice. Don't worry; she's very good, better than many male doctors I've worked with."

Bill didn't like this. It was bad enough having his belongings searched and confiscated like some common criminal (*but isn't that what you are?*) and having to undergo questioning and a physical exam, but to have it performed by a *woman*! If it was to be a standard physical exam like the ones he'd had before, he was going to be very uncomfortable.

The attendant was going through his suitcase with a thoroughness that spoke of his having done it many times. He removed Bill's aftershave and a bottle of Advil, put them in labeled plastic bags, and wrote Bill's name on them.

"Do you need help removing your clothes?" he asked.

"No," Bill said curtly and began unbuttoning his shirt without getting up. The attendant took it from him, checked the pocket and lining, and draped it over another chair on the other side of the examining table.

With a little difficulty, Bill managed to get his shoes and pants off without having to stand and the attendant carefully examined them as he had the shirt.

"You want my socks and shorts, too?" Bill asked jokingly and was taken aback when the attendant said yes. Bill removed them, and the attendant examined the soles of his feet.

"William, this will be a little embarrassing for you, but I must ask you to stand and bend over so that I can make sure you haven't hidden anything in your rectum."

"What!" Bill said angrily.

"I'm sorry, but it's part of the admission procedure. Everyone goes through it."

"Not me! No way. Uh-uh."

"Look, I'm just doing my job."

"I don't give a sweet fuck!" Bill swore.

At that moment the doctor, an elderly, plump woman with short, graying hair, walked in. "What's the problem, Jeff?"

"No one, not him, not you, is going to look up my butt!" Bill shouted before the attendant had a chance to answer.

The doctor looked Bill over, causing him to cover his privates with his hands and blush, then she turned to the attendant. "I think we can forgo that part of the examination in this case, Jeff." She turned to Bill. "Of course,"— she consulted a clipboard that she carried in with her— "William, if you are smuggling drugs in, we will find out, and you will be immediately discharged and turned over to the local police."

"Fine. And call me Bill," he replied, relaxing a little.

The attendant left and Bill grabbed his shorts. "Okay if I get dressed?" he asked the doctor.

"You can put those on," she answered with a nod to the underwear in his hand. "I have to give you a physical, then a staff nurse will take your history."

Bill endured the standard physical in silence, answering the doctor's and then the nurse's questions about his drug and alcohol use in as few words as possible. He was growing extremely tired, and paranoid about being there. He found himself trying to conjure up excuses to get out, if even just for a little while—just long enough to get a bottle.

"Take these," the doctor said, handing him two pills before she left. "They'll take the edge off and help you sleep. You'll be under detox restrictions for five days, meaning you can't go outside unless a staff person is with you. You'll also be accompanied to the dining hall. I imagine you'll spend most of the next five days sleeping, and that's normal. From what you've told me, you have a lot of rest to catch up on."

Bill nodded wearily. He recognized the pills as Valium and took them. Some sleep would be nice. He could think about how to get out of there after he caught some shut-eye. He put his clothes on, and five minutes after taking the Valium he could barely keep his eyes open. The attendant came back and helped him down the hall to his room, number 113. On the way they passed a greasy, longhaired, bearded man who proclaimed to Bill: "The king is dead! Long live the king!"

"What the hell was that about?" Bill mumbled sleepily as the attendant helped him take his shoes and pants off again.

"That was Alex. He's under the delusion that he's the reincarnation of Elvis," the attendant told him.

"*Jesus!*" Bill remarked, smirking. "I didn't know you took nutcases here. I thought this was strictly an alcohol and drug rehab."

"With the economy the way it is, we've been taking more and more mental/emotional cases like Alex as long as there is also addiction involved. You wouldn't believe some of the nutcases we've had in here. Two years ago there was a guy in here that believed that eating bugs would cure him of his alcoholism. And just last year one of the patients went psycho, thought the head nurse was his dead mother come back to haunt him. He attacked her, then tried to kill himself. The weird thing about that one was, he had no history of mental problems other than being a drug addict. But I guess that shit can mess you up big time, like Alex there."

"Yeah? What's he hooked on?" Bill asked.

"He took anything he could get his hands on, but mostly he was a speedball junkie."

Bill fell back on the bed and started to ask the attendant another question, but was asleep before he could get a word out.

Bill remembered little of his first three days in the clinic. He slept for twenty hours straight, with the help of the Valium, and was roused by a nurse. Groggily he ac-

companied her to the nurses' station, where she took his
pulse, temperature, and blood pressure.

He didn't realize he was hungry until she asked him if
he wanted to eat. His stomach gurgled loudly in answer
and he nodded sheepishly. She took him to the cafeteria, a
large round room past the reception area that had a
domed glass ceiling. The room was full of people dining,
few of whom took note of him as the nurse helped him to
get his tray and silverware. The serving line was short and
soon he was having his plate heaped high with a thick slab
of roast beef, mashed potatoes, gravy, broccoli, and butter-
milk biscuits.

Bill was amazed. The food looked and smelled good
enough to have come from a four-star restaurant. He wondered how much his stay there was costing if they were
serving prime rib.

Cost. He hadn't thought of that before. How was he
paying for this? Since being fired from K mart security he
had no benefits. He was going to have to ask someone
about it, but he imagined it was being paid somehow,
otherwise he doubted they'd let him stay.

The nurse led him to a small corner table where a couple of older men sat eating. "Jim, Bob, this is Bill. He
hasn't been assigned a group yet, so can he eat with you?"

One man nodded. "Sure," said the other.

Bill sat after assurances from the nurse (Betty, he
thought her name was) that she'd be back in half an hour
to get him. Once he started in on the food, he didn't care.
He forgot about why he was there, how he'd got there,
and how he was going to pay for it. He became completely
immersed in the meal. Bob and Jim made casual conversation, asking questions that Bill responded to with nods
and monosyllabic answers. They laughed knowingly at his
voracious appetite. Jim even got up and got him a big dish
of strawberry shortcake smothered in whipped cream that
he almost had an orgasm over.

Bill had forgotten how good food could taste, especially since he hadn't eaten since God knows when, he reminded himself. He was sipping a cup of hot decaf—no caffeine or any other type of drug, except for cigarettes, was allowed—when Nurse Betty returned for him. Bill was glad. He was stuffed and getting very sleepy again.

She led him back to his room, prattling on about what he could expect once he'd detoxed. He'd get a counselor, become a member of a recovery group, and attend classes and AA or NA meetings every day.

Bill half listened. At this point he didn't care. He didn't want to care. He would do everything they told him to because, as it had been at the height of his coke use, he liked not being in control. He didn't want any responsibilities. He just wanted to sleep. Sleep and forget.

19

 I am back. I am born again. I am new.

He whispers the litany over and over as he has done continuously in his mind since arriving at the halfway house.

The person he was for all those years in prison is almost gone, shriveled within him, hiding in the tiniest corner of his mind, his soul. The person he was becoming—the immortal God he was becoming before the cop destroyed his life—is returning. As he had in the few months before his arrest, he can feel the change, the metamorphosis taking place within himself. As he had fifteen years ago, he can feel himself evolving, rising above the substandard existence and awareness of average people.

He can't remember how it had started back then, has no recollection of a gradual process taking place or of his even thinking about it. One day he simply awakened, both literally and figuratively, to realize that he was changing, had changed, and moved on to a higher level of existence.

Now he remembers! It was the day after his mother's funeral. Attending her burial had brought back all the bad feelings he'd grown up with—all the torments and ridicule he had suffered at the hands of his father while his mother was too afraid to interfere. Even though he had got revenge against his old man, the bastard had ruined any hope he might have had of being a normal, self-respecting person. But when his mother died, the sniveling, inferior *person his father had made him died with her. It was then that he realized he had been superior, not inferior, to all others from the moment he had put an end to his father's abuse. It was then that he began to understand his true identity. It was then that he began to develop his special insight, and hunger, for the human soul. It was then that he began to search people's eyes and could tell who was worthy of life and who was not.*

And now he is back, ready to carry on the work that has been postponed for fifteen long years of degradation and humiliation during which he had to submerge his true being. But before he can continue the role fate chose him for, he must take care of the one who interrupted his divine metamorphosis. He must put step one of his plan into action and make his final transformation absolute. He must take his revenge against the cop, Bill Gage, and possess his soul, and then he can be free to destroy and consume all those fate has assigned to him.

First, he needs a car. And a nonperson. The car is easy, the right nonperson is more difficult. He leaves the halfway house at dawn each day, supposedly to spend the day seeking employment, but instead walking the streets of Crocker and Fitchburg, visiting the places where the poverty-stricken live, and where the homeless hide.

And on the sixth day (God created man!) he finds him.

It is near the Fifth Street Bridge that the feeling suddenly comes upon him. The prey is near. Close. Very close.

He jumps the iron railing that leads to the walkway over the bridge and stumbles down the embankment past the huge concrete bridge supports and into the cavernous darkness beneath the giant stone and metal span.

The riverbank under the bridge looks empty, but he knows the one he seeks is down here somewhere—or will be soon. There is evidence everywhere: littered cans and bottles, a large makeshift cardboard-box shelter covered with a tattered blanket, the remains of a campfire with a burned-out can of Sterno in the middle of it.

He feels eyes watching him, but doesn't look around, doesn't seek them out. Not yet.

The only place to hide is in the narrow shelf atop the riverbank where the bridge begins. He ignores it, turns his back on it, and sits facing the river. With the patience of a fisherman he waits, casting stones into the water, and sets his bait—a bottle of cheap Scotch. He pulls it from under his coat, holds it up to the light so that the eyes behind him can see it. Slowly he undoes the paper band and unscrews the top. He sniffs it, inhales it, running it under his nose as though it were a vintage wine and he a connoisseur. Finally he brings it to his lips and tastes it—not much—but from behind he knows it looks as though he has guzzled it.

He sighs, grunts, smacks his lips, and wipes the back of his hand across his mouth, accompanying the gesture with a little shiver.

There is a scraping sound above and behind him. He ignores it, pretending to be too intent on taking another swig. The scraping gets louder—the sound of a body moving over a rough, pebble-and-trash-strewn surface. A few stones and a can rattle down, skittering across the rocks behind him. Still he doesn't turn.

The fish is nibbling at the bait. Not quite close enough to hook. He doesn't want to scare him away with a premature jerk of the line.

He pretends to drink some more, loudly savoring each pretended gulp.

The scraping sound stops. There is a grunt of exhaling air, and something heavy hits the embankment behind him. Litter scatters as do muttered curses.

And suddenly he's afraid to turn—afraid that he has made a mistake—afraid that this won't be the one he seeks. And if that's true . . . his exposure here could be a major blunder. But not one that can't be corrected.

*He steels himself for disappointment, and the not un-
pleasant task the disappointment will force him to do, and
swivels around to look at the man getting shakily to his feet
a few yards away. Their eyes meet.*

*I love you, Lady Luck. Together we will give birth to
havoc, destruction, and revenge.*

The man is perfect.

20

Bill Gage slept another twenty-eight hours and woke feeling rested but groggy. Nurse Betty had given him another couple of Valiums after his meal, even though he didn't need them to sleep. He woke feeling thickheaded from the drug.

He rolled over in the narrow bed, thinking to doze off again, and saw, across the room, his roommate on his knees by his bed, deep in prayer.

Oh, Christ! Bill thought. *What have I got myself into? Just what I need—to be rooming with some born-again fruitcake.*

The man finished his prayers and crossed himself. He stood and looked at Bill. "Good morning," he said, his voice thick with a French-Canadian accent. He nodded at Bill and proceeded to straighten his blankets and make his bed. "You slept good, eh? You been out a long time."

"Yeah. How long?" Bill asked, his mouth dry and his voice raspy.

"Let's see. You came in on Friday afternoon and today's Sunday. A couple of days, eh? I don't know how many hours. I'm not too good at numbers." The man finished making his bed and turned, crossing to Bill with his hand out in greeting.

"Hi. I'm Alex."

Bill didn't get up. His legs felt too rubbery and his body

too heavy. He shook Alex's hand and took the opportunity to size him up.

Alex was a little taller than Bill—maybe five feet ten. He had thick, curly black hair that hung to his shoulders and framed a face nearly hidden by an equally thick black beard. He wore thick, Coke-bottle-lens glasses in nerdy black plastic frames. The lenses magnified his eyes enormously but gave them the disconcerting illusion of being separate from his face. They looked disembodied and appeared to float an inch or two out of their sockets.

He had a faraway, unfocused look to his eyes also that Bill wasn't sure was an illusion created by the glasses. Even when he looked right at Bill he seemed to be actually looking over his shoulder at the wall, or even through him. He had weird eyes.

His build was stocky, wide in the shoulders with big arms, thick forearms and wrists, but surprisingly small hands with short, stubby fingers. He had a small beer gut that sagged a little over his belt and legs that were ridiculously thin compared with the rest of his body.

He wore a wrinkled black T-shirt and blue jeans with carefully frayed holes at both knees. On his feet he wore leather sandals that were held together in spots by black electrical tape.

"You're Bill, eh?" Alex asked when Bill didn't introduce himself.

Bill nodded, his eyes returning to Alex's face. There was something familiar about it. He was sure he had seen it somewhere else recently.

"I'm off to breakfast, eh," Alex said, heading for the door. "I'll tell the nurse you're awake. They asked me to anyway, eh," he explained without looking back. He began singing "Love Me Tender" as he went out the door, and Bill remembered where he had seen Alex before.

On the day he was admitted, Alex had been the nut raving about being Elvis reincarnated. No. That wasn't it.

That was what the attendant had told him. What Alex had said was "The king is dead! Long live the king!"

Bill remembered the attendant's story about the drugged-out crazies that the hospital took in because of a financial need for patients. He shook his head wearily. What the *hell* had he let himself be talked into?

21

He strolls casually through the vast mall parking lot, appearing to be just another shopper searching for his car in the maze of chrome, metal, and glass. And why not? He is searching for a car, though it's not his own . . . yet. He's spotted several suitable models, but the timing isn't right. He must wait until there is no one around.

As he nears the end of a long row of cars, a woman with child in tow comes along, proceeding to a Jeep Cherokee parked in the next row over. When they leave, he goes to work quickly, picking the door lock of an old Toyota, getting in, and ducking under the dash to hot-wire it.

Everything is ready. He is ready. At long last his carefully constructed wheels are in motion. He heads for the old abandoned warehouse near the bridge in Fitchburg where he told the homeless drunk, Joe, to meet him.

Joe is perfect. The right height, the right build, the right color eyes through which he can see the complete desolation of the man's soul. But most especially, his teeth are right—rotting and loose looking. Perfect.

He looks at his own perfect machine-made pearly whites in the rearview mirror and laughs, wondering what Joe will say when he learns that he has a dentist appointment.

Probably won't say much, he thinks. But I'm sure he'll scream.

He makes a stop in an alley near the halfway house. In

an old, rusted Dumpster behind a vacant restaurant he has been collecting gas cans lifted from car trunks at night, and plastic one-gallon milk jugs filled with gasoline siphoned from cars in the predawn. He has been hard at work since getting out of prison. There are a lot of containers in the Dumpster.

He loads them in the trunk and piles them in the back and front seats until there is room for only two people in the front—Joe and himself.

He pauses, running down his mental list carefully to be sure he hasn't forgotten anything: He has Joe; he has the car; he has the gas; he has confided in one of the other cons at the halfway house, telling him his concocted story of how he is going to scam some big-time drug dealers to get enough money to get out of the state—making sure to also impress upon the con that if they find him out they will kill him. While there he also picked up his clothes and the special thing that will complete his transformation. That, with a pair of pliers, is everything he needs. He is ready.

Driving to pick up Joe, his mind races, going over everything repeatedly in detail. He reruns his meeting with Joe, checking carefully to be sure it went as he thought it had. The homeless drunk is a godsend, but he is also the most dangerous and risky part of the plan. Joe is perfect, with no family, no friends, and he's been in the area for only a week and a half after riding a freight train in from Albany.

It has been all too easy to ply Joe with the cheap Scotch and coax him with the promise of more waiting behind the warehouse when they rendezvous.

He pulls into the cracked-tar lot of the old warehouse and drives around the back. He sees no traffic, no pedestrians, no one to remember seeing him. It is almost too perfect.

No. He smiles. It is too perfect.

I am perfection.

"What's with all this?" Joe asks through the open window when the car pulls up to him. With a palsied finger he indicates the gas cans and plastic containers crowding the interior of the Toyota.

"It's for a friend," he replies, innocent as milk. He's not lying. "You're my friend now, aren't you, Joe?"

"Did you get another bottle?" Joe asks cagily.

He pulls it out from under the seat and holds it up.

"I'm your best goddamn friend, buddy!" Joe reaches eagerly for the bottle and he lets him take and drink. Joe passes the bottle back to him a couple of times and he feigns drinking. But when he doesn't ask for it, Joe stops offering and greedily polishes off the rest of the bottle.

"You gotta 'nuther bottle, buddy?" Joe slurs, swaying on the verge of toppling.

"Yeah. Get in."

Joe squeezes onto the seat next to him, and they drive off. The spot he seeks is not far. He has reconnoitered it completely.

He drives the car to the outskirts of Crocker, turning up the steep hill that runs behind the hospital. There is a stretch at the top called High View Cliff where the trees hug the road on one side and on the other is a drop of over three hundred feet down a cliff of rocky granite and shale ledges.

He drives slowly, obeying all the traffic signals, until he is almost at the designated spot. He pulls the car into a deep thicket of trees just below the rise in the road leading to the cliff. He steers the car into the deep shadows cast by the trees until it is invisible from the road.

"Looks like strawberry spring is over," he says to Joe, who is passed out, snoring softly next to him. He nudges Joe and the wino stirs, smiling drunkenly.

"You know, you really should do something about those teeth," he says softly as he reaches for the drunk.

* * *

The first few—the front ones—come out easily with nary a whimper from Joe. They were ready to fall out on their own, they are so rotted. It isn't until he gets to the side and back teeth, the ones with the deep roots, that Joe reacts to the pliers ripping the teeth from his mouth.

Joe screams, but he mashes the drunk's face with his fist, sending a gusher of blood out the nose and down the wino's throat, suffocating the scream into a bloody gargle.

He rips a tooth free and holds it up for Joe to see.

"She loves me," he says.

He pockets the tooth and yanks another one.

"She loves me not."

He is disappointed. It wasn't as satisfying as he'd hoped it would be. Joe passed out too soon and nothing could revive him. He did the rest of the teeth quickly then. When it is finished, he takes his own dentures from his mouth and pushes them carefully and securely into Joe's. From his pocket he takes his spare dentures and clicks them in place over his gums.

He pulls the top from one of the plastic jugs of gasoline and douses Joe liberally with it. For a second, he is filled with doubts. What if it doesn't work?

"It will work."

He throws the empty jug into the backseat and gets out, walking to the road and checking it. All is clear. One last look over everything and he backs the car out.

He pulls the car to the shoulder of the road overlooking High View Cliff. Putting the car in neutral and engaging the emergency brake, he gets out. One more check of the road in both directions and he is ready. From his pocket he takes a book of matches, lights one, and uses it to ignite the entire matchbook.

He tosses the flame onto Joe and is delighted with the whoosh of flame that engulfs the wino. Holding his right arm over his face against the heat, he leans in the open driver's window and releases the brake. The car begins to roll. It hesitates on the edge for a second, then with a metallic scraping sound not unlike a scream as the underside of the car rubs against the rocks at the edge of the cliff, the car goes over.

A plethora of wonderfully violent sounds fills the night, and his ears drink them in: crunching and buckling; glass popping and shattering; metallic groans that could rival the bellows of dinosaurs.

"C'mon!" he breathes.

The car rolls over and over, flames from the burning Joe licking out the broken windows.

"C'mon!"

The car is halfway down the cliff, crunching and smashing, tires flying, glass tinkling . . .

Come on, goddammit!

Metal screaming and . . .

Fourth of July!

The explosion is not what he had hoped it would be, but the fire is dazzling. There is a soft, muffled wallop and fingers of fire reach out of the windows followed by a loud exhaling sound punctuated with metallic poppings. The interior of the Toyota sprouts flames as the car flips clear of the last rock ledge and free-falls another thirty feet to the bottom.

He grins and is about to turn away when he is rewarded by the boom he'd hoped for on contact. The Toyota's gas tank goes with a heavy clap on impact with the bottom, fire blazing from it like laughter at having been scared by the loud noise.

He laughs too. Death is a wonderful thing.

So is birth.

Carefully removing a bundle of rags from inside the small army surplus knapsack he bought at a thrift shop, he takes out his new identity, drops his pants, and straps it on. Leaving the sharp edges of the thing wrapped in cloth, he undoes the hinge at its base so that it will lie flat against his stomach. He smiles as he pulls his pants back up and admires the bulge it makes.

Dawn finds him standing on the corner across the street from the cop's house. The urge to exact revenge here and now is nearly overwhelming, but he is disciplined if he is anything.

No. He doesn't want this to end now. All his planning will be for naught if he gives in to the murder lust boiling inside him. There are other ways to appease that lust, other avenues. And the torture they will bring the cop will be delicious and make the final act of his plan so much more satisfying.

Fear is a wonderful thing too.

By noon he is outside the city of Crocker, heading west. It would be easy to steal a car again, but he has no need for machine transportation anymore. He has legs, and his legs will lead him on the path to all that he desires.

Nobody walks anymore. Oh, they do it for exercise, walking round and round on some path in a park like hairless gerbils on a giant flat wheel. But nobody really walks anymore. Not anywhere. This world was made for walking and he will walk all over it.

The paths paralleling major thoroughfares are numerous. Most people never see the urban wilderness that abounds in this country. They're all traveling too fast to notice. Granted, it's not true wilderness, it's more a wasteland, a discarded land. But it is there, hanging on, sometimes in narrow strips no wider than a supermarket aisle amid the ever-expanding asphalt blight.

Dressed in blue jeans, a sweatshirt, lined denim jacket, and with a new pair of Nike Cross Trainers (courtesy of the halfway house) on his feet, he travels these paths, discovering them anew. Some have so long been discarded by anything other than vermin and the occasional exploring child

*that they are overgrown to the point of being nearly im-
passable.*

But pass he does.

*By sunset two days after Joe's Fourth of July celebration,
he is outside Williamsville, nearing the New York border.
New York is where he'll begin, Albany in particular as a
sort of tribute to Joe, who was from there and who so
graciously gave up the mortal coil so that he could be
reborn.*

*By the end of the week he is in the suburbs surrounding
Albany proper. He cases neighborhoods carefully, invisible
in the throwaway wilderness. In an affluent suburb lit by
pseudo-gas-lamp streetlights, he finds the perfect family:
parents, two daughters, one son. The first practice for the
real thing is about to begin.*

*Entry to the house isn't difficult. He waits until well
after midnight and puts on the plastic gloves he stole from
the halfway-house kitchen. His hand goes through a small
pane of glass in the back door. The sound of nearby traffic
covers the sound.*

*He lets himself into the kitchen, listening intently for any
sign that his break-in has been heard. All is quiet. He un-
dresses quickly, leaving his clothes in a pile on the kitchen
floor, unwrapping the sword between his legs last of all. It
stands eternally erect on its hinged metal base, gleaming in
the darkness, waiting for flesh to cut and blood to feed on.*

It will wait no longer.

*He explores the house, carrying several electrical cords
he has cut from kitchen appliances, and easily and soundlessly subdues, gags, and binds the children. Tying the last
cord, securing one of the girls' legs to her bedpost, he hears
a noise from the adjoining master bedroom. He goes to the
door and looks out. The father is up, plodding in his boxer
shorts to the bathroom.*

*He grabs a heavy cheerleader trophy from the girl's
dresser and pads silently after the father. The door is open*

and he can hear the soft fizz of urine striking water. The man's back is to him. The father never knows what hits him as the base of the trophy cracks into his skull. He doesn't omit a sound as he topples forward over the toilet and into the bathtub.

"Honey? Are you okay? What was that noise?" The woman's voice comes from the bedroom. He checks the man quickly, pleased that he is still breathing, and goes to her.

"It sounded like you fell," she says as he enters the room. She thinks he is her husband. Light from the digital clock on the bedside table reflecting off the metal strapped to his groin is the first indication that something is wrong. Getting his fist in her face as she sits up is the second.

She lies moaning, semiconscious on the bed. He leans over, places the bloodied trophy on the night table, and turns on the lamp there.

The woman is attractive, raven haired and thin. Her large breasts push against the cotton flower-print night-gown she wears. He kneels next to her on the bed and rubs himself against her, slicing the gown from her body with the thing between her legs, not caring if he takes a little or a lot of flesh in the process.

22

Pain brought her fully conscious. Something sharp and hard was cutting into her legs, stomach, arms, and breasts. In a panic she remembered the man striking her.

Her eyes flew open as the top of her nightgown was cut away and her right shoulder slashed painfully. The man was bent over her, rubbing his groin against her clothing. She tried to lash out and roll away from him but received another, lesser blow to her face for the attempt.

She lay with her eyes closed, struggling not to lose consciousness, and felt him straddle her chest, pinning her shoulders to the bed with his knees.

He's going to rape me, she thought. She wondered wildly where her husband was and why wasn't he saving her from this when she remembered the crash from the bathroom. The conviction that he was already dead came over her, bringing hot tears to her eyes. Another thought put her in a state of panic: *What will this man do, maybe has already done, to the children? Oh, my God! Please, no!*

Eyes still closed, summoning every ounce of courage she had, she pleaded with him. "Please. I'll do anything you want, just don't hurt my kids. I'll do anything you want."

"I know you will," he answered.

She opened her eyes and then her mouth as a scream started involuntarily from her throat. She had expected to see his penis thrust in her face but instead was shocked at what she saw. Before the scream got halfway out of her mouth, the man shoved the thing between his legs into her mouth and down her throat, shredding her lips, breaking her teeth, ripping her tongue open, and silencing her forever.

23

Bill was in physical therapy class learning about trust. The latter was supposedly bestowed on those who could fall backward off a table, their eyes closed, and expect their fellow group members to catch them. As usual, Bill was participating as minimally as possible. He'd stationed himself at the end of the catching line in the hope that the instructor would tire of the exercise and move on to something else before Bill had to catch anyone, or even worse, depend on others to catch him.

He was next in line to catch and climb atop the table when the chief of staff, Dr. Phyllis McRegan, entered the small gymnasium and beckoned to Bill after having a word with the therapist.

He went cautiously over to her. She had a reputation for being a no-nonsense, tough old broad, and he'd already seen proof of that when she bawled out a patient who had refused to join in the nightly gratitude meetings.

"A Chief George Albert of the Crocker, Massachusetts, Police Department is here to see you, Bill. Normally, we only allow visitors on Sundays, but when he explained the importance of the matter, I agreed to bend the rules a little. Just remember, Bill, no matter what he says or does, if it's going to interfere with your recovery and sobriety— you've got to ignore it. You've got to look out for number one from now on, understand?" She gave him a thrust-out-jaw look that defied him to argue.

"Yes, ma'am," he said, feeling like a schoolboy.

"Call me Phyllis, Bill. Everyone does. Even the people who hate me call me Phyllis."

Then I guess everyone *does,* Bill thought.

Chief Albert was waiting for him in McRegan's office. She led Bill inside and left them alone, closing the door on her way out.

"That's one tough bitch," George commented with a chuckle. "She almost wouldn't let me in to see you. So, how are you doing?"

Bill shrugged. "How am I supposed to be doing? I'm just doing, I guess."

"Dr. McRegan says you're not making much of an attempt to get with the program here."

"Maybe when I find out what the program is, I'll be able to get with it," Bill answered sarcastically.

Chief Albert smirked. "You're too stubborn for your own good, Bill, always have been."

"Alcoholic cops are like that. Yeah, they are," Bill replied in a childlike voice.

"So what don't you get?" George countered.

"Nothing. Everything. Ah, shit! I don't know. It's too hard to explain. I feel like a moonie, like I'm being brainwashed."

"The program here has proven itself. It works."

"Yeah, I know." Bill gave in and slouched. "Hey!" Bill sat forward in his chair. "That brings me to another question: How am I going to pay for this? I don't have any benefits anymore since I got canned, and there's not much in my bank account."

"What about Cindy's life insurance money?" George asked.

"Just about gone."

"Where'd it go, Bill? Up your nose?"

Bill bowed his head in embarrassment.

"Don't you see? That's why you've got to get with this program here. Look at what that stuff did to you, that and the booze."

When he'd been with Darlene he had spent money left and right, never thinking twice about it. He thought about it now and for the first time realized the financial impact his coke use and drinking had had. He reluctantly did some mental arithmetic. Over $25,000 in two months. Could that be right? He and Darlene and her constant entourage of friends had gone through an average of two to three ounces of coke every two weeks. At $2,500 a pop, plus what he'd spent on booze, it added up all right.

Bill sighed and looked at his friend. "So, how am I going to pay for this? I'll have to sell my house."

George smiled and shook his head. "The Crocker Policeman's Fund is picking up the tab for you. I had to pull some strings—mostly making the mayor feel like he owed you a *lot* for the Video Killer case—and he finally gave in."

Bill nodded and said, "Thanks," softly.

"But that's not why I came here," George said. "I'm actually here in an official capacity."

Bill winced. He'd been afraid of this. The family he'd smashed into had decided to press charges, or sue, or both!

"I need your help with a case that concerns you."

Bill raised his eyebrows in puzzlement.

"The FBI came to me with a strange case this week. Their coming to see me was strange enough to begin with after we snubbed them on the Clayton case. Actually, it was the mayor who pulled some strings with politicos in Washington that kept them out of the investigation. The mayor figured that if the FBI got involved, it would look like our police department was inept. He did the same thing with the state police. His uncle's a senator."

"So what's that got to do with me?" Bill asked.

"Plenty. Last week a family was brutally murdered in a suburb of Albany, New York. Mouths and throats torn up, bodies tortured and mutilated. Every one of them had their teeth pulled out. The baby had his eyes removed. A real horror show." Chief Albert paused.

"Like I said, what's that got to do with me?"

"And like *I* said: *plenty!*" the chief shot back, irritation in his voice. "Your name was written in the victims' blood all over the walls."

Bill swallowed hard and blinked. "What?" he cried, half rising.

"If you hadn't been in here, you'd be a prime suspect, I imagine. And that's not all. The day after the FBI visited, this arrived in the mail at the station, addressed to you."

George held up an eleven-by-seven-inch manila envelope, the kind with a metal clasp on the flap.

"Addressed to me?" Bill asked, bewildered.

George tossed the envelope to him. "Open it. There's a photocopy of a letter to you inside and some pictures taken by the FBI of the murder scene. They kept the original of the letter for their forensics department."

Bill caught the envelope and looked at Chief Albert as if this were some kind of gag.

"I'm not kidding. Open it. I can't describe to you what's in there, and I wish I didn't have to involve you in this, considering your condition and surroundings right now. But you are already involved, and this guy is a real sicko, and somehow he knows you. The FBI wants you to study this and try and think of anybody you've known or busted that could do this."

Bill opened the envelope and pulled out a three-folded sheet of white paper with black ink scrawled in tight lines on it. As the chief had said, there were photos in the envelope, but Bill ignored those for the moment. He unfolded the letter and began to read.

Dear Bill,

Long have I dreamt of this moment. I am sure by now that you know of my recent debauchery. But what you cannot know is that you committed these crimes. You are responsible for these deaths and will be responsible for many more like them. You see, this is just a prelude, a hint of delicious things to come.

Puzzled? Don't be. All will be made crystal clear in good time.

Wondering who I am? I'll tell you that much now at least. I am Death walking. I am Death. Death on two legs. The Walking Death. Stalking the unsuspecting who wear your brand. I am the grimmest of reapers. I am the night stalker, walking by day, feeding by night. You cannot stop me. You cannot find me. But I will find you. Because you are my provider. You have given me everything I have today and made me what I am. I owe you. Enjoy the time you have left. I'll be in touch.

Sincerely,
The Walking Death

Bill read the letter a second time, then placed it on the desk. He swallowed hard, his mouth and throat suddenly very dry, the kind of dry that only a stiff whiskey could alleviate. Bill tried to ignore that compulsion and looked at George. His former boss was staring out the window at a group of patients having a snowball fight.

Bill didn't want to look at the pictures, but he couldn't *not* look at them. Slowly, his hands trembling and his brow sweating, he pulled them from the envelope.

The first photo was of a young girl, about the age of his twins. She was lying naked on a bloodstained bed, her legs spread-eagled, left arm resting over her head, her right across what was left of her stomach and chest. He looked closer. As George had said, her mouth and throat were mutilated, torn to jagged shreds as if attacked repeatedly with some clawed sharp instrument. All her teeth were missing, and her body—the parts that weren't covered with blood—was a mass of bruises and cuts. Her groin area was as mutilated as her mouth, ripped open as if she'd had intercourse with a chain saw.

He flipped to the next picture, that of another young girl, roughly the same age as the first girl, but with darker hair, and in almost the exact same pose. What had been done to her mirrored the first victim. She, too, was missing her teeth.

The next picture was of a woman—the mother, Bill guessed. She was lying on a bed. She bore the same mutilations as her daughters. Broken, jagged slivers of some of her teeth remained in her mouth, but most of her teeth were gone.

The next picture showed a man, naked in a bathtub. His body was even more mutilated than the others'. The skin on his arms, chest, and legs had been flayed. Though his head was turned three quarters away from Bill, he could see how badly disfigured the face was. It looked like a mass of hamburger with eyes set into it.

He looked at the last victim's picture and felt his stomach turn, a gorge rising in his throat, the urge to drink doubling. It was a little boy in a crib. A little boy. Younger than Devin, but not by much. His small hands were tied to the side bars of the crib and there was not a patch of skin left unbloodied on his tiny body. His stomach and chest had been ripped open. What few teeth a boy of his age would have had been pulled. His eye sockets were blood-encrusted, empty holes. The rest of the photographs were of the various walls in the house where the perp had smeared *Bill Gage* in blood.

Bill threw the photos on the desk. He couldn't look anymore. Tears welled and flowed from his eyes. He wanted a drink so badly he was trembling and ashamed of it. He covered his face with his hands. He could hear

George picking up the pictures and putting them back in the envelope, but he didn't look up until he had himself a little under control.

"I really didn't think it was a good idea for you to see these right now," George said. "Neither did Dr. McRegan. But the FBI guys came with me. I was able to compromise by getting them to let me see you alone. These guys can be real assholes, and I knew this was going to be hard enough without them in here.

"I managed to convince them to wait a week and give you time to go over the evidence before talking to you. I know it's a lot to throw at you right now, what with the condition you're in and being here, but I had no choice. They're pushing hard on this."

"So what do they want from me?" Bill asked, his voice raspy. He cleared it.

George frowned. "You have to ask? It's obvious this family was chosen for its likeness to your own. They want to know if you have any idea who the perp might be. Someone from the past who'd want revenge."

It was Bill's turn to frown. "How the hell should I know. And this family isn't *exactly* like mine. I don't *have* a wife anymore, remember? And those girls aren't twins. One's obviously older than the other. And the boy's a lot younger than Devin. . . ." His voice trailed off, his convictions weak.

"Close enough," Chief Albert answered. "The feds want to know who you've put away during your career who would want to do this to you."

"Shit! I don't know," Bill mumbled. "What about someone who knew Wilbur Clayton? Someone from NAMBLA?"

"We're checking that out, but why go to the trouble of killing someone in upstate New York?"

Bill sighed. His head was reeling, and he felt a near-uncontrollable urge to start crying. That last picture of the little boy had really got to him. If he'd had a bottle within reach, he would have downed it in record time.

"Maybe they're just trying to throw the feds off track," he said softly.

"They?"

"They, him, her, *it*, whoever the sick fucker is who did this!" Bill spat out and the tears came.

Chief Albert looked out the window some more until Bill was under control. "Through the massive exposure you got due to the Video Killer case, the feds are aware of your special talents. They want you to study the letter and police photographs and give them some leads. I'm supposed to leave them with you. They don't expect anything right away—"

"They were tortured slowly before they were killed," Bill interrupted, his voice dry and cracking. "They were bound and gagged and tortured slowly one at a time. The genital wounds on all but the mother were inflicted before their throats and mouths were ripped open. The boy and the girls were already dead by the time the perp got around to pulling their teeth and removing the boy's eyes. The guy's probably left-handed and well built, tall—he'd have to be to overpower an entire family. It looks like he used something long and sharp on them, thrusting it repeatedly into their mouths and other orifices. Could be a double-edged knife."

George looked at his friend. Everything he'd said, except for the description of the perp and his being left-handed, had already been confirmed by the autopsies. But Bill hadn't seen those.

"How do you know he's left-handed?" George asked.

"By the way he tied the knots on their binds," Bill replied wearily. "Left-handers tie knots opposite of the way right-handers do."

"I see you've still got it," George said with admiration.

"Fat lot of good it does me," Bill muttered. "Because of me, those people are dead."

George stood and leaned over the desk toward Bill. "Stow it, Gage. You know and I know that's a crock. This wasn't your fault, any more than Cindy's death was your fault. You just have the bad luck to be involved here. The last thing you want to do is take responsibility for what this sicko has done. That's the whole point of the letter. It's what he wants. He's playing mind games with you. He *wants* you to feel responsible. If you play his game, you're fucked."

Bill heard his friend, but the words wouldn't sink in. The nasty little voice of the addict within kept whispering that it *was* his fault and the only way to deal with this was to get royally fucked up.

George left him with the letter and pictures and promised to return in a week with the FBI agents. Bill was noncommittal about studying the letter and photos, and George didn't push it.

Bill walked him out to his car then went back to his room. He stuffed the envelope under his underwear in the top drawer of his dresser and tried to forget about the pictures. It was like trying to forget about a hangnail while putting on woolen gloves. He spent the next half hour futilely searching the room and bathroom for anything that might contain alcohol. He ended up curled into a ball on his bed, hugging his knees to his chest and trembling violently.

24

 Ivy got off the bus, hoisted the pack to his shoulders, and proceeded on his daily diversionary backyard route to the garage behind his tenement house. All looked quiet as he made the approach through Wilbur Clayton's backyard. He hopped the fence and scooted around the garage to the back door. As soon as he opened it, he had the feeling something was wrong. When he walked in and saw his mother sitting on the boxes that he'd made Henry's nest from, and holding his dog on her lap, he knew it.

"Leave my dog alone," he said curtly, angry that she had discovered his hiding place so quickly.

She released Henry, and the dog bounded off her lap to Ivy, whining and jumping at his legs. He reached down and picked the dog up, holding him waist high to keep Henry from attacking his face with his wet nose and tongue.

"Ivy . . ." his mother started to say, then faltered.

"What are you doing here?" he asked vehemently. "Why don't you just leave us alone, and we'll leave you alone. That's what you want, isn't it?"

"No," she replied, her voice thick. Tears began to stream down her face. "No, honey. I don't. I . . . I want you back."

She cleared her throat and Ivy said nothing.

She's drunk, he thought, though she didn't look drunk

and he couldn't smell the cheap wine emanating from her as it usually did.

"I'm sorry," she said, her voice a little stronger, but still soft. "I . . . I've been a real . . . jerk," she finished with a sigh.

Ivy was taken aback. He hadn't expected this.

"I really screwed up and I'm sorry," his mother went on. "I don't know what else to say. Things were going so good for us for a while there, and I screwed them up. I don't blame you for leaving, and I don't blame you if you can't forgive me right away, but I want you back. I *need* you back."

She began talking faster as if trying to get all the words out before her tears silenced her. "I'm going to change. Things will be good again. Debbie at the restaurant has got me into Alcoholics Anonymous, and I've been going to meetings for almost a week now. With their help I know I can change. It's the booze that screws me up. You've got to believe I can change, Ivy. I need you back so bad. I love you. Please give me the chance to make it up to you."

She began crying, sobbing loudly. Ivy scrutinized her carefully. She sounded sincere enough. The aching in his heart made him want to believe her so badly.

"What about Henry?" he asked, keeping control of his voice despite the emotions that raged inside him.

His mother let out a short laugh amid her tears. "Yeah. I want him back, too. I want both of you back."

Against his better judgment, Ivy gave in to his feelings. He put Henry down and ran sobbing into his mother's arms.

25

He has walked for this day and night, putting good distance between himself and the capital city of New York. In the thick tangle of briar near an abandoned factory outside of some nameless small city, he finds a resting place for the night. It is cold, but he doesn't mind. He builds a fire of litter and deadwood and spends half an hour meticulously sharpening a stick. When it and the fire are just right, he carefully opens the Saran Wrapped package of chicken he has carried with him all the way from the house in Albany. Skewering the meat, he sets it on the fire to cook.

From his knapsack he pulls his large leather pouch, liking the sound of the teeth rattling in the bottom of it. He opens it slowly and removes each of his victims' teeth gently. In the bottom of the pouch, wrapped in foil, is a special treat. He takes the foil out carefully, letting the teeth fall from his hand, clattering back into the pouch. With trembling fingers he unfolds the foil and sighs. A shiver of excitement thrills his flesh.

"I have become," he whispers softly to the objects cradled in his palm. In silent prayer he intones, "The eyes are the windows to the soul." As though consuming delicate hors d'oeuvres, he eats the first eyeball slowly, thrilling at the ecstasy the consumption of the child's soul brings him.

"The eyes are the windows to the soul" is a statement he had always believed, but it wasn't until he had stood over

*the baby boy, crying in delicious pain in the crib, that he
realized that the eyes are the embodiment of the soul, the
chalice that holds the soul.*

*He brings the second eye closer and peers into it. Yes, it's
there. He can see it. So young and pure and innocent. He
places the eye containing that virginal soul into his mouth
and feels the power it contains transfer into him.*

*Refreshed and rejuvenated, he takes the stick from the
fire and consumes the chicken, replenishing his body as he
has just done his spirit. As he eats, he rattles the teeth in
the pouch and runs over the Albany murders in his mind. It
was almost perfect, but not quite. He wishes he had taken
the souls of all his victims, but his revelation had come late,
and he was afraid he'd already spent too much time in the
house. He also realizes, now, that the family wasn't quite
right. But he had been in too much of a hurry—almost a
frenzy—to kill and put his plan in motion. He knows now
that he should have chosen a family without a mother. He
knows the cop's wife is dead, killed by his soul brother,
Wilbur Clayton (Way to go, Wilbur!). At the time he had
justified it with the notion that it would mislead the cop a
little, just to keep him off balance.*

*Now he thinks not. He wants the cop to know, to feel, to
see, to understand that each family he kills is a mirror
image of his own. Only that way will the cop truly know
and believe in what is coming for him and his family.*

*He must be more careful, more selective, next time, he
thinks as he finishes his meal and pulls his thin blanket
from the pack. He wraps it around himself and curls up on
the cold ground, close to the fire, to sleep.*

Next time it must be perfect.

*Dawn and he is on foot again, heading south, easily
finding the paths through the discarded patches of wilderness that run like veins through the urban countryside.
Within one day and night he is in the Catskill Mountains,
where much of the wilderness is real. He bathes in ice-cold*

streams and sleeps beneath stars that fill the sky from horizon to horizon, with barely enough room left over for the near-full moon.

On the fourth day, he catches sight of a sign near a winding road. It reads: TANNERSVILLE—12 MILES. He likes the name—it feels right. A tanner is one who cures the hides of slaughtered animals.

A delicious idea occurs to him.

The town is small, no more than a village, really, built around and dependent upon a ski resort at the base of Mount Tanner, which looms over the area like a massive breast. He camps on the mountainside and spends his nights watching snow machines spew forth powder. His days are spent among the town's populace as he watches, waits, and catalogs.

After three days of fruitless searching he is ready to move on when Lady Luck deals him another winning hand. He is outside the town's sole department store—a run-down old place by the name of Gracie's 5+10—when he spots them. A father, toddler son, and two daughters—identical twins, no less!

Yes, Lady Luck is shining on him with all her love-light. Though he knows the cop's daughters are not identical twins, what better way to get his point across and leave no doubt as to his intentions?

He follows the family through town, hoping with all his might that no mother shows up for this family. After watching them for a while, he surmises through the father's actions, by the way he dotes on his kids, that the man is a divorcé having his children for weekend visitation.

Perfect.

He follows the family into a coffee shop where they lunch. He orders coffee, sitting at the table behind them. The father strikes up a conversation with the pretty young waitress, obviously interested in her, and tells the girl he is renting a chalet on Hobb Road, right outside of town.

It is all he needs to hear.

The walk is short, Hobb Road easy to find. Within fifteen minutes he is outside the sloping drive of an A-frame chalet not far from the ski resort. The family Jeep Cherokee is parked out front. He hides himself in the nearby bushes to bide his time. Half an hour later the family comes out again. The twins and father carry skis, the toddler is bundled up so much he can barely walk.

He waits until their car is out of sight before casing the chalet. Breaking in is easy—less than child's play. He raids the refrigerator for a bottle of Perrier, ignoring the other food inside. He cannot consume normal food until he has purified his body and spirit with more souls.

26

"Okay, Bill, would you like to share with the group how it is that you came to Birch Mountain?"

The question came from his group counselor, Irving Fredd, a white-haired, wrinkled, wiry old guy with thick glasses. Bill was sitting in the daily discussion meeting Irv liked to have. Irv had asked this question of him daily since his arrival at the clinic.

Usually Bill declined, but today he hesitated. Today he felt an urge, no, a need, to talk and tell his story. Maybe it was the returning urge to drink and drug that had come upon him since seeing the pictures of the victims George had shown him, and maybe it was just time to unload. Whatever the reason, he needed to get it off his chest.

"I don't know where to start," Bill said to the floor, keeping his eyes and head down.

"Start anywhere," Irv counseled. "The beginning's always a good place."

Others in the group chuckled.

"I'm not sure about the beginning," Bill stammered. "But I think I'd have to go pretty far back for that."

"You going somewhere? Got a pressing date?" Irv asked jovially. "We don't, so go ahead."

Bill started after a deep breath. "Without dragging my childhood into it, I started drinking heavily when my dad died." He debated a moment whether or not to open that can of worms and declined. "I became a real drunk, a gutter drunk, for ten years. I didn't care if I lived or died. I quit the state police, moved back to my hometown in Pennsylvania, and fell into the bottle, headfirst. Into a lot of bottles."

He glanced at Irv, who nodded, and Bill went on. "I went back to the town of Crocker where I had lived while working for the Massachusetts State Police, a little over four years ago, trying to sell some property, a condo, I had bought when I lived there. I wanted the money for drinking, because I was practically living on the streets as it was. But I met Cindy where she worked at a bar, and I fell in love with her. I knew she'd never love a drunk, so I quit drinking that night, got myself cleaned up, moved back into my condo, and got a job as a store detective at K mart.

"I started dating her and she fell in love with me, too. Within a year we got married. We were married four years and in all that time I never had a drink. I just quit, cold turkey, without a second thought because I had to have her." He stopped speaking, his emotions and memories of Cindy sweeping over him.

"Then what happened?" Irv asked.

The phone on Irv's desk rang before Bill could answer. "Yeah, he's here, but we're in the middle of a group session, for Christ's sake." Irv sounded perturbed. "Yeah. Okay. I'll send him up." He hung up the phone and turned to Bill.

"You're wanted up at Dr. McRegan's office right away. We'll continue this tomorrow."

Bill hesitated to leave. Part of him was happy to have been literally saved by the bell before he'd had to reveal the shame of the past couple of months, but a larger—and getting bigger every day—part of him was disappointed at not being able to finish his story, at not being allowed to unburden himself.

Reluctantly, he got up and left the office, which was in the old mansion nestled under the mountain peak below the clinic proper. The road up to the clinic was at a near-forty-five-degree angle, and by the time he reached McRegan's office he was huffing and puffing.

He sat heavily in the same chair he'd sat in during his last meeting with Chief Albert. George was there again. With him were two FBI agents. Danvers, a tall, broad-shouldered, blond-haired Californian type, handed Bill a manila envelope as he sat.

Bill cradled it in his lap, barely touching it. Chief Albert sat behind McRegan's desk. Danvers stood against the wall closest to Bill while the other agent, Willis, a muscle-bound, clean-cut African-American man, sat in the chair next to Bill and operated a fancy tape recorder. He wore headphones throughout the meeting.

"There's been another family killed," Danvers explained, motioning to the envelope Bill held gingerly as if it were burning hot. "Same M.O. Your name was written in blood all over the scene. Chief Albert received that envelope three days after the murders. It was addressed to you care of the Crocker Police Department. The letter it contained was written on a nine-by-eleven piece of skin cut from one of the victims—the little boy. Needless to say, we've kept it for our lab boys. There's a photo of the letter in the envelope."

Bill didn't want to open it, didn't want to read the sick words and see the even sicker pictures he knew were inside. He was afraid of the compulsion to drink that had overwhelmed him the last time, but he also knew he had to look. Hands trembling worse than at any time in his life, he undid the clasp and pulled out the photo of the letter, leaving the other photos inside. His stomach turned when he saw the roughly square piece of child's skin with the following words written on it in blood:

Dear Bill,

Hello again. Did you miss me? I think not, but hope springs eternal. I'm sure you know by now that I got the family right this time. Perfect. Is there any doubt in your mind now of what the future holds? I think not.

I'm out here, Bill, walking the walk and talking the talk. Death on tour. Next stop? Who knows?

How long will it take to get to you? Another question mark. I'll get there when it's time and not before. You'll know it when I arrive. Oh, how you'll know it. Soon, but not too soon, you and your family will be dirty dancing with Mr. D.

Me.

Death.

The Avenging Angel

Sweet Dreams,
The Walking Death

Bill placed the photo of the letter on the desk. With the back of his hand, he rubbed his suddenly dry lips. He reached into the envelope and brought out the crime-scene photographs. There were four victims this time, unlike the five from last time. The first four photos depicted the victims with their mouths void of teeth and their throats and genital areas ripped to bloody shreds. The only difference this time was that all the victims were missing their eyes, not just the baby boy.

As Bill looked at the first photo—that of a man tied to a bed, barely a square inch of uncut skin left on his body—Danvers spoke. "This happened in Tannersville, New York, in the Catskills, a couple hundred miles southeast of Albany. The guy was divorced. Had his kids for a week and had rented a chalet to take them skiing."

Danvers went on speaking, giving family background, but Bill had stopped listening. He sat staring at the next two photos, one in each hand. They were of twin girls, *identical twin girls.* They were lying on a bloody shag rug, bound together side by side, their bodies mutilated horribly, but not so much that Bill couldn't tell they were twin girls—*The bastard wants me to know that.* He made a rough guess that they were approximately the same age as Sassy and Missy.

The words in the letter—*got it right this time. Perfect*—flashed in his mind. There was no doubt about it now. There was no denying now that The Walking Death was choosing families to murder for their resemblance to Bill's own. He was practicing on them in preparation for a final showdown. The twin girls and the absence of a mother proved it.

"Oh, God!" Bill groaned and dropped the pictures on the floor. He sat back heavily, eyes closed, breathing deeply and mumbling "Oh, God" over and over. The addict's voice inside him, which he had managed to silence after George's last visit, spoke up louder than ever. *Get out of there!* it said. *This ain't your problem. Get out, get drunk, forget about all of this. It's not your problem!*

Bill wanted to heed that voice so badly, wanted nothing more than to drink and drug himself into oblivion and forget all this. If it was just himself that was involved, just he that the perp was after, he would have walked out of the clinic and headed for the nearest bar without a moment's hesitation. But his family *was* involved, and no matter how bad his compulsion to drink and drug became, he couldn't, *wouldn't,* let them down again.

Danvers stopped speaking and gave George Albert a questioning look.. He didn't like dealing with local law enforcement—and dealing with drug-addict/alcoholic cops in recovery even less. But he had no choice. Bill Gage was obviously an integral part of this case. The perp was bent on revenge, and Gage *had* to have some idea of who would have it in for him.

"He's going to kill my family," Bill said, opening his

eyes and sitting up. "You've got to protect them, George. They're staying with Cindy's sister, Evelyn."

George held up his hand. "Way ahead of you. It's all taken care of. I've got two officers staying with them, and we're keeping a round-the-clock surveillance on her condo. The kids are being escorted to and from school and day care, and Evelyn is driven to and from work each day by one of my men."

It suddenly occurred to Bill that The Walking Death didn't know about Evelyn, but that didn't help his kids at all. "I have to get out of here," he said, standing. "I've got to be there."

Danvers stepped forward as if to restrain Bill. He was a tall, heavyset man who looked as though he might have played college football.

George was on his feet quickly and moved between the two men. "Take it easy, Bill. You're better off here. Your family's safe, I won't let anything happen to them. And you're safe here. You can't go to them now. You might be drawing the killer right to them if you do that. If he comes around and doesn't see you with them, my guess is he'll wait until he can get you all together."

George made sense, and Bill listened in spite of himself. It was evident from the perp's choice of a family without a female adult that he didn't know about Evelyn, so the kids were probably safe with her. Safer with her than they'd be with Bill. It also made him think the perp was not someone local. Since Evelyn had never been mentioned in the media stuff about him when he was working on the Video Killer case, the perp had probably got his information about Bill strictly from the news.

"And we don't need you going off the deep end and getting drunk," Danvers added. "You're no good to anyone messed up, especially your family."

I guess I know what he thinks of me, Bill thought. He tried to give the federal agent a cold stare, but his heart wasn't in it. Despite the put-down and dislike apparent in Danvers's words, the man spoke the truth. The way he was feeling, he was much better off remaining in the clinic, removed from temptation. He knew that no matter how much he might want to do the right thing, the addict within him had a powerful will of its own.

"The best thing you can do now, Bill," George said, ignoring Danvers, "is to study the letters and photographs and try to come up with a name. Someone you put away who would be capable of this type of revenge."

Bill sighed and sank into his chair. "I've been trying to do that," he lied, "and I keep coming up blank." The truth was, he had avoided thinking about it because every time he did, the desire to drink and drug had come on so strongly it had frightened him. Still, he could truthfully say: "I can't think of anyone I put away who'd do this. This guy's a serial killer, and the Clayton case was the first serial killer I've ever dealt with."

"This guy's not a classic serial killer." Willis, the other agent, spoke up for the first time. "He's operating with a definite revenge motive."

"Wilbur Clayton killed for revenge, too," Bill said.

"Yes, but this perp's target is very specific. He's not angry at all women, or men, or authority figures. Classic serial killers usually have a generalized vague body of people that they make their victims, either consciously or subconsciously, usually the latter. This guy has focused on you for something he perceives you did to him in the past. This perp might never have killed anyone before this, but I'd say the chances are pretty good that he has, but maybe was never caught. You might have put him away for something altogether different and unrelated to anything like this. Something trivial, even. Maybe this guy has no record at all, never been arrested. He could be someone from your personal life. Someone looking for revenge against your father through you."

"Oh, that's just what I need," Bill groaned. It came as no surprise to him that Danvers and Willis knew about his father's having been a serial killer himself. They would have checked him out completely by now; it was their job. Still, that didn't help the anger he felt rising in him. He tried to calm himself. It made sense to pursue any ties to his father, considering what he had done. Maybe his father had had accomplices? It would explain a lot about how he was able to carry on killing and covering up for so long, but Bill's instinct told him no. This guy, this *Walking Death*, was someone connected to himself somehow.

"If his motive was revenge against my father, why doesn't he mention that in his letters? Don't you think he'd want me to know why he was doing this so as to torment me some more?"

"Maybe," Willis replied. "And maybe he's waiting to tell you face-to-face so he can enjoy your reaction in person."

Bill had to give Willis credit. He was sharp. Bill took a deep breath and let it out slowly. No matter how much he didn't want to be involved in this, and no matter how much the situation made him want to drink and drug, he was involved—*had* to be involved. His family was in danger. "I'll need to see the initial investigation reports on both murder scenes," Bill said to George. "I'll also need to see the coroner's reports on all the bodies, too."

George looked at Danvers for confirmation. The agent hesitated, then shrugged and nodded.

"You got it," George said.

"I'd also like to see my case files from when I was with the state police," Bill added. "They're on microfilm, but they can be copied. I can't remember every perp I've ever put away, so I'd like to go through the files to refresh my memory."

"We've already got someone on that, reviewing your files for suspects," Danvers said.

"Yeah, but they won't be able to put faces and backgrounds with them, or gut feelings based on memories. I can. If I'm going to help you, I need to see those files of my old cases."

"All right," Danvers agreed reluctantly. "We'll send a courier with everything you need tomorrow." He leaned over Bill. "Just remember, time is of the essence here. With every day you take looking at files another family, or two, or three, or a dozen, comes closer to being killed by this nut."

Bill met Danvers's eyes. "I know that. You don't have to remind me. *You* remember that I've got my family at stake here, so don't try and push me around. I don't need your shit."

Danvers straightened and gave Bill a begrudging grin. "As long as we understand each other."

"Oh, yeah. I understand you perfectly," Bill said coolly.

Back in his room, Bill put the envelope in the drawer with the other one and lay on his bed. He closed his eyes and tried to clear his mind, but fearful thoughts for his family's safety kept racing nonstop. He couldn't relax, much less concentrate on who from his past might be capable of committing these crimes.

A nurse's voice over the PA system announced it was time for the daily gratitude meeting in patient lobby A. Daily gratitude meetings were mandatory, and Bill hated them. Expressing gratitude for his blessings was the last thing he felt like doing.

Gratitude meetings were a staple of the recovery program at Birch Mountain and, as Bill understood it, of AA in general. All patients gathered in the large A lobby at the front of the building. A designated chairperson started the meeting with the Lord's Prayer, then explained that the purpose of the meeting was to remember and express thanks for the things he or she was most grateful for in spite of the problems addiction had caused in each person's life.

The chairperson started with a self-introduction and a statement of gratitude, and so it went around the room to the chairperson's right until all of the fifty-five patients had introduced themselves and expressed gratitude.

Not everyone participated fully, and Bill was one of those. A lot of the patients merely introduced themselves and passed on the gratitude part, but that was okay; the others still clapped for them just as they did for the grateful ones.

"Hi. I'm Dave and I'm cross-addicted," this week's chair said after leading in the Lord's Prayer. "And I'm grateful to be here and for all of you here with me. I'm grateful for the support of my family and the people I work for."

Everyone applauded. Someone shouted, "All right Dave!"

"Hi. I'm Bonnie and I'm an alcoholic," the next one in line said. She was a young girl; Bill guessed her not to be more than sixteen. She was grateful to be alive and for the love of her parents.

The gratitude went on, but Bill didn't listen. The photos of the dead families occupied his thoughts. He couldn't get the image of their toothless and eyeless faces out of his mind. He knew that most serial killers tended to keep mementos of their victims, which might account for the teeth, but he also had the feeling they were more, that they were some clue the killer was taunting him with. What really bothered him was the eyes; why remove the eyes of his victims? The Walking Death didn't seem to have any remorse about the murders; in fact, he seemed to enjoy them gleefully, so he couldn't be removing the eyes because he felt guilty under their staring. Bill shuddered. What the hell could the perp want with the eyes of his victims? It was too bizarre. What did it mean?

As if in answer to his thoughts, a short, fat man named Ralph spoke in a whisper next to him. "I wish this would hurry up and get over so we can go to dinner. I'm starved."

A strong intuitive feeling came over Bill, and though he couldn't give a plausible reason for it, he suddenly knew what the perp wanted the eyes of his victims for. He decided to pass on dinner.

A small woman on the other side of him grabbed his arm. He looked up. Everyone was staring at him and he realized it was his turn. Words came harshly from his mouth without thought.

"I'm Bill, and I haven't got a goddamned thing to be grateful for." Embarrassed at the shocked looks he got from the others in the room, he rose brusquely from his chair and stalked out of the room.

27

Ivy's life had become one pleasant surprise after another. The second day back with his mother she brought home a grocery bag full of dog food and treats for Henry. She actually began doting on the dog, coaxing him into her lap to pet, and taking him on the porch to be brushed with one of her old hairbrushes.

Henry loved it and so did Ivy.

Four days after returning home he was putting clothes away in his closet when he noticed his leather pouch had been returned to its hook on the inside wall. He took it down and opened it. All the money his mother had taken was inside.

Ivy felt ashamed. He felt small at having made such a big deal over the money. He took the pouch into the kitchen where his mother was making supper.

"Mom, I want you to take this money to pay for Henry's food," he said, leaning against the fridge and placing the bills on the counter next to the stove.

His mom went on cooking and ignored him.

"Mom, I really want you to take this money. You were right. I should be helping out around here. Earning my own way."

"Thanks, Ivy," his mother said without turning around, "but you keep it for us in case of an emergency. Okay? I'm getting more hours at the restaurant now, so we're doing okay, Lambsy."

Ivy frowned at being called by the despised nickname and placed the pouch firmly on the counter next to his mom. "No. It's about time I turned over a new leaf, too, and stopped being so selfish. I *want* to help out. Please?"

His mother turned and caressed his face. "Thanks, hon. But we *really* don't need it right now. It would help us a lot more if you kept it and keep saving for hard times so we'll have something to fall back on. You never know what can happen. I could get sick and miss work, or get laid off. Save it for when we need it."

"Really?" Ivy asked.

"Really," she assured him.

"Okay. And I'm going to save a lot more, too. I haven't collected bottles and cans for a while, but I'm going to start again. Before you know it, I'll have enough so we can go on a vacation somewhere. How would that be?"

His mother turned and embraced him unexpectedly. "That'd be great, Lambsy. I love you."

This time Ivy didn't mind her calling him by his baby name at all.

28

It's time to cover some miles. Put some distance between the first two kill sites and the upcoming third. He is tempted to steal a car, but there is too much danger of detection that way. If he trusts to his feet and legs and sticks to the forgotten pathways, he is virtually untraceable.

Feasting on his victims' souls, followed by stolen meat roasted over an open fire, has fortified him for the walk ahead. He wants to make good time. He is eager for another practice session in preparation for the moment when he will pay the cop a visit.

"They'll be waiting for you."

The voice comes out of the darkness and he is caught off guard until he realizes the voice is his own.

Yes. He's tipped his hand. Told the cop and the FBI and anybody else involved what he plans to do. All they have to do is wait for him to show up in Crocker. That's all they'd have to do if they were smart, that is. But they aren't. Their wits are dulled by humanitarianism. They will frantically try to catch him before he can kill more innocent people, and he will lead them on a wild-goose chase.

He sleeps that night secure in the knowledge that all is right with his world. Before dawn he is walking at a brisk pace, his mind focused, steeled for the journey ahead.

He covers nearly one hundred miles the first day, surprising even himself. By sunset of the second day he is well

*into New Jersey. He finds a large, dry drainage pipe near a
river and crawls inside, falling immediately to sleep.*

*The city by the river is Nontuck, a dirty, factory-littered
metropolis. He blends in easily with the city's many homeless wandering the streets and carries out his search meticulously.*

*Within hours of hitting the streets he spots a likely fam-
ily. There is a father and a mother, but maybe he can work
around her. What's more important are the children, two
girls, close enough in age and resemblance to pass for
twins, and a five-year-old boy.*

*He spies them in a Piggly Wiggly parking lot, loading a
station wagon with groceries. When they leave the lot, he
runs down the sidewalk, following for several blocks before
losing them.*

*Frustration tries to overwhelm him, but he won't let it. If
anything, Death is patient. After all, is he not immortal? He
can afford to wait until the time is right.*

*And wait he does. At night he sleeps in an alley across
from the supermarket. During the day he circles the lot
endlessly, perusing each car and shopper. He calculates it
will be a week before he sees them again, and he is right.
Exactly one week from the day he first saw them, almost to
the hour, they return in their station wagon for what must
be the weekly shopping excursion.*

*He is ready for them. He cleans himself up in a public
rest room at the bus station around the corner and follows
them into the store. He keeps his distance, throwing a few
things into his hand basket just for appearances, until they
head for the checkout line. Then he is right behind them.
And his hunch pays off. To pay the grocery bill the man
pulls out a checkbook. It is an easy thing to do to glance
over and read the address as the man writes the check. He
leaves his groceries in front of an astonished register clerk
and follows the family outside.*

Back at the bus station he consults a wall map of the city provided for nonexistent tourists. He pinpoints the street, Walleye Avenue. Not far into the suburbs surrounding the squalid city. Not far at all, compared to the miles he has traversed.

It takes him less than two hours to find Walleye Avenue. He walks its length casually, noting every detail of its layout, especially around the house numbered 54.

He finds a stand of thick maple trees and laurel bushes in a vacant lot a block from number 54 and waits until dark. He approaches cautiously from the rear, keeping to the thick shadows.

He peers in a window. The children are gathered around the TV set playing Nintendo. The girls hog the controls while their little brother tries to worm his way into the fun.

He goes to another window. The man sits at a computer in a small study, his eyes intent upon the screen.

Another window. The woman is in a bedroom. She is half naked, wearing only white bikini panties. Her breasts are large and full, and she almost has to pour them into her heavy-duty bra.

He watches without feeling, without arousal. Mere flesh cannot excite Death. Arousal for him can come only through the act of soul taking. Then and only then is he aroused. Then and only then is his entire being racked with orgasm.

Yes, Death likes to get his rocks off.

The woman continues dressing, all in white. He sees that she is donning a uniform—that of a nurse. A clock on the dresser reads 9:45 P.M. There's only one reason she'd be putting on a nurse's uniform at this time of night: she works the eleven-to-seven shift.

Again Lady Luck is shining on him.

He retreats to the bushes and waits until he sees the woman leave the house after putting the children to bed and kissing her husband.

For the last time, he thinks, but pity does not accompany

the thought. He returns to the windows. The living room is dark. The kids are in bed. The father grabs a beer from the fridge and returns to his study.

On the left side of the house is a deck with sliding glass doors that open on the dining room. It is nothing for him to slip the latch and enter soundlessly. It is nothing for him to surprise the father and knock him unconscious with a heavy pewter candleholder he takes from the dining room table. It is nothing for him to subdue the children while they sleep and bind and gag them. It is nothing for him to scoop out their eyes, yank their teeth, and force his razored member into their mouths and other bodily openings. He takes excessive time and pleasure with the father, making him watch his daughters' mouths, vaginas, and rectums being torn up. He relishes the pain apparent in the man's eyes. He imagines it is the cop's children he is mutilating, and it is the cop that he is forcing to watch. The fantasy gives him extreme pleasure. But the best comes when he rapes the man's little boy and hears the moans of inhuman pain emitting from behind the father's gagged mouth and sees the eyes fill with rage, then madness.

Yes. Now he knows what will cause the cop the most pain, and he works slowly and brutally on the boy.

After all, practice makes perfect.

29

Bill's roommate, Alex, woke from his nap and sat up. Alex was supposed to be in physical therapy, but he'd been too tired to go and had slipped back to his room for forty winks.

He woke with a half-remembered dream swimming around in his head. He'd been someone else in the dream, but who he couldn't remember. It wasn't Elvis, though. He knew now that he wasn't Elvis. He'd thought he was, but his psychiatrist at the clinic, Dr. Sloan, had told him it was the side effects of the medication they had him on. They changed the medication, and he changed his mind about being Elvis.

Now he was almost Alex again, but not quite. He felt as though there was someone else inside him waiting to emerge that was not anyone he had ever been before. Or maybe it was *outside* trying to get *in*.

He tried not to think about it. His shrink had told him to avoid paranoid thoughts and occupy his mind with something else. He got out of bed and reached for his cigarettes on the desk by the bed. The pack was empty. He shuffled to Bill's side of the room and checked his desk and drawers. Bill always had butts, but Alex could find none. He went to the dresser and opened the top drawer, moving Bill's underwear and socks aside in his search.

He spied the two manila envelopes at the bottom of the drawer. Since he was a man without a whit of conscience, he had no qualms about removing the envelopes. He closed the drawer and took the envelopes into the bathroom in case Bill should return unexpectedly.

He turned on the light, locked the door, and sat on the closed lid of the john. He opened the first envelope, saw it contained pictures and a photocopy of a letter, and ignored the letter in favor of the photos. His eyes widened at the gory scenes depicted.

He licked his lips.

Could these pictures be real? They certainly looked real. Though he hadn't talked much to Bill, he'd overheard one of the nurses say that his roommate was an ex-cop. If that was true, then the photographs had to be real. They must be pictures of a crime scene.

Hurriedly he opened the other envelope and pulled the pictures out. He stared at the pictures in detail, comparing them against one another. This was incredible. He'd never seen anything like this before. The pictures touched something deep inside him—something dark and hidden, but waiting for its moment.

After a long time he reluctantly put the pictures away and looked at the photocopied letters. He read each one intently, lingering over the one that appeared to have been written on a piece of skin, then read them again and again, studying every word. There was an irresistible familiarity to the words, the sentences, the handwriting. He experienced a sense of déjà vu and more while looking at them. It was as if each word, each letter held a secret meaning and was trying to reveal itself to him. There was some special code here that he couldn't quite grasp. Almost, but not quite. It was just beyond his understanding.

He stroked the papers, running his hands and fingertips over the words, lingering on the signature, *The Walking Death*, at the bottom, as if he could pull the hidden message from the paper.

30

It was 8:00 P.M., time for the mandatory evening AA meeting in the old house down the hill. Bill took his usual spot at the back of the room and watched his fellow drunks and drug addicts file in and take their seats.

He'd made no friends yet, even among the members of his own group. Every other patient seemed to have found a clique or a special friend to hang out with, but not Bill, and he preferred it that way. These people were nothing to him. Once he was out of there, he'd never see any of them again. And with the added burden and pressure of worrying about his family, he had no time or emotion to spare for them.

During his free time each afternoon from one to three, he sat on the patio with its splendid view of the Green Mountains, chain-smoked cigarettes, and watched his fellow patients. There were a lot of young kids in the clinic, kids no more than nineteen or twenty, and as many girls as there were boys. There were a lot of Canadians, too, down from Ottawa since their government's national health insurance footed the bill for their treatment and all the clinics in Ottawa were full.

And when he took the time to notice, there were a lot of beautiful women. Some had approached him but had given up after a few minutes of his monosyllabic responses to their questions.

The speaker for the meeting entered the room and went to the podium. The audience twittered with anticipation; the speaker was Louis A., an extremely funny guy who spoke at least once a week at a meeting. Bill had already heard him twice and had enjoyed both times immensely. It looked as though this meeting was going to be okay after all.

Louis A. was around fifty and from New York City. He'd been a fledgling wise guy with the mob in Bensonhurst at one time, but his excessive drinking had made him unreliable and thus an outsider. Not, as he liked to say, that he'd ever had a chance to be an insider since he was half Irish and half Jewish. He had grown up in an Italian neighborhood and hung out with Italian kids so much, he'd thought he was a *paesano*. Though raised Jewish, he even attended Catholic Church with his Italian buddies.

Louis A. started speaking in his rapid-fire, raspy voice, and soon the room was full of laughter. Bill laughed, too, but not as often, nor as heartily as he usually did when listening to Louis. It wasn't because he'd heard most of Louis's jokes before—they were truly funny every time he told them—but he couldn't get The Walking Death out of his mind.

He'd been putting off doing any work on the case. A special courier from the FBI had delivered their reports on the homicides so far, and his old state police files. Rather than have all the files delivered on paper copy, which would have filled Bill's room, Danvers had arranged to have a microfilm viewing machine brought to the clinic. Though she told Bill she was against it, that it was bad for his recovery, Dr. McRegan allowed them to put the microfilm machine in an empty office where Bill could use it and work on the case in private. There it sat, unused so far by him.

What was he waiting for? He didn't know. Better to ask what he was afraid of. That hit closer to the truth. And the truth was, he was afraid of the urge to drink and drug. After all, drinking had been a constant part of his police career for many years. For a long time, before his father's exposure and death, Bill had thought he did his best work with a few whiskeys under his belt. Now the problem was that he was afraid the task ahead of him would drive him to seek a drink or a drug at any cost. The addict within, having been silenced for the short time between his arrival at the clinic and the first murder, was very much alive again and vocal. Whenever he tried to think of The Walking Death case, it whispered and wheedled, prodded and poked, giving him numerous reasons why a drink or a snort of coke would help him solve the case PDQ. And if that didn't work, the addict would whine that it wasn't his responsibility and insidiously coax him into ignoring and forgetting it all, looking out for number one, and escaping into oblivion.

But ignoring the problem wouldn't make it go away. The Walking Death was still out there, and sooner or later he was going to descend on Bill and his family. The addict inside wasn't strong enough yet to convince him otherwise, but Bill was afraid to fuel his arguments.

A thought occurred to him. Maybe the perp knew he was in the clinic and was just waiting for him to get out so that he could pounce. That would mean he was working with someone in Crocker while he traveled. And the only people who knew he was in the clinic were members of the Crocker Police Department.

He thought again. If the perp knew he was in the clinic, why not send the letters and photos directly to him? No. It was obvious that the perp had heard of his working for the Crocker police during the Clayton case and assumed he was still on the force.

Bill had an encouraging thought. If the perp knew where he lived, wouldn't he send the letters and pix there? So he probably didn't know where Bill lived; or he wanted Bill to think that so he'd feel safe and let his guard down at home.

Yes. That's what he wants. Bill felt sure of it in his gut. The Walking Death wanted to catch Bill and his family at home. Just as he was doing with his "practice sessions."

But all in all it didn't matter. He wasn't home and neither were the kids. Maybe the perp knew that, maybe not. More than likely the latter, but whether he did or not wasn't going to help Bill figure out who he was. And procrastinating over getting to work on the case, no matter what his fears were, wasn't going to help either.

Louis A. finished his speech and invited everyone to stand and join hands for the Lord's Prayer. Mechanically, Bill stood, clasped the hands held out to him, and recited the prayer. On the last line, *Deliver us from evil*, his voice caught in his throat and he had to leave the room quickly so no one would see him crying.

That night, after he was sure his roommate, Alex, was asleep, Bill crept from his bed, got on his knees, and said a halting prayer asking God to protect his family. He still couldn't bring himself to look at the files on the case, but for the first time since entering the clinic, he slept soundly through the night.

Little by slow, Bill started to get the program of AA. He started getting on his knees every morning and night, albeit out of sight of his roommate or anyone else. He started really listening to the speakers at the nightly meetings and began hearing variations of his own story told over and over by different people.

Where before he had always compared himself to others, refusing to admit he wasn't unique, now he began to see the similarities. He began to listen to and believe his counselor when he stressed that alcoholism was a disease. As Irv liked to say: "It's a terminal disease, but it's the only terminal disease that you don't have to die from. You can put yourself in remission and stay there. You'll always have it, but you and you alone can decide whether it runs rampant and kills you, or whether you keep it in remission."

Bill had never looked at it that way. Now that he did, it made sense. Just as the twelve steps to recovery were starting to make sense.

Daily step meetings were part of the clinic's recovery program, but until recently Bill hadn't paid much attention to them. He went and sat and barely listened to the readings from the step book and the discussions afterward. The only step he'd truly accepted was the first, admitting he was powerless over alcohol and drugs, and that had been hard as hell. He was still having trouble with the rest, but he was working on steps two and three, believing that a power other than himself could help him, and accepting that power as God. As for the rest—making a list of past wrongs and making amends to those he'd hurt were the ones he dreaded—he was a million miles away from attempting them.

Things had started to change for him one morning while praying. He began to reflect on his life and saw that the first step did indeed apply to him—in spades. He *was* powerless over alcohol and drugs, and when he used them his life *was* unmanageable. And if he accepted that, then step two wasn't that hard.

It was as they said over and over at the meetings: He'd already come to trust in a power greater than himself, i.e., the rehab clinic and the AA program. How much harder could it be to trust in a *higher* power? In God?

31

Music on the warm night air. A mournful dirge. A wailing soul. The voice of the wind moaning through the icy fog coming off the patches of melting snow.

A harmonica.

Its eerie, whining notes float to his ears and set his skin atingle, raising goose bumps on his arms. He is tired and he is hungry. It has taken him a week to travel from New Jersey to the Rhode Island border. It took three days alone to get out of the Jersey swamplands with all the cops and feds swarming around. That told him the bodies of his latest practice session had been found shortly after he'd left Nontuck.

The harmonica music is invigorating. It lightens his heart and soul, and puts a little bounce back in his steps. He stops and stands perfectly still in the middle of the abandoned railroad yard. He swivels his head slowly from side to side, like radar, trying to pinpoint the exact location of the harmonica player. To the right he can see an old depot station shrouded in fog, its roof caved in. Farther along are the dim, blurred lights of a small city built around a cluster of old and abandoned textile mills. To the left are the railroad tracks, almost invisible in the ground fog, reappearing sporadically through the thin spots of mist as they curve out of sight at a bend in the near distance.

Overhead, the sky is the white of bone freshly relieved of its meat.

The harmonica music is coming from a wild tangle of brambles just over the rise of the next rail line. He recognizes the song as the quintessential harmonica tune—"Red River Valley." As he moves closer, the music pauses, then breaks into an old blues tune the name of which he can't remember. It brings back memories of the squalid housing project in Roxbury where he grew up and the tortures and humiliation he endured there. The images bring anger, furious anger. He rails at himself for lack of control, but there is no denying the anger. He focuses on the harmonica player as the source of his torment.

He hurries toward the brambles. The scent of boiling beef and vegetables drifts to him. His stomach gurgles hungrily, but not from the smell of the stew—it is the strong scent of human flesh that now reaches his ultrasensitive olfactory receptors. He strokes the cloth-wrapped, hard-metal bulge in his pants in anticipation.

The brambles are thick and strong, but he moves gracefully and silently through them, contorting his body to flow smoothly through openings of various sizes with nary a rustling of wood or leaf.

The thicket begins to thin out. Ahead, he can see the flickering light of a small campfire. Closer, he can see two small figures silhouetted against the light of the fire. One of them is swaying slowly back and forth while playing the harmonica. It is hard to tell since they are sitting, but they appear to be small enough to be—

Children!

Can it be true?

His mouth waters at the thought.

But it can't be children. What would children be doing out here at this time of night, in the middle of March?

Runaways!

But would a child know that old blues tune and be able to play it so well?

He knows he knows the name of the tune—remembers old Sam, his first cell mate, playing it on the harmonica his first year in the pen—but he can't think of it, and that adds to his anger.

Crouching, he pushes through the last of the brambles and stands ten feet from the fire and the two figures. The harmonica player sees him and stops playing. He lowers the instrument and stands, and the other follows suit. Neither one is taller than three feet.

Flashing on a memory from childhood of standing outside the Roxy Theater and staring at a poster for Disney's Snow White and the Seven Dwarfs, he heads for the campfire.

32

The man appeared suddenly out of the surrounding fog like a shade materializing. It caught Gunther Torkelson in midnote. His brother Karl looked up at the silence, followed Gunther's gaze, and saw the man too. Survival instincts tensed Gunther and Karl to run, until they saw that the man couldn't be a cop or a railroad dick. His clothing was as disheveled as their own. His hair was unkempt, his face unshaven and dirty. He was just another tramp.

"Welcome," Gunther said. "We got some stew on. Ain't much, but you're welcome to join us."

The man was tall, but then nearly everyone was, except small children, when compared to the dwarfed Torkelson brothers. He smiled at them, and Gunther thought there was something strange about his smile.

"I'm Gunther Torkelson. This is my brother, Karl," Gunther said by way of introductions. Karl nodded and grunted a greeting. The man said nothing but sat cross-legged by the fire next to Karl.

Gunther looked long and hard at the man, who sat and stared at the fire as though mesmerized. He looked to be simpleminded, smiling that strange little smile of his constantly, Gunther decided after a few moments. Just another of the multitude of deranged people dumped out of the state hospitals and living on the road or on the streets of the cities.

"What's your name, friend?" Gunther asked slowly. The man looked at him, but Gunther felt as though the man was looking right through him.

"Call me Mr. D.," the man said in a strong but low voice.

Gunther nodded. "Pleased to meetcha, Mr. D.," he said and raised the harmonica to his lips. Karl was about to taste the stew, but Gunther stopped him.

"Karl, don't be rude. Give our guest first taste."

Grudgingly, Karl held up the steaming tin can he'd poured stew into. "Wanna taste?" he grunted.

"No, thank you. I'll give you a taste instead," the man said. Moving casually, bordering on slowly, the man stood and dropped his pants. Gunther almost laughed when he saw the man's huge penis was wrapped in rags. He nearly screamed when with one swift motion, the man removed the rags, revealing a cruel-looking, razor-adorned pipe worn like a dildo. The man knocked the can from Karl's hand and grabbed him by the back of the neck. The man looked over at Gunther and opened his mouth in a wide, cruel smile.

The harmonica dropped from Gunther's fingers, and a freezing jolt of panic coursed through him as he realized what the man was going to do.

Mr. D. winked at Gunther and shoved the razored pipe into his brother's face, missing his mouth and scraping his cheek in a spray of blood and flesh. Karl screamed once, a short and painful screech, before the man pulled the pipe-cock from Karl's cheek and plunged it into his mouth. There was a worse sound now, a crunching, snapping, squishy sound—much like the sound of a sharp knife cutting through a very juicy apple.

Karl's scream became a bloody, warbling, muffled gurgle. Gunther didn't react. He sat frozen by blind, all-consuming terror. Never before had he known such fear, such panic. He felt as if a massive hand of ice had been shoved down his throat. It grabbed hold of his guts and squeezed them until he thought he would shit in his pants. He had trouble breathing and sat there openmouthed, staring at his brother's legs kicking madly in the air. The only sounds other than his own wildly beating heart were those awful wet noises coming from his brother's mouth and throat being cut to ribbons.

The man broke from his thrusting and looked over at Gunther. If Gunther had been able to summon enough wind, he would have screamed much louder than his size would indicate he was capable of. The man's groin and legs were smeared with blood. He smiled and pulled his bloodied metal member from Karl's mouth, grabbed Karl's head with both hands, and plunged the rod into Karl's left eye. Karl howled a gurgling scream of pain and died. With a wretched sucking sound, the man pulled the pipe out of Karl's head and turned toward Gunther. At the end of his gory rod, hanging from a tendril of raw tissue, dangled Karl's piercing blue eyeball. It was looking directly at Gunther.

"Now it's your turn," the man said and winked. He plucked the eyeball from the razored end of the bloody pipe and popped it into his mouth.

That was when Gunther lost his mind to fear. He lunged to his feet and headed for the small opening through the brambles that he and his brother had used to get in and out of the clearing. The only problem was that the man was between Gunther and the opening. Gunther tried to skirt him, leaping over a boulder that had been pulled close for a seat. Just before his feet touched the ground, he felt a large hand close on his ankles, and he fell on his face.

"Don't be so impatient!" the man scolded in exaggerated tones.

Gunther squirmed, kicking at the man frantically, but it was like kicking a stone statue. He clawed the wet earth in an attempt to get away, but the man pulled him closer. Gunther's head bumped against the boulder-seat. The man mounted him from behind, thrusting the razored edge of the pipe against him, slicing through Gunther's jeans. He pulled back and stabbed the thing deep into Gunther's rectum, ripping him open with a level of pain Gunther had never known and would thankfully never know again.

In his uncontrollable terror, pain, and desire to escape this nightmare, Gunther raised his head and smashed his forehead repeatedly against the rock until blessed unconsciousness saved him from the horror that had hold of him.

33

He is satiated. Content. Full with the warm after-
glow that always follows the delivery of death
and the taking of souls. It feels good.

After removing the dwarfs' teeth and placing
them in his pouch, he has consumed their souls before
sitting down to eat their hobo stew. It's been days since
he's eaten, but now he has overdone it, made a pig of
himself. A full stomach slows him down and takes away his
edge.

He is walking along the railroad tracks, heading north.
His clothes are wet from washing the blood of the dwarfs
off him with snow. He'd tossed their bodies deep into the
bramble thicket to hide them.

The cold night air feels like ice on his wet skin and
clothes, but he welcomes the feeling. It helps to dispel the
food-induced lethargy that slows his step.

He begins to pick up the pace, lengthening his stride. He
wants to make up for lost time. He is just getting into a
good fast rhythm when he missteps, trapping his right foot
between the rail and a rotting tie. Not able to stop his
forward momentum, he plunges forward, arms outstretched to break his fall, but not preventing his ankle
from twisting severely until he hears a loud pop and feels a
spear of pain shoot through his foot and all the way up to
his hip. He falls writhing on the tracks, feeling the broken

ends of bones in his ankle grind together as he tries to pull his trapped foot free. With a superhuman effort he yanks the ankle furiously from the rail, pulling his foot right out of his sneaker and sock, and passes out from the pain.

34

Ivy pulled a chair over to the kitchen counter next to the refrigerator. He placed the back of the chair against the counter and climbed on it to reach the high cabinet.

He was going to make dinner, simple spaghetti with bottled sauce, for his mom. She was due home any minute from her afternoon AA meeting. He wanted dinner ready so she could eat and have time to relax before going to work at the restaurant at five.

He retrieved a package of spaghetti from the top shelf and placed it on the counter before climbing down and putting the chair back against the table. He opened the package, measured enough spaghetti for two by the circular graph on the back of the box, and dumped the pasta into the pot of boiling water on the stove.

The sauce was heated, and he was just getting ready to drain the spaghetti when his mother came home, slamming the door and going directly to her bedroom. Ivy's bright hello was lost in her wake.

A chill went through Ivy. He didn't like this. His mother looked as she did whenever she was getting ready to tie one on. She'd been sober over two weeks now, and it had been the best two weeks Ivy'd had since Christmas.

He covered the pots of cooked spaghetti and sauce and went to his mother's room. Henry, who was sleeping on the living room sofa, woke as he went by and followed him after a yawn and a stretch.

Ivy knocked softly on the door and pushed it open when he got no answer. His mother was lying curled up on her bed. Ivy went in and Henry followed, sniffing around a pair of Ivy's mother's shoes near the bed.

"I made some spaghetti for supper," Ivy said softly, going to the bed. "It's all ready if you want to eat."

"No. Thanks anyway. I'll get something to eat at the restaurant," his mother replied without looking at him.

"Is anything wrong?" Ivy ventured.

His mother sighed and looked at him. "I ran into Lavinia Washington on my way home from the meeting. American Plastics has hired back everyone they laid off—except me, that is."

"No way! Why?"

His mother looked at him and shook her head. "Don't you know? Because I showed up hung over too much and was drunk again by lunch one time too many."

"You drank in the mornings at work?" Ivy asked. He'd had no idea of the extent of his mother's drinking problem.

"Yeah," his mother replied softly with shame. "I could hide it pretty good from you and from most people, or so I thought, but my boss at the shop knew. She used to try and cover for me."

Ivy sat on the edge of the bed. Henry abandoned the shoe he was chewing on and jumped on the bed also. He went to Ivy's mother and began licking her face, bringing a smile.

"That place isn't worth it anyway," Ivy said. "We're doing okay. You should consider yourself lucky. You can find a better job if you need one, but you don't need one now, do you?"

"No," she said, looking at Henry, whom she held and patted.

"Then don't let it get you down. I mean it's nothing to . . ." Ivy hesitated, not wanting to embarrass his mother.

"It's nothing to get drunk over? Is that what you were going to say?" she asked him.

He nodded.

"You're right, it isn't." She laughed and sprang from the bed to embrace him. "Have you been following me to my AA meetings?"

"What?"

"You sound just like the people there. That's one of the things they say: 'It's not worth drinking over.'" She hugged him again, and Ivy returned it warmly.

"Did you say something about spaghetti?" she asked. He nodded, and arm in arm they went to the kitchen to eat, with Henry trailing at their heels.

35

Alex lay very still in bed for what seemed like hours. His eyes were closed and his breathing was as shallow and quiet as he could make it. He was listening to Bill's breathing, waiting for a sign that he was asleep, but Bill was restless tonight, tossing and turning.

Alex was patient. He waited without moving, trying to will his roommate to sleep. Finally Bill's breathing evened and deepened. Alex held his, listening intently. When he caught the light buzz of a snore, he let his breath out.

Quietly he pushed the covers back and got out of bed. On tiptoe he crossed the room to Bill's dresser. Lifting up on the handles to keep the drawer from squeaking, he slowly opened it.

He paused, looking over his shoulder at Bill. He waited a moment to be sure Bill was still asleep, then began pushing aside the clothing. He found the first two envelopes—the ones he'd already looked through—and underneath them was a new one.

His heart jumped with excitement. He took the envelope out, placed it on top of the dresser, and closed the drawer, lifting up on it again as he did so. He checked Bill again before taking the envelope into the bathroom. He locked the door and turned on the light. He was so eager to see the contents of the envelope that he almost ripped it trying to open it.

He stopped and held the envelope in his trembling hands, trying to will himself to calm down. If he ripped the envelope, Bill would know it had been tampered with. He must leave no evidence.

He took several deep breaths and tried the envelope again, carefully opening the clasp and flap. He sat on the closed john lid and removed the photocopied letter first. He wanted to read the letter before looking at the photographs this time. He placed the envelope with the pictures still inside it on the floor at his feet and unfolded the letter.

He read it slowly, his lips moving soundlessly. He read it again, lingering on each word, trying to drink the letter in. That feeling of intense excitement, of being on the edge of a great revelation, was overwhelming. He brought the letter close to his face and breathed of its air, hoping its message could be inhaled.

Reluctantly he put the letter in the envelope, but not too reluctantly—he still had the pictures to look at. These he removed by their corners from the envelope so as not to smudge them or leave his prints on them.

He held the pictures in his cupped hands and relished each and every detail of their artistry.

He realized he'd been in the bathroom a long time. Though he would have liked to spend more time—hours, days, months—studying the pictures, he couldn't risk it. The longer he spent in the bathroom the greater the chance that Bill would awaken and catch him, or the night nurse would come by on her rounds.

With great care he replaced the pictures and letter in the envelope and sealed it. He turned off the light, unlocked and opened the door, and peered out. All was quiet in the room, but through the small window on the door he could see the flash of the night nurse's light as she made the rounds. She was only a couple of rooms away. He didn't have much time.

He crossed the room and repeated the drawer-opening procedure. Bill snorted loudly once in his sleep, and Alex thought he was caught for sure, but his roommate just rolled over. Alex closed the drawer and hurried back to his bed, getting under the covers just as the night nurse came in and passed her light over the two beds.

When she was gone, he relaxed. He lay awake for a long time, running the letter over in his mind and conjuring up the images from the photographs. Eventually sleep overtook him, and he lapsed into a series of dreams filled with mutilation and murder where the shadow of The Walking Death was always nearby.

36

He wakes to a rumbling sound in his head. He is cold and stiff, and his body is racked with a pain that he cannot locate. It permeates his being.

The rumbling grows louder and vibrates against, and inside, his head. He opens his eyes and is blinded by sunlight so bright it makes his eyes water. He lifts his head from the rail and the rattling in his head stops, but the rumbling sound goes on.

A train is coming.

He remembers where he is and what happened. His vision clears, and he sees the swollen wreck of his right foot and ankle lying at an awkward angle to his leg. Less than a mile down the track he can see the source of the rumbling. A freight train with two diesels pulling the load is heading right for him. He tries to rise, but the pain suddenly erupts, traveling up his leg and forcing him down again. His head is swimming and his eyes swarm with black spots.

The train roars closer.

He looks at his foot again and notices it is missing the sneaker and sock, which are still trapped between the tie and the rail.

The train is bearing down on him. He reaches for the sneaker, but the pain is a wall preventing him.

The world shakes at the approach of the train.

Screaming with agony, he forces himself to his knees and rolls over the side of the tracks just as the train explodes *past him. Bits of his shredded sneaker pelt him as he writhes in pain, oblivious to the roar of the train going by.*

It is sunset when he wakes, shivering from the cold. His right leg is numb from the thigh down, but when he tries to move it, the pain is there like an obnoxious relative who doesn't know when it is time to leave.

A few feet down on the gravel, he spies a piece of rotting two-by-four that looks just big enough to act as a cane. Shuddering with the pain that each little movement brings, he crawls to the piece of wood.

Each foot, each inch is excruciating. He growls deep in his throat with every stab of pain but keeps going. It takes him half an hour to crawl ten feet, but he does it, passing out from the effort as his hands close on the piece of wood.

Voices wake him. It is dark. All he can make out are the pale blur of his hands clutching the paler blur of wood. The voices are off to his right, too far away for what is being said to be comprehensible.

With great pain, he shifts closer to the tracks, biting his lip against the agony the movement causes him. On one elbow he lifts himself to peer over the rail.

A light blinds him and he ducks. He pokes his head up again, eyes squinting. It is just one of the railroad-yard lights on an old telegraph pole. He scans the tracks, sees no one. Laughter drifts to him from farther down the tracks behind him, and he sees two hunched silhouetted figures walking away from him.

He relaxes as best he can with the pain in his foot and leg. He pulls the board to him and hugs it, waiting for the pain to subside a little before attempting to stand. That proves to be quite the chore, taking four tries over several hours, during which he passes out twice from the intense pain.

Standing on his good foot, leaning on the board, he tries to clear his head and consider his options. He is angry at this development, angry at himself and at Lady Luck for allowing Lord Loser to step in and throw a monkey wrench into his plans.

He pushes the anger down, knowing that now is not the time for it. There will be plenty of time to vent his anger later, if he can overcome this problem and continue.

He stops and examines his sockless foot. It is so swollen that if it didn't have toes and wasn't attached to the end of his leg, he wouldn't have known it was a foot. He pulls up his pant leg to examine it more closely. The swelling extends to the knee, but the ankle is the worst, blown up like a melon, a shiny, black-and-blue melon.

This is a serious setback. He moves on gingerly, crossing the last set of tracks in the yard. The first thing he needs is a place to recoup. He debates whether to see a doctor and decides against it. The heat was so high in Jersey that he can no longer afford to take any chances. He can't assume the cops don't know where he is or what he looks like.

He knows he'll have to set the ankle himself. He shivers and wishes he had warmer clothing. Eventually he'll need another pair of shoes, too. He looks back over the railroad yard to the city beyond. That would be the easiest place to get what he needs—clothes and shoes from a Goodwill box, a hot meal and some medical attention at a mission. It is tempting, but he denies the temptation. He must be strong. He heads into the stretch of woods off to the left of the tracks.

He spends the night in the hollow of a huge oak tree. He dips in and out of sleep according to the intensity of pain that periodically wracks him and the cold that numbs him. In the morning his body is stiff from the cold, and the pain in his foot and leg is a constant slicing agony.

Walking limbers him up a little but brings the pain back worse than before. Hopping on one foot with the makeshift crutch, he can take only ten steps before he has to stop and lean on a tree and rest. The biting cold of the day—winter's last gasp before spring—doesn't help either. But he *keeps moving, counting ten steps, fighting the pain all the time, then resting.*

The forest is larger than he'd thought in the dark. There isn't much evidence of people about either. Near midday he begins to see the first bits of litter signifying humanity. He finds a trail after a short while that runs in a straight line through the woods and is cluttered with empty cigarette packs and candy wrappers.

He assumes the trail is used by teenagers and kids on their way to and from school each day. He squints at the sky, locating the sun through the leafy canopy. Just after noon. He shouldn't have to worry about running into any of them now, but he still doesn't want to take any chances. He hobbles across the trail and into the brush again.

A granite rock outcropping makes a good place to rest when he can't stand the pain anymore. He stretches out atop its flat surface, letting his bum foot hang over the edge. He is beginning to despair. With his mangled foot, dirty, bloody clothes, and hobbling on a rotting two-by-four, he will stick out like a neon sign wherever he goes. He needs a hermitage, a place away from people where he can mend.

He looks around, peering through the trees, trying to determine if any houses are close by. Maybe he can shack up in someone's garage or toolshed. Another thought occurs to him. Why not break into a house, kill its inhabitants, and make himself comfortable? No. Too risky. Too many unknown factors like neighbors and relatives, not to mention the fact that he doesn't think he can overcome anyone with his leg in the condition it's in.

His eye catches something in the trees off a ways to his right. A dark shape, a structure of some kind that appears to be suspended in the branches of a large maple tree. He gets up slowly despite the excitement building in him. He hobbles through the forest, not pausing, making his way to the tree.

It is as he hoped—a tree house. Maybe Lady Luck has kicked Lord Loser out and is back in his life again. He thanks her, then sees there is no apparent way to get up to the hut. He searches the tree for a ladder of some kind and spies a knotted rope tied off behind the tree. Beneath it is a rock that is just the right height for a kid to stand on to reach the rope.

He reaches the rope easily, but climbing it is another matter. His arms are powerful, but without the help of his legs it is an arduous task to reach the entrance hole to the tree house. But at last he does. He almost loses his grip and falls at the top as he is reaching for the rim of the hole to pull himself up. He hangs for several desperate moments, weak and praying for one last burst of strength to pull himself up and into the tree hut.

In tremendous agony, he pulls himself up and through, twisting his bad foot as he does and passing out on the floor of the tree house.

37

Bill was sitting on the patio, chain-smoking and looking at the afternoon sun on the mountains. It was his free time in the schedule, and he knew he should be using it to go over his old cases and the evidence from the most recent Walking Death homicide, this one in New Jersey. But with his recovery finally making progress, and with the program really starting to work for him, he couldn't bring himself to look at the files and risk reawakening that monster of an addict waiting inside him. Plus it was just such a beautiful day; the sky was a deep blue with high, thin, wispy clouds dancing above the mountains on the horizon. The sun was warm, but the air still had a chill of winter to it. The weatherman had said a cold front was moving in, and he told himself to enjoy the good weather while he could.

"Hi. Mind if I join you?"

One of the other patients, a tall dark-haired girl, stood before him, leaning against the iron rail enclosing the patio.

"Feel free," he replied. He knew her name was Kelsey, but this was the first time he'd spoken to her, or she to him. She was extraordinarily beautiful. Her hair was a lustrous raven black. Her eyes were light blue, the color of pale turquoise. Her nose was small but noble, and her lips were full with the corners upturned, giving her the appearance of having a perpetual smile. Hers was a sunny face, not the kind of face you'd expect to see on a drug addict or alcoholic.

"I'm Kelsey," she said after pulling a chair over from a nearby table.

"I know," Bill replied. Though he'd generally discouraged or avoided conversation with the other patients— even the pretty ones—he welcomed it this time. It was another excuse to avoid working on the case.

"You're Bill, eh?" she asked, her Ottawan accent showing.

"And you're Canadian, eh?"

She laughed. Bill liked the sound and the way her face and eyes lit up even more than usual.

"Where you from, eh?" she asked, exaggerating the *eh*.

Bill smiled. "Massachusetts. Couple of hours from here. A small city called Crocker."

"I could tell you're from New England. We Canadians aren't the only ones with accents."

Bill laughed. "Want to hear me say, 'Pahk the cah in the Hahvid Yahd'?" Bill quipped, bringing forth her lovely laughter again.

"When did you get here?" she asked.

"Almost two weeks ago. You?"

"It will be a month this Thursday. That's when I go home. I can't wait."

"Congratulations," Bill said. He couldn't wait to go home either, but at the same time, because of The Walking Death, he dreaded it too.

"Your roommate Alex told me you're a police detective."

Bill couldn't recall mentioning that to Alex. In fact, he rarely talked to his strange roommate at all.

"I used to be," he told Kelsey. "What did you used to do?" he asked, a little more sarcastically than he had intended.

Kelsey blushed beautifully. "I'm a writer. Well, I should

say I'm *trying* to be a writer, eh. I support myself by working at a nightclub."

"Not the best job in the world for an alcoholic," Bill commented.

"No," Kelsey answered, blushing again.

"What do you write?"

"I like mysteries. Detective stories, you know?"

"Oh. I see. Is that why you wanted to know if I was a cop?"

"Well, yeah. I've been working on a detective novel for a long time, you know? But I've, like, never met a real detective."

"So, you want to pick my brain, is that it?" Bill asked, smiling.

"If you don't mind, I would like to ask you some questions, eh?" she asked so sweetly that she could have been asking him to cut off one of his arms and his only reaction would have been to ask which one and how far up.

They talked for an hour, until the floor nurse came out and told them it was time for their group meetings. Before that happened, Bill told her about his experiences with the state police and realized as he did that it was a good way to get himself in the mood for going over his old cases. It was like approaching the task from the side instead of head-on. He told her about as many of his old cases as he could remember, reviewing each for clues that the perp involved might be The Walking Death.

After the nurse chased them out, they walked down the hill together to the old house where all the group meetings were conducted. Bill talked all the way and Kelsey listened attentively. At the old house, she asked him if he'd meet her on the patio after the evening AA meeting to talk more, and he agreed.

That night he returned to his room after the meeting and showered. Halfway through getting dressed in new jeans and a nice sweater, he found himself wondering why he was getting all dolled up, so to speak. What was he doing, trying to impress Kelsey? She *was* beautiful, but she was also at least twenty years younger than he, maybe more. She couldn't possibly be interested in him for anything other than the fact that he was a detective and a source of information for her writing.

Grow up, he told himself. *Even if she is interested in you, she goes home in three days to Canada.* If nothing else, that fact alone doomed any chance they might have at a relationship.

He decided to change his pants and put on an old pair of paint-stained sweats. Now he didn't look so preened. Grabbing his cigarettes, he went out to the patio.

Kelsey was sitting at the far end of the porch with a group of other patients. They were gathered around Gary, a young guy from New Hampshire who'd brought his folk guitar to the clinic with him. He was strumming old Beatles tunes, and the others were singing along. They were just finishing "Yellow Submarine" when Kelsey noticed Bill hesitating by the door, looking as though he was going to turn and go back inside.

"Bill, over here," she called, standing. Everyone turned to look at him, making him feel very self-conscious. They were all so much younger than he that he felt very uncomfortable joining them. He would much rather have slunk back to his room, but Kelsey came over, took his arm, and led him to the group and into a chair next to hers. She introduced him around the group, most of whose names he knew but had never spoken to. There were Denny and his cousin, Kip, from Toronto; Lucy from Connecticut; a black kid, Dwayne, from New York City; Linda, Lori, and Kathy from Vermont; and Gary with the guitar from New Hampshire.

None of them looked over thirty.

"Any requests?" Gary asked Bill when he was seated.

Bill shook his head.

"Come on. There must be some song you'd like to hear. I know a lot of songs," Gary said.

Bill cleared his throat. "What you just played is good. Beatles songs. I like Beatles songs."

"Cool," Gary replied and began strumming. He broke into "Let It Be," and everyone except Bill joined in.

Bill listened to the song and was struck by the reactions of many of the group to the words. Several of the girls had tears brimming their eyes, while Denny and Kip looked on the verge of tears themselves.

Bill listened more closely to the words and understood why. The faith and cry for help expressed in the song did a good job of summing up how he supposed they all felt—how all addicts must feel when they reach bottom. An inexplicable feeling of closeness to these people came over Bill, and for the first time since being admitted to the clinic, Bill felt he belonged.

By the last verse of the song, Bill was singing along, too, and feeling his own eyes misting. Kelsey took his hand as the song ended and squeezed it in hers.

"Let's go for a walk," Kelsey whispered to him. Gary was taking a break to have a cigarette, and several of the others had got up and gone inside for sodas. Bill nodded and followed Kelsey inside and through the reception area and outside via the front entrance.

The night was cloudy and cold. Kelsey was wearing a parka, and Bill wished he had brought his coat with him.

"Feels like snow," Kelsey said, looking at the sky. At that altitude it had snowed several times a week since he'd arrived, but it hadn't stayed on the ground for long. As soon as the sun came out it melted away. Bill had heard from the nursing staff that it had been a very mild winter for Birch Mountain. Normally, they said, the mountain received several feet of snow at a time and it stayed on the ground well into April and sometimes even into May. Here it was late March and nearly all the snow was gone.

Though it still snowed often, it was light flurries compared to the raging blizzards of winters past that the nurses spoke of.

Bill and Kelsey walked up the slope of the summit directly behind the clinic, the night shadows deepening with every step, until they came to a path leading around the top of the mountain and into the woods. The path was wide and well trodden, but the darkness of the moonless night made it very difficult to see at first. Kelsey produced a small penlight from her pocket, and though its illumination was weak, it served to keep them from stumbling.

"Where are we going?" Bill asked Kelsey.

"The Money Tree," she answered.

"The Money Tree?" Bill repeated, puzzled. "What's that?"

"You'll see," she said and led on.

Bill followed, and with the help of Kelsey's light his eyes began to adjust to his surroundings. He sneaked sidelong glances at Kelsey and began to appreciate her beauty even more. Her hair was so dark and full it seemed almost liquid. She was wearing a bulky parka, but it went only to her waist, serving to accentuate her slim waist, trim behind, and shapely, long legs that looked as though they had been poured into her tight-fitting jeans.

Bill was suddenly embarrassed to catch himself wishing he was twenty years younger. But what the hell? Maybe Kelsey had a thing for older men.

Fat chance!

What was he thinking? He was far too old for her, not to mention the fact his wife had been dead for less than four months.

So what were you doing with Darlene? the nasty side of his conscience spoke up.

A revelation struck him. He saw with sudden and complete clarity what he had been like when he was drinking and drugging. A rush of memories flashed through his mind. Shame consumed him as he remembered the things he had done with Darlene and her friends.

In complete contrast, he saw what he was like now, clean and sober. He understood that when he was straight, he never would have done the things he had done when he was using and drinking.

A sense of remorse so deep and painful it brought tears to his eyes came over him. He was glad it was dark so that Kelsey couldn't see. As she led him deeper into the woods, he mulled over his revelation. He realized he never again wanted to be that person he'd been for the past few months. He didn't like the person he became when he drank and used coke. Understanding that, he also understood why he'd been avoiding working on the Walking Death case—police work was a part of that past, a part of the person he had been. To go back to it would be like the first step in going back to being the addict he had been. But what choice did he have? He found himself fervently hoping the FBI would catch The Walking Death soon, without his help.

"We're almost there," Kelsey said, interrupting his thoughts. She added, "Are you okay? You're awfully quiet, eh?"

"I'm fine," he replied quietly.

She looked at him a moment, then shrugged and led him along a narrower path that branched off from the wider main one. They could not walk side by side here, so he followed behind her, trying not to stare at her swaying buttocks in front of him.

She stopped next to a huge old elm tree that looked to be covered with ribbons.

"This is the Money Tree," Kelsey explained, shining her light over the tree. Bill went closer and saw that the ribbons were really patients' identification bracelets hammered into the bark of the tree with coins.

"It's a tradition at Birch Mountain that before you go

home you have to come up here and put your bracelet on the tree with a coin." She handed Bill the penlight, took the plastic bracelet from her wrist, and took a quarter from her pocket. She leaned against the tree and took off one of her sneakers. Holding the bracelet to the tree with a coin like a nail, she hammered it into a crevice in the bark with the heel of her sneaker.

She put the sneaker back on when she was done and stepped back to view her effort. The wind picked up, making the bracelets flutter in the dim light.

"So, you go home Thursday. That's great," Bill said, trying to put some enthusiasm into the words, but they came out flat.

"Yeah. But to tell you the truth, I'm kind of scared, eh?" Kelsey said softly.

"Why?"

"Oh. You know. Seeing my old friends and going back to work at the club serving drinks."

"Maybe you should get a new job," Bill suggested.

"I don't know. I make really good money on tips, you know? Right now I can't afford to give that up."

Kelsey touched her bracelet on the tree. "I guess what I'm really afraid of is seeing my boyfriend again. He's a drug dealer. He doesn't know where I am. I left while he was out, and I didn't tell anyone except my mom where I was going. And she won't tell him cuz she hates his guts, eh?"

"Is he dangerous?" Bill asked, concerned.

"No," she said hesitantly. "He's no big-time dealer or anything. He deals to supply his own habit. But he's real possessive, you know? He's not going to like it when I tell him I can't live with him anymore. Not if he's going to keep dealing and using drugs. I just can't put myself at risk like that anymore."

"No," Bill agreed.

"So, what about you, eh?" Kelsey asked, changing the subject.

"What about me?"

"What do you have to go home to? A wife? Family? Girlfriend?"

Bill told her about his family and before he realized it he was telling her about Cindy and how she died; the Video Killer case; and even going back to how he and Cindy had met. It all came pouring out, even stuff about his father.

Kelsey was a good listener. By the light of her small flashlight, Bill could see her nodding on occasion and looking at him so intently he knew that she was really hearing what he was saying. They started walking back to the clinic as he spoke. She took his hand about halfway down the path when he became choked up talking about Cindy's death and how he felt responsible for it. Despite his attraction to Kelsey, Bill took her gesture for exactly what it was, an offer of comfort from a friend, nothing more. If he'd been drunk, or high, he would have taken it as a come-on and would have tried to jump her bones.

They rejoined the group on the patio for more sing-along and stayed up late talking after everyone else had gone to bed. The night head nurse came out and chased them to their rooms at 2:00 A.M.

Bill walked slowly to his room, past the nurses' station. He undressed, went into the bathroom, and washed his face and brushed his teeth. He got into bed without ever turning on a light, so he never saw that the top drawer to his dresser was half open.

38

Alex lay as still as possible when Bill came into the room. He willed his roommate not to notice the open drawer and was not surprised when it worked. He felt a new power within him—a power given to him by The Walking Death. When Bill went into the bathroom, Alex thought of getting out of bed and closing the drawer, but Bill left the bathroom door partially open and he didn't dare for fear of being caught. He had to lie and suffer through Bill's preparations for bed and wait until his roomie was asleep before he could get up and close the drawer.

Alex had fretted most of the night, lying in bed, wondering where Bill was. He wanted to look at the letters and pictures but was afraid Bill would walk in on him and catch him.

Around midnight he had gone out to the lobby and peered through the large glass windows to see Bill and Kelsey sitting at the far end of the patio. He hurried back to the room and took the pictures and letters into the bathroom.

He had spent over an hour deep in communication with the words and pictures sent by The Walking Death. He had come away from them convinced that The Walking Death had been sent by God. And he carried a special message just for Alex. Every time he looked at the photos and letters, he came a little closer to understanding what The Walking Death—what *God* himself—wanted of him.

Not having any idea how long he had spent absorbed by the contents of the envelopes, he began to sense that Bill would be returning soon. He was right. He had just managed to get the stuff back into the drawer but hadn't been able to shut it all the way before he heard footsteps in the hall outside the door. He had rushed back to bed, diving under the covers as Bill opened the door.

Now he lay very still, waiting for the deepening sounds of breathing from Bill that would tell him Bill was asleep. When he was certain of it, he leapt from the bed and closed the drawer. He was still burning with the desire to look at the letters and pictures again, but he didn't want to press his luck. He returned to bed, curled up, and worked at re-creating the photos and the events that must have led up to them in his mind until sleep overtook him. His fantasy carried over into his dreams, and he slept with a smile.

39

In the other bed, Bill was slipping into the dream state and found himself in a terrifyingly familiar place. Darkness filled with whispered pleas for help.

"Oh, Lord, please help me," he whispered in the dream.

A soft laugh came in answer.

Everything happened according to form. He felt the building anxiety, saw the bright strobe light and the appearance of Wilbur Clayton. But Wilbur didn't hold a bottle in his hand this time. Instead, he reached out and grabbed Bill by the balls with his dead hand. The light got brighter.

"You like it, don't you, Billy-boy?" Wilbur asked, only it wasn't Wilbur's voice anymore, it was someone else's, but he didn't want to know whose, didn't want to know anything. He just wanted to run, to hide, to escape—*to wake up.*

He did, sweating and shaking. He got up and threw the covers off. Still trembling, he got dressed and grabbed his cigarettes.

40

Alex slept with the instincts of an animal. As soon as Bill sat up, Alex woke, every fiber of his being alert. He marveled at this and at his entire improved state of consciousness. Ever since The Walking Death had come into his life, Alex had felt the growth of new powers—of a new *being*—within him.

He feigned sleep, watching Bill through slitted eyes as his roommate got dressed and left the room. Alex got up immediately and dressed quickly. He was tempted to use Bill's unexpected absence to peruse the envelopes again, but he was more curious about where Bill was going at this time of night.

One of the puzzles of The Walking Death for Alex was why Bill had been chosen for destruction. He was pretty sure by now that he, Alex, was meant to be the instrument of that destruction, aiding The Walking Death, but he had to know why. When he knew why, he'd know *how* he was supposed to serve.

He opened the door and stepped into the hallway. It was empty in the direction of the nurses' station. He heard a soft metallic click behind him. He went to the metal fire door at the end of the hall. Through the wire-mesh glass, he saw Bill outside heading around the clinic toward the road leading down the mountain.

Alex cast a quick look back in the direction of the nurses' station, saw no one, and followed.

41

Bill lit a cigarette as soon as he was outside. The night was clearing and cold. He went around the building, careful to stay out of the lighted areas, crossed the driveway, and headed down the road.

He wasn't sure where he was going and didn't really care. He just needed to walk and get away from the clinic, his room, and that awful dream. He decided to walk to the long, low shed that contained the art studio, behind the coach house. Sometimes Old Jim, the resident art therapist, stayed there all night working on his own sculptures.

He started down the road at a fast pace, inhaling the cold air deeply between long drags from his butt. Neither the walk, the night air, nor the cigarette did anything to dispel the sense of terror that still clung to him from the dream.

A loud crashing of branches in the woods off to his left made him jump. Just an animal, he thought until a few seconds later there was a loud snap and the rustle of bushes. Bill began to listen more intently and heard the continuous snap of twigs and the rustle of leaves as though someone was following him.

The irrational conviction that the follower in the woods was Wilbur Clayton, or worse, the thing behind the light in the dream, possessed him. Despite the cold air, he began to sweat profusely. He walked faster and heard the follower in the woods pick up speed to match. He walked faster, his breathing matching his pace. The thing in the woods—animal or haunt of his dreams—was sounding closer.

Just ahead through the trees at the bend in the road, Bill could see the lights of the studio. A very loud crash of brush and the snapping of wood came from the woods. Giving in to terror, Bill broke into a headlong run to the coach house.

42

It was amazing!

Alex could see everything around him in the night as clear as day—clearer.

It's a gift from The Walking Death, he thought. He must be getting closer to discovering the true message, the true power, hidden in the letters and photographs. For the first time Alex felt it was all within his grasp. Revelation was imminent.

He started around the clinic, following Bill. His roommate was out of sight, but that didn't matter, Alex knew which way to go. The path was lit for him. The ground and bushes glowed brightly, showing him which way to go, and he followed, plunging into the woods.

The brush was thick, but he didn't mind. He crashed right through it. He was not surprised that the noise he made sounded muffled and faraway. It was part of his newfound powers. He could pass through the forest like a silent spirit.

To his right he heard footsteps on asphalt and knew that he was traveling parallel to Bill on the road leading down the mountain.

The footsteps speeded up and Alex matched them, pushing through the underbrush. Though his night vision was so crystal clear, he never saw the root that caught his foot. The last thing he *did* see was a close-up view of the papery bark of a fat birch tree just before his forehead struck it and he went down.

There was a rainbow explosion of light, and everything around him shimmered, seeming to disperse into a thousand shining particles and come back together again. He lifted his head from the forest floor and marveled at the display.

To his left, the light grew intensely bright and hot. There was someone standing there in the light. The figure moved toward him, and Alex gasped with delight. It was *He!* The Walking Death was standing there only a few feet away.

Alex bowed his head in silent worship, too excited for words. He raised his eyes again after a few moments, and The Walking Death had moved closer, close enough to touch. Alex looked up at the long black robe and into the deep black shadow of the hood-shrouded face. He could see no features, no eyes, but he knew they were there—could feel them staring out at him, into him. The power he felt emanating from the figure was incredible.

"Tell me," Alex gasped. He was so full of joy that he was near tears. "Tell me what you want from me. Tell me how I can help you."

The Walking Death said nothing. Slowly the figure raised his right arm. From out of the belled sleeve of the robe there slithered a thin, white hand. With increasing exhilaration, Alex saw that it was a skeletal hand.

"Yes," he whispered fervently. "Tell me. Tell me."

The hand came closer. The Walking Death—The *Angel* of Death—touched Alex's forehead, and he was consumed by a fireball exploding in his brain.

43

Bill reached the art studio out of breath and sweating. He stood on the doorstep, bent over, hands on knees, catching his breath and listening for any sound of the follower in the woods. He heard nothing and felt a mixture of relief and shame at having been so frightened.

Maybe it had just been his imagination, he wondered, but didn't really think so. He was quite sure that there had been either a very large animal (a bear?) or a person in the woods following him. His gut instinct told him that it was no bear, but thinking rationally now, he could not accept that it had been some wraith from his dream. It had to have been a human being, but who?

It could have been one of the security guards following him along a path through the woods . . . only he knew of no path that followed the road. And why would a security guard do that, anyway? Besides, whoever had been following had not been treading any path. It had sounded as though someone was crashing through thick brush, unmindful and uncaring of the noise he was making.

The door to the studio opened suddenly, causing Bill to start nervously again. Old Jim peered out at him through thick-lensed, black-rimmed glasses.

"Who's that?" he inquired in his tough, no-nonsense-tolerated voice.

"It's me," Bill replied, stepping out of the shadows into the light and feeling childish. "Bill Gage."

Old Jim smiled. "Oh, yeah. You were down here for the first time the other day, right? Couldn't get the hang of the pottery wheel, if I remember."

Bill nodded.

"You always prowl around this time of night?"

"No, I couldn't sleep."

"I know what you mean," Old Jim grumped. "I haven't had a good night's sleep since they took my prostate out in '82, though I doubt that has anything to do with it. Well, come on in. I'm not heating the whole goddamned mountain."

He stepped aside, holding the door open for Bill.

"Got some of that herbal tea crap they push on you up at the clinic. Supposed to help you sleep, but that's only because it's decaffeinated. Caffeine's a drug, you know. Can't have drugs in a rehab clinic," Old Jim said sarcastically. " 'Course, nicotine's a drug, too, but I don't see anyone trying to ban cigarettes up here. They *couldn't.* They'd have a full-scale riot on their hands if they tried. Christ, these hypocrites even *encourage* you to smoke if it helps you stay sober. The goddamned tobacco companies ought to supply cigarettes to places like this, and AA in general, at a discount. We're the ones keeping them in friggin' business. Ah!" Old Jim finished in disgust. "What's the use?"

Bill listened politely to Old Jim's tirade, nodding his head whenever Jim looked at him. He'd heard the stories about how ornery Old Jim was, but Bill thought the artist was just the type that couldn't stand bullshit of any kind, nor did he suffer fools lightly. Bill had seen a good example of that on his first visit to the studio.

He had walked down with a nineteen-year-old kid from Toronto by the name of Joel. Joel was a real character. A born bullshit artist, he was short, five feet five or so. He'd had a shotgun blow up in his face on a hunting trip with his dad when he was twelve and now bore a disfiguring burn scar across his throat and up the left side of his face. He had also lost his left eye in the accident and wore a glass one.

Joel had barged into the studio talking big about how he knew everything about making clay pottery and using the pottery wheel. Old Jim had been skeptical, but had allowed Joel just enough rope to hang himself. It had quickly become apparent that Joel knew a lot less than he claimed, and Old Jim had chewed him out good when he'd wasted several lumps of clay on the wheel.

"I didn't get to show you around much the other day," Jim said to Bill. He sat on a wooden stool before a workbench that ran all the way around the room. "Too many goddamned people here. I keep telling those bozos up there not to send more than four at a time, but no one listens."

He turned to Bill and motioned for him to sit on the stool next to him. "You got any artistic talent? Ever do anything with art before?"

"No," Bill answered.

"At least you're honest, not like that fool kid was with you the other day. I guess you've already learned the pottery wheel ain't your thing. And since you have no inbred talent, the easiest thing'll probably be to learn how to make stained glass gizmos. Pull your stool over here, and I'll get you started."

Bill got up and pulled his stool over next to Jim's. He didn't really feel like learning to make stained-glass gizmos, as Old Jim had called them, but he welcomed the chance to get his mind off the dream.

"I'm not supposed to do this," Old Jim said, giving Bill a conspiratorial wink, "but I've got some *real* coffee brewing in the other room. I sometimes stay on the mountain all night working and I can't stay up without it. You want a cup? Probably keep you up all night, but you sure as hell don't look sleepy."

Bill nodded eagerly. Real coffee was the one thing he'd really had a craving for at the clinic. Bill had always been a confirmed coffee drinker.

Old Jim went into the other room to get the coffee, after giving Bill a book of patterns for making stained glass to look at. He came back with two mugs of steaming black coffee.

"Hope you take it black," Jim said, setting the mugs on the workbench. "Got no cream and sugar. Used to have a refrigerator, but it died and the cheap bastards who run this place won't cough up the money for another. I thought about bringing in my small one from home, but the missus would have none of that, so I got used to drinking my java black."

"That's fine," Bill said.

"You see anything in there you'd like to make?" Jim asked, sitting again next to Bill.

"Yeah," Bill answered. "I guess I'd like to make some things for my kids. I thought this clown and the unicorn would be good." He indicated patterns depicting a bow-legged clown holding a bunch of balloons and another of a prancing unicorn.

"Well . . ." Old Jim gave Bill a penetrating look. "I guess if you're good with your hands, you can give it a try. It's a pretty difficult piece for a beginner, though."

Bill wasn't very good with his hands, had never had an affinity for tools or nimble finger work, but he didn't admit that to Old Jim. He really wanted to make something for his kids—felt an overwhelming *need* to make something for them.

Old Jim instructed him in what to do. He started with

the clown. First, he had to trace the pattern and cut out each of its parts. He then had to search the glass bin for pieces of glass he could use in the colors he wanted for the clown and balloons. The next step was to cut out the pattern into pieces and glue them to the pieces of glass. Using a pen with a diamond razor wheel on the tip of it, he traced the pattern on the pieces of glass, cutting them into the shapes he wanted.

Bill worked slowly, methodically, and listened carefully to everything Old Jim had to say. He soon became absorbed in the work to the point of forgetting his coffee. He didn't notice when Jim took the cold mug away and dumped the coffee in the sink.

At one point, while Bill was busy cutting the glass into balloon shapes, he became overwhelmed by a sense of loss toward his children, all due to his drugging and drinking. His eyes filled with tears and he began to sob soundlessly. The emotion grew stronger and so did its release. Soon he was crying openly and couldn't stop. Old Jim must have noticed, but he never said a word. He'd seen patients break down while creating things for their families before. There seemed to be some sort of catharsis in creating something for loved ones you've hurt, which is why the art studio—whether he'd openly admit it or not—was one of the most effective therapies at the clinic. He went on with his own work and let Bill get it out.

Eventually Bill got himself under control, and Jim came and sat next to him, inspecting his work. "Not bad," he said, nodding at the head and body of the clown that Bill had cut out of colored glass. "You know," he said, placing his hand on Bill's shoulder, "you can't keep beating yourself up. Sure, you've made a mess out of your life, we all have up here. Every nurse, doctor, and counselor in this place is a recovering alcoholic or addict or both. Me, I liked Scotch. Drank the stuff day and night until it rotted my gut, gave me ulcers; then I drank 'white Cadillacs'—Scotch and milk mixed together."

He laughed at the face Bill made.

"Disgusting, huh? Listen. What I'm trying to say is, you're not alone, because you're no different than anyone else up here or out there in the world. Even so-called normal people have their secret addictions, but most of them are never lucky enough to get help for them the way you are. And most of them don't have the courage to take that help if it's offered.

"You can't change the past by brooding over it. You *can* make up for it by changing the present and the future. But you've got to do it one day at a time, Bill. That's how it's done, one day at a time."

Jim picked up the clown's head and felt the edge. "Pretty rough here. Bear down on the cutting tool a little more. When you finish the rest of the pieces, I'll show you how to sand and polish the edges nice and smooth."

He went back to his own work, leaving Bill to his. Bill felt better. He'd heard other patients say that everyone working at Birch Mountain was a recovering addict of one kind or another, but it felt reassuring to have it confirmed. It ruled out falling back on the excuse that no one up there understood what he was going through. In fact, it was just the opposite—everyone knew what he was going through.

The rest of the night went swiftly. Bill got into a rhythm with the work as Jim led him through the steps of sanding the edges of the glass, applying flux with a brush, wrapping the edges with copper strips, and then soldering the pieces together. By dawn his clown was done. The head was a little crooked and the soldering was rough and bubbled in spots, but overall it was a decent job. Bill held it up to the light and smiled at the glowing glass clown he had created. He could picture it hanging in the window of Devin's room, and the thought brought a burning singe of tears to his eyes again. The feeling passed quickly though and didn't leave him with the lingering sense of sadness he'd previously felt whenever he'd thought of his children. Instead he felt hopeful, something he hadn't felt in a long time.

44

Alex was walking on air. He was floating, filled with elation. Pure joy coursed through him like live electricity. He felt as though he must be glowing with it, but no, when he looked at his hands and body, he appeared normal. The difference, the *glow*, was inside. He held within him the essence, the very mind, of The Walking Death, which possessed him now.

Alex was awed by the power that had taken up residence inside him. Now everything was clear—so vividly clear—and he knew what The Walking Death wanted him to do.

He made his way out of the woods, back to the clinic. He went in the front door and was stopped by the night guard. It was 4:00 A.M. The guard, seeing the bloody gash on Alex's forehead, immediately radioed the nurses' station.

The guard made Alex sit down in the lobby until a nurse came. Alex couldn't understand what all the fuss was about—he was unaware of the wound on his head until the nurse showed him his blood on a wad of cotton she had used to clean the wound. He dismissed it as a scratch, but the nurse thought it was deep enough to tape several butterfly stitches to it and to schedule an appointment with the staff doctor as soon as he came in.

She led Alex back to his room, which was where he

wanted to go anyway. The poor nurse, already on edge, became completely unhinged when she saw Bill was missing from his bed. She checked the empty bathroom and left the room quickly, running to the nurses' station to report Bill absent.

Alex floated over to Bill's dresser and opened the top drawer. He took out the manila envelope but had to quickly put it back as the head nurse returned to the room to question him about Bill. She wanted to know if Bill had been outside with him, but Alex lied and said no, he hadn't seen his roommate all night. When the nurse left, he took the envelopes out of the drawer again and floated to the bathroom.

He was filled with an incredible ecstasy when he looked at the pictures and letters—an ecstasy greater than the contents of the envelopes had previously provided. Now he knew, really knew, why The Walking Death had chosen him. It was because of what he now understood Bill to be.

His roommate was the Antichrist. It was so very clear to Alex. And now he knew how he was to be The Walking Death's instrument in making the Antichrist atone.

As Alex gloated over the material, what The Walking Death wanted him to do became crystallized in his mind. He had to prepare Bill for the arrival of The Walking Death. And the way to do that was to destroy the minions of the Antichrist.

45

Birds talking to him. Chirruping words. What are they saying?

He moves.

"Pain!" is what they say. "Don't move!"

Head swimming, he glances down at his leg. It is swollen inside the pant leg like some half-deflated, deformed watermelon. It radiates with a steady hot pain.

He puts his head down and loses consciousness for several moments. When he comes to, the birds have stopped talking to him. There is someone there with him—his father.

"You little freak," he says through his battered face. "I knew I should have killed you when you were born and I saw that you'd never be a real man."

"Go away," he mumbles at the ghost of his father. "You're dead. I pushed you off the fourth-floor porch."

His father laughs, and his head hangs to the side on his broken neck.

"Go away!" he screams at the hallucination and passes out from the pain the effort causes him. When he comes to, he lies very still for a long time, eyes closed, drawing on his will to blot out the pain and any apparitions that might be waiting for him.

He opens his eyes. He is alone. He lifts his head and surveys his surroundings. For a moment he cannot remember where he is or how he got there, but slowly it comes back to him—the fall, the track through the woods, and the excruciating climb to the tree house.

So far so good, or bad, depending on how he chooses to look at it. His leg and foot are definitely in a bad way, leaving him immobilized, but at least he has found a decent shelter. If he can reset the broken bones, he may be able to get back on the road and continue with his mission in a few weeks. That puts him behind schedule, but the more he thinks about it the more he thinks that breaking his ankle might just be a good thing, a gift from Lady Luck.

What better way to throw the cop a curve and get the heat off his scent by disappearing for a while? Then he can strike when they all least expect it. It will be the ultimate triumph. Of course, it all depends on whether or not he can set the ankle properly by himself. He looks at it and winces at the thought of pulling the bones apart and resetting them. If he can do it before passing out, he will need something to splint the ankle while it heals.

Despair overcomes him and he tries to fight it. Despair wants to tell him it is over, to give it up. He reaches deep inside himself to find the special strength that has always sustained him. Deep down he knows he can overcome anything. Hasn't he always been able to do that in the past? Yes. And he can do it again.

He is immortal. He is The Walking Death.

He spends the rest of the day resting and sleeps fitfully through the night, troubled by dreams that he cannot remember upon waking. By morning his leg is numb and swollen so much more that he has to rip the pant leg open from the knee down. The numbness in the leg has a chilling effect on his body, and he shivers, which brings the pain back to life in his foot and leg. He is soon in agony. Hallucinations visit him as the tree house melts away around him and is replaced by the stark concrete walls of the strip-search room at the prison.

This isn't real, he tells himself. I have a fever. I'm hallu-

cinating, but that knowledge doesn't make the scene go away.

It is his second day in prison. A guard leads him to the strip-search room where six men—four black and two white—wait. A large black man pays the guard money, and the guard leaves, locking the door behind him.

The black man orders him to take his clothes off. He refuses. The man punches him in the stomach and he doubles over, going down. Again the black man orders him to remove his clothing. Again he refuses. The black man kicks him again and again. Suddenly they are all on him, kicking him senseless and ripping the clothes from his body. And when he is naked and his deformity is revealed, they laugh, oh, how they laugh.

"Lookee that thing! T'ain't no bigger'n my fucking thumb!"

They grab at his tiny penis, pulling on it to see if it grows larger when it gets hard, but it doesn't. They think it is the funniest thing they have ever seen and he is shamed. He had thought that when he'd killed his father, no one would ever again see his deformity and he would never again have to be subjected to ridicule and abuse concerning it.

They grab him roughly and drag him to a bench. Though he is big and strong, they are just as big and just as strong, and there are too many of them. The black man who paid the guard pries his mouth open and forces himself inside. He bites the black man and is beaten for it. The others hold him while the black man uses a homemade jackknife to pry each and every one of his teeth from his mouth. Nearly unconscious from the pain, he is draped over the bench, and they take turns sodomizing him and forcing him to perform oral sex on them with his bloody aching mouth.

Through it all, one thought repeats itself in his mind: The cop did this to me! The cop who betrayed me! *The threats of revenge against the cop that he made at his trial are nothing compared to what he feels now. From that* moment on, he lives for the day when he can make good on those threats, and more.

The scene fades and he sinks into a fevered stupor. To his advantage, the day grows unseasonably warm. He comes to and drags himself to a patch of sunlight shining through the tree house's single window cut high into the south wall. It helps remove the chill that pervades his body. He lies in the sun and meditates, trying to forget the hallucination by performing his breathing exercises, focusing on removing himself from the pain of his physical body in preparation for what he must do. He'd rather wait, but knows that he cannot. If he waits any longer, the bones will begin to heal improperly and he will be a cripple.

By midafternoon his mind is clearer, the fever lessened, the hallucinations forgotten. He is as ready as he'll ever be. He undoes his trousers and removes his special sword of vengeance from his waist. He wraps it in rags and sets it down on the metal base that fits over his groin. It stands erect in the sunlight, the rags covering it making it appear to be a work of art waiting to be unveiled.

He drags himself to the corner of the tree house and wedges his twisted foot diagonally between the corner two-by-four studs. The pain beats upon his senses, but he keeps it out and steels himself for the worst of the pain that he knows is coming.

Several deep breaths, grit the teeth—he stiffens and, bracing his arms on the floor, pulls his body away from the corner. He feels bone rubbing against bone accompanied by an intensely nauseating wave of pain. He begins to lose consciousness, but manages to hold on just long enough to hear a loud snap followed by a splintering crack. He feels the bones click back together. Intense waves of hot and cold pain batter him, subduing and submerging him in the fathomless black seas of unconsciousness.

Whistling wakes him. Not birds whistling this time—human whistling. Kid whistling. He lifts his head and the *pain forces it back down again. His foot is still wedged in the corner, but the swelling has gone down a little. By the emptiness in his stomach and the stiffness in his bones, he gauges that he has been out for at least two days.*

He nearly drifts off again, but the sound of the whistling brings him back. He recognizes the tune: "Pop Goes the Weasel."

The rope ladder!

Did he pull it up?

Despite the pain, he twists his body until he can see the opening in the floor. He didn't pull up the rope. And now the young whistler is directly below the tree house.

He tries to free his foot too quickly, and the effort punishes him with monumental pain, and he blacks out again.

"Hi," a voice says when he comes to. He looks around and sees a young boy sitting against the opposite wall. For a moment he is sure that he is having another hallucination, though he doesn't recognize him as anyone from his past.

"What happened to you?" the boy asks, showing no fear.

He rubs his eyes, willing the apparition to disappear, but it remains, convincing him it must be real. He has to think fast. He cannot afford to be found, yet he is in no position to kill the child to silence him. Instead, he tells the boy the truth, or most of it, of how he fell and broke his ankle and found this tree hut to get out of the elements. He explains that he is homeless and can't afford professional care.

"Well, you're in luck. I'm a Boy Scout," the boy says with pride. "I've got my first-aid badge. I can splint your leg for you."

He smiles and nods at the youth, silently thanking Lady Luck for rolling the dice in his favor once again.

"What's that?" the boy asks, pointing at his rag-wrapped weapon standing like a monument near the wall.

"That's my good-luck charm," he answers with a smile, and the boy smiles with him.

46

Ivy and his mom got off the bus at the Searstown mall and walked across the parking lot to the cinema complex. It was a cloudy yet mild late-March day. Heavy rain had been forecast for the afternoon, and with nothing better to do, his mother had suggested they take in a movie matinee.

Ivy was only too happy to agree. He loved movies, plus this gave him the chance to use some of the money he'd been saving in the leather pouch in his closet. His mother, seeing how important it was to him, didn't argue when he said he wanted to pay.

Ivy wanted to see *Dracula*, but his mom was more inclined toward *Home Alone II*. Actually, Ivy didn't care what they saw. He was just happy to be spending a normal afternoon doing something fun with his mother.

Ivy felt good using his own money to buy the tickets, soda, and popcorn for the two of them. The movie was okay—strictly for kids, Ivy thought, one of which he did *not* consider himself to be.

The best part of the whole afternoon was seeing his mother happy again, actually laughing, which she did a lot during the film. It was dusk when they left the theater complex, walking arm in arm to the bus depot.

"What do you want to do now?" Ivy asked his mother while they waited for the bus.

She looked at her watch. "There's an AA meeting at the

Lutheran church here in Leominster in a half hour that I'd like to go to."

Ivy's shoulders slumped a little in disappointment. He had hoped they might spend the rest of the evening together and maybe go to Friendly's for supper. His mother noticed and put her arm around him and gave him a hug.

"I've got an idea," she said, lifting his chin with her finger to look into his eyes. "Why don't you come to the meeting with me?"

"Really? Are you sure? I mean, will it be okay? Will they let me in?"

His mother laughed. "Of course! It's not an exclusive club, you know. People bring their kids all the time."

Ivy thought for a moment and nodded his head. "Yeah, okay. I left enough food and water for Henry, so he'll be all right until we get home. Yeah, I'd like to go with you and check it out."

"Good," his mother said as the bus pulled up. "Let's go."

Mother and son, beaming happily, got on the bus.

47

The boy—his name is Tommy, he discovers—is as good as his word. He brings back slats of wood, rolled bandages, and surgical tape. He does a very professional job of splinting his ankle. The boy even brings some Tylenol III—Tylenol with codeine—for the pain, and amoxycillin, an antibiotic, for his fever. The boy explains that his dentist gave them to him when he had an abscessed tooth, but he hadn't needed to take them all.

He doesn't like to dull his mind with drugs, but the pain is dulling it anyway, so he takes the pills. Waiting for them to work, he looks the boy over. He appears to be no more than fourteen. His hair is black, his eyes dark brown, and his skin has the dark coloring of Mediterranean ancestry. He is a slight boy, but tall. When he fills out, he will be a big man.

The two talk a little about the boy's school until the pain pills take effect. At first he is surprised that they do not dull his faculties as much as he thought they would, but before long he is dozing. Tommy covers him with a blanket and leaves him to the first truly restful sleep he has had since the accident.

Tommy visits every day after school, and though he eyes the erect bundle of rags, he never asks again what it is. He brings clothing—including sneakers, only one of which he can wear because of the swelling in his left foot—food, drink, more medicine, and magazines he pilfers from his parents' house.

"Dave"—that is the alias he is using with the boy— "have you ever wanted to kill someone? I mean really kill someone?" Tommy asks on his third visit in as many days.

"Dave" is caught off guard by the question and shrugs in answer.

"I have," Tommy says softly, not meeting "Dave's" eyes. Without any prompting, Tommy begins talking, telling the sorry tale of his life at the hands of parents who don't care about him.

"Mom's all wrapped up in her career, and Dad's too wrapped up in his girlfriend," he explains. "Sometimes I think about killing the both of them, making it look like an accident, and getting the insurance money. I could live free then."

Tommy looks guiltily at him. "I guess you must think I'm pretty sick, huh?"

Before he realizes what he is doing, "Dave" is talking. "No, I don't think you're sick. It all depends on what you do with the feelings, or let them do with you." He knows he shouldn't go on, shouldn't reveal too much to Tommy, but he can't help himself. Maybe it is hearing the boy speak so candidly about wanting to kill his parents that makes him feel a special kinship to Tommy. Maybe it is just the need to talk to someone after being alone for so long.

But that is a sign of weakness, and he knows it. It is a dangerous thing, weakness. The boy is now a liability. He knows he will have to kill him when it comes time for him to move on again. Strangely, knowing that compels him to open up even more to the boy and tell him the story of his life.

"I killed my father."

Tommy's mouth drops open in amazement.

"Yes, I did. When I was fifteen. He was a bastard. A real piece of shit. My mother was too, but I could control her.

She was a drug addict, he was an alcoholic. He was dangerous too. He would come home drunk and start beating on my mother and work his way around to me. He was big too. Sooner or later he would have killed one of us, so I decided to kill him first." He declines telling Tommy of the sexual abuse and humiliation his father subjected him to because of his deformed sexual organ.

"Wow!" is all Tommy can say. "How'd you do it?"

"That was the hard part. I knew I had to make it look like an accident, or at least like someone else killed him. We lived on the fourth floor. One night when he was sitting on the back porch, drinking, I went out and told him someone was in the backyard trying to steal his car. When he leaned over the railing to look, I pushed him. The cops believed it was a drunken accident."

"But weren't you scared? Didn't you feel guilty?"

"No," he answers simply. "Emotion is negative. I learned that early on in life. If you allow yourself to have emotions, you get hurt. They're nothing but a drawback. Emotions are useless, they cloud the intellect."

"But didn't your conscience bother you?" Tommy asks.

He laughs. "Tell me something. What is conscience, Tommy? Do you know? Can you give me a definition?"

The boy thinks for a moment. "I guess it's knowing what's right and wrong. And when you do wrong, your conscience bothers you."

"Do you think killing my father was wrong? If I hadn't, he would have killed me or my mother or both of us sooner or later. Would it have been right to let him do that? Who's to say what is right and what's wrong? What's right for one person is wrong for another. Right and wrong are not black and white. Nothing in this world is. You have to make your own right and wrong to survive."

The boy thinks about that and says nothing.

* * *

The desire to tell Tommy more gnaws at him. He is eager to tell the boy of his secret, deadly manhood; to unwrap it and show it to him. He knows the boy is curious about it, has seen him looking at it standing in the corner. He wants to tell him about the thrill of the kill, the joy of consuming souls, and the way it has changed his life. That would lead to telling Tommy how and why he made the thing as an instrument of death to compensate for his lack of manhood. And, of course, that would lead to telling the boy about his transformation while in prison. The years of being the chameleon and, like a lizard, how he has waited and waited for the perfect moment to pounce. But now is not the time, he thinks. I will show it to him soon, and it will be the last thing he sees.

He is surprised at how much he wants to tell his story, to share with the boy all that he has felt, done, and understood. He supposes it is because it is a way of reliving the miraculous and heady moments of his life. A way of feeding his spirit, much the same way his fantasies while in prison had kept him going.

He tells himself that he feels nothing for the boy, that when the time comes for him to leave, he will dispatch the boy quickly and painlessly—his way of saying thanks for all the boy has done for him. But knowing that the boy will die brings even greater temptation for him to unburden himself. Tommy will never live to repeat anything he is told, so what's the big deal? Could it be that he is getting soft? That deep that he harbors affection for the boy? That when the time comes, he will let him live and it will be easier to do that if the boy knows nothing of him? But the boy already knows too much. Surely he will have to die. Again he is tempted to open his soul.

The days run on and Tommy continues to visit, faithfully bringing supplies and clothes for him to wear. The boy does most of the talking, about school, TV, his parents. He listens, says little, but the desire to talk doesn't leave him.

It grows stronger. Soon he can't resist it. He rationalizes and gives in, telling the boy all the deep and dark secrets of his life—all except one. That he will save for last when he removes the rags cloaking it.

48

Bill walked back to his room as the sun was rising in the east over the summit of Indian Head. He was tired, his eyes sore and his fingers cramped from working on the stained-glass figures. He'd managed to make two of them—a clown and a pony. He planned on returning to make another pony. He'd give the clown to Devin and the ponies to the twins. Old Jim had mentioned that he could also make jewelry like earrings and pendants, and he was considering making something for Evelyn.

He stopped in the road as though he'd run smack into some invisible barrier.

What if his family wouldn't accept his gifts?

He was pretty sure Devin would. He was too young to understand what a shit his father had been. But what of the twins? Of Evelyn? For the first time since getting clean and sober—perhaps for the first time in his life—he realized that the twins and Evelyn meant as much to him as Devin, his own flesh and blood.

He had a family, goddammit!

What a wonderful, yet painful, feeling! He let out a sudden whoop of joy at the realization. How could he have been so blind, so stupid? During the four years that he had been married to Cindy he'd had only fleeting moments of a sense of family. With a deep sense of sadness he understood now that he had been on what is called a "dry drunk" by those in Alcoholics Anonymous. He had let go of the drink, but the drink had not let go of him. He hadn't dealt with the causes of his drinking, hadn't dealt with the fact that he was a bona fide, dyed-in-the-wool alcoholic. The thought struck him that that was why he'd dreamt of his father all those years.

But why did he now dream of Wilbur Clayton? Obviously he hadn't resolved anything, only changed the face of his inner ghosts. Wilbur had replaced his father as the bogeyman of his dreams.

Tears came to his eyes. He sank to his knees in the middle of the road and crossed himself. Overhead, clouds moved swiftly, driven by the wind. The sky was aglow with sunshine, as were the mountains in the distance. Bill felt overwhelmingly at one with God and the universe.

"Please, please, God," he mumbled. He cleared his throat and shouted, "Please, God! Give me back my family! Give me back my life!" He broke down and huddled on the road, sobbing.

49

The first sacrifice!

It was all so clear to him. Completely and irrevocably, he knew what he must do—whom he must kill. The Walking Death demanded it. *Commanded* it. And he, Alex, loyal servant, would obey.

Salvation was at stake. He knew he must not fail.

Kelsey. She would be the first. She was closest to Bill at the clinic, so she would be his first clue that The Walking Death had found him; that there was no escape; that The Walking Death was *everywhere.*

Alex replaced the envelopes in Bill's drawer and floated back to his bed. He pretended to be asleep when the day guard and nurse escorted Bill into the room. He watched through slitted eyes as Bill undressed and got into bed, and smiled at the knowledge of what was to come.

50

Kelsey couldn't sleep. She lay motionless in bed and stared at the ceiling, and the feeble light coming through the window. Knowing that she had only one more day to spend in the clinic made her too anxious to relax, much less sleep. Tomorrow she would go home.

She couldn't say she was overly excited or happy about leaving. She had come to love Birch Mountain. She felt so safe there, safe from the real world and its problems. She was afraid to leave the only sanctuary she had ever known in her life. She was afraid of the temptations of the real world. Shit, it was easy to stay off drugs and booze if you couldn't get any and had professional counselors at your beck and call twenty-four hours a day. And not just professional help either; the constant support and acceptance she'd received from the other patients was something she had never experienced before in her life. It was going to hurt deeply to give that up.

She was a little surprised at herself to realize that she was also going to miss Bill very much. With it came the knowledge that if she stayed, her liking of him could very easily grow into love.

She got dressed and left her room early in the morning, after spending most of the night either lying in bed and staring or pacing as quietly as possible between the night nurse's rounds so as not to disturb her sleeping roommate.

She went out to the patients' lounge around 8:00 A.M. It was empty.

Through the tall windows overlooking the valley and the mountains beyond, she watched the day come to life beneath the rising sun.

She missed her apartment, but other than her friend, Sue, and her mother, she couldn't say she really missed anyone else from home, including her boyfriend. She wrapped her arms about herself and hung her chin on her chest. She had asked herself over and over again how her life had become so screwed up, and she still hadn't been able to come up with an answer. It was all so complicated sometimes it actually, physically, hurt her head to think about it.

She left the patients' lounge and wandered out to the main lobby. Noticing the guard wasn't at his post by the door, she took advantage of the moment to take a walk in the woods behind the clinic.

51

After the guard and the nurse put Bill to bed, Alex went out walking. He had been trying to find the spot in the woods where The Walking Death had appeared to him the night before last, but was unsuccessful. He was returning to the clinic, walking up the drive, when he saw Kelsey heading for the path behind the building that led to the Money Tree. She was alone.

This is it.

He cut across the road and up the gravel embankment into the woods. He ducked behind a tree, his heart thudding wildly in his chest, and peered out to see if anyone had seen him. There was no one in sight, but still, he knew he would have to be careful.

He made his way into the woods in a parallel direction to the path Kelsey was on. As he walked, he began to feel lighter, more energetic. His senses became acute, expanding beyond their normal levels of perception. He began to detect microscopic levels of life in the crevices of bark on the trees around him and in and under the pine needles, leaf rot, and detritus that made up the forest floor. Spring was awakening on the mountain, and life was being reborn all around him—and he could *feel* it.

But more importantly, he could detect Kelsey's presence in the woods. Her life force had a delicious scent to it, and the sound of her blood pumping through her heart was like the pounding roar of some massive piston working inside an incomprehensibly large machine.

It's just her heart, he told himself. Her heart, beating. Thump-a-thump! *Thump-a-thump!*

He followed the sound through the forest and began stripping his clothes off as he did, leaving them behind, keeping with him only the steak knife he had pilfered from the cafeteria the day before.

He didn't notice the cold air. His body was hot with excitement, filled with the burning spirit of The Walking Death. He noticed that the sound of Kelsey's heart began to change. It became clearer, more articulate. He realized with a shock that it was speaking, forming words with its rhythmic pumping, and it was speaking to him, calling to him. It said:

Alex! Eat me! Thump-a-thump!

52

It felt good to walk in the cold morning air, smelling the mountain forest around her. She felt the tension leaving her body bit by bit with every step she took. She picked up the pace, breathing deeply of the invigorating air.

Kelsey had enjoyed jogging at one time, before she'd become involved with drugs. She had taken pride in her body and caution as to what she put into it, or did with it. What had happened to that pride? she now wondered. How had she got away from it? How had she allowed herself to succumb to drugs and alcohol?

Her father had been an alcoholic, and she'd sworn at an early age that she would never be like him. Yet here she was, *worse* than he ever was because he had been only an alcoholic while she had the dual addictions of drugs *and* alcohol.

Doug got me here, she thought and felt an immediate pang of guilt. That was a lie. Well, maybe not a lie, but certainly not the truth. He had something to do with it, but he hadn't forced her to use drugs and drink, had he? And wasn't it just like her to look for someone else to blame? She had done that all her life, blaming her problems on someone—anyone—else but never accepting responsibility for her own actions.

She had been lured by Doug's magazine-model good looks, his Porsche, his bankroll, and eventually his steady supply of cocaine that made her feel better than she had ever felt before in her life. It had been easy to give up exercising since she hardly ever ate—she didn't need to exercise to stay thin and in shape on the coke.

Oh, you stayed thin, all right, but you didn't stay in shape!

That was true enough. She had got thinner and thinner and had thought she looked *great.* Upon her admission to the clinic, she had weighed ninety-eight pounds, standing five feet six. After detoxing she had been horrified by her image in a mirror. She had looked like a concentration camp victim. After a month at the clinic, she had put some weight back on, getting up to 110, and now she looked more like her old self.

She began to take longer strides, stretching her leg muscles with every step. Soon she was jogging.

You can't run from things anymore, and you can't hide from responsibility, she thought in rhythm to her stride. She smiled and ran faster. For the first time she felt as though she might just make it outside of the clinic, back in the real world.

She was so wrapped up in the exuberance of her new-found strength and resolve that she didn't pay attention to the snapping of twigs and the rustle of bushes from the woods bordering the path. Just as the noises were becoming loud and close enough to get her attention, causing her to slow her pace, Alex came flying out of the woods, a growling, diving, naked man with wild eyes. He knocked her to the ground, punched her, and grabbed her by the throat tightly with his left hand.

He's going to rape me, she thought frantically as he lowered his mouth to hers and kissed her. She tried to scream when he lifted his mouth, but it never came out as he brought up a knife in his right hand and slit her mouth open from cheek to cheek.

53

Bill got up, showered, shaved, and dressed. He went to the cafeteria. Lunch was just getting over, but he was able to get a sandwich before the kitchen closed. He was tired, having slept only four hours, and would have liked to have stayed in bed, but this was Kelsey's last day at the clinic and he wanted to spend it with her more than he wanted to sleep.

He ate his lunch quickly, looking around the caf and out at the patio for any sign of her. He saw a couple of the girls from her group—one was her roommate—sunning themselves on the porch. He finished eating and went out to ask them if they'd seen her.

"Gee, now that you mention it, I haven't seen her all morning. She wasn't at group meditation today," Angela, Kelsey's roommate, replied. "Her bed hardly looked slept in this morning when I got up, either."

"Wasn't she supposed to go home today?" the other woman, a middle-aged, dowdy-looking woman whose name Bill couldn't remember, asked. "Or is that tomorrow?"

"She's not supposed to go until tomorrow," Bill answered. "I think I'll go check with the nurse on her ward."

54

Alex found a patch of unmelted snow and washed the blood from his body. He had tossed Kelsey's body into the woods, not bothering to conceal it any further. The Antichrist would know what had happened to his minion when he received the message Alex was going to leave for him. He retraced his steps through the woods, retrieving his clothing as he went and picking shreds of flesh and muscle from his teeth. He stopped and had to vomit once, which surprised him. He had enjoyed the taste of Kelsey's flesh. He had a moment of fear, thinking his weak stomach would be seen as a betrayal by The Walking Death. He fell to his knees, half clothed, and prayed for forgiveness. A sense of calm came over him, and he knew that if he carried through the rest of his task properly, all would be forgiven.

He arrived back at the clinic fully clothed, not a speck of blood on him, not even a shred of flesh stuck in his teeth—he had used his long fingernails to clean them just to be on the safe side. He entered the clinic by the main door just as Bill was coming in from the porch on his way to the nurses' station. Bill barely acknowledged Alex in his hurry to check on Kelsey.

Alex followed discreetly, stopping at the row of pay phones near the nurses' station and pretending to make a call while he eavesdropped on Bill.

"Excuse me," Bill said to the nurse behind the desk. He

had never seen her on the ward before. Her name tag said
LAURA. "I'm looking for Kelsey. Her room's on this ward."

"Everyone is at their afternoon therapy groups, where
you should be," the nurse replied without looking up.

"Can you tell me where her group is?" Bill asked, a
little annoyed with her indifference.

"No, I cannot."

"Thanks for nothing," Bill said and stalked off.

Alex hung up the phone, smiled, and patted his pants
pocket, which was beginning to become wet with blood.

55

What am I getting so upset about? Bill asked himself. Kelsey probably *was* in her group therapy. He had spent a good deal of the day before with her and she had seemed fine. Why was he so worried about her now? He went back to the porch to ask the two women where their group met, but they were gone.

He looked at his watch. Group therapy sessions had started fifteen minutes ago. He was supposed to be in a physical therapy session. He debated whether to go late or to go to the office that had been set up for him by Dr. McRegan and look over his old files from his years with the state police. The feelings of guilt about not looking at the records the FBI had supplied for him had been growing day by day until they were now stronger than his fear of a relapse if he did the work. A lot of people had gone to a lot of trouble to set up the microfiche machine. George had called him yesterday to see how he was doing, explaining that the feds were getting antsy, and he had lied, saying he'd found nothing yet. Of course, it wasn't technically a lie. He *hadn't* found anything, but then he hadn't told George he hadn't started looking yet either. George had reminded him that his family's safety was at stake, and that had been the final straw—the guilt then became overwhelming.

What was he thinking? George was right, his family's

safety was at stake here. He decided it was time to get cracking on those files no matter what it did to him, no matter how much it wakened the addict sleeping inside him.

He let himself into the small office with the key McRegan had given him. The office was just around the corner from the nurses' station on his ward. He turned on the light and went over to the stack of four boxes on the table next to the microfiche machine.

The label on the top box read: CASE RECORDS—GAGE WILLIAM R. 1968–70. His first three years as an investigator with the state police. He pulled out the first roll of microfilm and loaded it into the machine and turned it on. Opening the small window a crack, he lit a cigarette and settled into the chair in front of the screen.

Dr. McRegan knocked on the door at 4:00 P.M., rousing him from the seat.

"I thought I'd find you here," the doctor said upon opening the door. "Your counselor complained that you didn't show up for group this morning. And I checked— you haven't been to any of your scheduled therapy sessions or classes today. You were out most of the night, I hear. Down at the art studio with Jim?"

Bill yawned and stretched. "Excuse me. Yeah. I couldn't sleep. Old Jim was up and he helped me get my mind off things. As to not being in group or sessions today, I've been avoiding this too long." He looked at his watch. "I didn't realize it was so late."

McRegan closed the door, took out a cigarette, and lit it. The clinic did not allow smoking indoors, and she gave Bill a look that said she wouldn't tell on him if he didn't tell on her. She sat on the corner of his desk.

"Do you think it's such a good idea, you working on this case while in recovery?" she asked him.

"I've got no choice," he answered.

"Spoken like a true addict," she shot back.

"What's that supposed to mean?"

"Just what I said. That's typical addictive thinking. 'Stinking thinking' is what we call it. I'm sure you've heard that at AA meetings. You ever use that same excuse, 'I have no choice,' when it came to your alcohol or drug abuse?"

That comment hit home.

"But this isn't the same thing. My family is at stake here. There's a madman killer out there, and he's targeted me and my family," Bill argued.

"No difference. It all comes down to the same thing. When are you going to learn to do what's best for you? You can't protect your family, or be of any use to them until you do. The FBI is very competent. I'm sure they can catch this person without your assistance."

"Maybe. But then again maybe I can help them find him a little faster and save some innocent people from a gruesome death. You're wrong on this, Doctor. I am finally taking responsibility, and I am taking care of myself. If I don't do everything I can to help, I won't be able to look myself in the mirror the next time he kills."

"Okay," she replied after a few moments of thought and several drags from her cigarette. "So, if you are choosing to do this, why did you say you had no choice?"

Bill smiled. "Now, on that you were right. That was stinking thinking. To have no choice makes me into a martyr, right. Lets me get on the 'pity pot.'"

Dr. McRegan laughed. "As long as you can keep it in perspective. But be warned, Bill. If it starts to get to you, stop. Don't let it get in the way of your recovery. You owe yourself that."

Their eyes met and Bill nodded.

"Good. Maybe you should knock off for a while. They're starting up a volleyball game out back. Go play for a while before dinner. Doctor's orders."

"Yes, ma'am," Bill replied with a smile.

Bill went out to the volleyball court, which was in the woods behind the clinic just off the path to the Money Tree. There was a game in full swing with a four-on-four contest taking place on the small basketball court next to it. A small group of spectators stood nearby smoking and watching. The day had warmed up considerably, and the volleyball and basketball players had taken off their jackets.

Bill saw Joel and went over to him. "Joel, have you seen Kelsey around?"

"Yeah, I think so," he said, rubbing the scar on his neck, a gesture he did habitually. "I think she went up the path to the Money Tree with a couple of girls in her group. Debbie, and that good-looking blonde—you know. The one with the big wazoos." He cackled as though he'd just said something extremely funny.

"Thanks," Bill said, feeling relieved and wondering why he had such a sense of urgency about finding Kelsey. He was debating whether or not to go after her as the volleyball game ended and sides for a new game were being chosen.

"Hey, Bill. Wanna play on my team?" The invitation came from the Canadian kid who'd been out on the porch with the sing-along the other night.

Bill decided not to chase after Kelsey. If she wanted to see him, she would find him. He had to face that maybe seeing him on her last day wasn't as important to her as it was to him. She'd probably got all the information from him she'd needed, and that was that. Feeling a little sorry for himself while at the same time chiding himself for making more of his relationship with Kelsey than what it truly was, Bill joined the volleyball game.

Taking the serving position, he noticed a small flock of crows and turkey buzzards circling a spot a good distance off in the woods. Thinking it was odd for them to be circling like that in winter, he popped off a good serve and the game was on.

The first thing Bill wanted when he got back to his room after the game was a long hot shower. But first he had to move a pair of Alex's jeans from over the rod holding the shower curtain in place. They were dripping wet as if Alex had hand-washed them in the sink. Bill removed his towel from the rack on the back of the door and hung Alex's pants up to finish drying. He noticed a fading stain on the right pocket that looked as though it had been scrubbed hard with a bar of soap. Bill figured a pen must have leaked in his roomie's pocket.

He turned on the shower, undressed, and stepped in, letting the hot water soothe his aching muscles. It had been a long time since he'd done anything athletic. Though he'd always thought of volleyball as a girl's game, he now had a different view. He was sore all over. He began washing himself, gingerly at first, and looked forward to dinner, and maybe seeing Kelsey later.

Knock it off! When will you learn?

56

Ivy followed his mother into the basement of the church in Leominster. It was a small gymnasium with a low stage at one end. Racks of folding chairs lined the four walls. In the middle of the floor was placed a ring of chairs. All but three of them were occupied.

His mother led him to a couple of the empty chairs and they sat. She waved to a woman sitting across from them and said subdued hellos to the other people there.

Ivy was a little surprised by the collection of people gathered for the meeting. They didn't look like alcoholics to Ivy. He had some vague notion of alcoholics being tramps, dirty and incoherent, but these people were normal.

The guy sitting next to Ivy looked like a businessman. He had gray hair, wore a dark brown, double-breasted suit, and had a thin gray moustache. He reminded Ivy of Vincent Price. Next to him was a woman in her sixties. She looked like someone's grandmother as she sat knitting what looked like a scarf. There was a young guy next to her. He looked as if he wasn't a day over eighteen. He had long hair and an earring and wore a Guns 'n Roses T-shirt. He was holding hands with a red-haired girl who had a bad complexion. Across the floor from him and his mother were two women, one of whom had waved to his mother. They both appeared to be about the same age as his mom.

One had bleached-blond hair and wore too much eye makeup, the other was thin and mousy looking, with stringy black hair and thick glasses. The latter held a blue vinyl notebook in her lap. She opened it and cleared her throat.

"Welcome to the 'Keep It Simple' group of Alcoholics Anonymous. My name is Sheila, and I'm an alcoholic."

"Hi, Sheila," everyone except Ivy responded.

"Hi," Sheila said again. She read from the book, something called "How It Works," explaining the philosophy of AA. Ivy tried to pay attention but quickly lost interest. Partly it was because of Sheila's voice, which was very nasal and had a droning quality to it; the rest of it was that he'd discovered the ceiling of the gymnasium was criss-crossed with beautifully carved beams depicting angels and devils in conflict. He traced the intricacies of the carvings for some time while Sheila continued to read from the notebook.

"Can we go around and have everyone introduce themselves?" Sheila asked, closing the book.

The woman next to her said, "Hi. I'm Mary. I'm an alcoholic."

Ivy's mother introduced herself next, speaking softly but clearly and proclaiming herself to also be an alcoholic, getting Ivy's attention. It was the first time he'd ever heard her say it out loud. She took Ivy's hand and said, "This is my son, Ivy."

"Uh, hi," Ivy said quickly with a little self-conscious wave of his hand.

Everyone smiled and said hi to him. The businessman next to him patted him on the back and introduced himself as Vick. The introductions went on. The old woman was Irma, the longhaired young man was Tom, and his girlfriend was Debby.

Sheila spoke again, recounting the history of her alcoholism, and Ivy returned to gazing at the ceiling. He was trying to figure out if the beams were merely decorative or served as real supports for the ceiling when he realized Sheila had stopped talking and now his mother was.

"I started drinking heavily when my husband, Otis, was killed in a car accident. Actually . . . I drank pretty heavily even before that."

Ivy's ears perked up. This was news to him.

"I was a closet drinker," his mother went on. "I started right after my son Ivy was born." She tilted her head to the side a little to indicate Ivy, but kept her eyes on the floor. "I suffered from postpartum depression, and it seemed to be the only thing that helped get me out of the doldrums. A couple of stiff belts of vodka and I was fine. I drank vodka because I'd heard it didn't smell on your breath. At the time I thought I was getting away with something; I thought my husband had no idea what I was doing.

"Since I've been sober, I've had a chance for a lot of 'remember whens.' And now I remember things he said or did, or the way his mood would change after I'd had a few drinks.

"He knew. He always knew." She paused, her breath hitching in her chest, and spoke haltingly and emotionally. "I wish he was here now so I could tell him I'm sorry." She sighed, her shoulders drooping. "But I can't do that now, so I'd like to do the next-best thing."

She turned to Ivy and took both his hands in hers. "I'd like to tell my son, Ivy, how sorry I am for all the pain I've caused him and for all the promises I've broken and all the times I wasn't there for him." Tears streamed down her face. "I'm sorry, Ivy," she mumbled, turning to him.

Ivy fought back tears and glanced around at the others with embarrassment.

"It's okay, Mom," he blurted out. She took him in her arms and hugged him. The others applauded.

57

Bill dressed and dried his hair with a towel. It was a quarter to six, fifteen minutes until the cafeteria opened for dinner. He decided to take a walk through the patients' lounge out to the porch to see if Kelsey was around, berating himself all the while for doing so.

She wasn't in the patients' lounge. The usual patients were there, playing cribbage and Monopoly, watching TV. He walked out to the porch, and she wasn't there either among the cliques sitting at the round tables, smoking and talking and enjoying the unusually balmy air.

He saw her roommate, who said she hadn't seen Kelsey all day, but she hadn't been back to her room since lunch. She guessed that maybe Kelsey was in the room packing her things for her discharge tomorrow.

Bill thought about going to her room but immediately discarded that idea. He didn't want to look as if he was chasing her, and men were not allowed on the women's ward. It was as he'd decided earlier—if Kelsey wanted to see him, she'd find him.

He went to his office and began going over the files again, finishing those for the year 1969 before shutting off the microfiche machine and going to the cafeteria for dinner. The line was long but moved quickly; the service was very efficient. He got his tray and silverware from the carts along the wall and scanned the cafeteria for Kelsey while he moved slowly toward the serving counter.

He didn't see her.

He began thinking about one of the perps from the file he'd just gone over. He was a possible suspect for The Walking Death—a huge black guy who had liked to rape and beat women to a pulp. Bill remembered when the guy had been convicted, he had vowed loudly in court to get Bill, who'd busted him, someday.

Bill doubted the guy was really The Walking Death. If his memory served him properly, he'd heard something about the perp getting knifed in prison a few years back, leaving him paralyzed. Still he made a mental note to tell George or the feds about it next time he spoke to them so they could check it out.

He got his dinner, fried chicken, mashed potatoes, and string beans, with chocolate pudding for dessert. He was just sitting at his group's table when Sheila, Kelsey's friend and fellow group member, came over.

"I think Kelsey's missing," she said, running up to him. Bill stood and noticed a group of staff, nurses, two security guards, and Dr. McRegan, gathered in the lobby outside the cafeteria. McRegan was giving instructions to the security guards and they left by the front door. Bill got up from the table and he and Sheila went out to the lobby. A lump of fear filled his throat and his chest felt tight.

"I want you three to search every room on the wards," Dr. McRegan was telling several nurses. "The rest of you search the therapy rooms downstairs and the gym. And I want to talk to you," she said, noticing Bill. "And someone call down to the coach house and the art studio, see if anyone there has seen her."

"What's wrong? Where's Kelsey?" Bill asked McRegan.

"That's what I'm trying to find out. Come to my office."

She led the way and Bill followed. She told him to close the door after him and motioned him to a seat.

"When was the last time you saw Kelsey, Bill?" Dr. McRegan asked, settling into the large upholstered chair behind her desk.

"Last night. We sat on the porch till after midnight or so," he answered. "We took a walk up to the Money Tree around nine thirty."

"And then you were reported missing from your room from three until seven this morning."

"Yeah, and you know I was at the art studio. Check with Jim, he'll tell you I was there all night. Besides, Kelsey was seen yesterday by me and others and Joel saw her going for a walk in the woods earlier today." He squirmed in his chair, a little nervous at McRegan's insinuations and a lot irritated that she was wasting time asking him questions.

McRegan picked up a pencil and made a note of that. A knock at the door was followed by Clara, the head night nurse, opening it and poking her head in.

"All the patients are accounted for except for Alex and Joel. And, of course, Kelsey."

"Great!" McRegan said. "Where the hell are those two? What's going on? Call more security guards in. Get on the radio and tell Harris to drive down the mountain and into town to look for them."

"Right," the nurse answered and closed the door.

"Why don't you call the police?" Bill asked.

"If I can contain this and keep it on the mountain, I'd rather not involve the police. I'm sure Kelsey is okay."

"Look, lady! She is missing! She has been for a whole day! In a small place like this that's a long time," Bill said loudly. He had a bad feeling about this. Suddenly, out of the blue, he had an overwhelming urge to drink. He quashed the feeling as best he could.

"Not really," McRegan answered quietly, controlling her anger. "Having been a policeman, you should know a person has to be missing for seventy-two hours before the police consider them missing. We have no reason to think something has happened to her. She may have decided to go home early, for all we know. She was due to leave in the morning. Maybe someone—her boyfriend—came and got her early."

"She wouldn't leave without telling someone. And besides, she told me her boyfriend didn't know where she was. Have you checked her room?"

"Yes."

"And?"

"And what?"

"Were her clothes and luggage gone?"

"No," McRegan said with a sigh. "Everything was still there. But all that means is that she hasn't left the mountain. It doesn't mean anything has happened to her."

"So where is she? I think you're wrong. I think something *has* happened to her. And if I were you, I'd call in the local police, if not the state police, to assist you with the search. This is a pretty big mountain. She might have fallen in the woods and hurt herself."

McRegan considered what he said for a moment. "If our own search of the grounds doesn't find her, I'll call them."

Bill had to be satisfied with that. Dr. McRegan was not someone who could be told what to do.

"Well, what can I do to help?" he asked.

"Nothing. I'm sorry, but our insurance policy would never allow a patient to assist us in anything like this. There's too much liability. Besides, since you are someone who was closest to Kelsey, I'm going to have to ask you to remain in your room until she is found. Or I have to call the police in."

"You're talking like I'm a suspect, and that tells me that you think Kelsey has been the victim of foul play," Bill answered. The urge for a drink bubbled up again, but this time he found it easier to submerge it.

Dr. McRegan laughed. "Spoken like a true policeman. No. I don't think that, but it is something I have to take under consideration."

Bill looked as though he would protest, then thought better of it. McRegan was right. She was only following correct procedure, and he knew what a bitch that could be. "Okay," he said with resignation. "But you've got to promise me you'll call the state police if your search is unsuccessful."

McRegan looked down at her desk for a moment, then back at Bill. "I don't have to make any deals with you, Bill."

Bill said nothing, but returned her stare unflinchingly. "Okay," she said finally.

Bill went to his room and began pacing. The desire to lose himself in a drink to escape all this hadn't completely left him, but it hadn't overwhelmed him either. He realized he could live with it, and wondered, a little fearfully, if he would have to do so for the rest of his life. McRegan herself brought him a sandwich and soda from the cafeteria, which he had no stomach for. She reported there was as yet no sign of Kelsey, nor his roommate, nor Joel.

"Will you call the police now?" Bill asked her.

"In a little while," she answered, looking him squarely in the eye. "Security hasn't finished searching the trails behind the clinic yet."

Something clicked in Bill's mind. Something about the trails, but he couldn't quite put his finger on it.

"You'll be the first to know when I call," McRegan answered and left. Bill scowled at her exit and continued his pacing. Several turns around the room later, he threw himself on his bed in frustration.

He stared at the tiled ceiling and ran over everything Dr. McRegan had told him. There was something he was missing, or forgetting, concerning her comment that security was searching the trails behind the hospital.

It was no good. He had a mental block. The harder he tried to think, the more confused his thoughts became. He tried a different tack and reviewed everything he'd done since last seeing Kelsey. Several people had said they'd seen her—now he remembered. At the volleyball court. Joel had said he'd seen Kelsey go for a walk in the woods.

And now Joel was missing, too. Was there a connection? But something else had happened at the volleyball court, too, hadn't it? He'd noticed something in the woods . . . *birds!* And not just any birds! He'd seen a flock of crows and turkey buzzards circling. They were carrion birds, and the only time they circled like that was when they had found something dead for them to feed on.

He jumped off the bed and ran to the door. There was a burly attendant standing outside.

"I have to see Dr. McRegan," Bill exclaimed when the attendant blocked his exit.

"Sorry. She's busy. She says you're to stay in your room."

Bill sized the attendant up. He was about thirty years old, six feet tall with broad shoulders. He looked as though he worked out regularly, but Bill knew that a hard jab to his solar plexus or balls would take him out fast.

"What's going on?" It was Dr. McRegan, coming down the hall.

"I know where in the woods you've got to search for Kelsey," Bill told her excitedly.

"What?" McRegan said, stopping outside the room. Bill told her about the birds. McRegan looked doubtful.

"Bill, they could have been flocking over anything. It's starting to snow, and the weather report says we're in for our last big storm of the season. I've just called off the search to be resumed in the morning."

"The state police have the capability to search the area, storm or not. Have you called them?"

"No," McRegan answered, avoiding his eyes this time.

"No? No? What the hell do you mean, *no*?" Bill demanded.

McRegan stiffened. Her eyes narrowed on Bill. He knew immediately that he had taken the wrong tone with her, but he didn't care.

"You listen to me," she said through clenched teeth, her eyes flashing anger. The attendant took two steps away from her. "I run this hospital, and I don't answer to you. *I'm* in charge here, and *I* make the decisions, and *I* will take responsibility for those decisions. Now we will wait until morning, when the storm should be over, and we will complete our search with *clinic* personnel. If we still find nothing then, I will call in the authorities."

Bill couldn't take it. "You are *fucking* nuts, lady! What if she's hurt out in those woods. She'll freeze to death before morning. And if she is dead, you'll never find her under the snow that's falling."

"I don't think that's the case, Bill. I think she's left the mountain, for whatever reason," McRegan returned, her arms folded stiffly across her chest.

"Have you been drinking, Doc, or using drugs?"

The question caught McRegan off guard and angered her even more. "I don't have to listen to this. You've heard my decision." She turned to leave.

Bill was right behind her. "You're a walking contradiction, you know that? You must be on something, Doc, to think she'd leave the clinic on her own and leave all *her stuff behind*!" Bill screamed at her, throwing his hands up in frustration.

Dr. McRegan slammed the door to his room shut in his face. "Lock it," she instructed the attendant. "And remain on guard here the rest of the night. Don't open that door for any reason."

Bill lost complete control of his temper. "You stupid bitch!" he screamed at her through the small glass window in the door as she walked away. "You goddamned stupid fucking bitch!" He punctuated the last with his fists pounding against the door.

58

Ivy and his mother cleared the supper dishes from the table and put them in the sink. "I'll do these, Mom, so you can get ready for your meeting," he said to her.

She kissed his forehead. "Thanks, hon. You want to come with me?"

Ivy thought of his embarrassment at the AA meeting he'd attended earlier with her. "Uh, no. Thanks anyway, but I've got a lot of homework to do."

While Ivy did the dishes, his mother got ready. "Is someone picking you up?" Ivy asked as she was putting her coat on.

"No. I'm just going to the church down the hill a few blocks. There's a new meeting starting there tonight."

"Be careful," he told her. "The weatherman said we're going to get freezing rain, and it'll be real slippery out there tonight."

She opened the door and groaned. "Looks like the weatherman was right. It's raining already."

"Why don't you call a cab?" Ivy asked. "I've still got money left in my stash. I'll pay for it."

"Oh, no, hon. It's okay, really. I've got my hat and rubber boots, and I'll take the umbrella too. I'll be fine."

Ivy didn't like the idea of her going out in the freezing rain and tried to insist that she use his money to take a taxi, but she assured him she'd be all right. Despite his arguments, she prevailed, kissing him and hugging him before leaving for her meeting.

Ivy finished the dishes, dried them, and put them away in the cabinets. He got out his schoolbag and began working on his math homework, all the while keeping an eye on the clock. When an hour had gone by, he got up, went into the front room facing the street—his mother's bedroom—and looked out the window for her.

After fifteen minutes of watching for her he began to get worried. The AA meeting should have lasted only an hour. He went to the kitchen closet and put on his coat, hat, and boots and went out looking for her. At the bottom of the stairs he heard a siren and saw flashing lights coming from the street. He felt icy fingers squeeze his heart.

He hurried down the driveway to discover a small group of people huddled around something in the middle of the road. There was a police car diagonally in the road, its lights flashing. The officer was standing in the car's open door talking on the radio. As Ivy approached, he overheard the cop speaking.

"We got a hit-and-run on Leighton Street. Just occurred and I was a block away and happened on the scene probably seconds after it happened. No sign of the hit car, though. Witnesses said it was all over the road. Drunk driver probably. Send an ambulance, but I think the victim's dead. I couldn't get a pulse."

Ivy hurried to the crowd and pushed through. The first thing he saw was his mother's hat and umbrella lying a foot from her head. There was blood on the wet road between the two.

"She's dead as a doornail," someone nearby said. The words came to Ivy as if from far away. His legs grew weak and he felt faint. As the sound of the siren from the approaching ambulance grew louder, he backed away from the crowd, turned, and ran back to the apartment.

He scurried up the stairs, falling several times as hot

tears blurred his vision. He burst into the apartment and fell on the floor, sobbing hysterically. Henry jumped on him, licking his face. Ivy hugged the dog to himself, squeezing the puppy so hard it whimpered.

He didn't know how long he lay there, senseless with grief. Eventually a clear thought made its way through the pain—he was alone. His father was dead, and now his mother. What was going to happen to him? He had no one now.

Suddenly he sat up. He knew what happened to kids who lost their parents—who were suddenly made orphans. They were sent to a foster home, or worse, an orphanage.

Well, that wasn't going to happen to him. He got up, grabbed his knapsack, dumped out his schoolbooks, and took it into his bedroom. He randomly stuffed clothes and some of his favorite books into the bag. He strapped it on, picked up Henry, and headed for the door.

He stopped in the kitchen. Where was he going? Tears overwhelmed him again. He felt as if he could die—drop dead right there on the floor. He just couldn't believe this had happened, couldn't believe his mother was really gone. He was completely, irrevocably alone.

Unsuccessfully fighting back tears, he went out alone into the night.

59

It is time to go. He can feel it; he is ready. Though he still wears the splint the boy made, the ankle feels better, and he has wasted enough time. The plan is behind schedule. He must move now.

What to do about the boy? He knows he has told him too much, but in doing so he has found a kindred spirit, a reflection of the way he was, the way he thought when he was that age. Can he trust the boy to remain quiet? A loud inner voice tells him no, but an equally loud one says yes. What to do?

He must leave tonight. The boy's visit this evening will be the last, either way. He knows he must make a decision, but he puts it off, waiting for the boy to arrive, hoping he will know what to do on instinct when the time comes.

60

Bill Gage paced the room, furious at Dr. McRegan and cursing her under his breath. He had to do something, he knew, but what? He had to get out of the clinic and search for Kelsey where he'd seen the flock of carrion birds earlier in the day. He had no doubt he could take out the attendant, but all that would do was bring security down on him. No, he had to get out of the room and the clinic without anyone knowing for a while.

He stopped in the middle of the room and glanced at the tiled ceiling. It looked new, and from the metallic framing that ran around the edges he could tell it was a false ceiling with the real one above it.

He stood on his bed, reached up, and pushed one of the Styrofoam-like tiles up and to the side. He couldn't see much. He went over to the desk and climbed on it, pushing the tile over it up and out of the way. With the added height of the desk beneath him he was able to stand with head and shoulders above the false ceiling, but still he couldn't see much. He took out his lighter, flicked it to life, and held it up, inspecting the original ceiling a foot or so above the new one.

There. A few feet from where he stood was a ventilator shaft. The rooms were all air-conditioned by baseboard vents now, which was the reason for the new ceilings. He tugged on the metal framework holding the ceiling and wondered if it would support his weight. He doubted it.

He climbed down from the desk and went over to the door, looking through the small window. The attendant was sitting to the right of the door. Bill turned and looked back at the desk. It was partially hidden by the large portable closet next to it. Hidden just enough, he hoped, that the attendant, when he looked in to check on Bill, wouldn't see it clearly—and maybe that would give him the time he needed.

He went back to the desk and put the chair on top of it. Glancing back at the door, he climbed up. Standing precariously on the back of the chair, he was able to get most of his body, up to his knees, above the false ceiling, and just barely reach the ventilator shaft. With the chair teetering beneath him and his upper body hunched over between the old ceiling and the new, he stuck his fingers into the bottom slats of the ventilator grate and pulled.

It wouldn't budge. He tried again and felt it give a little, sending a small shower of dust and grit into his face. He sneezed and almost lost his balance. He pulled again, and the grate gave a little more, sending more stuff at him, but he was ready this time and kept his face turned away. He pulled again, and the vent grate came free with a screech of rusted metal. His momentum from pulling at the grate almost sent him crashing backward off the chair, but he managed to right himself before that could happen.

Now came the tricky part. He carefully placed the grate on a crosspiece of the ceiling's metal support frame. Grabbing the edge of the open shaft with both hands, he pulled himself up slowly. God! he was out of shape. He was thankful, though, for having lost so much weight from his cocaine use. A few more pounds and he wouldn't have been able to pull his body up an inch, never mind all the way up and through the ventilator shaft opening.

His feet came off the chair and he lifted them, placing

them carefully against the false ceiling's frame, using it lightly as leverage to push himself the rest of the way into the opening. He managed to get his belly over the edge of the opening and rested, pulling his legs up behind him. It was going to be tight. It looked as though there was barely enough room for him to fit into the shaft. He hoped its other end hadn't been blocked up, but there was only one way to find out.

He lifted and pushed himself into the vent and immediately regretted it. Claustrophobia overcame him in the tight space, and he had trouble breathing. Plus the fact that the vent was dusty and filmy with cobwebs, and he was very near a panic attack. He wanted desperately to go back and get out of the shaft, but he didn't think he could, not without tumbling out of the vent and crashing through the ceiling anyway. He had to push on.

He began to sweat. It trickled down his nose and into his eyes. He tried to wipe it out but couldn't bend his arms enough to get his hand to his face. He gripped at the soldered ribs of the ventilator shaft sections and, pushing with his knees and feet, squirmed along a few inches at a time.

Something with many legs crawled down the back of his collar and he nearly shrieked. Frantically he pushed his back against the top of the shaft until he felt the thing squish wetly against the skin of his back. His sweat turned cold, and his breathing became even more shallow and rapid. He felt light-headed as he scrambled wildly to reach the end of the shaft.

A terrifying thought occurred to him. The shaft was like a tunnel—a very tight tunnel—but a tunnel nonetheless. Like the tunnel in his dream. The thought filled him with dread, though he knew he was being foolish. He had to get out of there. *Now!* He scrambled forward, knees hurting and back aching, but he didn't care. All he thought of was getting out of there.

* * *

His hands came up against a barrier. He felt around it. The end of the shaft. He pushed against it but it wouldn't budge.

Please, God, don't let me be trapped in here!

He scrunched up closer to the end of the shaft and put all his weight into pushing. From behind him came the sound of voices echoing down to him. For one awful moment he thought he heard Wilbur Clayton's voice, but then realized it was the attendant who had been guarding his room. Another voice joined his—Dr. McRegan's.

"The ceiling," the attendant said. "Looks like he went out the ventilator shaft."

"Call security," McRegan said.

Bill pushed harder and began pounding the cover over the end of the shaft. With a loud metallic wrenching sound the cover came free and flew away from him. Bright light from the outside floods blinded him, and cold air hit his face. He grabbed the edge of the shaft and pulled himself out, toppling head over heels eight feet to the ground on his back.

He lay there stunned for a moment, his breath coming in short gasps, snow falling in his face. He forced himself to his feet despite the pain in his back and legs. He had to get moving. The security guards would be out there any second.

Slipping on the fresh snow, he awkwardly ran up the embankment toward the trails behind the clinic. It was very cold, and the wind factor reduced the temperature even more. He wore no coat—would never have fit into the shaft if he had remembered to put one on. He heard the emergency door at the back of the clinic open as he reached the trail to the Money Tree. He sprinted up the trail, looking back but seeing no one in pursuit yet.

It was one of those strange stormy nights where the cloud cover was low, thick, and white and had the same effect of illumination as would a full moon. Bill had no trouble seeing his way up the path. But he had to get his bearings, remember where, exactly, he'd seen the carrion birds flocking and try to find the spot. He stopped at the volleyball court and looked at the white sky. He tried to remember where he'd been standing when he'd seen the birds. He'd been about to serve the ball in the first game. He went over to the rear of the court and scanned the tree line. There, at a ninety-degree angle to the bench, was where he'd seen the birds, maybe a half mile into the woods.

It was hard going through the thick underbrush of the woods. After a hundred feet or so he could no longer see the lights of the clinic behind him and became unsure whether or not he was still heading in the right direction. Hoping that his usually good sense of direction wouldn't fail him now, he went on.

A splash of light played over a tree to his left. He looked back to see bobbing lights pursuing him. Security was on his tail. He hurried on, searching the ground as he went. He figured he had to be getting close to the spot where he'd seen the carrion birds.

He came to a thick stand of laurel and pushed his way through, finding nothing but air on the other side and tumbling down a small embankment onto the middle of the trail to the Money Tree. He cursed himself. He could have taken the path and reached this point a lot quicker. He looked around, trying to get his bearings. If he remembered correctly, the path wound away to the right from where he stood. That meant the spot he was searching for was to the left of the path.

He crossed the path and pushed through the underbrush, hearing voices calling to one another close by. Some of security had obviously taken the trail to try to cut him off. They had very nearly succeeded. He ducked behind a tree, and lights came up the trail and a security guard and clinic attendant ran past. He was just about to thank God for their not seeing his footprints in the snow when the security guard stopped, backtracked, and played his flashlight over the spot where Bill had crashed through the bushes, fallen, got up, and crossed the path.

"Through here," the guard said to the attendant. He raised his radio to his lips and told the rest of the search party what he'd found.

Bill pushed away from the tree and ran. He slipped and fell several times, soaking his clothes with the deepening snow. He heard several shouts each time he fell and knew that his pursuers were close enough that they could hear him. The thought distracted him from watching his footing. He tripped over something and crashed into a thicket of brambles, sending snow and broken twigs showering down the back of his neck, and scratching his face and hands badly.

He crawled out of the bushes and shook the snow off. He stood and looked around. What the hell had he tripped on? The spot was clear of trees so it couldn't have been a root. Then he saw what it was that he'd tripped on. A deep groan escaped from his lips and he fell to his knees in the snow, sobbing.

Charlie, the night attendant who'd been assigned to guard Bill's room, was cold and miserable. McRegan was going to have his head for letting Bill escape the way he did. He was wondering if he would be able to get his old job at the mill in Barrington back when his thoughts were interrupted by a noise ahead in the woods. He flashed his light in that direction and called to the security guard a few feet away.

Bill Gage was there, in a small clearing, on his hands and knees. The body of a naked girl lay before him.

"Get the fuck away from here," Bill growled as the guards approached. "Watch where you step!"

The guards stopped at the edge of the clearing. Bill was

sifting gingerly through the snow around the girl's body, his head scanning back and forth.

"Give me some light!" he ordered. Charlie, the attendant, shone his light on the spot where Bill was searching.

"Come on, goddammit, come on! Why isn't it working? There's got to be something here. Got to be some clue. Why can't I see it?" Bill muttered as he searched the snow-covered ground.

"Is that the girl who's missing?" the security guard asked Charlie, indicating the naked corpse. The attendant nodded.

"Okay, let's go," the guard, a burly ex-marine, said to Bill.

"Leave me alone," Bill growled when the guard put a hand on his shoulder. "I've got to examine the scene while it's still fresh!"

"Leave it for the police," the guard commanded. "You're coming back to the clinic with us." More of the search party arrived, and two of the bigger security guards grabbed Bill's arms and hauled him to his feet.

"Let me go! You don't understand! There's a clue there! I know it. Give me time and my tunnel vision will come back. I'll be able to see it!" Bill shouted as they dragged him away through the woods. The guards exchanged a glance that was becoming common between them: "Another nutcase," it said.

With Bill struggling and protesting the entire way, the guards took him back to the clinic, followed by Charlie, the attendant. The rest of the search party stayed at the site of the body, waiting for the police to arrive.

The guards deposited Bill in the clinic lobby. The scene was pandemonium with the lobby full of patients who'd heard of Bill's escape and the search for him. Several of the female patients screamed and burst into tears when Bill was dragged in and the guards announced that Kelsey's body had been found. Dr. McRegan was there, look-

ing very pale and scared, but to her credit she took immediate control of the situation and ordered the attendants
and security guards to escort all the patients back to their
rooms.

"You still want to wait until morning before calling in
the police?" Bill asked sarcastically of McRegan. His eyes
blazed at her through tears.

"Maybe you should tell me first why you killed Kelsey."

Bill laughed, a barking, harsh sound. "Save it, lady," he
said fiercely. "I didn't kill her and you know it. And if you
still won't call the local and state police in, I will. We've
got major trouble here. The serial killer the feds came to
see me about is on this mountain."

McRegan was clearly shocked by that. "What? How can
that be?"

"How the hell do I know?" Bill nearly shouted at her. A
rage was burning so intensely inside it threatened to in-
cinerate him, but he managed to keep under control. "All
I know is, Kelsey was murdered and mutilated. And from
the photos of the other victims, the mutilations look close
enough alike to have been done by the same guy. Now,
whether you agree or not, I'm calling in the police and
FBI."

"You can't do that," McRegan said flatly.

"What the hell is wrong with you?" Bill did shout at her
this time. "Haven't you fucked this situation up enough
already? You want to try for obstruction of justice?"

"I mean," McRegan said with a sigh, "that the phone
lines are down because of the storm."

Bill looked at her doubtfully. "Because of the storm,
huh?"

"That's right," McRegan returned, anger flashing in her
eyes. "What's that supposed to mean?"

Bill ignored the question. "Your security people have
radios, right?"

"Yes, but their radius only covers the mountain. I've

sent two men into town in one of the Land-Rovers, but with the storm I don't know how long it will take them to get there and get back here with help."

Bill started to say something but was interrupted by a nurse and an attendant running up. They were white-faced and shaking.

"Dr. McRegan. You've got to come quickly. Another patient has been murdered," the nurse blurted out.

Bill followed McRegan, the nurse, and the attendant, who led them to Joel's room. His rage dissipating into horror, revulsion, and fear, Bill took in the scene. Joel lay naked and spread-eagled on his bed. His face was covered in blood from the mutilations it had endured. His eyes, the real and the glass one, were missing. The rest of his body was drenched in blood from the jagged, gaping tear down the middle of his chest.

While the others stared at the body on the bed, Bill noticed something else. On the wall above Joel's bed words were scrawled in blood:

I've come for the Antichrist.

Below that was a scrawled signature:

The Walking Death

Bill backed out of the room as Dr. McRegan barked orders at the nurse and attendant to close off the room and keep everyone away from there.

This can't be happening, thought Bill. It wasn't possible. How did The Walking Death find out he was at the clinic? Besides that, there was something wrong with all this, something that didn't fit, but he was too shaken to put his finger on it. His head was swimming and he felt sick to his stomach.

Bill turned away from the room and walked down the hall. He rubbed his face, trying to clear his head and figure out what he was missing here.

"Wait a minute," he said softly, stopping in the middle

of the hall. Kelsey and Joel weren't the only ones who'd been missing. Alex!

Bill hurried to his room. He didn't notice that the bathroom door was closed, so sure was he that he'd find Alex dead on his bed. His roommate's bed was empty, and the room appeared normal except for the missing ceiling tiles where he had made his escape.

Bill sat on his bed and put his head in his hands. He forced himself to concentrate, to review what had happened, to examine every detail.

The mutilations of Kelsey's and Joel's mouths and throats! That was it! In the photographs the FBI had given him, it was obvious the throats of The Walking Death's victims had been repeatedly punctured by a large, sharp instrument, not slashed as had Kelsey's and Joel's. It wasn't the same M.O. It *couldn't* be The Walking Death. A killer like that never changed his M.O.

But then who could it be? He thought of the letters and photographs he kept in his dresser drawer, and his eyes went to it. The bloody fingerprints on the drawer knobs made the sick feeling in his gut worse. He knew now that The Walking Death had not come to the clinic.

He got off the bed, went to the dresser, and opened the top drawer. Sitting on top of the manila envelopes, blood seeping into the paper, were two pairs of eyeballs. One of the orbs was made of glass. Bile rushed into his throat and he had to force the vomit back into his stomach as he heard the bathroom door open.

Bill turned slowly. He thought he knew whom he would see, and he was half right. Alex came out of the bathroom, but he wasn't alone. He had his arm around the neck of Sheila, Kelsey's roommate, and pressed to her throat was a bloody knife.

"Alex—" Bill started to say.

"I'm not Alex. I am The Walking Death," Alex said calmly. "And you are the Antichrist."

"Alex, listen to me," Bill said softly, taking a step forward. In Alex's deadly embrace, Sheila was white with fear and trembling. Mascara-stained tears trailed down both cheeks of her face.

"Shut up and don't come any closer!" Alex shouted.

Bill stopped. Sheila whimpered like a hurt puppy.

"Get down on your knees," Alex ordered.

Bill didn't move.

"I said get down on your knees before The Walking Death," Alex shouted.

Bill did as he was told.

"Now you will pay for the evil you've spread," Alex said, calm again. "But first you will watch another of your minions die." With that he pushed the knife into Sheila's left eye. Blood spurted from her face.

"No!" Bill screamed and was on his feet charging Alex. Alex quickly raked the knife across Sheila's throat and tossed her aside. She spun against the wall, painting it with her blood, and fell to the floor. Bill reached Alex just as his roommate spun back toward him, the knife up. Unable and unwilling to stop, Bill impaled his right shoulder upon the blade. In his rage he hardly felt it. He thrust his left fist up hard, catching Alex under the chin. Bill drove him back against the wall. The pressure of Bill's fist snapped Alex's head at an unnatural angle, tilting it so far back his forehead struck the wall. Bill shoved harder and had the pleasure of hearing Alex's neck snap.

Bill Gage heard nothing after that as unconsciousness flowed over him like the blood that flowed from Sheila's neck and his own shoulder.

III

Recovery

*Made a decision to turn our will and our lives over to the care of God
as we understood Him.*

—Step Three of AA's 12 Steps
to Recovery

*Maybe I'm not the person I should be,
Maybe I'm not the person I could be,
But thank God,
I'm not the person I used to be.*

—AA slogan

61

He can't walk anymore. His vision dances, and he is dizzy and befuddled like a sleepwalker. He can feel his ankle swelling inside the laceless sneaker. The old cane the boy, Tommy, gave him helps, but it is not made for the wooded terrain.

Tommy.

He stops, leans heavily against a tree, and wonders what the boy is doing at that moment.

Then he remembers.

The boy is dead. Or is he? He tells himself that the pain in his leg is clouding his memory. Of course the boy is dead. It would have been too dangerous to let him live.

Then why can't I remember killing him?

He pushes the thought away. He knows he must cleanse his mind of everything but the completion of his plan. But walking back to Crocker, Massachusetts, is out of the question.

Not too far away he hears the rumbling of a passing train. It seems like decades ago that he was at the railroad yard and had his dwarfish feast of souls.

His pouch filled with collected teeth rattles against his side. He pauses and opens it. The boy's eyes are not inside. Did he consume them already? He doesn't know. Which teeth are Tommy's? He knows not that either. All he is sure of is that he has to get away from this area fast. He has stayed too long.

And if you didn't kill the boy he may be talking to the police at this very moment.

He tries not to listen to the warning inner voice, and hobbles on, hurrying through the brush toward the railroad yard.

62

Ivy and Henry huddled next to the heater in the
garage. Ivy sat with his back against the wall,
Henry in his lap, and the homemade heater
blowing warm air over them.

Ivy cried himself to sleep, staining Henry's sleeping
head with his tears. Shortly after midnight the heater
stopped running, dying without a whisper. Within fifteen
minutes, Ivy shivered into wakefulness.

He tried to fix the heater. Everything looked okay,
which led him to surmise that the battery was dead. Leaving Henry in the nest of boxes, Ivy went to the back door,
opened it, and peeked up at the third-floor apartment. It
was dark, as he'd left it.

He wondered if the police or social workers had come
looking for him yet. The cold bit into him. It was too cold
to remain in the garage, and there was nowhere else to go.
He decided to chance it.

He went back and got Henry. Surveying the house,
driveway, and street carefully before making his move,
he ran to the stairs and climbed them as quietly as
possible. He let himself in and put Henry down. The dog
immediately ran to his dish and began lapping nois-
ily.

Ivy carried his backpack into his bedroom and threw it
on the bed. Without turning on any lights, he went into

his mother's room and lay on her bed weeping until sleep temporarily relieved him of his grief. A few moments later, Henry padded into the room, jumped on the bed, and snuggled up against Ivy's chest.

63

Bill Gage was back in the ventilator shaft, crammed in the dark and spidery tunnel, able to move just enough to inch along.

He stopped, listened. He could hear a scuffling sound, as though something was scuttling through the tunnel ahead, crawling toward him. His first thought was a rat. But if it was a rat, by the sound of it, it was a pretty big rat. A worse thought entered his mind and became conviction.

It was *Kelsey* crawling through the tunnel toward him. It was Kelsey with her eyes gone and her slit throat gaping like a second mouth. Kelsey naked and bloody and coming for him, reaching for him.

He tried to back up but he was stuck. He couldn't move backward or forward. He was trapped. Kelsey's dead face would be in his in a few moments. He'd have no choice but to stare into those empty eye sockets, and that would drive him mad.

He closed his eyes and prayed from his heart for deliverance.

The scuffling sound changed, as did the quality of the air around him. He didn't feel closed in anymore, didn't feel stuck. He realized he couldn't feel the walls of the ventilator shaft pressing against him.

He opened his eyes. It was still dark, but he could move

his arms and legs. He got to his knees and reached an arm searching upward. He found nothing.

He stood. The scuffling noise had stopped. He fumbled in his pocket for his lighter, brought it out, and struck it. What he saw sent the lighter from his trembling hand and he was plunged into darkness again.

Terror pressed against him as thick as the air around him. Wilbur Clayton had been standing before him, blood running from the bullet hole Bill himself had put into him. Just like in his dream.

He couldn't breathe. The pressure on his chest was crushing. *It's just a dream,* he thought. Miraculously, the thought freed him of fear. After all, a dream was just a dream, it had no power. It had no danger as long as he recognized it for what it was.

Just a dream.

Nothing to be afraid of.

He realized he could wake up if he wanted to. It was his dream. He could wake up, could even change the dream if he wanted to. He bent to the floor, feeling around for his lighter. He found it and lit it again. The tunnel was empty, but he noticed something new. A pinpoint of light had appeared far off in the darkness.

Suddenly, without moving his legs or feet, he felt himself being propelled forward. The lighter flickered out, and he dropped it as he picked up speed in his flight forward. The pinpoint of light got bigger and brighter.

He flew onward toward the light at the end of the tunnel. He thought about waking up again, or changing the dream. He didn't think he wanted to see what was in the light. The closer he got, and the brighter the light became, the more he knew he didn't want to see what was at the end of the tunnel. He wanted to wake up.

He didn't. He couldn't.

He tried to stop his flight forward, tried to change the

dream, and had the same result. He could do neither. The end of the tunnel rushed at him, the light blinding him.

Without warning, he ran up against a glass wall. His body striking the glass made a loud splat. His breathing created an expanding and contracting steam spot around his mouth.

A growing sense of fear and recognition came over him. He knew where he was, knew what he was looking at, understanding both in a flash of memory that made him tremble.

He was inside a camera lens, his father's camera lens, to be exact. And the scene before him was one he had witnessed only once, but had been shocking and terrifying enough to make him block it out of his memory for years until this moment.

Wanting to turn away but unable to free himself from the glass, wanting to close his eyes but finding them frozen open and unblinking, able only to water with tears, he watched and relived the most horrifying experience of his life.

His father was standing behind a bright photographer's light set upon a tripod. He was dressed in nothing but a leather G-string with studded chains hanging from it. Tied to a cot in front of the lamp was a young naked woman, blood streaming from her nose, mouth, and nipples, which were pierced with safety pins. And huddled in the corner behind the chair was Bill himself, age seven.

It all came back to him in a sickening series of flashbacks. His father had come home early from work one summer day and told his mother he was taking Billy to the playground. Bill remembered being excited—it was rare that his father took time off from work just to be with him.

But in the car he had become nervous, sensing that something was wrong. There was a strange odor in the car, a sour human-sweat smell tinged with something else. He had looked in the back of the station wagon and noticed some stained rags that seemed to be the source of the odor.

"Leave those alone and sit down," his father had ordered, his voice strange, almost mechanical sounding. That was when Bill noticed they had gone past the playground.

"You missed it," he said teasingly to his father, who did not answer. "Dad, you missed the playground."

His father took a long time to answer, and Bill was just about to repeat himself when his father said, "Don't worry about it."

That was all.

Bill started to ask where they were going, but didn't. Something about the look on his father's face, a faraway yet stern look, and the way he was gripping the wheel, hands white-knuckled, stopped him.

Bill began to get nervous when they passed out of the town limits and into the countryside. Eventually he summoned enough courage to ask his dad where they were going but got no response. Several miles out of town, his dad turned the station wagon down a dirt road that ran for many miles through dense woods. At the end of the road was what looked like an abandoned farmhouse.

Ignoring Bill's questions, his father got out of the car and roughly dragged him to the cellar storm door at the back of the ramshackle house. Despite Bill's objections and struggles against entering the cellar, his father forced him into the darkness, closing and locking the door behind them. He stood shivering in the damp blackness as his father left him, moving off out of sight into the cellar's darkness.

Bill whimpered, crying softly for his dad to come back, when a chilling moan came out of the darkness followed by a whispered plea: "Help me!"

Bill was about to turn tail and run when a blinding bright light came on, dazzling him. When his vision returned, he found himself in the room he was now dreaming about.

Aghast at the sight of the tortured girl and his father's strange apparel, the adult Bill tried to push away from the glass again but could not. He knew what was coming and did not want to watch. He was helpless to do anything else.

"Come here, Billy-boy," his father commanded, stepping from behind the photographer's lamp.

Billy, who had retreated, cowering, to the wall, shook his head.

"I said, come here!" his father demanded.

"I want to go home, Daddy," Billy whimpered.

"If you don't come over here right now, you'll never go home again!" his father threatened. The tone of his voice and the look on his face told little Billy that he meant it. Reluctantly, he went to his father, trying not to look at the frightened, pleading look in the girl's eyes.

His father positioned him in front of the cot, adjusted the light to shine more directly on his son, then went to the camera and began focusing it. He took a picture, and the flash hurt Billy's eyes.

"Take off your clothes," his father commanded as he took another picture of Billy next to the girl tied to the cot.

Billy didn't want to. He wanted to run and hide, but he was too afraid of his father to do so. His father was changed, was not the man he loved as his daddy. He had become something else, something horrible—he had become a monster. Billy could see it in his eyes and in the terribly distorted features of his face.

With trembling hands and tears streaming down his face, Billy removed his clothing while his father snapped picture after picture of him.

"Now get on top of her, Billy-boy," his father ordered when he was naked.

"I don't want to, Daddy," Billy protested, sniffling.

His father came forward quickly and grabbed him roughly. He picked his son up, shook him hard, and put him on top of the bound naked girl.

"You do what I tell you to. This is very important to me, you hear?" He continued shaking Billy as he yelled. "There is a man who will pay a lot of money for these pictures, so you do what I say or else I'll give you to the man and he'll take *you* away and *torture* you and you'll never see home or your mother or me again. Do you understand?"

Billy started crying. His father slapped him hard, bringing a ringing noise to his ears.

"Stop your sniveling, Billy-boy. You hear me?" His father raised his hand to strike Billy again. Billy cowered on top of the girl, stifling his tears with great effort.

"That's better," his father said, returning to his camera. "Now lie between her legs."

Billy did as he was told and his father snapped more pictures. He repositioned Billy several more times, making his son bury his face between the girl's legs, straddle her face, and pull on the pins through her punctured nipples, taking pictures of every scene while Billy tried not to hear the moans and screams of pain the girl let out.

"You like it, don't you, Billy-boy?" his father asked repeatedly, chuckling each time.

Inside the camera, hearing the words that had been spoken by Wilbur Clayton in his dream, made the adult Bill remember what had gone on inside his young mind throughout the ordeal. He remembered withdrawing deep inside himself until the things his father was making him do didn't seem to be happening to him at all.

Until the final scene.

His father went to a box on a table in the corner of the cellar. He came back with a long butcher knife and placed it in Billy's hand. Billy dropped it, and his father slapped him so hard he knocked him off the cot and onto the floor.

Billy lay there dazed and crying soundlessly, unable to catch his breath, unable to move. His father picked him up and placed him back on the girl. He tried to place the knife in Billy's hand again, but Billy was shaking so badly he dropped it. His father picked the knife up and put it in Billy's hand again, squeezing the boy's fingers around the handle so hard he cried out in pain. He put Billy's other hand on the handle as well and positioned his son's arms so that the knife was raised over the girl's chest as if to strike.

"Stay still," his father ordered.

Billy closed his eyes so that he didn't have to look at the terror in the girl's eyes. His father took a few more pictures, then paused. He seemed about to say something, then changed his mind. He went over to Billy, put his hands over his son's around the knife, and without warning plunged the blade between the girl's breasts. Blood spurted from the screaming girl and the child and adult Bill added their screams to hers as his father hurried back to his camera to get it all on film. All three victims of his father's madness lost consciousness in the blinding strobe of the camera's flash.

64

A banging noise woke Ivy from a deep, grief-exhausted sleep. For a moment, in that sleepy disoriented stage of initial waking, he thought his mother was in the kitchen, hammering a frozen ice-cube tray against a counter as she had often done. That thought faded quickly when he remembered his loss of two nights before.

His mother was dead. She wasn't in the kitchen, she'd never be in the kitchen again. The banging sound came again, and he knew it was someone at the door. He'd spent the last two days mostly sleeping, withdrawing from the grief that waited to engulf him. Groggily, with fresh tears in his eyes, Ivy got out of his mother's bed so as not to wake the still-sleeping Henry and started for the kitchen.

He froze at the bedroom door, coming fully awake. No one *ever* came to visit him and his mother. So who could be knocking at the door? There was only one answer that he could think of—people from child welfare or the police come to take him to a foster home, or worse, to an orphanage. He'd read enough Charles Dickens novels to know that he'd rather die than go to an orphanage. And he'd seen on TV and read in the papers enough about child abuse to know that he didn't want to go to some foster home either, where strangers who neither loved him nor cared about him would be in control of his life. Not to mention the fact that Henry would be taken away from him and sent to the pound, where he'd more than likely be put to sleep.

Ivy crept through the living room until he could see the kitchen door without being seen himself. Anxiety tightened his chest and throat muscles when he saw a police officer's head and shoulders framed in the glass of the door.

He ran back to his mother's room, scooped the just-waking Henry off the bed, and frantically tried to think of someplace to hide. From the kitchen he heard a key rattling in the lock and the door opening.

"Hello?" called a male voice. "Hello? Ivy Delacroix?" the voice asked hesitantly, as if reading his name from a piece of paper.

Being as quiet as possible, Ivy crept to the closet and pushed his way through his mother's clothes—the scent of her so strong in them he wanted to burst into tears at the memories they invoked—and scrunched himself and Henry down into the rear right corner. There was a pile of old dresses on the floor that he pulled over himself and his dog to further conceal them. He breathed shallowly, stroking Henry in the darkness and praying that the dog would not whimper, whine, or bark and give their hiding place away.

He strained to hear and was rewarded by movement in the living room. Again the male voice called out to him. Henry growled deep in his throat, and Ivy immediately grabbed the dog's mouth, keeping his jaws clamped.

A different male voice called his name again, sounding closer to his mother's room. Footsteps approached the closet door and Ivy held his breath. The door opened; clothes were shifted back and forth on the rack before the door closed again.

"Well, the kid ain't here," the voice said, retreating from the room.

"Maybe a relative or neighbor came and got him when they heard what happened to his mother," the other male voice answered. "Let's go."

Ivy held his breath until he heard the kitchen door close, then let it out in a long heart-wrenching sob. After several minutes of giving in to grief, he gathered himself together and crept out of the closet with Henry still clenched in his arms.

It wasn't safe there anymore, he knew. He had to get out of the apartment and find someplace else to live—someplace warm. Going to his bedroom, he packed his shoulder bag with as much clothes as it could hold, leaving room for food at the top. He went to the kitchen and filled the pack the rest of the way with cans of dog food, a jar of peanut butter, and two cans of Chef Boyardee ravioli.

65

Once at the railroad yard he realizes that hopping a train in his condition will be impossible. The first one to rumble through, shortly after his arrival, does not slow down at all. Not that it is moving at any great speed, but his splinted ankle prevents him from running to catch it.

He breaks into the dilapidated, abandoned depot, finding a dry corner with the roof still intact overhead. He tries to make himself comfortable, propping his leg on a pile of broken wood and brick, but the cold is brutal, the coldest it has been since the last time he was at the railroad yard. The cold makes his leg throb with pain, and the pain clouds his thoughts, keeping him from figuring out what to do and making him frustrated and angry.

It is in the dead of the following night that the solution to his predicament comes to him. He is awakened by a train passing by and hobbles to a hole in the wall to peer out at it. Between the broken-down depot and the passing train, there is a large trash bag lying on the near track. At first he thinks it is a body, but when he realizes what it is, the idea strikes him.

Making use of the darkness, he wastes no time. He does not know when the next train will be through, or whether another one will pass through tonight, but he knows he must be ready.

Lady Luck shows her helping hand right away when he

finds a tattered, discarded coat in the rubble around the depot. He uses it to wrap around the trash bag and arranges it on the tracks the last train passed by on. There are four sets of tracks through the yard, but the other three are in a state of decay and disrepair with broken ties caked with ice and snow. He figures they aren't used at all.

It doesn't take him long to fix the fake body on the tracks. He hobbles up the line a hundred yards and turns to view his work. It is nothing but a dark lump on the tracks, but it is noticeable, and with the train lights it will be visible enough.

Now comes the hardest part, waiting in the cold for another train to come by. He would prefer to wait in the relative shelter of the depot, but he knows he has to be as close to the tracks as he can get. He lies on the cold ground next to the rail line, staring at the cloud-covered sky and rubbing the deadly bulge in his pants. It begins snowing lightly, and he passes the time catching snowflakes on his tongue, trying to ignore the increasing pain the cold brings to his leg.

He hears the train before he sees it. He tenses, rising to a sitting position, looking up the tracks for the lights of the approaching engine.

Something is wrong. His ears tell him first, then his eyes. The sound of the train is coming from behind him. He twists around, causing excruciating pain to his leg, and curses softly, seeing the glow of the train lights coming from the wrong direction, heading south toward New York rather than north.

He must move quickly to remove the fake body from the track, then throw himself to the ground beside it so as not to be seen.

After the train has passed, he gets up slowly. It is snowing harder now, portending a major storm. The eastern sky is showing the bleak gray light of dawn and he decides to wait another day. He drags the makeshift body to the de-

pot, where it makes a fairly comfortable bed, and sleeps
fitfully on it throughout the day.

It is still snowing when he wakes. Seeing how deep it is
outside, piled even higher in drifts across the tracks, he
knows there will be no trains that night. He is cold and
hungry, but he can deal with that. What is harder to deal
with is the intense pain in his leg. He allows himself two of
the Tylenol and codeine pills the boy gave him, refusing to
let them remind him of Tommy and bring back his doubts
about how he left the boy. That is not important now.

The pills help him sleep through the night and well into
the next day. He is awakened by the sound of a plow diesel
clearing the tracks. Soon afterward a train rumbles
through, heading north.

He waits for darkness before returning the "body" to the
tracks. Again he places himself fifty yards down from it,
lying in the deep, freezing snow, and waits. Shortly after
midnight he hears a train approaching, feels it rattle the
ground, and this time it is heading in the right direction.
He closes his eyes against the flying snow as the diesel
roars by, followed by the rattling cacophony of a long line
of freight cars. He opens one eye, praying to Lady Luck for
the train to stop. Just when he thinks it won't, he hears the
shriek of the brakes as the train slows down.

He sits up, scanning the passing cars quickly. The train
screeches to a halt. Three cars away he sees what he needs,
a freight car with its cargo door partly open. He hears
voices and glances to see two engineers disembarking from
the diesel to inspect the "body" on the tracks. He gets to
his feet and hobbles as quickly as he can to the open cargo
door. He looks over his shoulder several times, praying to
Lady Luck that he won't be seen.

His prayers are answered. He makes it to the freight car.
The cargo door is open just enough for him to squeeze
through after using its edge as leverage to hoist himself off

the ground. He pays a big price in renewed pain as he pulls his leg inside, but it's worth it.

The train begins to move after several minutes, and through the haze of pain that envelops him, he strokes himself and fantasizes about the deeds ahead.

66

 Bill Gage finished telling the psychiatrist about his dream and wiped tears from his face with his good arm. He stared at the floor and at the Van Gogh print on the wall—anywhere but into her eyes.

"And you're sure the dream is an actual memory and not just a dream?" the psychiatrist asked after a few moments.

"Yes," Bill answered quietly. "When I woke from it, I remembered everything clearly. It wasn't just a dream."

"How did you feel when you woke?"

"I cried," Bill admitted after a moment's hesitation, a lump in his throat. "I felt a sense of relief, too. I mean, I was glad I remembered. It explains a lot of my behavior."

"How do you mean?"

"I think the incident had a lot to do with the way I've acted over the years. My fanatic dedication to law enforcement, my alcoholism, my obsession with freeing myself of my father's ghost. I think it was the main motivator in my killing Wilbur Clayton when I didn't have to. I thought I had exorcised my father with that act, but my relapse showed me I hadn't. I think now that the real reason I killed Wilbur wasn't because he was like my father; it was because he was like me, and I wanted to kill that part of me that those bad things had happened to, just as they had happened to Wilbur."

"You say 'those bad things.' Have you recalled any other, similar incidents?"

Bill thought a moment. "No. I don't think it ever happened again, but I'm not really sure. And to tell the truth, I'm not sure if I want, or need, to know. I think it was a one-time thing. He needed the pictures that one time to sell to someone for a lot of money. That's what he said." Bill paused. "That makes me think he must have been involved with NAMBLA—the North American Man/Boy Love Alliance. They're an organization that believes child pornography is acceptable. Especially concerning his threat that he knew men who would come and take me away and I'd never be heard from again."

"And how do you feel now?"

"Okay, I guess. Like I said, I feel a lot of relief. I'm glad I got this out. It feels like a weight has been lifted off me. I think this will help me stay clean and sober. I think I can now, finally, put the past behind me and get on with my life."

The psychiatrist tapped her pencil against her teeth a few times. "It may not be that easy. I think you're going to need continued counseling. Just because you've faced the past doesn't mean everything will be okay now."

Bill sighed. "Maybe. Hell, I know you're probably right, but I'm being discharged tomorrow, and The Walking Death killer is still out there. I've got to help find him and protect my family. I've got to put all this behind me now, at least for a while."

The psychiatrist asked him if he wanted to talk about Kelsey's death and what had happened with Alex, but he declined, feigning tiredness. She gave him the phone number of one of her colleagues in Worcester for him to call when he got home and reasserted her opinion that he should continue counseling.

Bill thanked her and left the office. He crumpled the card with the number on it and tossed it into the nearest trash can.

67

Ivy walked quickly, Henry cradled in his arms, and stayed close to the inside edge of the sidewalk. He kept his eyes peeled for police cars, and when one went by soon after he left his house, he ducked behind a hedge until it had passed.

He didn't know where he was going, hadn't had time to figure that out yet. His main concern had been to get out of the apartment before the cops or a social worker returned.

Ivy heard a car approaching and turned to see another police cruiser coming up the street. It seemed to slow down by his tenement house, but he could've imagined it. He quickly ran into the alley next to Watson's Market and ducked behind the trash barrels.

The cop car pulled up and stopped at the end of the alley. Ivy tensed, ready to run out the other end. A policeman got out of the cruiser, looked around—his gaze passing quickly over the alley—and went into the market. Ivy rose slowly, waiting to be sure the policeman wasn't coming right out again, before quickly running out the opposite end of the alley.

They're searching for me, Ivy thought. *I've got to find someplace to hide, and fast.* Staying outdoors anywhere was out of the question. It was still too cold, and the sky was a leaden gray, heavy with snow clouds. As he hurried down the hill toward downtown Crocker, flurries began to dance from the heavens.

An idea came to him. What about the cop, Bill Gage? Though he hadn't seen him in months, the guy owed him. After all, Ivy had lied for the guy at the inquisition into Wilbur Clayton's death. Ivy had been in the tunnel under the hospital, having been chased there by Wilbur Clayton, and had seen Bill Gage kill Wilbur in cold blood. Gage *was* a cop, but he did owe Ivy a huge favor, and Ivy was just desperate enough to cash in on it.

He stopped at a phone booth outside a gas station near the Putnam Street Bridge and looked Bill Gage up in the phone book. He found the address and felt lucky that he knew where the street was.

"It's going to be okay now, Henry," he said to his dog. He set off across the bridge. "This guy's going to help us. He's *got* to help us."

The storm was in full swing by the time Ivy reached Bill Gage's street. Clouds of snow swirled and danced in the glow of the streetlights, which had been turned on early in the storm's gloom.

Ivy walked along the sidewalk, Henry zipped up inside his coat, his furry head sticking out at the top. He walked slowly, checking the house numbers, looking for 77, Bill Gage's house. Near the middle of the street, he found it and was disappointed. The house was dark. It looked as if no one was home.

He walked up the steps to the front door and rang the bell. He waited, but no lights came on, and he could hear nothing from inside. He rang the bell again, silently praying for Bill Gage to answer the door.

Nothing.

He turned away and looked at the sky. The snow was falling heavily. Several inches had already accumulated on the ground. Where was he going to go now?

He looked back at the house and wondered if he could

break in. The sound of a car door opening on the street behind him distracted him. Parked opposite the house was a dark sedan with two men inside. The one on the passenger side got out.

"Hey, kid. What are you doing there?"

Cops! Ivy leapt down the stairs and ran up the street. The cop tried to cross the road and nab him but slipped on the snow-slick surface and fell.

"Hey, kid! Stop! Come back here!" he yelled and followed it with a stream of curses when he hit the ground.

That was an unmarked police car, Ivy realized. Had they followed him there? No, that couldn't be. He would have seen them, and they most certainly would have grabbed him before he made it to Bill Gage's house.

Then what were they doing there?

Maybe they have the house under surveillance because they expected me to show up there. He immediately dismissed the thought; they hadn't called him by name, which meant they didn't know who he was and weren't expecting him. Whatever the reason, he knew he had to keep moving just in case they came after him or sent another car out to nab him.

He ran to the corner and around it, stopping to look back. They didn't seem to be following him, further reassuring him that they weren't there waiting for him. That was good, but he still had to find a warm dry place to hide.

Again he thought of breaking into Bill Gage's house. Could he do it without the cops seeing him? Normally, probably not, but with the storm raging, he had a chance. He could sneak around and approach the house from the rear and break in without the cops out front seeing him, couldn't he? It was worth a shot.

You'll get caught, a voice inside warned him. He figured the voice was right, but he was too cold, tired, and hungry to care anymore. He had to try it. Even if he did get caught, at least the cops would take him someplace warm.

Jail would be better than spending the night out in this storm. Even an orphanage would be better. He could always escape later.

He decided to go for it.

After ducking into the driveway of a house on the street behind Bill Gage's, he made his way via backyards to Gage's house. He was thankful for the heavy snow, which reduced visibility and muffled any noise he made.

He paused at a low hedge separating Gage's yard from the one next door. He couldn't see the unmarked police car from there. He found a hole in the hedge and crept through, careful not to snag his backpack. Everything looked quiet. Staying low, he scurried to the rear of the house and flattened himself against it. He sidled along to the corner near the driveway and peered around. He could barely see the police car and the men inside but couldn't tell if they had seen him. There was no movement that he could see, no appearance that they were coming out after him, but he decided to wait and be sure.

He counted slowly to one hundred three times, waiting to be sure the coast was clear. At three hundred he checked the cop car again. Nothing had changed, They were still inside.

Ivy went to the back door. It was locked, which didn't surprise him. There were no first-floor windows low enough for him to reach. But there were cellar windows.

He went to the cellar window nearest the driveway and pushed on it. It wouldn't budge. Looking through the glass, he could see that it was securely latched. He went to the other window at the opposite corner of the house, but it too was locked.

"What do we do now?" he muttered to Henry, who had fallen asleep inside his coat.

Break the glass!

He thought about it for a long time, afraid the noise would attract the cops out front. But maybe the snow would take care of that. He had to try. Scooping snow with both hands, he piled it thickly against the window. Sitting in the spot he'd cleared, he raised his foot, counted to three, and kicked the snow-covered window.

Nothing happened.

He kicked again. Nothing. He tried again and again and on the fourth kick he was rewarded. There was a dull crack and his snow-covered foot went through the window. The noise wasn't loud, but to his nervous ears it sounded like an explosion.

He got up and returned to the corner of the house to check on the police car. Nothing had changed. He went back to the cellar window and cleared away the snow, picking the shards of glass from the wood of the window frame. He reached in and turned the latch. The window opened easily. He slipped off his backpack and pushed it through, hearing it tumble to the floor but unable to see where it had landed in the utter darkness of the cellar.

Taking Henry, who was awake and whimpering now due to being jostled about, from his jacket, Ivy went feet-first through the window, holding on to the sill with his free hand for as long as he could before dropping into the darkness.

68

He sleeps fitfully on the train, waking when it slows, crawling to the door to try to determine where he is, dozing off again when the train moves on. He spends two days this way, in a half-awake, half-asleep fog. He awakens clearheaded and in a panic on the morning of the third day, certain he has traveled too far.

The train has stopped; there is no thrum of the engine beneath him. Hearing voices, he goes to the door and looks out cautiously. There is activity in the railroad yard. Fork-lifts are unloading from a freight train on the far tracks.

He looks around for a sign, some indication of where he is, but there is none that he can see. He scans the terrain beyond the railroad yard. A forest with mountains in the distance tells him he's not in Massachusetts—the mountains are too big. Must be New Hampshire, or even Maine.

He curses himself and Lady Luck, then takes the latter curses back. It's not her fault. If he hadn't been in so much pain, he wouldn't have needed to take pills the boy had given him, and he would have been able to keep better track of his location.

Now he must wait until darkness falls to leave the train and either find another train heading south, or some other way to get back to Crocker.

Night seems to take forever to arrive. He whiles the hours away leaning on the cane and pacing the length of the boxcar, exercising his leg, trying to limber it up from the stiffness that settled into it while he slept on the train. At dusk he lets himself out of the car carefully, checking the yard to be sure it is clear. Testing his leg, he sets off at as fast a pace as he can for the lights of a nearby town.

Outside the railroad yard he comes upon a major highway that circles the town. A road sign tells him the next exit is for Dublin, New Hampshire. He was right in his guess that he is in the Granite State.

He hides in the deep snow behind some bushes near the highway, watching a steady stream of night traffic pass by. He contemplates what to do. He realizes now that hopping the freight train was a mistake. It was too hard to determine where he was and could have been fatal in his condition if he had tried to jump from the moving train when it passed through Massachusetts.

No, the train is out. He must find a more direct route to Crocker, which is less than an hour away by car. He watches the traffic go by awhile longer and knows that a car is the best way to travel now. Limping, he crosses the highway during a lull in traffic, and heads for the town of Dublin.

69

Bill Gage greeted Chief Albert and the two FBI agents in Dr. McRegan's office. The doctor had been relieved of her duties by the clinic's board of trustees in the wake of the murders and her handling of the situation. The new director was a short, fat, owlish man by the name of Dr. Krimpe, who was only too willing to accommodate Bill in anything he needed. Bill suspected those orders had come from the trustees, who were worried about a lawsuit.

The thought of suing Birch Mountain Hospital had crossed Bill's mind several times since his confrontation with Alex. A lot of what had happened immediately following that incident was hazy. He barely remembered being bandaged and carried to one of the clinic's four-wheel vehicles for a bumpy ride off the mountain to nearby Vermont State Hospital, where he underwent emergency surgery.

The day after his operation two members of the clinic's board of trustees had visited him, apologizing and offering their condolences, telling him of Dr. McRegan's dismissal. They also told him that the clinic would pick up the tab for his surgery and stay at the hospital and pay any insurance deductible owed for his stay at the clinic itself.

The trustees had been very relieved when the doctor treating Bill came in and told them he thought Bill should remain at Vermont State Hospital until his discharge date from the clinic. But Bill had burst their bubble by insisting that he be allowed to return to Birch Mountain to recuperate where he could also review his case files on The Walking Death case.

There was another reason Bill had wanted to go back to the clinic, one he didn't tell the trustees or the doctor. It had been while he was under surgery that he'd had the dream in which he remembered what his father had done to him. The memory had shaken him deeply, more deeply than he would ever let anyone know, and though he hated to admit it, he knew he had to talk to someone about it and confront it. He knew the best person for that was Dr. Laura Lorenzo, the psychiatrist who had been treating him all along. He had developed a good relationship with her and trusted her. He felt secure telling her just about anything, and felt better now after having talked to her.

Of course the trustees had given in, willing to do anything to please him, and the next day he had been returned to Birch Mountain by ambulance. The patients and staff had greeted him with a party that had touched him, all the more so because Kelsey, Joel, and Sheila were not there and he felt responsible for their deaths.

Now it was discharge day. The FBI agents had been in and out of the hospital all week conducting interviews in their investigation to determine whether Alex had been at all connected to The Walking Death. They had come to the conclusion that all had happened just as Bill said it had and that Alex was suffering from a psychotic delusion. When he wasn't in sessions with Dr. Lorenzo, Bill had spent the week hunched in front of the microfiche machine poring over the case files from his days with the state police. Surprisingly, he discovered that the urge to drink and drug diminished the more he worked, rather than the other way around. Bill put it down to the fact that he had finally put his faith in a higher power and every morning asked God to keep him sober for that day. It was working, and that was all he cared about.

He'd come up with a dozen names of possible suspects, and each had been checked out and eliminated by the FBI as being either still in prison, known to be far away from the scenes of the murders, or dead. The latter surprised Bill. Of the twelve suspects he had uncovered, five were dead. Three had been child molesters or rapists and had been killed in prison, a common fate for that type of criminal.

Bill had expected George to send one of his patrol officers to pick him up today and was surprised when George came himself, accompanied by agents Danvers and Willis. The three men sat in chairs around McRegan's desk while Bill sat behind it.

"We've got a problem in The Walking Death case," George Albert said. Agent Danver took a folded newspaper from his briefcase and tossed it on the desk. Bill opened it and read the headline:

FBI STALKS "DEATHWALKER" SERIAL KILLER!

"Deathwalker?" Bill asked, confused.

"As usual the media screwed up the information they got, or maybe they just made up the name because it makes a better headline," Agent Danvers said. "That's not our problem. Our problem is that we have a leak in this case. Someone very close to it has decided to feed information to the media. Read the story. You'll see that except for calling the perp 'Deathwalker,' their information is pretty accurate."

Bill read the story, feeling a chill when it described him and his family as targets of "Deathwalker" and reprinted portions of the letters he had received. He became angry when the story went on to say that though he had once been famous as the cop who'd tracked down and killed the Video Killer, Wilbur Clayton, he was now in a rehab clinic, location unknown, recovering from a drug and alcohol problem brought on by his involvement in the Video Killer case and by the facts coming to light about his own father. His anger turned to rage when his family members' names were given.

"I don't believe this!" Bill said through clenched teeth. "Where the hell did they get this information?"

"That's what we'd like to know," Danvers said in an accusatory tone.

"You think I leaked this?" Bill asked incredulously. "You fucking idiot!" he exploded a second later. He stood, looking ready to lunge across the desk and pummel the FBI man.

"You're the only loose cannon in this investigation," Danvers replied matter-of-factly.

"You must have shit for brains, pal," Bill shot back. "If I was leaking info to the press, do you think I would tell them I was in fucking rehab with a drug problem? You think I would give them the names and descriptions of my family?"

"You might to cover your ass," the agent said dryly, a goading smile on his face.

"And what motivation would I have for doing this, bright boy?"

The agent rubbed his thumb and forefinger together in the age-old sign for money and his smirk widened. "Moolah. Let's face it, you're a drug addict, and addicts will do anything to get money to support their habit."

"Fuck you!" Bill thundered. Despite his injured shoulder, he started around the desk toward Danvers, who stood quickly, ready to go at it with him. George came out of his chair like a shot and grabbed Bill while the other FBI agent restrained Danvers.

"Take it easy, Bill," George placated him.

"No! I won't take it easy. This asshole can't come in here accusing me of this shit! If he and his whole fucking bureau didn't have their heads so far up their asses, they'd know I didn't leak this, and they wouldn't be wasting time with it. If you guys were as good as you think you are, this perp would have been behind bars after the first murder," Bill shouted, pointing his finger at the FBI agent.

"And if you weren't so fucked up, you might have been able to finger this guy for us, since it's obvious you know who he is," Agent Danvers gave back as good as he got. "But maybe you don't want to do that, huh? Maybe you know who the perp is, but you figured you'd get your name in the papers again and grab some of the limelight when you reveal who he is. Then you'll look like a fucking hero again, won't you?"

Bill lunged at the fed and it was all George could do to hold him back.

"Get him the fuck out of here," George yelled at Willis, the other agent, who grabbed Danvers's arm and tried to pull him to the door. Danvers resisted and shrugged him off. He straightened his jacket, gave Bill a look of undisguised disgust, and calmly walked out of the office, Willis trailing behind him.

"Calm down, Bill," George said when they'd left. Bill walked to the wall and punched it hard enough to knock a glass-framed print by Degas to the floor, shattering its glass. "Do you believe that guy?" Bill asked, ignoring the mess at his feet. He looked at George. "You don't believe . . ." He didn't have to finish the sentence.

"No I don't," George said, cutting him off. "You should know better than to even ask. I told them you didn't leak the info, but Danvers wanted to confront you himself, yank your chain just to be sure. I don't think he believes it himself, but he's frustrated and just the type of asshole who looks for someone else to blame when things don't go right for him.

"Nothing's been heard of The Walking Death, or 'Deathwalker,' for weeks now. He's just vanished. No killings, no letters, no trace. Danvers is afraid that this guy is a standard killer after all, and this cycle of murder is over. If that's true, it could be months, even years, before he kills again and we can get a lead on him."

Bill took a deep breath and let it out slowly. He had to remember not to let his temper get the best of him. He had to remember the danger signs to relapse: H.A.L.T. Don't get too Hungry, Angry, Lonely, or Tired. Though he didn't feel the urge to drink right now, he could easily see it steamrolling over him if he let things bother him too much. His motto had to be, as an old friend from the state police used to say, "Don't sweat the small stuff and remember it's all small stuff."

"I don't think so," Bill answered, calmer. "He's not a run-of-the-mill serial killer, if there is such a thing. He doesn't fit the standard profile. His motivation is very clear—revenge against me. He's not moved to kill for any other reason. He has a definite plan. This lull in his activities may be a part of that plan. Either that, or something unexpected has happened to him. Maybe he got hit by a car, or had an accident, or he came down with the goddamned flu and is holed up somewhere getting better. Who knows? I do know that if he's not dead, he's still out there, and he won't stop until he can get his revenge on me, for whatever twisted reasons he has. He wants me, he wants my family—he wants to see us suffer."

George looked at his friend. "I learned a long time ago not to doubt your instincts, Bill, and I won't start now. Of course, I can't say the same for our government friends. If you and your family weren't personally involved in this, I'd say fuck 'em, let them figure it out for themselves. But we can't do that. They think, and I have to honestly agree, that you know who this guy is. It's just a matter of jogging your memory."

"I know," Bill said. He picked the newspaper up from the desk and looked at the headline again, mouthing the name *Deathwalker*. He felt a twinge of familiarity concerning the name, but when he tried to pinpoint it, all he could come up with was *Skywalker,* as in Luke Skywalker from *Star Wars,* one of the twins' favorite movies.

That must be it, he thought, but in the back of his mind he really didn't believe so, and didn't let it go.

70

Behind a noisy country music bar, he finds what he needs—a battered old pickup truck with the keys under the floor mat. He helps himself to it, and within the hour he's crossing the state border and heading into Massachusetts.

Back at the bar, when the owner of the truck discovers his truck missing, he believes it is his bitch of a wife who has taken it in retaliation for his being out getting drunk with the boys. The truck is so old and beat up it never crosses his mind that it might have been stolen. He proclaims loudly to his drinking buddies that if the bitch wants to play games, he will too, and vows to stay out all weekend getting really fucked up.

71

Getting out of the cellar proved to be a major endeavor for Ivy. It was pitch-black in there, causing him to stumble over unseen things on the floor and bump into the water heater and support posts in his effort to find the stairs leading up to the first floor. Just finding his knapsack on the floor took a good ten minutes.

Feeling his way along like a blind man in the dark, he cursed himself for not packing a flashlight.

He made a blind search of the rear of the cellar first, stumbling often and falling to his knees twice. Henry, whom he had returned to his coat, whimpered constantly and barked when Ivy fell. In the dark of the cellar, each bark sounded humongously loud to Ivy. He froze on his knees, barely breathing, straining to hear any sound of the cops outside entering the house.

His search of the rear of the basement proved futile (though he couldn't be sure that he wasn't just going around in circles). He worked his way carefully around the furnace and started on the front of the cellar. Near the left front corner, he stumbled over a wooden step and sighed with relief. Feeling each step in front of him with his hands, he climbed to a narrow doorway at the top and let himself out of the cellar.

He closed the door carefully behind him and stood listening and looking around. There was more light up here from the streetlamps outside shining through the semicircle of glass in the front door. He saw that he was in a hallway. Next to the cellar door was a long table with a mirror on it and a coatrack on the wall opposite it.

The only sounds in the house were the ticking of a clock and an occasional ping and click that Ivy surmised came from the refrigerator in the kitchen. Slowly and carefully he started walking down the hallway.

He came to an open archway on the right and discovered the living room. He started in but pulled back quickly. The windows in the living room looked out the front of the house, and the shades weren't drawn. He continued a short way to the kitchen on the left. He was glad to see the windows here were on the side and rear of the house.

He put his backpack on the kitchen table and unzipped his coat, freeing Henry, who immediately did his puppy squat and piddled on the kitchen floor. Ivy cursed softly but couldn't really blame the pup. The poor thing had been cooped up in his jacket a long time. He was just thankful Henry hadn't peed on him. He retrieved some paper towels from a dispenser near the sink and cleaned it up. Next he searched the kitchen drawers until he found a manual can opener. There was an electric one on the counter next to the microwave, but he didn't want to risk the noise.

He fished a can of dog food from his pack, opened it, and holding his nose against the disgusting odor of it, dumped it onto a small saucer that was in the sink. Henry attacked the food voraciously, spilling some of it on the floor, which Ivy cleaned up with more paper towels. While his dog ate, Ivy checked the refrigerator and was surprised to find it empty except for a half dozen eggs and some processed American cheese. It made him wonder if Bill Gage even lived there anymore. He took the jar of peanut butter from his knapsack and using his fingers, scooped it out and had his own supper.

Their meager meal over, Ivy cleaned the dog's dish and left it in the sink exactly as he'd found it. He picked Henry up and proceeded to investigate the rest of the house. What he found didn't exactly confirm that Bill Gage no longer lived in the house, but it didn't dispel the idea either. The closets and bureau drawers in what he rightly guessed to be the girls' room were nearly devoid of clothing, but not completely. Some clothes also seemed to be missing from the master bedroom. The nursery had next to nothing left in it, as did another bedroom which he figured was a guest room and rarely used. The upstairs and downstairs bathrooms were still stocked with towels and washcloths, but the medicine cabinets were nearly devoid of the usual toiletries kept there.

It looks like he took his family on a trip or a vacation, Ivy thought. Well, that was fine. So much the better. It meant he didn't have to worry about confronting Bill Gage right away and risk having the cop turn him over to the child-welfare people. It meant he and Henry had a warm place to stay for a while.

The only thing that still bothered him was the un-marked police car out front. Would the cops put the house under surveillance like that if Bill Gage was just away on vacation? He didn't think so.

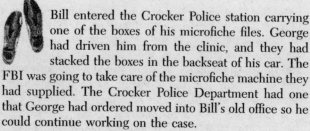Bill entered the Crocker Police station carrying one of the boxes of his microfiche files. George had driven him from the clinic, and they had stacked the boxes in the backseat of his car. The FBI was going to take care of the microfiche machine they had supplied. The Crocker Police Department had one that George had ordered moved into Bill's old office so he could continue working on the case.

Two patrolmen carried the rest of the boxes in and stacked them next to the microfiche machine. George came in after they'd left and closed the door. Bill sat at his old desk. The chief tossed the latest edition of the *Crocker Sentinel* on the desk. The headline blared:

DEATHWALKER SERIAL KILLER STALKS LOCAL COP TURNED DRUG ADDICT!

"Jesus!" Bill swore.

"Sorry," George commented. "I figured it was better if I showed you this now."

Bill scanned the article. "For Christ's sake, George, they not only give Evelyn's and the kids' names, but they've printed her address, too."

"I know. But I've had them moved to the Sheraton Hotel by the airport this morning. They're under guard there. I've got my men and the FBI has a couple of guys staking out her condo. And I've got two men watching your house. Tomorrow the FBI's going to start a stakeout of your place, too. But to tell you the truth, I'm still not sure that we're not just wasting our time. The perp hasn't made a move in over three weeks. I'm really not sure the feds are wrong about him. Maybe he has had his fill for a while. Maybe he just wants to keep you on edge for a few months. I don't know."

"Yeah, but maybe Deathwalker's doing it so we'll let down our guard." Bill paused, surprised at his use of the new name the media had come up with for The Walking Death. Again he felt that sense of familiarity over the name—something about it that seemed to fit the perp more than the name he had chosen for himself, and it was more than just the fact that *Deathwalker* was more catchy than *The Walking Death*. His intuition told him he was onto something, that this feeling was important.

"You think this lull in his activities is on purpose; a diversion?" George asked.

"Why not? Like I said at the clinic, this guy's no ordinary serial killer. His sole purpose is revenge against me. He has a very intricate plan, and I think this just might be part of it. Most serial killers don't kill for a specific reason, nor have a particular goal or plan. They kill when the urge to kill becomes too overwhelming. They might know that certain things set them off, or that they kill certain types of people who remind them of people who've hurt them in the past, but even that is pretty rare. A true serial killer is kind of like a drug addict, or an alcoholic. For one reason or another they commit their first murder and get hooked. They like the taste of it, they like the high it gives them, and the desire for more won't let them go. Like a druggie or a drunk on a binge, they feel powerful, on top of the world, when they're stalking and killing a victim. The rest of their lives might be a shambles, but when they are in the killing mode they can convince themselves that every-thing will be fine. Like the alcoholic and drug addict, they use killing, instead of booze or drugs, to escape the boredom or fear of their daily lives.

"But not this Deathwalker. He's deliberately working at this. I don't think he's a natural killer, but he's working hard at becoming one. It's like they say in AA: some drunks are born that way, others are made. I think this guy has made himself into a serial killer, and I think he's really hooked. Like with the removing the victims' eyes. He didn't remove the eyes of all his victims in the first killing, just the little boy's. He did remove all their teeth. I think he removes the teeth to send me some kind of weird clue as to his identity. But by the second killings he removed all his victims' eyes. That's a standard serial-killer trait; it's common for them to keep mementos of their victims.

"Don't ask me why, but I think he eats the eyes, another common trait for serial killers—eating some part of their victim—and carries the teeth around with him, laughing at me for not being able to figure out the clue to his identity they clearly represent, in his mind at least. The teeth have probably become like a good-luck charm to him.

"I'll tell you this, if he does catch up with me and get his revenge, and escapes, he won't stop killing. He might not have a specific reason to go on, but he will because he likes it now. He's had a taste of the power, and he wants to keep on feasting on it.

"I just find it hard to believe that he's out of the killing mode for a while, the way a regular serial killer would go. He's been too methodical, killing not on urges, but step-by-step. The only thing that would stop him is, like I said before, he had an accident, got sick, or got killed somehow. My gut instinct tells me he's not dead. And I don't think he disappeared deliberately either. The ferociousness of the killings and the wording of his letters tells me this guy is hell-bent on revenge and he can't wait to get it.

His last killing was in Jersey. We don't know where he is now. For all we know, he could already be in Crocker, biding his time and waiting for the right moment to strike, when we're lax, when we least expect it."

George nodded thoughtfully. "Oh, a couple more things I forgot to tell you. Doesn't have anything to do with this. Your girlfriend, Darlene, left town the day after you went into the clinic. She took your grand, too, I guess."

Bill frowned and shrugged. He knew he had waited too long, until just last week, to tell George about Darlene and ask him to try to get his money back. Deep down, he hadn't really expected to see the thousand dollars again.

"And remember Ivy Delacroix?" the chief went on.

"Yeah. The kid who testified for me at the inquest."

"Right. Something terrible has happened. His mother was struck by a drunk driver. Now the kid's disappeared."

"Oh, God!" Bill murmured. "Is she dead?"

73

He takes the long way to Crocker, traveling on Route 13 through Townsend before bad luck strikes again. On a dark stretch of Route 13, just after passing through Townsend Center, the truck runs out of gas. He lets it coast into the parking lot of an abandoned roadside diner, getting just enough roll out of it to hide it behind the building.

Twenty yards down the road is a house, a sign out front proclaiming it is the office of Lussier Real Estate. He goes to it, looks in the windows, but the house is dark, no one home, no car in the garage. No other cars on the dark stretch of road for him to siphon more gas from. There is a short private drive next to the house with another, smaller house, at the end of it, the lights on.

He approaches it carefully, leaning heavily on the cane. Parked out front are two cars, a beat-up white Ford sedan, and a red convertible sports car, the make of which he can't identify. He creeps to the front of the house, where the flickering light of a TV screen shines through a large picture window, and looks inside.

The first thing he sees is the television, reruns of The Wonder Years. The next thing he see is a small kitchenette beyond the living room. A tall, beautiful blond-haired woman with ice-blue eyes is standing at the table next to a man who is sitting. There are candles on the table. The woman is wearing a long, flowing silk robe of a blue that enhances her incredible eyes. She leans over the man and they kiss, long and tenderly, then she sits opposite him and they raise glasses of wine in a toast to each other.

He feels the hard metal bulge in his pants as he stares at the woman. An overwhelming urge to break in and screw the two of them to death just for being so happy and in love comes over him. He fights it. He's too close to Crocker now; too close to the culmination of all his plans to do anything stupid. And siphoning gas from either of the cars or stealing them is out of the question, too. They are parked too close to the house, and he has no hose to siphon with, nothing to put the gas in. Even if the couple is too preoccupied with each other to hear him hot-wire and drive one of the cars away, they will notice it missing too soon for his needs.

Reluctantly he backs away from the window and returns to the highway. The night is cold and his leg is throbbing too much for him to hike the ten miles or so farther to Crocker. A strange feeling comes over him, a feeling of uncertainty. For a long moment he questions the very reality of his being, his very immortality. Breaking his ankle has done this to him, that and the uncertainty about what to do with the boy, Tommy. (*Did I kill him or not? He still doesn't know.*) He tells himself to stop it. Death has no doubts. Death is never uncertain. Death fears nothing and no one.

He knows he must finish the business with the cop as soon as possible. That will restore his confidence. And to do that, he has to take a chance. The chance comes along almost immediately in the form of a semitrailer. He is glad for the new clothing and warm jacket Tommy gave him. He looks like any normal guy whose car has broken down on the road. He sticks out his thumb and the truck slows, brakes squealing, and picks him up.

"Pretty fucking cold to be hitchhiking, buddy," the trucker, a large, beer-bellied, greasy man says when he *climbs awkwardly into the cab, pulling his cane in after him.* "What the hell are you doing way out here this time of night?"

"My car broke down back there. I'm on my way to see an old friend," *he replies, smiling.*

74

Ivy was asleep in the guest room with Henry cuddled in his arms when a noise disturbed his sleep. He woke slowly, unsure of where he was at first. He could hear a car outside, but it wasn't until he heard the front door downstairs opening that it came back to him where he was.

He jumped out of bed with Henry in his arms, his left hand holding the dog's mouth closed so he wouldn't bark. Moving as quietly as possible, he went into the closet, leaving the door open slightly so he could hear.

There were several voices downstairs, one of whose he was sure was Bill Gage's. He heard Bill thanking whoever was with him, and they in turn were telling him they'd be right outside if he needed anything.

Must be the cops in the unmarked car, Ivy thought. He heard the front door close and then noises in the kitchen. Soon after, footsteps came up the stairs and he heard water running in the bathroom.

"Now or never," Ivy whispered to his dog and left the closet. Light from the bathroom spilled into the hallway illuminating his way. He went to the bathroom doorway and looked in at Bill, who was awkwardly brushing his teeth with his left hand.

"Excuse me," Ivy said. Bill Gage literally jumped and let out an involuntary shout, dropping his toothbrush and scaring Ivy as much as Ivy had scared him.

"Ivy! For Christ's sake, you scared the bejeezus out of me," Bill exclaimed and laughed nervously. "What the hell are you doing here?"

Ivy started to speak but was overwhelmed with emotion. In tears, he blurted out, "My mother's dead!"

Before Bill could say a word, Ivy tearfully told what had happened and why he was there, speaking rapidly as if afraid to pause or slow down for fear of not being able to finish. When he was done, he dropped Henry, who whimpered at the fall, and ran into Bill's arms.

"I didn't know where else to go," he sobbed. "I don't want to go to an orphanage."

"It's okay, Ivy. It's okay. Listen to me. I don't know where you got the idea your mother's dead, but she's not. She's alive."

"What?" Ivy cried, unsure that he'd heard Bill correctly.

"That's right. She's alive. She's in the hospital and she's pretty banged up, but she's going to make it."

"But I saw her lying in her own blood on the street. I heard the cop say she was dead."

"Well, he was wrong. She almost did die, but the paramedics revived her and she pulled through. Come on. I'll take you to the hospital and prove it to you. I'm sure she's been worried sick about you."

75

Under the Fifth Street Bridge all is quiet. Nothing much has changed since the last time he was there. A little more snow and ice has gathered at the edge of the river, there is a little more litter—mostly empty bottles of Mad Dog 20/20 and other rotgut brands of dubious vintage that are favorites of the wino population.

The trucker dropped him off in the center of Crocker. Deeming it too late and himself too tired to be going by the cop's house, he headed for the bridge, underneath which he can escape some of the wind, even risk a fire, and plan his next step, the first of which will be to reconnoiter the cop's house in daylight.

He is surprised there is no one in residence under the bridge, but he is also glad for it. He is hungry, hasn't eaten in days, but that is all right. He can live with the hunger, enjoy it even, knowing how good his next meal—after consuming the souls of the cop and his family—will taste.

Huddling against the base of the bridge foundation, he allows himself to doze. The morning will bring the culmination of all his plans.

76

For the first time in months, Bill Gage felt good, really good. He had just left Ivy at the hospital, by his mother's bedside. Watching their tearful reunion had given him a warm feeling. But it had also reminded him of the poor state of his own family relations.

That was going to change. As soon as the Deathwalker case was resolved and he was sure his family was no longer in danger, he was going to straighten things out with Evelyn and his kids. He had talked with Evelyn, Missy, and Devin over the phone—Sara refused—from the hospital a couple of times. On the advice of Chief Albert and the feds he wasn't going to have any contact with them now that he was out of the hospital, for reasons of their own safety.

He stopped his car at a red light on his way back to the station. He'd told Ivy he was going back to do a little more work and would pick him up in a couple of hours. What he really wanted to do, and needed, was to get to an AA meeting, but he was feeling as if his time was getting short, and he needed to spend every spare second on the Deathwalker case. He sat waiting for the light to change and began dwelling on the name *Deathwalker* so intently he didn't notice when the light turned green. The horn of the car behind him stirred him from his reverie and at the same time jolted him into finally recognizing why the name was so familiar.

"Jack Walker!" he said aloud.

He couldn't get back to the station quickly enough. He parked his car crookedly in a space and took the stairs inside two at a time. Once inside, he turned on the microfiche machine and began rapidly scanning the files of his past cases, starting with the year 1969, the last year he had reviewed while in the hospital. He wasn't sure which year he had arrested Walker, but he was certain—had a gut feeling—that Jack Walker was The Walking Death, aka Deathwalker.

It wasn't so much what he had been arrested for—manslaughter for killing a man in a bar fight—but what had happened after he'd been caught. Bill had got information that Jack Walker was working for the Rhode Island mob running drugs into Massachusetts. He offered Walker a deal to turn state's evidence against some of the bigwigs involved, but the deal had fallen through when the DA refused to go along because he didn't think what Walker knew was enough to get convictions. That and the fact that Walker was a bona fide weirdo, always talking about how people could just wake up one morning and be someone, or something, new and different, killed the deal. The guy just didn't have any credibility.

Bill had always been suspicious that there was more to it than that, namely that the DA had been bought off, but he could never prove it. What was important was how Walker had reacted when told the deal was off and that he was going to be prosecuted fully, especially since it had been discovered that Walker had threatened to kill the victim only days before the fight. He was convicted of second-degree murder.

Walker flipped and screamed about how Bill had betrayed him. The last time Bill saw him was in court when Walker was sentenced to fifteen to twenty-five years. Jack

Walker had vowed that he would be reborn, and when he was, he would get revenge on Bill Gage, the man who had betrayed him, no matter how long it took.

In the file from 1977 Bill found the case on Jack Walker. He called George Albert at home and told him he knew the identity of Deathwalker. George remained quiet while Bill filled him in on the particulars of the case but didn't get the reaction he was expecting.

"It sounds plausible, Bill, damn plausible, but there's one problem."

"What's that?"

"Jack Walker is dead."

"What?" Bill couldn't believe it.

"It's true. He was out on probation, at a halfway house on Water Street. A buddy whom Walker confided in at the halfway house said he tried to scam some of his old mob buddies in a drug deal to get some money. They must have found him out. They put him in a stolen car, stocked it with plastic jugs filled with gasoline, torched him, and pushed the car off High View Cliff. By the time the fire department got to it and put out the fire, there wasn't much left of Jack Walker except for his dentures. That's how his body was identified. He'd got the dentures from the prison dentist and the guy identified them as Walker's. We've been investigating it but haven't come up with anything yet."

Bill felt deflated. He'd been so sure.

"Shit!" was all he could say.

"No shit," Chief Albert replied. "Keep at it, though. You'll find the guy eventually. But it's late. Take a break and start again in the morning."

"Yeah," Bill answered, not really listening to his friend's advice. Something wasn't right here, but he was suddenly too tired and disappointed to figure it out. He said good-bye to George and, sighing, hung up the phone.

77

Ivy sat next to the bed and held his mother's hand. She was sleeping, covered from neck to knees in a body cast, her left arm and leg in traction.

Despite his mother's condition, Ivy couldn't have been happier. He had gone from heartbroken despair to joy. He still couldn't believe his mother was alive; he had to keep hold of her hand for fear she might disappear, or he might suddenly awaken to discover this had all been a dream.

Their reunion had been tearful and joyful, if tentative—with Ivy being very careful not to hurt her in his eagerness to hug her, touch her, and reassure himself that she was really alive.

And she was! Thank God! She was alive!

Everything was going to be all right now, really all right. Ivy could feel it in his bones, knew it as certain as he knew the sun would rise in the east tomorrow morning. The doctors had told him that his mother was going to be okay, though it would take a long period of recuperation, but he knew that he could help her with that. And Mr. Gage said that Ivy could stay with him for a while until arrangements could be made for him to stay at the hospital or with one of his mother's AA friends while she got better.

Ivy squeezed his mother's hand tightly. Yeah. Everything was going to be okay now. No more trouble.

78

The predawn darkness is cold, stiffening his leg so that every step, even with the help of the cane, is an excursion into pain. He hobbles out from under the bridge and crosses over it. There is no traffic on the road. As he crosses Summer Street, nearing downtown Crocker, a police car goes by, but the driver takes no notice of him.

An hour and a half later, as the first streaks of dawn are stretching across the sky, he is limping down the cop's street, toward his house and the fulfillment of his dreams of revenge. Normally the walk wouldn't have taken more than ten minutes, but with his leg so bad and only the cane for support, it is a struggle to go any faster than the proverbial snail's pace.

He notices the unmarked police car parked in front of the house while he's still a block away. The fact that the Crocker police are watching the house, lying in wait to trap him, does not bother nor scare him. It tells him the cop is afraid, that his tactics have worked, have struck fear into the heart of his enemy. Now it is time to turn the fear to terror.

He walks slowly past the house, scanning it and the adjacent driveway out of the corner of his eye, careful not to look once in the direction of the cop car. There appears to be no one home. Is the cop off to work early? Or have they moved him elsewhere for his own safety?

He continues to the end of the street, turns left around the block, and goes down the next street over, the one that runs parallel to the rear of the cop's house.

He walks until he comes to the house behind the cop's. A quick check around for surveillance and he is moving as quickly as possible down the driveway and alongside the garage. There is a low stone wall separating the two backyards, but it is no problem. What will be tough is the stretch of twenty yards or so of open ground between him and the wall and another fifteen at least between the wall and the back of the cop's house.

He carefully scans the surrounding area, but it is still too early for anyone to be out. There are lights on in the two houses on either side of the cop's, but he will have to trust in Lady Luck and hope that the police or feds have not set up surveillance in them.

He takes three deep breaths, pushes himself off from the garage, and hobbles as fast as he can to the wall, staying close to the side hedges and as low as his bad leg and the cane will allow.

The wall gives him more trouble than he thought it would. Without the injury, he could straddle it easily and not even break stride, but his leg and ankle are too stiff and sore to attempt it. He has to lift his bad leg over the wall with both hands, almost falling, and causing intensely sharp pains to shoot up the leg. In the process, he drops the cane behind him and cannot lean back over the wall far enough to retrieve it. He leaves it.

It seems to take hours to traverse the cop's backyard and reach the relative safety of the shadows at the rear of the house. Without the support of the cane, each hobbling step is agony, making him want to cry out.

He leans heavily against the house, resting, gulping air, trying to keep his weight off his ankle, and willing the pain to subside. Crossing the backyard, he had noticed the broken cellar window. He slides along the house, favoring his *leg, and leans over to peer inside. A feeling that something is not right comes over him.*

Why is the window broken? he wonders. And, more important, how long has it been broken?

His sense of survival tells him the broken window is a bad sign, but his desire to get into the house is stronger. He knows, even without checking, that all the other doors and windows will be locked. Besides, he doesn't want to have to pick a lock or jimmy a window, leaving any telltale signs of a break-in. After some consideration he manages to convince himself that the open window is really a lucky break. The cop, or the police, must know about it. He can use it to enter without leaving any traces.

But what if it's a trap?

Painfully he lowers himself to the ground. Lying flat on his chest, he looks inside. He can see little in the dim morning light, but his acute sense of hearing and smell detect nothing unusual. He decides it is a chance he will have to take. He has come too far.

Grabbing the frame of the window with both hands, he slowly lowers himself into the darkness.

79

Bill Gage lit another cigarette and pressed the scan button on the microfiche machine, moving rapidly on to the next case file. His eyes read the information on a perp he had busted for gunrunning and attempted murder, but his mind was still on Jack Walker. Despite what the chief had told him, he couldn't get Walker out of his mind. There was something about the whole thing that just didn't sit right, but he couldn't put his finger on it.

Frustrated, he clicked the machine off, pushed his chair back, and rubbed his tired eyes. He picked up the envelopes containing the letters from Deathwalker and the police photos of his deeds. As he looked at them, Kelsey's face kept flashing before his eyes until they were filled with tears.

He pushed the emotions away. He knew he hadn't dealt with everything that had happened at the hospital—and knew that was dangerous to his recovery—but he couldn't help it. He just couldn't afford to waste time on that now, no matter how important it was to his staying clean and sober. He had to concentrate on finding out who Deathwalker was and keeping him from killing again.

He held the last set of photos splayed in his fingers like a hand of poker. Without any conscious effort, he started dividing the pictures into grids and focusing on each detail in each grid.

He hadn't used his so-called tunnel vision in so long that he'd thought he had lost the ability, especially after finding Kelsey in the woods and being unable to use it then. He was pleasantly surprised to experience its return happening so easily now when he really needed it. He scanned each of the photos, his eyes lingering and focusing longest on the mouth and genital wounds of the victims.

Deep, large, roundish puncture wounds.

The coroner's report said the mutilations had been inflicted with either a large, double-edged knife or some type of round, blunt instrument with sharp edges to it.

Deep, large, roundish puncture wounds.

Unbidden, a memory from when he'd busted Jack Walker popped into his mind. He had been observing through a two-way mirror when Walker was ordered to strip for a search. He remembered his shock, and feeling of pity for the man, at seeing the deformed little stub of flesh that was Jack Walker's penis.

Deep, large, roundish puncture wounds.

A horrible thought occurred to Bill, so horrible that for a moment he refused to believe it possible. But it was all that he had to go on.

What had Chief Albert said about Jack Walker? That his body had been burned so badly the only way they could identify him was by his dentures.

Dentures! But when Bill had busted Walker he'd still had his own teeth. Sometime between then and his alleged death, Jack Walker had lost all his teeth, and Deathwalker removed the teeth of his victims in some weird ritual, that Bill was sure was the killer's way of teasing him as to the perp's identity. It might just be coincidence, but Bill didn't think so. Another thing occurred to him. Dentures could be removed, placed in the mouth of a stand-in, and fool the police. But another way to identify Walker would be to check for his deformity. Even though the fire had burned him badly, an autopsy report, or even an exhumation, might be able to show if he was deformed or not.

The first thing he had to do was find out when and how Jack Walker had lost his teeth.

At that moment Chief Albert entered the room. "Have you been here all night? Christ, Bill, it's six in the morning. Weren't you supposed to pick up the Delacroix kid at the hospital?"

"Shit," Bill exclaimed. "That's right." He quickly filled the chief in on his hypothesis.

"A razor-sharp dildo?" George said doubtfully. Bill agreed it was weird, but persuaded him to at least check into it and talk to prison officials to find out when and how Walker had lost his teeth, and if he would have been able to fashion a weapon such as Bill suspected while in the pen. He also agreed to talk to his halfway house counselors to see if they had noticed anything while Walker was there. If that information seemed to support Bill's assumptions, then he would get a judge to order that Walker's body be exhumed and examined for any genital deformities.

The chief thought it was a long shot, a grasping at straws brought on by Bill's fatigue and stress, but he didn't voice his opinion. Instead he agreed to everything Bill asked, under the condition that Bill would go and collect his ward Ivy at the hospital and go home and get some sleep.

80

He lies in the gloom of the cellar, wincing at the pain that exploded in his leg when he hit the floor. He had misjudged the drop from the window— had thought he was inches from it when he let go of the window frame, but he had dropped more than a foot.

Using the cold granite wall as a support, he carefully stands, keeping his bad ankle off the floor. Gingerly he tests the foot, putting a little weight on it, gasping at the pain just a little pressure brings. He steels himself against the hurt and takes a few steps. His head swims, his vision blurs, and he almost passes out. Only reaching out in the gray light to a support post saves him from falling.

He takes several deep breaths. He has to beat this pain —has to make it upstairs and learn the layout of the house so that he can choose the best hiding spot from which to make his attack when the cop shows up.

The sound of a car pulling into the driveway, and then the front door opening and closing, followed by voices from upstairs, kills that plan.

81

Bill looked over at Ivy sleeping in the passenger seat as they pulled into the driveway. The poor kid was exhausted. He had spent the night sleeping in the chair next to his mother's bed.

Ivy woke as the car came to a stop in the driveway. He looked confused and not fully awake yet.

"Come on, Ivy. Let's get you up to bed. It's been a long couple of days for you," Bill said.

"I'm okay. I'm not tired," Ivy said around a wide yawn.

"Sure."

"Uh, do I have to go to school today?" Ivy asked.

"Nah, I think you can skip it."

They got out of the car and went into the house. Henry was waiting at the door for them and jumped on Ivy frantically. Ivy picked the dog up and followed Bill into the kitchen. Holding Henry close, he flopped into a chair at the table.

"You want to go right to bed, or would you like something to eat first?" Bill asked, opening the refrigerator and inspecting its frugal contents. "There ain't much but eggs and cheese. I make a heck of a cheese omelette, though."

"Yeah, sure," Ivy mumbled, stifling another yawn. "I am kind of hungry."

While Bill whipped up the omelette, he questioned Ivy about his life since Christmas. In turn Ivy questioned him, and Bill, quite unexpectedly, found himself confessing everything to the boy, including the Deathwalker case.

"Wow," Ivy said as Bill served up the food. "Is that why your shoulder's bandaged?" he asked after Bill told him what had happened with Alex at the hospital. Bill nodded. "It's kind of weird how you and my mother were going through almost the exact same things," Ivy added.

"Yeah, but your mom did it on her own, the hard way, with no help from a hospital. You should be very proud of her for that."

"I am," Ivy answered, his voice cracking and his eyes watering. Bill made a point of concentrating on his breakfast so as not to embarrass the boy, and they finished their meal in silence, washing it down with water from the tap. Ivy started to collect the plates for washing, but Bill stopped him.

"I'll take care of those. You go on up to bed."

"Okay," Ivy willingly agreed. The food had done nothing to ease his tiredness. If anything, it had made him more sleepy.

"Oh. One more thing before you go to bed. I forgot to ask you how the heck you got into the house without the two officers outside seeing you?"

Ivy blushed with guilty embarrassment and stammered out how he'd broken the cellar window and got in. "I'm sorry. I'll pay for the window."

Bill laughed. "Don't worry about it. It's okay. Now go on up and get some shut-eye."

When Ivy was gone, Bill's smile turned to a frown. If a kid had found it so easy to get by the surveillance on the house, for Deathwalker it would be a piece of cake. It also made him doubt the effectiveness of the security on Evelyn and the kids. He was on his way to the phone to call George and express his concern when it rang. It was the chief.

"Bill! I think you might be right about Jack Walker.

Agent Danvers just called me. A kid in Rhode Island contacted the police and told them about a weird guy he kept sheltered in his tree house for several weeks. The kid became scared after the guy showed him a razor-adorned dildo that he wore and bragged of killing people with. He told the kid he was heading for Connecticut, so I don't think he's in Crocker yet. The feds and Connecticut State Police are putting out a sketch of the perp based on the kid's description of the guy, which fits Walker—I don't know why he let the kid live, but he did, and I'm glad. The bodies of two dwarfs were found in a railroad yard not too far from the kid's tree house, too, with Deathwalker's M.O. I also got ahold of the dentist at the prison, and he said that Jack Walker had a spare pair of dentures. He lost his teeth the second day he was in the pen when he was gang-raped and some sick bastard yanked them all with a penknife after Walker bit him. The warden told me Walker worked in the machine shop and had access to a lot of metal, but that the cons were thoroughly searched before leaving it each day. He says that even if Walker did manage to smuggle a weapon out, he wouldn't have been able to keep it hidden with weekly cell searches."

"And we know inmates manage to make, smuggle, and conceal all sorts of weapons," Bill interrupted.

"Yeah," George agreed. "It all seems to fit your hunch. Danvers and Willis will be here by noon for the exhumation. The original autopsy report makes no mention of an abnormally small penis. Can you get back to the station then?"

"Yeah, sure," Bill said, inwardly groaning at the thought of getting only a couple of hours' sleep. He was beginning to feel the effects of his all-nighter spent in front of the microfiche screen.

He told the chief how Ivy had got into the house, and George agreed to increase the guard on Evelyn and the kids, and even to move them to another motel out of town.

"And you'd better take care of that window," George added.

"Right." Bill sighed and hung up. Fixing a broken window was the last thing he felt like doing, but it had to be done. He found an old square of plywood behind his toolbox in the hall closet and hoped it would be the right size to cover the window. He didn't want this to turn into a major project, he just wanted to get the window covered and get to bed.

Picking up the board and his toolbox, he wearily headed down into the cellar.

82

He makes it to the stairs before he has to stop and rest. His leg is numbing, which doesn't really help his mobility. He knows he can't trust it, that it will buckle under him if he puts too much weight on it.

He hears the phone ring upstairs and strains to hear what is said but cannot. He is just about to start up, hoping to surprise the cop while he's on the phone, when the cellar door opens. Quickly he ducks back under the stairs.

Footsteps start down overhead. His arm brushes against something heavy—a crowbar hanging on a hook under the stair next to him. Using the sound of the heavy descending footsteps to cover any noise, he lifts the crowbar off its hook and clutches it in both hands.

The footsteps reach the bottom and stop. He waits, holding his breath, his hands sweating.

"Shit! This won't be big enough."

It is the voice of the cop! Joy surges in him. At last! At long last his moment has come. The culmination of all his dreams and plans is at hand. The cop begins to move and he leans forward.

There he is! Now!

He lunges out from under the cellar stairs, putting his weight on his good foot. He swings the crowbar, catching the cop on the side of the forehead, sending him crashing to the floor in a heap.

83

Ivy couldn't breathe and Henry was barking. The dog yelped suddenly in pain, and then was silent. Ivy struggled to breathe, struggled to wake up, but something was covering his face.

A hand.

"Sssh! Be quiet. Don't make a sound." The hand came partly off his face and he opened his eyes. There was a strange man standing over him, the man's hand clamped tightly over his mouth.

Fear shot through Ivy. The man was naked, and there was some kind of weird-looking pipe strapped to where his penis should have been. Ivy struggled against the man, who lay on top of him, putting the weight of his body on Ivy, completely immobilizing him. He felt his pajamas being torn as the pipe thing rubbed against him, also cutting into his skin.

"Be a good little nigger boy," the man growled through a smile that was predatory.

Ivy felt anger begin to vie with the fear. One thing his father had always impressed upon him was that nobody, but *nobody* had the right to call him "nigger."

The man looked at him quizzically. "What are you to the cop, anyway? His bastard son from some nigger whore? Where's the rest of his kids, those milky-white girls of his, and that delicious little boy?"

He obviously didn't expect Ivy to answer, since he didn't remove his hand from Ivy's mouth.

"No matter. I have you, and I have the cop. You must mean something to him or you wouldn't be living in his house. I'm sure if I'm patient—and I can be very patient —the others will come along soon. Then we'll really party."

The man oozed malevolence, and his words sent chills of terror through Ivy. He realized this must be the killer, Deathwalker, that Bill Gage had told him about. He had to do something to warn his friend. He struggled, but the weight of the man was too great.

"If you make a sound, I'll kill you," the man said calmly, adding in a voice mimicking the Wicked Witch of the West, "and your little dog, too."

Ivy could tell he meant it.

The man took his hand off Ivy's mouth, allowing the boy to breathe more freely. He wrapped his arms tightly around Ivy's chest, pinning his arms to his sides. Grunting, he pulled Ivy off the bed and winced with pain as he stood. Ivy's leg brushed against the pipe as he fell to the floor, and he felt it slice through the fabric of his pajamas again and into the flesh of his leg.

Something's wrong with him, Ivy thought, gritting his teeth against the pain in his leg and pushing his fear down. He had to try to figure out what it was that was hurting the man. Out of the corner of his eye, as the man dragged him by his shirt to the door, Ivy saw Henry sprawled in the corner of the room. He looked dead.

"Henry!" Ivy yelled.

The man swung him against the door frame, cracking his head hard against the wood and bringing sparks of dancing lights to his vision.

"I said shut up!" the man hissed in Ivy's ear. Limping and wincing with every step, the pipe cutting repeatedly into Ivy's leg, the man dragged Ivy down the hallway. Ivy struggled to remain awake, the sharp pain in his leg helping, aware of the lurching step of the man, but unable, with his head befuddled from the blow it had received, to figure out what was wrong with Deathwalker.

84

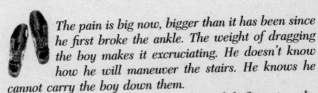The pain is big now, bigger than it has been since he first broke the ankle. The weight of dragging the boy makes it excruciating. He doesn't know how he will maneuver the stairs. He knows he cannot carry the boy down them.

He looks at the boy's face, sees the eyelids fluttering, the pupils threatening to roll up into his head. He doesn't care if he has hurt the boy, but doesn't want him dead just yet. He wants to have some fun with him first.

He reaches the top of the stairs and leans against the wall. The boy is not too heavy, but his weight and the awkwardness of dragging him are enough to make the pain in his ankle and leg brutal. He looks down, counting the steps—five—to the first landing. There are seven more after that to the first floor.

He pulls the boy down to his side, grabs him by the hair, and starts down the stairs, dragging the boy behind him. The boy grunts as he thumps off each step and is whimpering by the time they reach the bottom. His wounded leg leaves a trail of blood on the stairs that Jack Walker finds as beautiful as any work of art.

That worked well, he thinks. But the cellar stairs are much narrower. It will be harder to drag the boy without toppling himself. He will have to think of another way to get the boy down them. He glances down at his crotch and finds his answer.

"Of course!"

Still clutching the boy's wiry hair, he drags him to the cellar door and shakes him into consciousness. Placing the boy in front of him, he forces Ivy to stand on the first step. He pushes the point of his metal cock against the boy's neck. He presses it into the skin until blood is drawn and the boy's eyes are open and fearfully alert.

"We're going down the cellar now. Walk slowly. Make a sound or one wrong move and I'll fuck your head clean off. Understand?"

The boy nods slightly, his eyes wide with terror. That is an exhilarating tonic. He laughs and grabs the boy by the hair again. Grunting with pain, he pushes the boy forward. Holding the wiry hair, they start down the stairs.

85

Bill Gage woke with an intense pounding in his head. For a moment he had what those in AA call "a remember when" and thought that he was suffering from one of his killer hangovers. His mind was muddled, and he couldn't identify what time it was, where he was, where he had been, or how he had got to where he was now, wherever that might be.

He tried to open his eyes but found that only his left one worked and its vision was terribly blurred. He tried to shake his head in an attempt to clear it, but he could barely move. There was something very tight around his neck and something very hard against the back of his head. He looked around. He was in the cellar. There was the furnace and the water heater. Now he remembered. He'd come down to fix the window. What had happened? Had he fallen?

He realized he was sitting naked and had deep cuts all over his body. His hands were tied around the hard thing behind him—some kind of post. Blood was seeping through the bandages on his shoulder, and it hurt terribly. His legs were bound together in front of him. He tried to lean forward and choked. There was a rope around his neck also. He blinked several times, relaxing his neck muscles, and felt his vision clear a little.

"The cellar," he murmured, dazed, his throat dry and his voice raspy. *What the hell am I doing tied to a post in the cellar?* he wondered. A terrifying thought occurred to him, that his recent dream/memory of what his father had done to him had somehow become real. Only now, he wasn't a bystander watching things that had been done, he was in the dream as the victim.

The cellar door opened, throwing a brief shaft of dim light into the gloom of the cellar, and footsteps started down the stairs. One pair of the footsteps was light sounding, the other heavy and awkwardly off-balance. He tried to raise his head to see, but the rope cut into the flesh of his neck, making him gasp hoarsely in pain.

"Oh, good! You're awake," a deep voice said from the stairs. "Now we can party."

Bill managed to lift his head just enough against the constricting rope as the steps continued down, and had his worst fear confirmed. Descending the cellar stairs, with Ivy in front of him, the razored dildo that he had rightly guessed was Walker's M.O. against the back of Ivy's neck, was none other than Jack Walker, aka *Death-walker!*

86

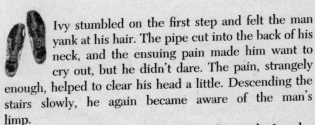 Ivy stumbled on the first step and felt the man yank at his hair. The pipe cut into the back of his neck, and the ensuing pain made him want to cry out, but he didn't dare. The pain, strangely enough, helped to clear his head a little. Descending the stairs slowly, he again became aware of the man's limp.

Despite the thing pressing against his neck, Ivy decided he had to do something now while they were still on the stairs. He had to use the man's disability to his advantage. The only problem was that he wasn't sure which of the man's legs was hurting. With the man behind him, and being unable to turn and look, he'd have to guess and take a chance.

They were halfway down. After the man stopped to speak to Bill Gage and they were continuing down, Ivy lifted his right foot as if to step down to the next step, but instead thrust it backward, striking blindly at the man's legs with his heel.

Ivy knew the moment he struck that the man had anticipated his move. The man yanked his hair, throwing Ivy off balance and causing his foot to merely glance off the man's shin. The man's reflexes were quick. Ivy screamed, feeling the man thrust the sharp pipe into the side of his neck. The only thing that prevented it from cutting deeply was that the man shoved him forward as he thrust at him. Ivy fell clear of the pipe and tumbled head over heels down the remaining stairs, landing at the bottom, unconscious.

87

"You fucking little bastard!" he rages as he pushes the boy down the stairs. His anger is tempered by the fact that the boy missed his bad leg and by the lovely sight of his metal cock slicing through the dark flesh, drawing even darker blood that now drips from his killing member.

He descends the rest of the stairs rapidly, keeping his bad leg raised and hopping from step to step on his good one. At the bottom he stands gingerly on his bad foot, leaning heavily against the railing, and delivers several kicks with his good leg to the boy's head. The sight of blood on the boy excites him greatly, but what excites him even more is that the boy is still breathing. He can still have fun with him.

With one last kick to the boy's head for good measure, he turns toward the cop.

"Hi, there. Remember me?"

88

Ivy had screamed as he tumbled down the stairs, and Bill struggled furiously against the ropes holding him. He almost lost consciousness as the one round his neck dug in, cutting off his air, and the pain in his shoulder flared. He was forced to stop and relax so that he could breathe again. He stared at the prone figure of Ivy lying at the foot of the stairs, sure that his young friend was dead. Tears of rage ran down his cheeks as Jack Walker gleefully kicked the boy.

Now he sneered at Walker. "Yeah, I remember you," he said through clenched teeth. "But I plan on forgetting you real soon."

"Ho! Ho!" Walker said, smiling, but his eyes were flashing anger. He leaned awkwardly and painfully over and punched Bill in his wounded arm. Bill groaned at the pain and his vision wavered for a moment.

"Brave words for someone in your position." He stood over Bill, the bloody dildo-pipe waving in Bill's face. Up close, Bill could clearly see how the thing had made the horrible wounds in Walker's victims. The pipe was eight inches long. Shards of broken razor blades had been soldered to the end, giving it a nasty cutting edge that reminded Bill of the way some people embed broken glass in the top of a stone wall. More broken razors had been soldered randomly all along the sides to the base, which was a cupped piece of metal that allowed the whole thing to fit right over Walker's testicles and tiny penis, effectively hiding it. The bottom of the pipe was soldered to a small hinge and latch attached to the metal base so that the pipe could be flipped up (and not be bulging out, or cutting through his pants, Bill guessed) or locked into an erect position, such as it was now.

Bill lowered his eyes from Walker's groin and noticed Walker was favoring his left foot.

Walker looked back thoughtfully at Ivy. "What's with the black boy anyway? Bastard son? Or maybe he's your boy-toy, huh?" Walker laughed obscenely. "You like to eat his little black cock, is that it? Like to bugger his black ass? A man of your high esteem. I'd like to say I'm shocked, but you know, I'm not. Being in prison makes you very liberal minded, sexwise. And I have you to thank for that."

Bending over slightly, he thrust the pipe at Bill's shoulder and missed, gouging a piece of flesh from Bill's cheek instead. Bill grunted in pain and watched in horror as Jack Walker picked the piece of bloody flesh from the end of the pipe, rolled it around in his fingers, and sniffed at it before flicking it away.

"Ah! I don't care what they say, revenge does smell sweet," Walker said, grinning. He turned and looked again at Ivy. "I bet your boy-toy smells very sweet."

Walker smiled at Bill and absentmindedly licked blood from his fingers. "I'm going to pull his teeth out one by one, Bill. Then I'm going to pluck his eyes from their sockets. Did you know the eyes are the windows to the soul? Actually they are much more than that—they *are* the soul, and I'm going to consume his. Then, while you watch and he's still alive, I'm going to fuck him to shreds. And when your kids get home, I'm going to do the same to them."

Walker laughed again and turned toward Ivy, his laughter turning to a grimace as he put his weight on his left foot. Bill saw his only chance to save Ivy. Walker took a step toward the boy. One more and he'd be out of range. Calling on all his strength and straining against the ropes to the point of cutting off his air, Bill swung his bound legs as hard as he could to the left, kicking Walker's left leg out from under him.

There was a loud popping sound and a simultaneous scream of rage and pain from Jack Walker. His bad leg crumpled under him and he went down sideways, arms flailing. The strap holding the pipe-dildo on snapped and the thing clattered to the floor. Walker twisted as he fell, grabbing for it, and struck his head against the side of the stairs in a bone-crunching crack. He hit the floor and lay still.

89

Consciousness returned to Ivy slowly. He could hear voices but couldn't make sense of the words. His head and neck hurt fiercely; the rest of his body hurt only slightly less.

He came awake a little more, his head clearing of the fog of pain enough so that he could understand the voices and remember where he was. He opened his eyes just in time to see the man he now knew as Deathwalker cut a piece of flesh from Bill Gage's face. He flinched but had enough presence of mind not to cry out. He closed his eyes and tried to control the sense of revulsion at what he'd seen. He thought he was going to puke.

When the man spoke of pulling his teeth and eyes and mutilating his flesh, Ivy kept his eyes closed and remained still, steeling himself for one last desperate lunge. He didn't know if his body would respond, *could* respond, but he had to try. He refused to just lie there and let this sicko kill him.

He opened his eyes a slit and watched the man turn and approach him. He was just ready to strike when Bill beat him to it. Adrenaline surged in Ivy at the sight of the man crashing to the floor and striking his head so hard on the stairs that Ivy could feel the whole structure shudder with the impact. He saw the pipe thing come free and clatter to the floor, and he lunged for it, feeling pain erupt in his neck, head, and back, but not caring. His hand closed on the straps, and he picked the bloody thing up. He stood unsteadily.

Ivy stood over Deathwalker and clenched the pipe tightly in his hand by its cupped metal base. Rage burned in him, a rage as hot as volcanic fire. Just when he'd been sure that everything was going to be all right in his life, this guy, this sick motherfucker, had tried to kill him. After all he'd gone through, he'd come within seconds of death. All because of this pervert.

Well, now it was his turn. Eye for an eye. Do unto others. He was going to do the world a favor and kill this sick bastard. He raised the pipe in both hands.

"Ivy! Don't!"

Ivy heard Bill's voice as if from far away, so intent was he upon killing Deathwalker. But the sound of Bill's voice was enough to make him waver.

"Don't do it, Ivy!"

"Why not?" His voice was edged with angry tears. "He tried to kill me. And you. Why shouldn't I? You killed Wilbur Clayton. Didn't that make you feel good to get rid of someone that sick?"

"No, Ivy, it didn't. It was wrong. Believe me, it will haunt you for the rest of your life," Bill said, pleading.

Ivy didn't want to listen to Bill, didn't want to listen to anyone. He wanted to hurt this guy the way he'd been hurt.

"Please, Ivy, don't do it," Bill begged him softly.

Ivy didn't respond. He clenched the metal base of the razored pipe tighter. All the bad things that had happened to him since his father's death whirled through his mind. Plunging the pipe into Deathwalker's throat seemed like a great way to strike out at everything.

"Ivy, put it down."

Ivy looked at Jack Walker's face. Wasn't that what this sicko was doing—taking out everything that was wrong with his life against the world? Hadn't he wanted to take it out on Bill and himself in particular?

If I do the same thing back to him, Ivy thought, *that will make me no better than him. That will make me as sick as him.*

The pipe trembled in Ivy's hands, then he lowered it. Tears streaming down his face, Ivy went to Bill and began using the razored pipe to cut the ropes holding his friend.

90

He swims back to consciousness. His body and head are on fire with pain. At first he thinks he's back in the strip-search room at the prison, about to be gang-raped again. Painfully he gets to his knees.

He looks around. No, he's not in prison. He turns to see the boy struggling to cut the cop free of the ropes and remembers where he is and what he has come there to do.

He can't let it all slip away from him now! He must have his vengeance!

All he can think about is stopping the boy. In his urgency and pain-fogged mind, he also forgets about his bad ankle. He struggles to his feet—hears the cop shout, "Ivy! Look out!"—and lunges forward.

His ankle explodes with pain, broken bones crunching together, and he is falling. The last thing he sees is the boy on his knees, turning and defensively thrusting Death's pride and joy up at him.

He is falling and can't stop.

He is falling and his wielder of death, clasped tightly in the black boy's frightened hands, is waiting to catch him.

And catch him it does.

He grunts softly as it impales him, plunging through his

solar plexus and ripping through his heart. His knees strike the floor, and he tumbles to his side.

A bloody bubble forms in his open mouth and pops as he emits a long sigh. His last.

91

Bill Gage, his face and shoulder heavily bandaged, sat next to Ivy's hospital bed and held his young friend's hand. In his good arm, he held the boy's dog, Henry, who'd been found unconscious but okay in the guest room of his house. Bill had smuggled the dog into the hospital to surprise Ivy, but the boy was sleeping. That was good. Sleep would help mend him, would help him get over what had happened to him both physically and mentally.

Bill knew Ivy hadn't meant to kill Jack Walker, and no matter what the boy had said, he knew he really hadn't *wanted* to kill Walker either. It would take a lot for Ivy to get over that. Bill knew from personal experience.

He sighed. At least the nightmare was over. Jack Walker was dead and out of his life, out of his family's life. Now, Bill knew he had to patch things up with his family no matter how long it might take or how hard it might be.

A noise behind him made him turn. In the doorway stood Evelyn with Devin in her arms, Sara and Missy on either side. He smiled tentatively at them and they all smiled back, even Sara.

"Hi," he said cautiously.

"Hi," Evelyn answered. Missy looked uncomfortably from her sister to her aunt to Bill. "Hi," she said softly.

"Hi," Sara added a moment later, still smiling but averting her eyes.

"Daddy!" Devin squealed. Evelyn put him down and he ran to Bill, who put the dog down and scooped his son up in his good arm. He hugged his son and showed him Ivy's dog. Evelyn and the girls entered the room and stood at the foot of the bed.

"So," Bill said slowly. "What's up? What are you guys doing here?"

Evelyn opened her mouth to speak, but Sara cut her off. "We came to take you home . . . Daddy."